MOUNTAIN SICKNESS

FRANK MARTIN

SEVERED PRESS
HOBART TASMANIA

MOUNTAIN SICKNESS

PART I

BLIZZARD

1

Still stuck between the rising sun and the darkness of night, the sky's thin air shimmered into a veil of white. A full sheet of overcast clouds covered the mountaintops, and neither the blue sky nor the black night could be seen beyond them.

It was still early morning by any standard of measurement. The air had yet to warm from the night's frigid chill, but Nellie Sheridan rather preferred her morning rides that way. At sixty-eight, she still felt better than most women thirty years younger, and waking up at the crack of dawn every morning to jump on a horse and gallop through the mountainside probably had something to do with it.

Riding before sunrise was a habit she'd grown accustomed to since she was a little girl. Growing up in rural Colorado was hard enough, but coming from a family with a long history of ranching didn't make things easier. Before the fancy restaurants and ski resorts. Before the hippies and counter-culture. Even before swarms of miners flocked to the area like locusts looking to rape the mountain for everything she had, Nellie's family had already set up camp on the outskirts of what would later become Telluride. And they've been finding a way to prosper ever since.

These days, Nellie's ranch was practically an institution in Telluride. She enjoyed owning a nice adventure services company that offered horseback expeditions in the summer and snowmobile tours in the winter. With an army of employees, local kids and seasonal part-timers, the business practically ran itself, leaving Nellie ample time to enjoy the outdoors with her husband any way she desired. And during their morning rides that usually meant waiting for him to catch up.

Already a few miles from their secluded home at the ranch, Nellie sat atop her horse, Providence, overlooking the Telluride valley. Although one of the most breathtaking areas in all of Colorado, the town was practically cut off from the rest of the world. But then again, that seclusion was probably what made it so appealing.

The rolling hills they stood upon composed the entrance to the boxed canyon and served as her primary riding territory. From her vantage point, she could see Highway 145, the main artery in and out of the area, buried beneath a steep ridge of cliffs.

At the end of the road down below rested Telluride, a town of less than one square mile at eighty seven hundred feet above sea level. Branching off from the road, a smaller pass took cars up to Mountain Village, the artificial community built only decades ago to cater to the

1

resort's wealthy visitors. She could barely see the luxurious village nestled amidst the trees and ski runs. In between her and them sat a jagged field of white snow covering a rocky path that most would consider dangerous. To Nellie, it was simply the way home. Although she rarely spoke on the subject publicly, simply knowing that her family had called this place home for generations made her proud.

Her husband, Billy, shared in her pride. And that was the reason he kept his own pace during their morning ritual. It wasn't that he lacked her ability to command his own steed. In fact, at three years her senior, he often bragged that he felt (and looked) better atop a horse than she did. But when it came to traversing the mountainside, William Sheridan just loved to take his goddamn time.

He eventually caught up to his wife and joined her in the beautifully serene view she still found time to appreciate. "We should get back, Eleanor."

Billy was the only person she'd ever known to use her full name. Even her parents never referred to her as such, but she liked that he did. It was almost like a reverse pet name that was special just to him.

The proud woman kept her eyes locked onto the peaceful scenery and had yet to acknowledge her husband's presence. They both knew that she understood why he'd made the suggestion to head home, but he further explained it just to emphasize its importance. "Denser clouds are rolling in. There won't be much time."

She finally looked up just to be sure. With the sun only slightly higher than when she arrived on the hill, the sky was still fully clothed in a pearly white sheet of overcast, but back behind her sat an army of rigid, dark clouds lined along the horizon. The overnight storm front was coming in from Denver and moved at a decent pace for something as massive as it appeared to be. Nellie swore to herself that she'd seen something bigger than it before. Problem was…she just couldn't remember when.

She was almost prepared to leave when a small, floating speck of white caught her eye. The graceful crystal weaved back and forth, and Nellie followed as it slowly fell through the air in front of her face. When it was finally ready to hit Providence's neck, Nellie put out her hand and carefully caught the snowflake in her palm.

She held it up to her face, examining its design. Nothing special. But a Cheyenne woman once told her that catching the first snowflake of a storm was often good luck. She tried to think of a wish, but nothing worthwhile popped into her head. And before she had a chance to try again, the tiny crystal melted into the ridges of her hand.

***

Without any warning, the radio suddenly clicked on, sending abrupt noise throughout the quiet bedroom. "Good morning, Telluride! It is six o'clock on the nose, and you know what that means? Another wonderful wake up block with your beautiful host: Miss Georgia Croft."

Chris Chambers slid his arm from off his girlfriend's bare hip and swung for the alarm clock by his bedside. His fist missed the snooze button and slammed the top of the nightstand, spilling a glass of water onto the floor. Instead of going for another attempt, Chris simply forced his eyes open and stared at the clock hoping it would turn off on its own.

It didn't, and the energetic DJ continued to rant. "Now, I know what you're thinking: 'But Georgia, you're on the radio. How do we know you're beautiful?' Well, that's why I chose my profession wisely, folks."

Chris finally summoned up the strength to raise his arm for another try. But as his fingers lifted from the nightstand, he felt Sarah lean against his back to stop him. She then moved in closer to his ear and whispered softly with her heavy Australian accent. "Leave it on. I like her."

"Really? She's intolerable."

"I think she's funny." With too much energy for having woken up only seconds earlier, Sarah jumped out of bed and scurried to the bathroom. "But you're more than welcome to change the station."

Although spoken with kindness, Sarah's comment was strictly sarcastic. TORO happened to be one of Telluride's few FM radio stations. Chris briefly debated changing it, but he and Sarah both knew his options were limited.

He ultimately decided to let the radio be as he rolled out of bed shirtless and strolled over to the window. His eyes then surveyed the beautiful view of the mountain he woke up to every morning. Ski runs that ran down into the town, referred to as the mountain's front side, were littered with steep moguls and cliffs. The challenging terrain buried in between the thin tree lines darted and curved underneath the gondola and opened up at the mountain's base. Like a ballplayer sizing up his stadium, the twenty eight year old never got tired of taking in the sight of the snowy trails that acted as his office.

In the background of his personal moment, the DJ continued her routine by relaying the morning's stories. "Not much today in terms of headlines. The president has issued a new call for peace talks amidst an increase in violence in the Middle East. Also, reports are coming in of an energy crisis in Southeast Asia that's set to hurt the international stock market. And lastly, chair four will finally re-open today concluding a series of scheduled maintenance checks performed throughout the mountain this month."

The morning show moved on into a different segment, but Chris had phased out the DJ's voice, choosing instead to focus on the mountain's other non-natural furnishings. From his bedroom window, which happened to be on the top floor of a two-family house he rented in the middle of town, Chris could see the gondola's base already up and running for the early morning commuters coming from and going to Mountain Village. Designed in an elaborate "A" shape that takes its passengers up to a mid-mountain station before going back down to either side of the mountain, the gondola served as the area's free public transportation system. It allowed residents and visitors to seamlessly traverse back and forth between the twin communities, turning this isolated Colorado valley into a modern skiing paradise.

Off to the side of the gondola rested the archaic two-person chairlift that took the role as Telluride's first means up and down the mountain. The lift was still operational and would turn on when the resort opened several hours later. But it was mostly a relic of the past. The ride took well over twelve minutes, way too long by today's standards, and was only kept running as a throwback for the locals, old-timers who still appreciated the mountain's first runs.

Chris's eyes followed those skinny trails up the mountain when Sarah came up from behind him, wrapping her arms around his bare stomach. "Stop stalling. You're going to be late for work again."

And she was right. For Chris, waking up at the crack of dawn was the worst part of being on the mountain's ski patrol. He never considered himself a morning person and getting to his outpost on time had always been a struggle.

Sarah, on the other hand, had always gotten ready for the day with an almost inhuman amount of energy. And it showed as she left his side to dance around the room quickly putting on her thermal ski clothes and then heading into the bathroom.

Chris simply stood dumbfounded watching her, still in the underwear he wore to bed the night before. "How are you almost dressed already?"

She answered him from within the bathroom while brushing her teeth. "Becauth I acthually enhoy my hob."

"I do too. Just not what time I have to be there."

Their conversation fell silent for a moment as the radio transitioned to a smooth jazz melody selected especially for the morning. Chris turned his focus back out the window and onto the individual snowflakes falling sporadically from the sky. He heard the sink turn off and continued the conversation, assuming Sarah had finished brushing. "What are the chances you can stop by the hut later this morning?"

Once again, she answered him from within the bathroom. "Not good. I have a full class at nine and then a private right after that."

With his back still to the rest of the room, Chris laughed to himself as a morbid thought popped into his head. "Why don't you take the rugrats down Revelation Bowl? Maybe one of them will break their arm and you'll have no choice but to see me."

He made the remark smiling but then looked over his shoulder to see Sarah standing in the doorway with a look of condemnation. "Not funny."

He shrugged his shoulders jokingly as a sign of his humble innocence, but she brushed the gesture off as she walked across the room to grab a pair of ski boots that'd been drying against the radiator. "Those kids are my life, Chris. They mean the world to me."

Still in his light-hearted demeanor, Chris put his hands to his chest, exaggerating the sarcasm in his words. "I thought *I* meant the world to you."

"Well, after last night's conversation…" Continuing to quickly prepare for the day, Sarah sat down on the bed with her boots. But before putting them on, she paused briefly enough to look up at Chris with eyes of uncertainty. "…I'm not so sure anymore."

She turned her attention back to putting on her boots while Chris approached the bed and sat alongside her. "Come on, babe. I love you. You have to believe that."

She kept her head down and focused on strapping up the hard plastic of her ski boots. "Then you sure do have a strange way of showing it."

Chris's head slumped into a sigh, bringing the conversation to a pause. Neither one would've classified the discussion they had the previous night as a fight. Their voices never rose above a casual tone, but the content of the talk had grave implications for both their lives.

Without missing a step, Sarah popped up off the bed to move about the room, grabbing the remaining red ensemble to her ski school uniform. "Look, I don't want to force you into anything. You know that. But you also know that we can't keep doing this forever. The season ends, we both head home and count the days until we can see each other again."

After putting on her ski jacket, hat and goggles, Sarah was fully ready to head out into the cold. "I gotta run. I'm meeting some of the other instructors for breakfast."

"Sarah, wait."

She stopped at the bedroom door and turned to look back into the room, waiting for some sort of apology or last ditch effort from Chris to salvage their morning. But when he just silently looked up at her with his big droopy eyes, Sarah couldn't help but laugh. Even in his moments of bashful shame, he still had the ability to make her smile.

She brushed off her inconvenient giggles and forced a serious (although joking) look upon her face. "Fine. We don't have to talk about this now. The season's far from over. But we will eventually, mister. I love you too much to spend another summer away from you."

Like wounded prey, Chris sensed Sarah's stern anger on the ropes and seized the opportunity to vanquish it for good. He stood up from the bed, still wearing nothing but his underwear, and strutted over to her in the most obnoxiously seductive dance he could muster. "You mean, you're in love with all this sexiness?"

She continued to fight off the growing laughter as he approached her and was rather successful at keeping a straight face to the ridiculous scene. By the time he reached her, Chris wrapped his arms around her puffy ski jacket and brought her bundled up face close to his.

Sarah was still subduing the last of her giggles, but Chris's demeanor had completely shifted from goofy to serious in the blink of an eye. "We'll talk about it later. This time, I promise."

A wide smile of infatuation grew across Sarah's face, and the two lovers stared into each other's eyes for several seconds before bringing their lips together in unison. The kiss was slow and the couple savored every moment of it. They were lost in each other's grasp, completely unaware of the fact that one of them was fully dressed to battle the snowfall outside while the other was nearly naked.

After separating, they once again looked into each other's eyes without saying a word. The smooth jazz still playing in the background amplified the romantic sentiment of the moment, and neither one of them wanted to ruin it. Instead, with nothing else left to say, Sarah gave Chris one last smile before turning around and heading out through the door.

***

The distinct smell of bacon flew into Paul Fallon's nostrils, waking him from the first peaceful sleep he had had in weeks. First his eyes fluttered open, followed by a long stretch and deep breath. Upon arriving in Colorado, he was worried that adjusting to the altitude would make the first night or two difficult but prepared himself by drinking plenty of water prior to the trip. The fresh mountain air rewarded his adamant planning with a peaceful slumber fit for a king.

After sitting up off the fluffy king sized bed, he found his wife, Cheryl, entering the room with a tray of gourmet breakfast. "Morning, sunshine."

She brought the food over to his bedside, placing it down on the nightstand. "How'd you sleep?"

"Beautifully. You sleep in too?"

She laughed a little at the question. "If you consider seven sleeping in? Mountain still doesn't open for a couple hours."

Paul then remembered the blessing that was the time difference between here and back East, which allowed him two extra hours of rest while still getting up "early." But that wasn't the only thing which made waking up this morning special. Besides the long sleep and breakfast in bed, Paul noticed their hotel suite was much quieter than it should've been. He soon found the lack of noise coming from the common room disturbing and leaned over his wife to look through the crack in the open bedroom door.

She read his mind and quickly answered his curiosity. "They're right behind me and should be back soon."

And just then, the loud click of the front door opening echoed through the suite, followed by the continuous prattling of children's voices. Paul smiled at the sound as he leaned over and picked up the breakfast tray. "Speak of the devils."

He placed the tray on his lap and surveyed its contents. A full plate packed of eggs, bacon and home fries complimented a cup of coffee and sliced-open grapefruit on the side. He assumed it was from the buffet downstairs and mouthed a thank you to his wife for bringing it to him. He prepared himself to dig into the food but was neither surprised nor disappointed when the slight crack in the door burst open, interrupting his imminent meal.

Paul's fifteen year old son, Joey, was the first of his two children to enter the room. "Dad, you should've seen this spread! They had like six different kinds of eggs, every juice and cereal imaginable. Waffles, pancakes, French toast..."

The boy could have gone on forever, but his father cut him off. "Good. For what we're paying for this place every meal should be a feast."

He was referring to the Cliffs Hotel and Spa, arguably Mountain Village's most luxurious resort. Frequented by celebrities and the super rich, Paul knew it was the place to stay. His family was by no means poor, but he had to admit that the trip's price tag surprised him. Yet from what he heard, visiting Telluride was a once in a lifetime experience, and he was going to get the most out of it regardless of the cost.

Next to walk in through the bedroom door was the Fallon's seventeen year old daughter, Stephanie. And like most seventeen year olds (regardless of being on vacation or not), Stephanie stayed busy typing away on her cell phone. "You would think a place this fancy would have better reception."

Her mother, displeased with Stephanie's dependence on the device, snatched the phone right out of her hands. "That's the point, young lady. To spend time with your family."

"Mom!"

Joey then unleashed an over the top laugh while obnoxiously pointing in his sister's face, which in turn sparked a cliché sibling spat routinely found in most households. Cheryl, always the referee, stepped in between her two sparring children and started shuffling them towards the door. "Alright. Break it up. Let dad have his breakfast."

Both kids let out a unified grumble as they complied in leaving the bedside. But even after submitting to their parent's wishes, the juvenile commotion continued from the common room. Cheryl closed the bedroom door while looking at her husband and tried to contain a laughing smile. "Well, the quiet was nice while it lasted."

He simply nodded his head with a defeated smirk. "At least they're doing something together."

Paul then reached over and grabbed the remote control resting on the nightstand. As he turned the television on, his wife strolled over to the blinds, opening them up and letting the morning light into the room. "This place really is beautiful."

The view from their hotel room overlooked the main courtyard of Mountain Village. A series of buildings, the Cliffs included, were built in a circle along the outskirts of the village's main pavilion. In the center resided a frozen fountain, empty now but always full of ice skating children around lunchtime. In the hours to come the clothing stores, ski shops and lift ticket booths positioned around the courtyard would open as the resorts' guests scrambled to get the first snow tracks of the day.

Designed to look like its namesake, Mountain Village represented the commercial age's growing fascination with antiquity. Each one tied into the next, the building's stone facades and terra cotta roofs piled on top of one another in a seamless transition from one structure to the next. In between them, pathways made up of carefully designed stone pavers shepherded all who walked on them to the gondola's base. Everything about the village echoed a sense of old time charm and class, but replicating such a style with new construction left the buildings looking overly fantastical and manufactured.

Cheryl's comment about the view's beauty was not so much focused on the artificial winter wonderland but more towards the natural scenery of the Colorado Rockies behind it. The majestic setting was only amplified by several white flurries gracefully gliding through the air. "Looks like it's starting to snow, too."

Already well into his breakfast, her husband was less concerned with the pitiful evidence of snowfall out the window than that of the forecast on the television. "With a lot more to come. Look."

She turned around to the sight of a Denver weather woman highlighting a massive storm front moving in the direction of southwestern Colorado. During any other situation, Cheryl might treat such circumstances with aggravation and concern. But because of their ski trip, the normally reserved mother nodded approvingly with pleased satisfaction. "We might be snowed in here."

Finally turning to look out at the mountain's pristine slopes through the window, a big smile stretched across Paul's bacon-filled mouth. "One can only hope."

2

Whatever little coffee Phillip O'Neil had in his mug was already cold. Completely dressed in his red ski patrol uniform, he sat waiting at a table in the small warming hut for almost half an hour.

The tiny cabins, strategically placed around the mountain, were used as outposts for ski patrollers to pass the time in-between calls. But the warming huts also acted as a resting spot for skiers looking for a blanket and cup of hot chocolate.

Considered to be one of the local old timers by the resort's seasonal employees, Phil had been saving lives on the mountain so long the job practically became second nature. He mastered the art of treating broken bones and open wounds to the point where he could do it on the steepest cliff in the dead of night. Mountain EMS had been his life's calling, but not every day was filled with action and excitement, so it helped to have a partner worth passing the time with. For the past couple seasons, Phil was glad to have a youngster with a good sense of humor and laid back approach to life. It made the downtime that much easier. But on days like today Phil wasn't going to put up with any bullshit, which made waiting for his partner to show up a frustrating experience.

Phil looked down into the mug and actually contemplated taking a final swig of his ice cold coffee when the door to the hut suddenly swung open. Chris entered followed by a few whirling flurries of snow trailing in after him. Already dressed in his gear, Chris quickly shut the door behind him and started preparing a pot of coffee on the counter. "I know. I know. You don't have to tell me how late I am."

Phil casually remained seated, still holding his mug. "Half an hour."

"I said you didn't have to tell me."

Without saying a word, Phil slowly stood and made his way over to the counter. Chris stared down at the brewing machine when Phil reached over and clicked it off. The young patroller threw up his arms with a confused expression. "Ummm, excuse you?"

But Phil just looked up at him with a blank stare, trying hard to hide his aggravation. "Have you seen the weather report?"

"Yeah. Blue skies and sunshine. Can I have my coffee now, please?"

Ignoring the sarcasm, Phil walked around Chris and moved towards the door. "I'm usually easy on you, kid, but we haven't even started our morning rounds yet."

Chris lowered his head and spoke without turning around to face his partner. "Phil..."

"Not today, Chambers. Not when there's a blizzard..."

"Sarah tried to have the talk."

Phil stopped his walk towards the door and paused for a second before slowly turning around. "I told you it was coming."

Chris humbly looked up at him with a sense of defeated innocence. "Yeah. Yeah. Yeah. You have the almighty age and wisdom. I know."

The old patroller took a deep breath while staring into his partner's helpless face. "Fine. Drink your stupid coffee. You have five minutes of my counsel."

Phil moved back over to the table and sat down. "You're lucky I don't charge for this."

After turning his attention back towards the brew, Chris began pouring a cup. "She's loyal. I'll give her that much. We've had five summers of this long distance crap."

He then moved over to the table and sat down opposite his partner. "And I love her, man. I really do. But the thought of settling down, kids and white picket fences. It's scary, ya' know?"

Phil smirked and let out a slight chuckle at the young man's ignorance. "Yeah. The whole prospect seems absolutely terrifying."

"It's not funny. This is my life we're talking about."

Tilting his head to the side, Phil continued to leer at his partner with a look of exaggerated sarcasm. "I know. It's so tough. You work in such horrendous job conditions skiing in one of the most beautiful places on Earth and have a wicked, gorgeous woman who wants to spend her life with you. Your world is in ruins."

Even though he sought out Phillip's advice, Chris knew beforehand he wasn't going to like what he had to say. A small part of him hoped that his experienced partner would have just told him what he wanted to hear, but it quickly became clear that wasn't going to happen.

So when faced with the option of overheating or taking off his jacket, Chris decided to ignore a possibly frustrating conversation. "You know what?" He then took a big swig of his coffee while standing up from the table. "The mountain's going to open soon. We should get out there."

Phil let out a big belly laugh as Chris dumped the rest of his drink in the sink and started towards the door. "Come on! Don't be like that. Yours is a very serious problem most guys have."

Ignoring his partner, Chris opened the door and headed onto the mountain, even as Phil yelled out to him from his seat at the table. "I'm sure they make medication for it and everything!"

***

Peter Hayden already had one foot out the door and his face into the light snowfall when his wife, Rachel, called him back into the house. "Forgetting something?"

He turned to see her holding up his briefcase in the kitchen, swaying it back and forth mockingly. After letting out a sigh, Peter walked back inside and took the briefcase from her with a smile. "What would I do without you?"

She kissed him on the cheek and whispered in his ear before pulling away. "Probably run this place into the ground."

They shared a silent look of mutual happiness only years of a joyous marriage could produce. But their little moment of peace was interrupted by the thunder of their ten year old son stomping down the stairs. "It's snowing!"

The boy, already fully dressed in his snowsuit, continued his stampede as he reached the floor and barreled into both his parents. They simultaneously let out a playful grunt, wrapping their arms around him.

Peter then knelt down and straightened out his son's silly jester-like snow hat. "You can wear this for now but don't forget your helmet out there."

"I will, dad. Jeez."

"I'm serious. You're in ski school to keep you safe, but the mountain is still twice as crowded during these winter breaks and twice as dangerous."

"Nothing's gonna happen. Stop treating me like a baby."

He couldn't help but smile at his son's remarks. "You'll always be my baby, Ryan. No matter what."

Rachel stood next to the sentimental scene with a smile of her own. Her eyes then drifted around the expansive living room and felt a sense of pride at how far her little family had come from their humble beginnings. Peter had been Mountain Village's Manager for decades, and thanks to his hard work, the town had steadily seen an increase in visitor traffic during the non-holiday blocks of the season, the hardest to fill. Recently he'd begun to morph Telluride's image as an exclusive mountain for the wealthy into an affordable vacation spot for the middle class. And the resort's owners had rewarded his family in kind for establishing that perception.

She looked down at the two most important men in her life and thought to extend their moment together. "I was going to drive Ryan up to the gondola base, but maybe you should take him, dad?"

The tails to his jester hat swung about as Ryan jumped with joy. "Yeah!"

Peter nodded his head in agreement as he ushered his son towards the door. "All right. But let's hurry before it really starts coming down."

The father and son exited the house, closed the door behind them and made their way through the large, chunky snowflakes falling in every direction. Peter walked with a brisk pace while keeping his head down and away from the snow. Ryan, on the other hand, danced his way to the car and embraced the winter wonderland of their front lawn. "It's like we're inside a snow globe."

Peter pointed to the SUV in the driveway, trying to keep his son focused. "Well, if you don't get in the car I'll turn you upside down and shake you like one. Did you remember the key to your ski locker?"

Annoyed by his father's pestering, Ryan rolled his eyes while finally entering the car's passenger side. "Yeah, dad. I keep telling you, I'm not a baby."

While opening the car door, Peter smiled again at his son's desire to grow up. But instead of stepping inside, his attention diverted to his neighbor's house. Or at least, the closest thing he had to a neighbor. In contrast to the old and decadent town of Telluride, the condos and mansions of Mountain Village, built seemingly overnight, represented the lavish and debonair lifestyle associated with high society.

The municipality was effectively a combination of the condos, hotels and stores clumped together around the gondola's base as well as a series of mega mansions spread out over the mountainside. Peter took pride in the fact that he not only called this winter paradise home, but that he was responsible for its creation.

Unfortunately, because of the clientele that the area's accommodations attracted, Mountain Village had few permanent residents. And the man who currently occupied the house closest to the Hayden's, which was almost a quarter mile down the road, never spent more than four days before heading back to his home in Los Angeles.

Peter watched as he saw the speck of a man in the distance exit the house and enter a limo that had been waiting in the driveway. Peter knew the man, who didn't ski and lived alone in the forty-two hundred square foot house, was Scott Brooks. As a leader in this unique community, a place where the cost of the average single family home approached five million dollars, Peter made it a point to know all the property owners in Mountain Village. What Mr. Brooks did for a living that allowed him to purchase a five million dollar home in cash was another mystery entirely.

As the limo drove off, Peter brushed aside his pending questions for Mr. Brooks and stepped inside the car. After backing out of the driveway and turning on the windshield wipers, Peter began a slow drive through the village's windy roads as they climbed the mountain.

After several minutes of passing by a series of sporadically placed mansions, the father and son both spotted another neighbor standing on a balcony. The bald man carelessly sipped from a mug and wore a white bathrobe that blended into the falling snowflakes surrounding him. He caught a glimpse of Peter inside the car and responded by lifting his mug to the sky with a wide smile.

Ryan kept his eyes on the man with a star-struck look of amazement. "Is that Austin Cage?"

"I think so. I heard he bought a place here recently. Just didn't know which one."

Ryan turned to his father with energized excitement. "So he's going to come to the film festival every year? That's awesome!"

"Don't assume, Ryan. Maybe he just wants a place to ski."

But the boy ignored his father's precaution and went on rambling. "Did you see his last movie where he's a marine in the jungle? There was this big explosion at the end, and he's thrown from a helicopter half way across…"

Ryan continued to talk, and Peter tried to listen. But he was too distracted by his son's assumption. Although great for the town, Telluride's film and musical festivals gave off a perception that it catered to famous celebrities. It was an image he was trying to move away from. Then again, rebranding the resort while keeping its reputation intact wasn't necessarily that simple.

As the economy spiked in the nineties, Peter led the charge to revamp Telluride's scrappy ski resort into a luxurious retreat of class and prestige. After years of planning, Mountain Village ended up becoming the physical realization of that dream.

But times had changed, and the need for expanding business forced Peter to push the envelope. Rachel, with her liberal mindset, was happy with his newest marketing campaign to make Telluride an obtainable paradise for all. But Peter was worried that by making the mountain more accessible financially, he'd alienate the wealthy that enjoyed the austerity that came with the mountain's steep price tag.

Then again, maybe he was too close to the issue and over-thinking the situation. Maybe residents like Austin Cage would always come to Telluride, not because of its perception as a high society retreat but simply because of the breathtaking views he, himself, was currently amazed by.

After all, the valley's natural beauty and wonder were unlike any other Colorado had to offer. Through the falling snow, Peter stared out at the trees, streams and mountaintops, mystified by its existence. And he had forgotten just how lucky he was to call this place home. It wasn't a metropolis like Aspen or a rest stop along a highway like Vail. It was a heavenly utopia, hidden from the world. Telluride truly was a special place. And it was his job to keep it that way.

**

At the moment, Johnny Prescott was thanking God he lived in a town where his commute consisted of a five-minute walk and a gondola ride. No matter how hungover or half-asleep he happened to be, as long as he made it to that base station he would be brought straight to work. But on this day, he happened to be neither. He woke up feeling strangely hot for living in the Rockies during the middle of winter. Combined with body aches and a series of intermittent chills, Johnny assumed he was feeling the after effects of Tiffany Miller's sexual escapades.

He knew from the moment he met her, that girl would probably be the end of him. But that's the problem with love. Even knowing of your own impending doom, you're still powerless to stop yourself. They'd been going steady for a couple weeks, but he knew she'd gone behind his back with other guys in the past. He cursed himself knowing the possibility of an STD wasn't completely absurd. Then again, they did roll around on the floor of a hundred year old mine. So Johnny reluctantly admitted that might've had something to do with it.

He sat alone in the gondola cabin as it turned a corner at the mid-mountain station and began its descent into Mountain Village. The boy normally enjoyed the morning sight of a pristine ski slope as the slow ride brought him gracefully down the mountain. But today he was too focused on keeping himself together that the scenic view didn't even register to him. Besides, in the ten minutes he'd been on the gondola, the light snowfall he walked through to get to the station had grown heavier and obscured the cabin's windows.

Johnny closed his eyes, huddled in the corner of the cabin and tried desperately to fight the alternating bouts of heat and chills. But a growing knot in the pit of his stomach was quickly becoming the more pressing problem. Not wanting to focus on the sickness, Johnny's mind started to drift and wonder if Tiffany was feeling the same way. He briefly considered calling her, but his train of thought was interrupted by a bump in the cabin as it pulled into the station.

The gondola doors swung open just as Johnny's eyes did the same. The boy then tucked his chin and arms into his chest as he stepped out into the glass station, preparing himself for the cold. Johnny's gaze was focused downward, but he could feel the gondola's attendant shoot him a mixed stare of morbid repulsion and grotesque fascination. Johnny didn't bother looking in the mirror before he rolled out of bed and left the house twenty minutes earlier but assumed that his outward appearance reflected exactly how he felt on the inside. He might've responded to the attendant if he had the strength, but for now, Johnny was more focused on not collapsing in the snow on his walk across the courtyard.

He figured in thirty seconds he would be safe inside at work, where he could rest up in the back with a blanket and coffee until the morning rush of skiers hit the mountain. But as he started walking, Johnny thought the smart move would be to take a short detour to the pharmacy across the way. He'd never been in the store before but patted himself on the back for coming up with what he considered the best decision he made all week. Johnny Prescott never took a sick day in his life, and he wasn't going to start now. All he needed was some cold medicine, allergy medication and a pack of energy drinks. It would be just the breakfast he needed to get him through the day.

3

"So with the weather as beautiful as it is today, I doubt any of you out there are grabbing some outdoor barbeque on the mountain. But just in case, could someone pleeeeeease bring me a rack of ribs from Joseph's later? I'm begging you."

Georgia Croft released her finger from a button on the control panel, clicking off her voice from the broadcast. The music slowly transitioned into another soft rock song, her preferred genre of choice for the late morning block. Then, after carefully removing her headset, Georgia placed them down and checked over her pre-set playlist one last time before standing up and stepping out of the sound booth.

The TORO building was practically an anthill compared to most radio stations with an audience their size, but Georgia took pride in that. It wasn't the number of listeners that impressed. After all, any radio station in a dense metropolitan area could pull huge figures. But it was how Miss Croft's audience listened in that intrigued her. Mainly servicing only Telluride and Mountain Village, the number of people within TORO's radio broadcast range was pretty pitiful. And with the mountains boxing them in on every side, their signal was even worse. But with the help of the Internet, TORO had the power to transmit their radio show to the entire world. And when they did, Georgia was surprised by just how many listeners tuned in.

As it turned out, people from all over the globe came to visit Telluride and departed with a love for its small town radio station. They went home, turned on their computers, and just like that, were listening to Georgia's radio show as if they never left.

And that's what gave Georgia pride. The fact that her audience didn't listen to her because they had to. They weren't forced to endure her voice simply because they were in the car and she just happened to be on, but because they wanted to. They made a conscious effort to seek her out and tune in from wherever they called home. And that was how in the absence of a mining industry, she helped turn TORO into Telluride's number one export.

As those prideful thoughts ran through her head, Georgia strolled down the hall with a smile on her face. About to turn the corner, she ran into a man's firm chest and bounced off as if hitting a wall.

Slightly stunned, Georgia looked up to see Malcolm smiling down at her with a to-go cup of coffee in his hand. She laughed at the expression on his face, knowing he was about to tease her for her clumsiness. But she quickly raised a single finger to cut him off. "Don't say a word."

Still smiling, he put his arms up innocently. "What? I wasn't going to say a thing. But ya know, most people say 'I'm sorry' when they bump into their boss. Especially when they almost spilled a coffee said boss had to wait in line behind a girl coughing up a storm to get."

Georgia quickly contained her giggles and put on an exaggerated show for her sarcastic response. "Oh, I'm so sorry, Mr. West. I didn't see your six-foot-three self standing in the middle of the hallway."

Malcolm's race and size were a constant source of humor for Georgia. In a mountain town with a population of just over two thousand, there weren't that many African Americans. But Malcolm arrived several years ago to produce shows for the radio station and found himself at home doing so.

The laid back and carefree atmosphere was a stark contrast to some of the other stuck up environments he worked at in the past. A punk girl like Georgia, with her purple hair and lip ring, would never have built a friendly, teasing relationship with a boss like Malcolm anywhere else. But in Telluride, their close friendship was more natural than any he had with a DJ in the past. And so they became quite the pair as they bantered back and forth, jokingly throwing insults to each other's stereotypes.

With the playful nature of the conversation still in effect, Malcolm shifted the topic to business. "Good thing I ran into you, too...even though...you know...you ran into me and all."

Georgia rolled her eyes, signaling him with her hands to get to the point. "Yeah. OK. Just get on with it already."

"I need you for the afternoon block today, too."

Georgia's jaw dropped in an over-exaggerated, girlish look of surprise. "What?! You gotta be kidding me."

Malcolm abruptly shook his head in a no-nonsense manner, ending the fun tone of the conversation. "Nope. Stew's flight from Vegas got delayed cause' of the weather. So that means we're out of DJs until tomorrow."

Georgia stomped her foot, once again expressing every bit of emotion in the action. "Come on, Malcolm. Why don't you do it?"

"Because I'm a producer. Not a host. Besides, my voice isn't as sexy as yours."

Georgia eased the intensity of her objections, but still protested her boss' order in her own way. "As much as I love to be flattered, I'm pretty sure there are kidnapping laws against keeping me here."

Malcolm chuckled as he sidestepped around Georgia to get passed her. "Have you looked outside lately? Most normal humans don't leave their house in a blizzard."

He continued down the hall, but that didn't stop Georgia from yelling out to him, trying to get the last word in. "Are you kidding? We live on a ski mountain. People wish every day was like this."

And with Malcolm already having turned the corner and out of sight, Georgia let out a deep sigh in mental preparation for the task ahead of her. But first, she needed to continue the mission she was on to get a cup of coffee. It was going to be a long day.

***

Sarah Warren always made it a point to arrive early for class. It wasn't that she had some rigid code that required her to be punctual. In fact, she would be the first to admit she's usually running late. But not when it came to her job. And there was one simple reason why she did it: the children. As cliché as it sounded (and she knew it did), the children were always her top priority.

At twenty-five, Sarah didn't have any of her own, not yet at least. If she and Chris ever managed to settle down then maybe she'd consider having a baby or two. But she didn't have to have any to know how important children were to their parents.

Growing up as an only child in the suburbs outside of Sydney, her parents smothered her with affection to the point where she couldn't wait to leave and head to the States for the winter snow season. But that love and caring taught her just how valuable a child's life is to parents.

In her role as a ski instructor, every day Sarah was given a group of children and entrusted with their safety. It wasn't just a babysitting job (as Chris sometimes liked to tease her about). It was a responsibility to be their guardian. A crowded mountain of snowboarders and skiers was a dangerous place, not to mention when you added a snowstorm to the equation. She took her job and the vigilance that was required of it seriously.

That was why she showed up early to the ski school meeting place by the gondola. So that when the parents arrived to drop off their children, they knew their loved ones were in good hands. And not some punk kid who could get them hurt…or worse.

The ski school meeting area was right in the thick of Mountain Village's base. A series of signs in the snow running parallel to the gondola designated the locations where various age groups should congregate. Having some of the younger children in her class, Sarah's spot was off to the side, and she rather preferred it that way. The beginning of the day was always a crowded mess in the village, and the weather planned for today promised to make things especially hectic. Since Sarah arrived in Mountain Village, the snowflakes had graduated from tiny specks to full balls of fluff, and she only expected it to get worse.

Luckily, she wasn't the only one who decided to arrive early. Of her six students, five had already shown up and were ready to get started. Their parents had dropped them off ahead of the morning rush and went up the gondola to catch the first tracks of the day. She was waiting on one last student and arguably her most important.

As the two boys and three girls in front of her played in the powdery snow, Sarah looked behind her and into the village courtyard for her final charge to appear. For now her other students, all bundled up in their ski suits and helmets, were content to fool around where they were. But she knew how quickly a child's attention could be lost. It won't be long before they became antsy and cold, nagging her to get started. And with the crowds beginning to gather and the other ski school classes starting to fill up, it was only a matter of time before the whining began.

Sarah looked up at the gigantic clock that rested at the top of the courtyard and saw that she still had five minutes before she could technically consider someone late. But it was then that she felt a small figure tackle into the back of her. "Sarah!"

She looked down to see the top of Ryan Hayden's helmet as he squeezed her thigh in a tightening grasp. She smiled as she knelt down to his level and returned the hug. "There you are, Rye-guy. We've been waiting for you."

Ryan released the hug and pulled back to reveal a snowy beard built up around his facemask. "Like my new look?"

The other children laughed, and even Sarah managed a small giggle as she wiped the bits of slush caked onto his goggles. "I love it. You ready to go?"

"Sure. But can we stop for hot chocolate today?"

Sarah stood up and answered the boy's question while helping the other kids gather their skis. "Hot chocolate already? But we haven't even done one run yet."

Like a contagious plague, the other children quickly caught on to their classmate's desire and started to nag in unison. "Please, Sarah! Please! One quick stop. Just a little later. Please! Pretty please!"

Sarah couldn't help but laugh as she finally gathered her own skis and started ushering the children over to the gondola line. "OK! OK! We'll see how well you guys behave."

They all cheered as one, and the kids' youthful excitement

continued to force a smile onto Sarah's face. But it quickly faded when she became curious as to how Ryan sneaked up on her all alone.

As they reached the line and waited, Sarah's eyes scanned the crowded village and eventually found Mr. Hayden standing at the edge of the courtyard where the pavers met the snow. Not wanting to step onto the mountain in his work clothes, Mr. Hayden watched to make sure his son made it to class safely. She acknowledged him with a wave, and he responded kindly with a friendly smile and wave of his own.

Despite it snowing as hard as it was, Mr. Hayden stayed watching as the line slowly moved forward and his son boarded the gondola. He was a busy man, but unlike the resort's guests, Mr. Hayden's stay in Telluride didn't have an expiration date and he could spare a few moments to see his son off.

From the gondola window, Sarah watched as Mr. Hayden turned around and disappeared into the crowded courtyard. She tried to follow him, but the gondola car quickly climbed up the mountain and the village disappeared into a cloud of snow.

As the children in the gondola jabbered on, Sarah let her mind drift away while continuing to stare into the whiteness out the window. She wondered if Chris would eventually share Mr. Hayden's qualities as a father. If he would be kind and compassionate. Patient and caring. It's true his profession was treating people when they were sick or injured, but showing affection to a child of your own was a completely different ballgame. Would he really be able to step up to the plate as a father when the time came? Hell, he couldn't even commit to the two of them living together full-time.

Sarah could feel herself growing frustrated and pushed the thoughts out of her mind. They were important questions but ones that would need to be answered at another time. For now, she had six children whom she considered her own to deal with. And they deserved all her attention.

***

Cheryl Fallon always considered herself the glue that held her family together. The rock that kept them grounded. And this was especially true when the time came for a vacation. Most people assumed that going away on a ski trip meant rest and relaxation. But Cheryl knew better. For her, a family retreat was when she actually had to work the hardest.

Even now, as her family was dressed and ready to head out onto the mountain, she kept a watchful eye on their movements in the Cliff's ski shop as they waited for their valeted equipment. Paul, standing in front of her at the other end of the store, had already made a friend with the store's owner. She couldn't hear their conversation but assumed it danced back and forth between last night's sports scores and the stock market. More importantly, Cheryl kept a watch on her children out the corner of each eye. They were both browsing the shops overpriced skiing equipment and, Cheryl surmised, never bothering to look at the price tags while doing so.

Joey, who had been nagging her for a new pair of snowboard boots since the trip was planned, window shopped along the store's left wall. While Stephanie drifted between racks of ski jackets and pants, completely disoriented without a phone to accompany her right hand.

Cheryl wished she didn't have to monitor her family's every move but was left with no other choice. Otherwise, they'd probably all just wander off, lost in their own little worlds. Then their time together would be thrown out the window and they might as well have just stayed home.

As Cheryl continued to watch her family, she became increasingly concerned with her daughter's growing agitation. Stephanie paced around the store's aisles, browsing through the racks of clothes in a fit of irritation. Sensing her motherly duties were needed, Cheryl decided to end her role as a passive observer and investigate her daughter's uneasiness.

Stephanie was so entranced sifting through a pile of snow hats that she didn't even notice her mother approaching until she stood alongside her. Even then, she only gave Cheryl a brief glance of acknowledgment before going back to her pointless activity. "Hey."

Cheryl couldn't help but laugh at her daughter's brevity. "Hey? That's all I get?"

Once again, Stephanie refused to commit to the conversation with more than a one-word response. "What?"

At which point, Cheryl looked down at her daughter with an expression that only a mother with years of practice could master. The combination of a smirk, raised brow and two glaring eyes gave Cheryl the uncanny appearance of a friendly parent that wasn't taking any bullshit. "Listen, missy: I've known you your entire life, and I'm pretty sure I can tell when something's bothering you. So what's wrong?"

This time, the girl answered without interrupting her search through the hats. "Nothing."

Cheryl placed her hand on the pile of clothes, forcing the teenager's attention to her. "Steph, no matter how much you mope, you're not getting your phone back."

The bluntness of her mother's comment hit Stephanie right in the face, and she let out an exhausted sigh of disappointment. Then, after composing herself from that world-ending realization, the pout of a princess smeared across her face as she pleaded her case. "But why? What's the big deal? Everyone on planet Earth has a phone. I'm seventeen. I think I deserve one."

Although it came off as a whine, Cheryl could tell that deep down her daughter was feeling genuinely mistreated. Like most new parents, Paul and her had spoiled Stephanie way too much as their firstborn child. But she would be graduating high school soon, and she would have to learn that the world wasn't as nice as mommy and daddy made it out to be.

Cheryl paused for a moment to analyze the situation and then resumed her parenting stare as she started to speak. "First off, I think you need to look up the word 'deserve' in the dictionary. And it's because you're graduating high school soon that I took the phone away."

Stephanie gave her mother a confused look as if she just had her mind twisted in a knot. And Cheryl struggled to hold in a laugh at her daughter's clueless expression as she went on to explain. "Look. College starts in the fall and then you're free of us. No parents or little brother to bother you at all. You can sit in your dorm and text all day if you want to.

"But trust me, you don't have it so bad at home. You'll see as you meet other kids your age. Your family loves and cares about you deeply. Not everyone can say that. So when you're sitting in bed trying to fall asleep at two in the morning because you have a class at eight, you'll miss us and be glad we spent this time together."

Cheryl stopped for a moment, allowing time for her words to sink in. And when a small, reluctant smile crept its way across Stephanie's face, she knew at least some of her speech got through. She smiled in return while wrapping her arm around her daughter's shoulder. "Then someday you'll have a daughter of your own and say to yourself, 'well, I guess my mom was right'."

Stephanie let out a laugh, playfully pushing her mother away. "Never!"

They both continued smiling together when a voice called out to them from the back of the store. "Fallon. You're all set."

Suddenly, a blur of a snowboard jacket ran by them as Joey darted across the room. They looked up to see him running towards the young boy that called their name standing in a doorway leading to the outside. Cheryl then turned to her daughter as Joey disappeared into the snowfall.

"Can you go after your brother and make sure he doesn't take off without us?"

"Sure."

In better spirits, Stephanie jogged through the store after her brother while Cheryl approached her husband, who was still lost in his conversation. "Paul. They called us."

"Oh, Cheryl. This is Martin Wells. He runs the ski shop."

Trying her best to be both polite and curt, Cheryl nodded her head while tugging on her husband's arm. "Nice to meet you. I wish we could chat, but we really should…"

With a big jovial voice, Martin cut off Cheryl's unnecessarily courteous gesture and ushered the couple out towards the door. "No. Of course. It's going to be a hell of a powder day. Don't waste a second on my account. Go. Have fun."

Half way out the door and into the snow, Paul gave the store owner a handshake and a friendly wink. "Don't forget about that stock tip. We'll talk more when I get back."

The two smiled as Martin gave them both a final wave goodbye and disappeared into the store. Cheryl then turned her attention towards the scene in front of her. The falling snow had rapidly picked up in the last hour and Cheryl was forced to drop her goggles onto her face just to see in front of her. She quickly realized the back door of the Cliff's ski shop actually led out onto a run of the mountain. Well, it wasn't really a run, but a carved out path to allow guests of the resort an easy ski in-ski out experience as they valeted their equipment at the shop.

She was also pleased to note that her skis and poles had already been set up in the snow and were waiting for her to just jump in and go. Next to them were Stephanie and Joey, already strapped in and ready to head out. Steph played with the straps on her poles while Joey chatted with the young boy that had called their name to come outside. Cheryl walked over to them, curious about their conversation. She heard them talking about waxing Joey's snowboard to make it faster, but as she got closer, Cheryl was almost horrified by the pale look of death engrained into the boy's face.

Despite wearing no hat or protection from the cold, beads of sweat poured down the boy's face. His bloodshot eyes were squinted barely open to protect from the storm, yet the teenager was still oblivious to the gigantic snowflakes smashing into him. He stood leaning over ever so slightly into his hands that were buried in his coat pockets. But Cheryl had a sneaking suspicion that his stance was just to keep him from keeling over on the spot.

There was definitely something wrong with him. That much was obvious. But Joey was so immersed in their discussion of snowboards that he didn't even notice. Cheryl could also tell that the boy didn't want to be bothered but was still kind enough to participate in the conversation rather than be rude. Besides, entertaining the resort's guests was probably part of the job.

Neither Paul nor Stephanie, both of whom were ready to leave, noticed the boy's condition, but Cheryl couldn't help but stare and wonder what ailed him. Could it be drugs? She assumed even remote mountain towns weren't devoid of their addicts. Or maybe he was just sick. Either way, Cheryl quickly jumped into her skis and shepherded her family down the mountain, thinking the best thing to do was to get away from the child as quickly as possibly lest they caught what he had.

4

"Seven million dollars?! Goddamn! Did he put grease on your ass before he shoved it in?!"

Several patrons in the small town French café turned disgusted at Scott Brooks sitting alone in the corner booth. In response to their stares, he removed the phone from his ear just long enough to mouth an insincere sorry to their judgmental eyes before putting it back and continuing his conversation. "The entire stock is worth at least twelve. He fucked you. You do realize that, right?"

As he spoke, Scott shuffled what was left of the breakfast on the plate in front of him into his mouth. A combination of eggs, cheese and vegetables, the dish was exactly the gourmet meal he'd come to expect from such a quaint restaurant hidden in the quiet mountain town. He didn't even know the place's name, but it was small town secrets like this that made Scott consider Telluride his second home.

Unfortunately, Telluride's friendly neighborhood vibe only went one way and failed to rub off on Mr. Brook's character. If it had, his loud mouth and foul language might not have offended his fellow restaurant goers enough for them to get up and leave mid-meal. He never understood that when you leave the city, you're also supposed to leave the city way of life behind as well. Or maybe he understood and just didn't care.

After witnessing customer after customer walk away from him and towards the exit, a young waiter approached the obnoxious man as humbly as he could. "Excuse me, sir. Could you keep it down? You're disrupting the other customers."

Scott gave him a look that barely qualified as a glance and continued on with his conversation. "No. Listen to me. You can still salvage this, but you have to do some serious damage control."

If the waiter was offended he didn't show it as he continued his attempt at curbing the unruly patron. "I'm sorry, sir, but I'm going to have to ask you to leave."

After dropping his fork, Scott finished chewing the food in his mouth, took a deep breath, and finally turned to the polite waiter with a large smile. He then spoke into his phone while staring intently into the waiter's eyes. "Don't make a move without hearing from me."

Scott dropped the phone on the table, continuing his obnoxious smile. "Of the customers who just walked out, how much do you think their combined bills were?"

The waiter's eyes followed Scott's hand as it reached into his expensive jacket. "It's not about money, sir, and honestly, I'm a little offended that you…"

The boy stopped midsentence when Scott pulled out a rubber-banded wad of money the size of his fist. He then unraveled the bills while looking up at the waiter with a look of condescension. "You were saying?"

The waiter opened his mouth to speak but was too focused on Scott's actions to form any words. So instead of being scolded, Scott decided to fill the silence while standing from the booth. "I noticed they all put money on the table before leaving, too. Probably because everyone's so fucking nice in this town. But you know what, I can be nice too."

Scott proceeded to drop several hundreds from his wad onto the table, way above any potential bill that a small town café could possibly generate. He then scooted out of the booth and past the waiter while giving him a friendly pat on the shoulder. "Call it an asshole tax."

Satisfied with his meal, Scott cockily strutted towards the café's exit. But just as he opened the door to leave, the waiter's voice turned him back around. "We appreciate your business, sir, but would also appreciate if you didn't come back."

With a wave, nod, and smile, Scott acknowledged the waiter's request before exiting the restaurant. "Fair enough, mon ami. Ciao."

Once outside, Scott pulled his jacket up and over his neck to protect from the snow while scuttling over to the double-parked limo waiting for him. With the car already running, Scott quickly opened the door and slid inside the warm cabin. His body bounced up and down on the limo's cushy leather seats, and Scott gave a violent shiver, shaking off all the loose snowflakes that accumulated on his jacket in the short time he'd been outside. "Brrrr! I'm out there two seconds and already my balls are frozen."

"I hear ya, Mr. B."

The response had come from Charlie Young, Scott's driver and bodyguard, who sat patiently in the front seat of the car. "How was breakfast?"

"Not worth what I paid for it. Come on. Let's get out of here."

Charlie put the car in gear and slowly pulled out into the freshly plowed street. But with inches of snow quickly re-accumulating on the pavement, the limo slowly made its way through Telluride's tight roads.

Besides a series of well choreographed snowplows, only a few other vehicles wandered the streets, most of them with better four wheel drive capability than Charlie's stylish limousine.

During the ride, Scott focused his eyes out the window as he took in the old Western architecture that dominated the town's buildings. "You ever get tired of coming here?"

Through the open partition between the front of the car and the cab, Charlie answered his boss while keeping his eyes on the road. "No. It's too beautiful. But I tell you what: after a week or so, I'm definitely ready to leave."

"Wouldn't be because of them, would it?"

Scott's comment forced Charlie to quickly look over to his side and catch a glimpse of Telluride's infamous free box. The charity spot was an outdoor cubby where people could donate their unwanted items in exchange for philanthropic gratification. The relic survived from the sixties when the hippie lifestyle of free love came to Telluride in droves.

Today, a series of rich bohemians, self-proclaimed trustafarians, were busy scavenging the free box for blankets and jackets. Young women and long-haired men scampered around in the snow, quickly trying to shield themselves from the cold. It was a sight that made Charlie shamefully chuckle. "Why didn't they get the clothes before it started snowing?"

"Because they enjoy the pity in it. Look at 'em all. It's almost a show. Trust fund babies picking scraps like cockroaches. Shit, I should've brought some popcorn."

Never one to let Mr. Brooks's pessimistic attitude bring him down, Charlie just shrugged his shoulders, letting his boss' comment roll off of him. "Maybe they just like free stuff. Doesn't everybody?"

Scott then turned, fell back onto the couch and stared up comfortably at the limo's black ceiling. "But that's the thing. Nothing's free in this world, Charlie. Everything has a price. Sometimes it's money. Other times it's dignity. Maybe even a part of your soul. The key to success, though, is making sure that whatever you're buying, you have enough of it in the bank to cover the cost."

***

Despite a steady snowfall outside, Bill Sheridan couldn't be happier. Sometimes the snow was good for business. Sometimes bad. Today happened to be the latter. After hearing the day's forecast (combined with their own intuitive predictions) the Sheridans cancelled all scheduled snowmobile tours and told their staff to stay home. Most of the guests understood why it needed to be done, however, a few argued the decision. Some people would always be destined to underestimate the danger of the mountain. But Bill would be damned if he were to facilitate their stupidity.

So the Sheridans decided to take the day off and simply bask in the peace and quiet of each other's company. It was a rare and brief glimpse into what their life would have been like if they chose to retire when most couples should. But even well after their children grew up and moved away to start families of their own, Bill and Nellie kept their business going.

As the morning puttered on, the couple sat comfortably in the living room of their ranch home. Furnished with a combination of modernity and Old West decor, the space emitted a surprisingly homey feel for being styled as a traditional hunting cabin. Stuffed game heads of boar and elk lined the walls alongside ancient firearms, pistols, and rifles that told a story of their nation's history better than any textbook. Despite the images of death all around them, the two old timers still managed to enjoy coffee and a light breakfast while the Denver news lightly muttered on a television in the background. Neither were really paying any attention to it, but the reporter's soft voice was soon overcome by the roar of a vehicle approaching the house.

Bill stood from his seat and went over to the window. Through a whirl of fluffy whiteness he could make out the headlights of a truck piercing through the snowfall. The engine stopped and out stepped a tall male figure who then approached the house. His face was obscured by the storm, but Bill could still make out the pristine Marshal's hat atop the man's head.

On his way to the front door, Bill called out to his wife, who continued on with her meal uninterrupted by the pending visitor. "It's Travis."

Nellie remained quiet, even as Bill opened the door to stop their guest from knocking. A trail of several flurries flew into the house, and Bill quickly waved the Marshal inside. "Come on in before you turn into a snowman out there."

A middle-aged man with a fully groomed mustache, Marshal Travis Walker entered the house and started stomping his feet on a horse-themed welcome mat. Bill swiftly shut the door behind him and extended his arms, offering to take his guest's coat. "Mornin', Marshal. Can I get that for ya?"

"Thanks, Bill, but I don't plan on stayin' long." The Marshal then turned his attention to Bill's wife still sitting in the living room. "Nellie, how've you been?"

She answered him with a cup of coffee held up to her mouth, eagerly waiting to finish her sentence so she could take a sip. "Just wonderin' what brings you all the way out here in such lovely weather?"

A hint of sarcasm rang in her voice, but both Bill and Travis picked up that it wasn't the weather aspect of her comment which it applied to. From a legacy of pioneers and ranchers, Nellie's family never did take too kindly to the law in Telluride. And that relationship only grew worse after the untimely and controversial demise of her brother.

So Travis took a deep breath and contemplated his words carefully before speaking again. "You know I would never bother you two unless it was important."

From comfortably in her seat, Nellie rapidly nodded her head with anticipation. "Then get on with it already."

"The lock on the gate to Tomboy was off this morning. I've had my suspicions someone's been headin' up there, but now I'm sure of it."

Bill scrunched his brow, trying to follow the Marshal's train of thought. "And you think we did it?"

Travis humbly removed his hat before shaking his head. "Absolutely not. I know you two have enough connections in town to head up to the settlement any time you wanted. But I took a drive up there to check things out before the storm."

A pause filled the conversation, and Nellie was once again forced to nudge the Marshal's story forward. "And?"

"The boards were off the mine. Someone was down there, too."

The sentence rung through Nellie like a shot to the heart, bringing back memories of Tomboy she would rather have forgotten. The old mining settlement, built high above the town upon a flat stretch of land nestled into the back wall of the canyon, was the reason Telluride existed in the first place as a means to house workers' families.

During the late nineteenth century, miners thrived exploiting the area's abundant deposits of gold, copper, silver, and tellurium, the element which would eventually become the town's namesake. But as the age of industrial mining slowed down across America, the crew working the Tomboy mines suddenly vanished overnight. It was a genuine Wild West mystery worthy enough to become the subject of lectures and books.

Nellie's reasons for being wary of the historical landmark, though, were a bit more personal than its apocryphal and legend, and that had nothing to do with the fact it was being used as a spot for late night hookups. "You think it was kids?"

Travis lightly nodded his head in the affirmative. "Probably. I checked inside but couldn't figure out who it was. Guests at the resort don't care enough to head up there, and adults in town still remember what happened to your brother."

The Marshal's words sent a shiver down Nellie's spine, and she could instantly feel past frustrations coming back to her. "I told them to cave in that damn hole years ago."

Travis shook his head in subtle agreement while at the same time trying to defend the town he was sworn to protect. "Tomboy's status as a historical site depends on that mine staying accessible. We were able to board it up, but the council won't seal it completely."

Echoing his wife's feelings on the matter, Bill stared at the Marshal intensely. "So, why are you telling us? We hate the place more than anyone."

Travis slowly put the hat back on his lowered head. "I just thought you should know. Out of respect for your history an' all."

Nellie nodded her head appreciatively, but with enough conviction that it showed her desire to end the conversation. "That's kind of you, Marshal. Now you should get back before the storm really kicks in."

Bill reached behind the Marshal and opened the door, once again allowing a snowy breeze to enter the house. Travis bundled up inside his coat and prepared to leave when he suddenly turned his head back inside. "I never knew your brother, nor do I know all the details about what happened. But if you really want that place shut down, trespassing kids is as good an opportunity as any."

It was more advice than any person wearing a badge had given to Nellie in the past. And she silently responded to it with a slight curl of her cheek, the only gesture small enough that could still be considered a smile. Travis took the awkward action as a sign of gratitude and proceeded to walk back out into the snow.

Bill moved back over to the window, watching the Marshal wade through the shin high snow back to his truck. "What do ya think?"

Nellie reached over and grabbed the remote on the table, turning off the television as she stood. "I think he's incompetent. But that doesn't mean he's wrong."

"Fine. But once you start fighting the town council there's no going back. You'll have to relive what happened to your brother all over again."

She then joined her husband's side, and together they watched the Marshal's truck back out through heavy snow before heading down the road into Telluride. "Well, let's hope whoever went inside that mine made it out all right. Otherwise, I don't think we'll have much of a choice."

***

The only thing worse than waiting in a lift line is waiting in a lift line during a blizzard. It was a lesson Stephanie Fallon had learned on more than one occasion. Everything's good and fun when you're zooming down the mountain, but once your body stops moving and you're forced to stand still, that's when the cold really starts to set in.

After sharing a gondola ride with her family, Stephanie followed her parents down to a mid-mountain chairlift while her brother uncharacteristically trailed behind them. Now, she waited in line next to the little brat while her parents stood behind them. The chair was only a triple, so the family was forced to split into two groups. And mommy dearest thought it would be a good idea for Steph to spend some bonding time with her brother. Which wouldn't be half as bad if the wind chill wasn't into the single digits.

To be fair, the lift line wasn't nearly as long as the one for the gondola, but being a couple hundred more feet in the air didn't help. The extra elevation came with a slight increase in wind and snow that made the wait a little less bearable. Sporadic gusts pounded into her jacket, forcing the girl's arms to wrap around her shivering chest. Big, fluffy balls of falling snow swirled around her from every direction, limiting her sight to just past the end of the lift line. Beyond it, she could see the base of the lift as the front of the line slowly moved forward into position. But after swinging around and scooping up the passengers, the chair began its long journey up the side of the mountain and disappeared into a thick cloud of falling snow. Seeing a chairlift wasn't anything special, and Stephanie had been on one a hundred times before, but it was currently the only sight she could focus on that could distract her from the cold.

She was beginning to feel a little bit sorry for herself, but that quickly changed when she glanced over at Joey standing next to her. His shivering body stood in much the same position hers did, but his jacket, mask, and goggles were all pulled down, exposing his face to the freezing elements. The color of his skin had faded to a shade of pallid whiteness, and a thick rock of frost had frozen under his nose.

Upon seeing his condition, Stephanie quickly leaned over to adjust his clothing. "Joey! What's wrong with you? Cover yourself up."

But as she got closer, Stephanie saw that the freezing air wasn't the only factor affecting her little brother. A frozen bead of sweat outlined his forehead, and his bloodshot eyes stood out from within his pale face. She wasn't a doctor, but Stephanie could easily tell something else was wrong with her sibling.

Upon hearing the commotion, the children's mother moved up from behind them to investigate the situation. "What's going on here?"

Their father then poked his head over his wife's shoulder to get a view of their son. "Is everything all...Joey! Are you OK?"

The boy simply stood motionless except for the steady shiver that consumed his body. "I don't feel so good."

Stephanie began rubbing her brother's arms in a futile attempt to warm him. "Yeah. No shit."

Despite the seriousness of the situation, Cheryl still snapped at her daughter's language. "Steph! Watch your mouth."

"But look at him. Something's not right."

Paul quickly popped out of his skis and crouched down in front of his son. "Joey, what's wrong?"

The boy kept his head down and eyes closed, trying hard to fight off the cold. "I...I don't know. It hurts all over."

Scott then removed a glove and pressed the back of his hand to Joey's forehead. "He's burning up."

Cheryl shook her head, unhappy with her son's appearance. "We should head back. It's getting bad enough out here without him being sick."

Stephanie was a little disappointed. Not so much that her mother suggested they head in. It actually made sense to call it a day. She just wished the weather wasn't as bad as it was. All winter long she prayed for a day out West with new snow, but a storm can only get so bad before getting fresh tracks wasn't worth risking your life.

Neither she nor her father objected to her mother's request. It was just understood that Joey's health came first, and he appeared in no condition to refuse them.

They all looked at one another, silently agreeing to the plan when the Fallon's concerns were suddenly interrupted by a yelling voice from behind them. "Come on! Stop holding up the line!"

They all looked up to see a big gap between them and the person in line before them. Paul quickly hopped back into his skis as he went over their planned course of action. "We can't get to the Cliffs from here. We still have to take the lift up before we can get down."

With her dad and mom all ready to go, Stephanie tucked both of her ski poles under one arm and wrapped the other around Joey's shoulder. "Come on, bro. One more ride and we'll take it slow back to the room. Just hang in there."

She then ushered her brother forward through the falling snow, and together they boarded the lift, which for the final time took them slowly up the mountain.

5

Hamburger or chicken? That was the grand dilemma racing through Ryan Hayden's mind at the current moment.

Throughout the whole morning, all he could do was daydream about Joseph's homemade pudding. In fact, the boy was so preoccupied with it that Sarah had to constantly look back to make sure he was staying with the group. It was hard enough keeping a class of six eight year olds together on a clear day, let alone in a blizzard, when one of them couldn't stop fantasizing about desserts.

Several times during the slow, cold rides up the chairlift Ryan tried explaining it to her. He wanted to make her understand that Joseph's, a cafeteria-like lodge located on top of the mountain, always used the right chocolate to whip cream ratio which made the pudding super sweet, but not so sweet that you got sick. She just didn't get it, though. And how could she? Despite being really cool, Sarah was still an adult. And adults don't understand the nuances of excellent pudding.

But now Ryan created a problem for himself. He was so excited about the pudding that he couldn't make a decision on the lunch itself. The special pizza wasn't that good. And he wasn't interested in all the extra veggies and stuff they put in the pasta. So, hamburger or chicken were his only options. He kind of wanted a hamburger, but had one yesterday and craved something different. On the other hand, he was also pretty sure his mom planned on cooking chicken for dinner. The whole situation was quickly becoming the hardest decision he had to make all day.

Undressed from his ski jacket and helmet, Ryan stood wearing his long sleeved thermal in front of Joseph's grill section, staring at the menu like a stupefied zombie. Behind him, the lodge was quickly filling up for the lunchtime rush. Aside from the kitchen, the building basically consisted of a single large dining room and serving area. Like many of the structures built around the mountain, Joseph's resembled a modern day log cabin outfitted with a high ceiling and wooden tables. But any of the antique furnishings decorated around the room were overpowered by the loud rambling of chatter and a cloud of mixed smells swirling about.

Swaying back and forth, Ryan's eyes scanned the words on the menu until an arm wrapped around his shoulder, snapping him out of the trance. "What happened to your pudding?"

The words were spoken in Sarah's light, caring voice, but Ryan was almost offended by the question. The boy turned and looked at her with a stern, serious expression worthy of the conversation's topic. "Pudding's a dessert. You can't have dessert as your main course."

"Why not?"

Again, Ryan looked to his instructor agitated that he had to educate her on such a basic subject. "Because then it wouldn't be as special. You gotta save the best for last."

Sarah smiled, nodding her head approvingly. "Ryan, my friend, you are wise beyond your years."

"I guess. But now I don't know what I wanna eat."

Someone walked by holding a tray filled with two slices, and Sarah was instantly repulsed by the brown color of the cheese. "Pizza sucks, right?"

Ryan nodded and looked over to Sarah, desperate for help. She looked back at him, unable to remove a new smile from her face. It was an unwritten rule among ski school instructors not to pick favorite students. But it was hard for Sarah not to fall in love with the boy's innocence.

She finally glanced over behind the grill counter and caught a glimpse of a friend who could help. "Come on. I have an idea."

Grabbing him by the hand, Sarah led Ryan to the side of the grill and then yelled out to a young girl by the kitchen door. "Hey, Tiff!"

The pale girl, dressed in the usual Joseph's uniform and apron, turned around and returned Sarah's greeting with a weak smile. She then slowly trudged over to them, struggling to keep the smile on her face. "Well, if it isn't my favorite Australian."

Ryan stood idly by, listening in to the conversation as Sarah continued. "You OK? You don't look so hot."

The girl waved her hand brushing off Sarah's concern. "Yeah, I'm fine. Long night. That's all."

"How's your mom? She hasn't come in for a lesson in a while."

"I don't know. I had a big spat with her this morning about staying out late."

"Don't take it too personally. She just wants what's best for you."

The girl obnoxiously rolled her eyes. "No. She wants to ruin my life. I hate that bi-"

Catching sight of Ryan anxiously looking up at her, the girl suddenly stopped herself short, forcing an overly gleeful smile upon her face. "Hey, little guy!"

Sarah put her hand on Ryan's head as she introduced the two of them. "This is Ryan, one of my students. Ryan, meet Tiffany Miller."

The boy bashfully leaned into his instructor, who cuddled him in closer to her with an arm around his shoulder. "Ryan can't seem to find anything to eat. Think you can help us out?"

Tiffany moved in close, kneeling down to Ryan's eye level. "Sure. So Ryan, if you were to have anything you wanted to eat right now what would it be?"

His eyes drifted to the ceiling, thinking as he rubbed his chin. "Ummm...tacos!"

As if literally hit from surprise, Tiffany pretended to be blown backwards, falling to her heels and catching herself on the counter. "Tacos!? Oh, man. You don't make it easy for a girl, do you? Hold on. Lemme see what I can do."

Ryan watched curiously as Tiffany stood and disappeared into the back kitchen. He was confused yet excited at the possible prospect of getting his choice food. He didn't know exactly why he picked tacos. Probably because he just wanted to see if she could actually make it happen.

A minute passed by and Ryan still silently stood in wait. At the cusp of disappointment, he looked up at Sarah and started to lose hope. Sensing his eyes upon her, she looked down and gave him a reassuring smile, winking to seal the deal.

Just then, as if the two women had planned it all along, Tiffany emerged from the back holding a tray of two steaming hot tacos. Ryan's face lit up with joy. Partly because of the tacos, but mostly because he felt special getting something that nobody else could have.

He accepted the tray with a smile, smelling the spices floating above it. "Thank you."

"No problem, kid. Enjoy it."

***

As the assistant to arguably the most important man in Telluride, Beth McCabe was accustomed to waiting. Coming from what some would call a privileged childhood, she didn't always have the skill. In fact, she would be the first to admit that she hated it. But one skill she did excel at was learning how to get what she wanted, and Beth understood very well just how much patience it often required.

Peter had been silently staring at the miniature building in front of him for about ten minutes, and he still didn't have a response to it. Beth could tell he really wanted to continue staring at the model, but she could also tell that he felt bad about making her stand by his side the entire time.

Peter pushed his chair away from the large conference table, giving up hope that he would eventually come up with something to say. "This was the best they could come up with?"

Beth just shrugged her shoulders innocently, reluctant to have (much less give) an opinion. "That's what they told me."

Peter looked at her smugly with his head tilted to the side. "Come on, Beth. You're thirty-three years old. It's time you started pissing people off. Tell me what you think."

She looked down at the model and analyzed it again, this time while formulating her thoughts into words. The sculpture was of a single bland building built alongside an offshoot to the road leading up to Mountain Village. The mock-up itself was meticulously crafted. Even the landscape matched that of the actual real estate site it represented. But the building and area of development it sat on appeared generic and dull. Any concept of architecture or design was lost and replaced with cheapness and simple functionality.

Beth looked back up at her boss and instantly spoke her mind. "They're sending you a message. They know there's no money in this project, so why should they put more into it than they have to?"

Peter threw his arms in the air to accentuate his frustration. "Exactly! They didn't even try to hide it. It's like they deliberately made it look as cheap as they possibly could."

Beth removed a notepad from the table and prepared to write. "You want me to put together a response?"

Peter rubbed his chin in thought as he turned around and strolled over to the window behind him. When designing his management office, Peter made sure the conference room view purposefully overlooked Mountain Village in its entirety. Most of the personal offices had gorgeous views overlooking the natural Rockies. But to Peter, the conference room was a different story. It was a place where the future of Telluride would be decided. Where decisions would be made that could lift the resort up to the best in the world. And while doing so, he and his colleagues needed to be able to look out and see what they created as a constant reminder of what they could achieve. It was usually a feeling of pride. But today, the dense snowfall clouded the glass enough so that Peter couldn't even see the building next door.

He turned back around with an expression verging on defeat. "I think we're just going to have to bite the bullet on this one."

Sensing that they were still far from a decision, Beth placed the notepad against her chest for the time being. "You don't sound so sure."

Peter let out an exhausted sigh. "Of course I'm not. We can't be the only resort in the world with this problem. Rich people like being catered to everywhere they go. Housekeepers. Garbage men. Busboys. Where do they all live?!"

"You wanted a secluded getaway."

Peter rolled his eyes as he approached the table. "Be careful what you wish for, I guess. It's almost comical. Multi-million dollar condos spring up around here like the plague. But ask someone to build low-income housing and its like you're pulling teeth."

He leaned forward onto the table, once again staring intently at the pitiful model. "What's our timeframe?"

Beth flipped through the pages of the notepad, eventually coming to a stop. "In order to have the building populated by next season the contract has to be signed in two weeks."

Another momentary pause filled the air as the gears in Peter's head continued to turn. He stared at the model building, examining every nook of its shape and structure. His face crept forward, getting closer and closer until he eventually slammed his hand onto the model in joyful excitement. "Screw it!"

Beth jumped from the sudden action and watched as Peter flipped the entire set off the conference table, flinging it across the room. He then turned to her with a gigantic smile of an almost eerie thrill. "We'll build it ourselves."

Although she was initially fearful by her boss' quick outburst of destruction, his latest proclamation left her with more confusion than terror. "Excuse me?"

Still reeling with enthusiasm, Peter threw himself down into a chair, allowing the wheels to roll back on their own. "We don't need a builder. We can manage the whole thing while keeping it under budget. Architects, unions, engineers. Why not?"

Unsure as to how she should respond, Beth took a deep breath before speaking. "If that's what you think is best, Mr. Hayden."

With swift exactness, Peter shot his arm forward, pointing a concerned finger at his assistant. "What did I tell you, Beth? You have an opinion. Now give it to me."

She swallowed before taking in another long sigh. "I think Telluride is too special to let one building ruin its appeal."

Peter's excitement simmered down after hearing his assistant's thoughts. He turned his head to see the destroyed model bent into several different pieces and leaning against the far wall of the conference room. The image was a symbol for everything he had accomplished over the last few years. Telluride would only allow the best for its guests and residents regardless of social class, status or wealth. Granted it wasn't a cheap place to be, but he still struggled to keep it as inexpensive as possible. His wife, Rachel, was proud of him, which in turn made him proud of himself. But a line eventually had to be drawn.

He couldn't keep up the charade forever. At some point, financial sacrifices had to be made. And that despite its almost heavenly appeal, even Telluride wasn't above the economic reality that came in a capitalistic society. It was just the nature of civilization.

Peter's head dropped into his chest as he finally submitted. "Tell the builder I approve his original budget request."

Hiding an excitement under the surface, Beth replied while making a note in her notepad. "What made you change your mind?"

Peter looked up at her with a forced smile on his face. "To be honest, I'm surprised it's taken us this long to actually have this problem. And I suppose it's a good problem to have."

"I agree. It means we're expanding."

Peter slowly stood up from his seat and proceeded to stroll along the large window behind him, once again staring out into the massive snowstorm. "Yes. You're right, Beth: Telluride is special. And for a long time I've struggled to allow people to experience this place who otherwise wouldn't have the chance to. But now that I've succeeded, I'm stuck with accommodating them all. And it will only get worse from here. Because the secret is out, and we just can't hide the truth from people anymore."

"And what's that?"

He then paused for a moment before turning to her with a subtle smirk of sincerity. "That Telluride is where God vacations."

***

Since it started hours earlier, the storm outside had only gotten worse. And for the first time since the Cliff's opened its doors, Martin Wells considered closing the ski shop early. Well technically, he wasn't allowed to close the shop whenever he wanted. As a valet service, Martin's contract with the hotel required him to stay open during mountain hours in order to allow guests access to their equipment. But he certainly could send a lot of his employees home and just run the valet with a skeleton crew. After all, it was a firm possibility that by the time the mountain closed they could all be snowed in.

Not that all of them would necessarily heed his advice anyway. Some of his more crazy employees (snowboarders mostly) might take the opportunity to hit the mountain and enjoy what weathermen were now calling the storm of the century. Forecasts predicted the blizzard to continue until late afternoon, and if someone wanted to risk their life that was their prerogative. All Martin cared about was giving them the option of safety.

But before even tackling that notion, Martin had to make sure the employees he needed to stay were even functional. Currently, there was only one local kid working the valet. In the past, Martin was always more comfortable hiring out of towners that came in for the season. They worked hard because there was a point to their existence in Telluride: to ski. But for locals, this place was home. The winter would come and go and they would still be here, waiting for the next batch of tourists to cater to.

But the chamber of commerce had come down on Mountain Village resorts to hire more local help. And so Martin filled his store with young kids who had nothing better to do than be resentful of the rich vacationers they worked for. And Johnny Prescott was no exception.

He did his job well enough and put a smile on his face for the customers. But Martin could see some type of chip on his shoulder.

Johnny wasn't always like that. Having shopped at the store in the past, Martin actually knew the boy for several years. He grew up snowboarding regularly, but the delinquent antics of juvenile youth quickly turned the boy from an occasional rascal into a troublesome slacker. Martin had his suspicions that a change in the boy's behavior came from his crush on the Miller's girl. But there really wasn't anything for Martin to do about it. Teenage boys were going to chase teenage girls. Martin was convinced that sooner or later Miss Miller was going to be the end of that kid, but it was up to young Mr. Prescott to figure that out for himself.

From the front of the store Martin walked across the retail floor and was a little disappointed only seeing one customer browsing through the merchandise. During a storm such as this, there was a fifty-fifty chance the resort's guests would take advantage of the fresh snow on the mountain or opt to stay warm inside. It would seem that today almost everyone decided to brave the cold and head out onto the slopes. Besides those who valeted their equipment, the store just wasn't getting any floor traffic. It was another factor to why Martin considered sending his employees home early.

Without any customers to help, the sales people alternated between gossiping amongst themselves and pretending to be busy. Like most store owners, Martin would prefer not to pay them for doing nothing. But once again, that decision was going to be made based on Johnny Prescott's reliability.

Martin made it to the other end of the store and slipped behind the counter into the valet storage area in the back. Contrary to the fancy decor of the retail side of the store, the back resembled a cramped warehouse lined with a seemingly endless rack of skis and snowboards.

As he entered the room, Martin found no sign of his young employee. And it wasn't until he walked through the aisles of ski equipment that he spotted the boy sitting down against the far wall of the space. Martin's first reaction was a mix of anger, frustration and disappointment. But then he remembered that the boy didn't look well when he arrived for work hours earlier and decided to give Johnny the benefit of the doubt.

Martin stayed at the opposite end of the room and called out to the boy, who could've very well been sleeping with his head slumped down to his chest. "Hello? John? Is it the middle of a workday or nap time?"

The youngster failed to move, and Martin was now convinced he was sleeping. "Mr. Prescott, I'm talking to you."

Again, the store owner failed to receive a response. He started to approach the boy, moving forward through the aisles of skis. As he got closer, Martin noticed that despite wearing a jacket in the heated warehouse Johnny's body still shivered, almost uncontrollably. As a valet attendant, Johnny would be exposed to the cold during his runs outside to grab and return equipment, but judging by the white tinge to his skin, Martin thought the boy had to be freezing.

Upon reaching his sickly employee, Martin knelt down in front of him in a final attempt to gain his attention. "Hey! I need to know if you're OK?"

Johnny slowly looked up, revealing two beady red, bloodshot eyes accentuated by a pale white face. "I'm not doing so good, boss."

If this was the first time he'd seen this, Martin might've had a little sympathy. But Johnny had come into work hungover before. "I can't deal with you like this, John. Not today."

Martin could see Johnny use every ounce he had just to sit up and stand from off the floor. "I need help back here. Where's Paul?"

"Couldn't make it in. You're all alone. So either suck it up or I gotta teach one of the salesmen to do your job. But if I do that, you might as well go home and not come back."

Shy and unable to look his boss in the face, Johnny kept his head down as he spoke. "Why are you such a jerk?"

Martin was furious at the show of disrespect, and by a punk kid no less. He lifted his finger and pointed it down at his employee in an attempt to belittle him. "Hey! You don't get to talk to an employer like that, young man!"

Just then, a sudden burst of energy overcame Johnny as he jumped into Martin's face, snapping back at him with an unchecked temper. "Then how about fuck you!? Is that better, asshole?!"

For a moment, Martin was struck speechless. He thought the boy to be lazy and ignorant, but this was a side of him he'd never seen in all the years he knew him. Johnny glared at him with eyes that spoke volumes of hatred when the boy had never before shown the slightest hint of anger.

In a slow and steady motion, Johnny turned his back on his boss and now leaned against the rack of skis that was behind him. It was a show of defiance that Martin never expected. He considered the boy apathetic, but never anticipated him to express an outward anger of rage. That kind of behavior couldn't be tolerated, and Johnny Prescott needed to learn his place.

Martin took a deep breath to compose himself before conveying a voice of authority. "You think this is a joke? That you have a right to be here? This job is a privilege, son. And the next time you..."

In one swift, fluid motion, Johnny spun around, swinging a ski pole and slamming it into the side of Martin's head. The man's sentence was immediately cut off as he fell back and into the metal ski racks surrounding him. The shelves toppled over, clanging together as they smashed into each other and onto the floor.

Dazed and disoriented, Martin struggled to lift himself off the uncomfortable pile of ski equipment. But he managed to gather enough energy to look up and see the deranged look on Johnny Prescott's face. The boy stood over his employer, panting heavily and baring his teeth like a crazed animal. And for the first time in his life, Martin felt true, unencumbered fear.

A series of stomps could be heard just outside the door. And a moment later, three store employees entered the storage room, stumbling upon the horrific scene. They stood in shock, unable to act or even speak. Still holding the weapon, Johnny leered over his boss, never bothering to look up at his coworkers who entered the room. And before Martin could utter another word, Johnny quickly lifted the pole and thrust the tip downward, impaling his boss in the chest. Blood spurted out from the wound in every direction, and the three employees screamed in unison as they stumbled back out of the room.

Snapping into action, Johnny leaped over the bloody body in front of him, chasing after his colleagues in a feral craze. With a sudden swiftness, he quickly caught a woman by the shirt as she barely reached the door, and Johnny continued her momentum forward, slamming her head into the store's counter. The sheer force of the blow caved in the front of her skull, and she immediately dropped to the floor, her head covered in a bloody mess.

Now, out of the back and into the main floor of the store, Johnny wasted no time hopping the counter and easily grabbing the next fleeing person he saw. In an instant, the ravenous boy's teeth sunk into the man's neck, tearing away flesh and skin with a single bite.

The action only took a moment, but it was long enough to allow the rest of the customers and store employees time to escape. Now covered in blood and bits of human tissue, Johnny dropped the body to the ground and looked up to find the store completely empty and devoid of life. The boy snarled his teeth and growled like a rabid animal craving for its prey. And then he once again pounced forward, exiting the store in search of his next victim.

6

It didn't take long for the calls to start coming in. But not surprisingly, Chris actually expected it to be a busy day. He knew the mountain wasn't going to close unless it was literally the end of the world. And given that people just loved to disregard blizzard warnings, he was undoubtedly going to have his hands full. But then again, he would probably be out there enjoying himself too if he didn't have to work. So he couldn't exactly blame them.

The storm had just started picking up when dispatch reported a middle-aged woman down on a Blue Square run, the designation for an intermediate trail. Still working through their second round of morning coffee, Chris and Phillip threw on their gear, jumped on their skis and took off down the mountain. As the veteran patroller, Phil took the med pack and left Chris to pull the stretcher sled behind him. Normally that wouldn't be such a big deal. Chris had taken the sled a hundred times before, but racing down to a patient while having a barrage of thick snowflakes pounding your goggles made maneuvering the cumbersome contraption all the more difficult.

Chris followed closely behind Phil, who tore through the mountain like he knew it better than his own home. And in less than a minute they arrived at the specified location. At first, Chris was concerned they weren't going to be able to spot their patient through the dense snowfall, but the heavy set woman's lime green jacket and hat made her easy enough to spot. It also didn't hurt that the woman's constant moaning drew the two patrollers to her like a wailing siren.

As they got closer, Chris noticed a tall man in skis standing next to the woman. He looked down at her with the concerned expression common amongst family members of a victim, but the young ski patroller couldn't figure out why. As far as he could tell the woman just fell over and bumped her knee. She was definitely holding her leg as if it hurt, but it was hardly an injury that required a call to the ski patrol.

Hoping for some type of exciting trauma to treat, Chris immediately felt annoyed by the sight of the woman. But as much as he hated it, she was now their responsibility, which was all the more frustrating when there would soon be more serious injuries requiring their assistance. Nevertheless, the patroller remained professional and would never abandon a patient.

After working together for several seasons, Chris and Phillip reacted to the scene without a word of coordination. Phillip bent down alongside the woman to examine her injury while Chris readied the sled next to her. Through the whiz of the bullet-like snow, Chris could hear Phillip begin the appropriate questioning. But their patient just continued her perpetual moaning.

Chris tried to block out the whiny, annoying noise, but she went on and on like a never-ending broken record. It was absolutely distracting, and what bothered Chris the most was that it wasn't a cry of pain but of illness. They were definitely called to the scene because she fell, but the woman sounded like she had a stomach ache more than an injured leg.

The noise caused Chris to finally turn his head and get a good look at the woman. It was then that he realized something was definitely off. Their patient's face was pale white, just a shade darker than the snow around her scarf. Her eyes were closed and her chapped lips separated just enough to let out the agonizing moan, which at this point became like nails on a chalkboard. Phil did the best he could to treat the leg and prepare her for transport, but the woman rolled back and forth uncontrollably, like some force was preventing her from sitting still.

As he put his finishing touches on the sled, Chris could tell Phillip wasn't getting much of a response from the woman and started questioning the male bystander. "Are you related?"

"Yes. She's my wife."

Chris took a break from the sled to look up at the man, who still looked down at the old patroller treating his wife with grave concern. "What happened?"

The worried man covered his mouth with a gloved hand before speaking. "I don't know. She said she wasn't feeling well on the lift so we were going to head back to the room. But on the way down she was swerving, could barely ski straight and then, all of a sudden, wham! She went down and grabbed her knee."

Chris assumed it was some type of food poisoning and went back to preparing the sled. "Does she have any allergies? Taking medication? Past medical history?"

"No."

"Nothing that could cause her to feel ill?"

"No. She woke up fine this morning."

With the sled all ready, Chris moved over to Phil, who was also prepared to move the woman over to the carriage. "What do you think?"

The old patroller shrugged his shoulders. "I don't know. Her knee is bruised but not bad. Looks like she's about to pass out, though."

"Stomach bug?"

"Not like any I've seen. Skin's pale and diaphoretic but burning up.

Her breathing rate's low but heart rate's up. It's like her body wants to go into shock but doesn't know how."

Chris looked the woman up and down and started regretting his earlier thought. She really was sick and needed their help. "Well, let's get her down to the doc and see what he thinks."

Without speaking another word, Chris and Phillip worked together to carefully lift the sickly skier and place her into the sled. Then, with her husband anxiously waiting by, Phil proceeded to strap the woman down, taking the time to make sure each band was secure.

As he did, Chris allowed his own attention to wander. Although fairly ill, the skier was by no means critically injured or even seriously hurt. They would just be giving her a free ride down the mountain to see a physician. In terms of intensity, the call turned out to be fairly routine if not flat out boring.

But while looking around at the mountain surrounding him, Chris's curiosity started to pique. Besides a couple of guests bent over in unusual positions by the trees, several other skiers and boarders passed by him acting similarly to how the man had described his wife. Swerving and teetering back and forth, they almost looked like they were in a daze or trance. It wasn't everyone, but almost half the people Chris could see through the storm barely managed to keep themselves upright. One woman skied down the mountain hunched over completely, as if about to leave a trail of vomit behind her while several others continually fell only to get back up and fall again.

Chris had been skiing long enough to spot a beginner, but none of the behavior he saw resembled inexperience. There was something else causing these people to act so strangely. Possibly the storm? The blizzard was surely affecting ski conditions, but not like this. Maybe there really was some type of stomach virus going around. But how could it infect so many people so fast?

Chris's mind continued to flip through explanations when a female voice screeched through the radio, suddenly breaking his train of thought. "Outpost Three. You read?"

Chris reflexively clicked the radio strapped to his shoulder harness. "Outpost Three on call, dispatch. Patient's almost ready for transport. We'll check back in when she's delivered."

"Great. But ski school instructor Sarah Warren just reported a disturbance at Joseph's."

Upon hearing her name, Phil paused just long enough to look up at his young partner and gauge the expression on his face. Chris looked back at him curiously concerned yet steady. After all, a disturbance could be anything. There was no sense getting worked up without knowing the details.

Chris took a deep breath in and pressed down on the radio once more. "What 'd she say?"

"Couldn't exactly tell. She was cutting out, and it was very loud in the background."

Phil noticed the look of worry on Chris's face grow. He quickly finished strapping the woman in and responded to the dispatcher on his own radio. "Who's taking the call?"

"No one right now. That's why I'm contacting you. Everyone's out including the off duty reserves. I don't know if it's the storm or what but we've been getting swamped."

Chris and Phil once again exchanged a silent glance that communicated volumes. They could also sense the husband's eyes patiently leering at them. He could see them paying more attention to the radio than his wife, and Phillip, being the veteran patroller that he was, didn't want to give the man any excuse to report them.

The old timer quickly threw his med pack around his shoulders and took position in front of the sled. "Chris, head down to the snowmobile dock and ride one up. Shouldn't take you long."

Then, before the man had any chance to chime in, Phillip turned to the husband. "You ready, sir?"

Confused but still overwhelmed with concern, the man just nodded his head. Phil then turned back around and pointed his skis down the mountain. "Good. Stay behind me."

Phil pushed himself downward with the sled right behind him and the man following closely by. Chris watched them for as long as he could before they disappeared through the thick cloud of snowfall. Once they were out of sight, he reported back into his radio. "We'll take it, dispatch. Just let us drop off our current charge and we'll be on our way."

He then hopped up, spun his skis in the opposite direction and pushed off down to the other side of the run.

***

The rumor mill at Peter's office had been working overtime. For the past hour or so he heard mumblings between his employees about some kind of sickness going around. But the tone in their voices wasn't of gossip but fear. His people were concerned, worried and afraid that something was going on which couldn't be controlled.

In less than a morning, both the Mountain Village Health Clinic and Telluride's Medical Center had been packed with patients all experiencing the same symptoms. It was still too early to make any kind of executive decision regarding the safety of the community. But Peter had already made calls down to two of Telluride's councilmen to discuss their options.

It was slowly becoming a crisis that demanded action, a situation unlike any Peter encountered during his tenure as Village Manager. He was thankful that Telluride never had to deal with a true health epidemic. Past accidents or tragedies, either in town or on the mountain, were isolated incidents that could be handled as they arose. In fact, the case-by-case issues had been taken care of so efficiently there was never any need to expand or rethink the area's emergency communication network. But the currently established system now strained under the pressure put on it by Telluride's emergency services. The small town infrastructure just wasn't equipped to coordinate and manage such a vast and complicated crisis.

It was a frustrating situation for Peter. He needed up to date real-time information from the ground, so he ended up turning to the best source of civilian communication he could think of: TORO.

He sat anxiously at his desk with his head buried in his hands, carefully listening to Marshal Walker's words through the FM radio. "The best thing for everyone to do right now is stay home and wait for further instructions. Between the blizzard and whatever illness has been going around, there's just no reason to take a chance by going outside."

Georgia's soft-spoken voice chimed in after him. "Are you issuing a statement for the mountain to shut down?"

"No. It's still a free country and people can certainly do what they please. But I want everyone to at least be aware of the risks if they choose to do so."

"Thank you, Marshal. Please call back if you have any news."

There was a click at the other end of the line, and the radio host moved on to give her own personal thoughts on the situation. "So, Telluride's a little hectic today. But I can guarantee you that once all this craziness stops I'll be the first one on the hill. Because God damn they'll be a lot of powder out there."

Peter wasn't acquainted with Georgia personally but knew her as the station's young, eccentric DJ famous for her straightforward attitude. It was a quality that probably wouldn't get her far in big city radio but made her a favorite here in Telluride. And today the girl handled her role with professionalism and class during a pressurized situation. She hadn't played a song in almost an hour and was doing a fine job handling the overwhelming amount of calls the station had to be receiving.

She readied herself to answer the next caller when Peter heard a solemn knock on the door. He lifted his head from his hands but kept his eyes closed from exhaustion. "Come in."

The door clicked open, followed by Beth's voice entering the room. "Some of the employees were wondering if they could head out early. Because of the storm and all."

Peter opened his eyes to see his assistant's head poking through the doorway with her body still in the hall. He opened his mouth to speak but was cut off by a loud man's voice booming through the radio. "Hey! Ya there, lady? Can you hear me? Hello!"

Georgia surprisingly responded to the obnoxious caller with mellow ease. "Sir, you don't need to yell. We can hear you just fine."

But the man's voice maintained the same level of volume as he continued to speak. "Of course I have to yell. It's like fucking Beirut out here! Except, you know, for all the snow."

"First off, sir, we don't have the censors running so please don't curse. Secondly, what's your name and what are you talking about?"

Peter remained staring at the radio, but saw the rest of Beth's body completely wander into the room out the corner of his eye. She then stood still in the center of the office grasping her notepad as the man's voice went on. "This is Scott Brooks. I live on the mountain, but I'm in town right now and it's like a warzone."

Upon hearing the name, Peter sat up in his seat and listened even more intently as Georgia conducted the interview. "Can you elaborate? We just had Marshal Walker on the line and he said everything was under control."

"Oh, he don't know shit."

"Mr. Brooks, please. Watch your language."

"Yeah. Yeah. Yeah. I'm just calling in to let you all know I'm blowing this popsicle stand."

Georgia's voice grew short and agitated, but she remained firm as she tried to press Brooks for information. "What do you mean? Can you at least give us details?"

"Some crazy bitch attacked my driver. Is that detail enough for ya?"

Peter kept his eyes locked onto the radio's speaker as Scott Brooks continued his rant. But once again, he caught Beth out the corner of his eye, clutching her favorite notepad like a security blanket. "She was raving about her slut daughter banging some hillbilly last night, and then just bit Charlie on the arm like a lunatic. I swear, between the nut jobs in this town and the snowstorm of the Apocalypse, I'm jumping on a plane and getting the hell outta here."

"No argument from me about the nut jobs. Hell, I'm one of 'em. But if you're headed to the airport, I doubt a pilot will take off in this."

"That's what I pay them for, sweetie. To be stupid and do what I say. I'm just calling to let you know that you heard it from me first: Scott Brooks is tellin' you to run like the wind, folks. Something's going down and I plan on climbing out while I still can."

It sounded as if Mr. Brooks wanted to continue shouting from his soapbox, but a firm click cut him off followed by Georgia's laughing voice. "Ooooook. Guess some people just aren't cut out for life on the mountain, huh?"

Peter briefly looked up from the radio to catch a glimpse of Beth's face. She too was staring at the radio, but with a look of anxious concern. Even as Peter continued to watch her, Beth remained fixated on the radio almost in a stare of disbelief. It wasn't until he said something that she was shocked out of her trance. "Beth, you all right?"

She jumped slightly, surprised that she was still in her boss' office. "Sorry. What were we talking about?"

Peter could see she was flustered, a state he wasn't used to seeing from her. "The storm. People want to go home, right?"

Finally remembering why she knocked on the door, Beth snapped back to reality. "Oh, yeah. Do you mind?"

Peter shook his head while casually waving her away. "Not at all. And you should, too. I'm going to stay here and try to manage this thing."

"You sure?"

"Absolutely. Just be safe out there."

She smiled at him as she turned towards the door and opened it to leave. But just before heading out, Beth took one last peek inside the room and back towards the radio with a worrisome expression. The look only lasted a moment and Beth was gone before he noticed, but something struck Peter as odd. The DJ had already moved onto the next caller, but he could tell Beth was still stuck on the previous conversation. Her expression wasn't a general feeling but a targeted reaction of personal concern. And come to think of it, Peter sensed that even before he identified himself, Beth displayed a hint of recognition at the sound of Brooks's voice. The sign was nothing overtly obvious but enough for Peter to wonder if she actually knew him?

It was a strange thought, Peter admitted to himself, however, he'd have to address the issue later. Mr. Brooks's purpose in Telluride had been a curious topic for him, but Peter had bigger things to worry about. Questioning Beth on the subject had to wait. For now, Peter's main concern was helping the sick people in his town and getting through to the other side of the storm.

7

The day was only several hours old and already Nellie had made it a productive morning. Utilizing the day off, she shuffled around the house, cleaning and organizing with the liveliness of a woman half her age.

During her chores, Bill sat comfortably on the couch and continued watching television straight through breakfast. A slight part of him felt bad about relaxing while his wife busily moved around. But then he remembered the truth: that they were both old and rich enough to hire a cleaning lady without feeling guilty about it.

Unfortunately, Mrs. Sheridan was never one to ask for unnecessary help when it came to work she could easily do herself. And even though she grew up a tomboy, working on the ranch and playing outside with her brothers, Nellie actually found a basic pleasure in performing what some would consider her womanly duties. But she didn't see the chores like that. And neither did Bill for that matter. She simply took pride and considered it virtuous to maintain a cleanly household.

Currently, she happened to be taking clothes out of a dryer in the laundry room at the far side of the house. Right above the machine rested a conveniently placed window, which normally overlooked a beautiful view over the ranch's rolling hills. Although today the weather allowed for little scenery other than a dense cloud of falling snow.

Knowing there was little to see, Nellie kept her head down and focused on her task. But from a quick glance upward, she happened to spot a fleeting, dark speck amidst the never-ending field of white. Confused and curious, the clothes slid out of her hand as Nellie slowly moved closer to the glass, hoping to confirm what she saw. A dense, white wall out the window continued to sway back and forth, but through the whirlwind of snow she caught another glimpse of the object. There was indeed something foreign on their property.

Without any sense of urgency, Nellie left the laundry area and entered the living room. She then proceeded to pile on layers of clothing for the trek outside. "There's something in the blizzard."

Confused, Bill leaned forward from his cushiony seat. "What do you mean?"

Nellie turned to him as she finished buttoning up her thick, snow suit. "I mean I saw something out there."

Bill was still unable to comprehend the situation. "So you're gonna check it out? Why?"

"Because it's odd. And I don't like odd things surrounding my home."

Bill didn't respond, hoping his wife would change her mind on her own. But when she failed to falter while strolling over to the front door, he gave a long sigh and reluctantly prepared to stand. "Well, I'm not gonna let you go out there by yourself. Give me a minute and I'll go with ya."

But Nellie's hand was already pulling on the doorknob. "Just meet me out there. And hurry up."

She could sense her husband wanted to continue his protests, so Nellie quickly slipped outside and shut the door behind her. She was immediately met with a blunt force of wind and snow smacking against her face. The tough, old woman prepared herself for harsh weather but was still caught off guard by the powerful bombardment of cold. Forever refusing to submit to the elements, Nellie responded to the chill by simply bringing her neck gaiter over her mouth. She then pulled the top of her jacket closer together by hand and fearlessly ventured out into the snow.

Mrs. Sheridan began her trek by circling around to the backside of the home where the laundry room was located. Despite knowing the ranch like the back of her hand, Nellie still had to use the house as a point of reference when traversing through the storm. Otherwise, there was a good chance vertigo could have set in and she might have lost her way.

Once in position, Nellie tried to recreate her point of view through the window and was almost surprised to see the speck bigger than she thought. In fact, the black object had now taken shape to form the outline of a humanly figure. Whatever it happened to be was still too far away to distinguish its features, but Nellie continued to move closer, never wavering from her direct path forward.

Slowly but surely the blurry figure, only visible intermittently through the falling snow, started to come into focus. First a ski jacket. Then pants. And finally Nellie could see a fluffy trapper hat and goggles on top of the person's head. It was hard to make out under all the layers, but by the way the figure moved Nellie assumed it to be a man.

Besides the entire scene being strange itself, the most peculiar aspect of the sight were the man's legs. Or more specifically, how he moved his legs when walking. With the snow almost passed her shin, Nellie was forced to put an abundant amount of effort into every step she took. She moved a lot slower than she wanted to, but the man continued on towards her without missing a beat. Instead of lifting his foot up and over the snow, he tread through it like butter. It was only when the stranger came within a hundred feet of Nellie that she noticed a pair of snowshoes strapped to his feet as well as a five-day Telluride lift pass attached to his jacket.

The man was a tourist. And by the looks of it, a lost one at that. Nellie's ranch was nowhere near the resort or any hiking trail offered to guests. In fact, she couldn't remember a time any visitor wandered all the way out to her house. Let alone during a blizzard.

Having discovered what her mysterious object was, Nellie stopped wading through the snow and called out to the man. "Good mornin'. How'd you get all the way out here?"

She received no response, and the man continued his steady march forward. Nellie thought she had spoken with a voice loud enough to carry through the whistling wind of the storm but, nevertheless, tried to contact him once more. "You lost, mister? It's too dangerous to be out here alone."

Again, the man issued no reply, but to Nellie's surprise, actually looked to be picking up speed. From a slow trudge, his feet sped up to a swift shuffle. The man's snowshoes easily parted the path ahead, and Nellie was forced to set her feet back in a defensive position. "Hey! This is private property. I'll help you but you gotta stay where you are."

The vague warning did little to deter the man, who had been steadily picking up speed. His arms and body began pumping to match the intensity of his legs. And before Nellie realized it, the man was in an all out sprint charging towards her. It wasn't much of a sprint, seeing as how he still had to move through the high snow in a cumbersome pair of snowshoes. But the sight was enough for Nellie to realize she was in danger.

As quickly as she could, Nellie removed one of her gloves and began fumbling with her jacket's zipper hoping to get it open. "Stop! Right now!"

But before she could reach inside, the charging man was right in front of her, ready to attack. Before their collision, the man's neck lifted up bringing his face to within inches of his victim's. And in that brief instant, what Nellie saw brought back a vivid memory of her brother's final moments.

Pale white and filled with rage, her attacker's aged face resembled a maniacal creature far from human. Leering like a savage old beast, the man stared down at her with bloodshot eyes. His mouth, outlined by a pair of dry, cracked lips, opened wide unleashing a ghastly hiss of terror.

In the instant before they connected, Nellie lifted her gloved hand and managed to stop the lunatic from sinking his teeth into the small opening of skin around her face. But the hard contact forced them both to fall backwards into the snow and roll around for position.

Their struggle ended with Nellie's attacker on top, and she was forced to push back against the man's chest as he continued his attempt at tearing away her flesh with his teeth. Nellie's bare hand, now covered in snow, burned from the cold, but she forced the pain aside, using every ounce of strength she had to keep the man's mouth at bay.

The stranger continued to bite and chomp his teeth down at her, but the hiss of his attacks was interrupted by a loud yell. "Get off of her!"

Nellie's fight suddenly stopped as Bill came full speed at the man, tackling him back down into the snow. The two men, both old enough to be grandparents, tumbled over flat onto their backs. His muscles not what they used to be, Bill was forced to take a deep breath and recoup from the blow. The crazed stranger, on the other hand, pounced to his feet right on top of his attacker. The man immediately shot his arms down, grabbing Bill's head with his frosted gloves. He then proceeded to lift Bill up off the snowy field by the temples and squeeze with all his might.

Bill let out a grunt, trying to fight his opponent's grasp when a loud bang rang through the air. The deranged man released his hold of Bill's head as he violently flew back into the snow.

With his mouth dropped open in surprise, Bill turned to his wife and found her aiming a revolver in her bare hand straight to where the attacker used to stand. "Eleanor, you brought a gun?"

Calm and confident, Nellie slowly lowered the weapon and approached the man's body in the snow. "I saw a strange object outside our home in a snowstorm. Of course I brought a gun."

Bill took another moment to recover before standing completely and joining his wife's side. Together they looked over the body of their strange visitor, who now lay lifeless, submerged into the snow. Another few moments went by in silence before Bill finally placed a caring hand onto his wife's shoulder. "You OK?"

She answered him while still leaning over the corpse. "I'm fine. He just...reminded me of Danny."

Bill released his hand from her shoulder and turned back towards the house. "I know. That's what worries me."

Nellie kept her eyes locked onto the man, staring deep into his frozen face of ferocious terror. "You think there's gonna be more?"

"Maybe. I don't know. Either way, we should probably head into town and tell someone. After all, you did just kill a man."

A slight smirk lifted itself onto Nellie's face as she turned and started walking back to the house ahead of her husband. "Fine. But maybe we should both bring guns this time...just in case."

***

He'd been sick more times than he could possibly count, but Joey Fallon never felt anything in his life remotely like this. With his body scrunched together into the corner of the chairlift, Joey tried his best to keep the wild snowfall from penetrating into his jacket. Although he couldn't imagine why he didn't just take the whole thing off and throw it away into the breeze. Ever since they got off the gondola he'd felt as if his whole body was burning up inside. And he had a continuous stream of sweat building up against his thermal underwear to prove it.

But that he went from feeling fine to near death in less than an hour wasn't the only shocking aspect of his predicament. Even more surprising was that his sister was actually trying to make him feel better. It's not that he thought she was evil or wished him any harm. In fact, if he weren't feeling well Joey would've expected his sister to actually leave him alone and not be the obnoxious princess she normally was. But today she was trying to comfort him, offering kind words and sympathy.

He could tell she wanted to cuddle him, to wrap him up in her arms and keep him warm. But the triple chairlift didn't allow for them to sit next to one another. If they wanted to have the safety bar down on top of their laps then one of them had to sit on each side. Otherwise, the unequal weight would've caused the chair to drastically lean. Normally, a slight dip to a chairlift wouldn't be such a big deal, but with the high winds from a mountain blizzard already blowing the siblings back and forth, it wouldn't be a good idea to add to the equation.

So, as the lift blindly brought them up the mountain and deeper into the storm, Stephanie sat helplessly watching her brother suffer on the opposite end of the chair. Joey was only a mere three feet away, but the bullets of snow whizzing between them made it feel like a hundred. Joey's eyes briefly looked up from within his curled over frame and caught a glimpse of his sister's face. Her eyes, barely visible through the fogged up ski goggles, reflected a concern Joey wasn't used to seeing.

As brother and sister, they felt it was their job to torture one another. It was just what siblings did. But they were still family, and Joey always knew his sister cared for him in some fashion. That deep down she loved him the same way he loved her. It was just an unspoken understanding between siblings. But never before had he seen it so outwardly expressed through her actions. He wasn't feeling well, and for the first time Joey could see she truly sympathized with his condition.

She wanted to help him, and Joey wanted to be grateful for that. But for some reason he just couldn't find the words to tell her. He searched down deep within himself for any semblance of affection, but the emotion was gone, replaced by a plague of doubt. The love for his sister slowly transformed into a source of anger and frustration. He looked at the compassionate hand she would periodically place on his knee and felt disgusted. Aggravated. Resentful even. He despised the fact that it took a blizzard and a near life-threatening illness for her to show any type of sentiment towards him. Why now? What was so special about this moment? After all the years they spent together had she finally decided that he's not the brat she thinks he is? That he's actually just a helpless little boy who can't take care of himself. That he needs mommy and daddy to look after him. So that's it, he thought. She felt sorry for him. Well, he didn't need her pity.

Joey sat silently as Stephanie continued to project soft-spoken words of kindness over the roar of the wind. "Are you gonna be able to board down or should we call ski patrol?"

But her brother took the words as a condescending insult. "Since when did you care so much?"

"Joey! You're my brother. Of course I care."

He lifted his bare chin out from within his neck gaiter and gave his sister a glare that caused her whole body to jerk back from shock. A moment earlier, Joey's pale, exhausted skin made it look as if he was about to pass out. But now, Stephanie was honestly surprised he found the strength to stare her down with such contempt. Combined with the bits of frost and snow covering his face, to which he was oblivious, Joey's pinpoint pupils gave him the appearance of a maddened fiend of terror. Red and bulging, his eyeballs pierced through his sister with a furious rage she never knew he had.

Unable to comprehend the sight before her, Stephanie's jaw dropped open in disbelief. "What...what's wrong with you?"

Despite the unfathomable surge of anger rushing through him, Joey could still hear the thoughts in his head. But each one only drove him deeper into a whirlwind of loathing. He was now completely convinced of his sister's betrayal. They were only family by blood. Not by choice. She never really loved him. Never cared about him. All she ever cared about was herself. He was just a pest to her. A rodent that she would throw aside the first chance she got. And every second Joey had to sit next to this bitch only fueled the inferno of hatred burning inside him.

With coldly vicious eyes, Joey continued to stare at his sister through the wall of moving snow between them. "I always thought it was a joke when we fought. But now I see the truth, I could've died at any moment and you wouldn't have shed a tear."

Stephanie let go of one of her ski poles, allowing it to dangle by the strap on her wrist. Then, sensing her brother's pain, she leaned over to place another calm hand on his shoulder. "Come on. That's not true."

But before she could reach him, Joey smacked the hand away and pressed forward into the center of the chair. "Stop pretending! You hate me! You've always hated me!"

Reacting to her brother's attack, Stephanie leaned back into her corner of the chair, unknowingly balancing it out as it lightly swayed back and forth. "No way. I'd do anything for you."

Joey took several deep breaths, calming himself from a rapid pant to a deep sigh. He then slowly backed down into his side of the chair and turned to face away from his sister. "Then just leave me alone."

The argument died down and the siblings retreated to their respective sides of the chair. Joey dazed off, allowing his simmering hatred to fester and boil under the surface. But Stephanie couldn't let go of her concern for him. She didn't say a word and respected his wish for silence. But he looked so angry, so full of pain. And it all happened so quickly. What happened to her little baby brother that was so fun and full of life?

The uneasiness within her continued to build until Stephanie couldn't take it anymore and had to make things right. "Joey, I..."

Upon hearing his sister's voice, all thoughts racing through Joey's head suddenly vanished. Like the flip of a switch, his consciousness was overcome by oblivion. Every feeling, every emotion, every ounce of himself faded away into nothingness. And his mind became an ultimate blank.

In that instant, the boy known as Joey Fallon lost all will of his being. And his body seemingly moved by itself, free from control as he unleashed a bloodcurdling, animal-like scream, lunging towards his sister in an all out attack.

His gloved hands swiped back and forth repeatedly just shy of her terrified face. Latched securely onto his left foot, the boy's snowboard couldn't move passed the chair's safety bar, keeping his body in place and his sister out of reach. But that didn't prevent him from trying over and over again, lunging and grasping for his sister like a crazed animal struggling for a meal.

On instinct, Stephanie had leaned back and away, but still sat frozen in place, completely dumbstruck by the fit of maniacal rage that had taken over her brother. "Joey...stop...please."

Her soft pleas faded into the storm, and in his maddened state, Joey wouldn't have heard them anyway. Stephanie wanted to cry, but sheer terror kept her from doing much of anything besides clutching the metal frame of the chair.

For several moments, Joey continued to swipe at his sister's throat in a wild and chaotic frenzy. His lunges back and forth caused the chair to continuously sway further and further, adding to his sister's paralyzing fear. It was then that Stephanie heard the faint remnant of voices echoing through the storm. She turned her head and saw an outline of their parents in the chair behind her, shouting forward towards the odd sight in front of them. Stephanie tried to scream to her mother and father, but Joey's beast-like growls and snarls distracted her from calling for help.

The formerly jovial boy had transformed into a ravenous creature devoid of logic or reason. He ripped at his clothing, throwing his gloves and hat into the storm. With cracked, pale skin covering his bare hands, Joey continued to flail about wildly. Spit and saliva flew all around him as the boy's teeth gnashed ferociously towards his sister.

Stephanie tried to back further away but was held captive alongside her brother inside the small, moving chairlift. The chair's thin safety bar still kept Joey from fully reaching his sister. He lunged and lunged, pressing his body further towards his prey. But every attempt was refuted again and again by his board caught onto the bar.

Like a frustrated child, Joey threw a fit in his seat, using his free right leg to repeatedly kick down onto the board. Stephanie watched the tantrum, unsure as to what he was trying to accomplish. The board was securely attached to Joey's left foot, and his leg would surely come off before it could be wedged free. It wasn't until Stephanie leaned forward for a closer look that she noticed the plastic bindings which strapped Joey's board to his boot were starting to break away.

The startled girl knew she had to act. She had to do something. But she couldn't believe the force and ferocity with which her brother stomped down onto his board. It was unreal for him to have such strength. But with every blow from Joey's boot, another piece of the binding flew off, loosening his foot from the board.

A combination of fear and disbelief had overcome the teenage girl, but her body suddenly shocked into action as Joey gave his board one final blow. In a solemn, explosive instant, the binding was destroyed, shattered into a million pieces, and his snowboard fell down toward the unseen mountain below.

Now free from the safety rail's restraint, Joey climbed his entire body onto the chair and lunged at his sister. With a rush of unexpected adrenaline surging through her, Stephanie lifted one of her ski poles, holding it as a barrier between her and her attacker. But undeterred by the obstruction, Joey pressed against the pole, swiping at his sister beyond it.

With her feet still locked into her skis, Stephanie did the best she could to leverage the pole in front of her and keep her crazed sibling at bay. Without any sign of letting up, Joey's assaults continued on, rocking the chairlift back and forth through the relentless snowfall. Perpetual gusts blasted them from every side, and through the roar of the winds, Stephanie could hear her parents' faint shouts of concern and worry. She tried to wiggle her body around, hoping to maneuver herself into a better position of safety. But her cumbersome skis kept her in place, a helpless victim to both her vicious brother and the pendulum swing of the chair.

Just then, the chair came to a sudden stop, ending the struggle as the momentum sent Joey stumbling backwards. Taking advantage of the small opportunity given to her, Stephanie grabbed onto the safety bar as Joey prepared to lunge forward once more. When he finally did, his sister shot the bar up and off of her, slamming the metal rail into the side of his head.

The blow dazed Joey for only a moment, but it was enough to allow Stephanie the time to move to the edge of the seat and peer over the edge. She couldn't see the ground through the veil of dense snowfall, but the risk never crossed her mind. Just as Joey regained his footing, Stephanie plunged off the chair and down into the storm underneath the lift.

She disappeared in an instant, and Joey never bothered to give her another thought. Just as she was gone, he turned his attention back towards the chair behind him and saw a glimmer of his parents' fearful faces. Reacting on a perpetual, bloodthirsty instinct, Joey stood on top of the chair and climbed the overhead bar connected to the thick, steel cable above.

In a frantic spasm, Joey grabbed onto the cable and jerked it about in every direction. With the help of the gale force winds surrounding him, Joey weaved the chair back and forth, swinging it around like a toy. The motion caused a chain reaction of building momentum, forcing the other chairs down the line to follow suit. Screaming and shouting for the boy to stop, Joey's parents held onto their chair as it tossed them around like ragdolls, but their desperate words were lost and pointless.

Their son continued to swing the chair side to side until the entire contraption twisted and tangled upon itself. The tension built up across the line until it finally dislodged the nearest pulley assembly from its pylon. Without being secured, the line wrapped itself around the main bullwheel, causing the cable to snap and the entire chairlift to topple over and collapse down to the mountain below.

8

Chris usually loved riding a snowmobile. Not today. The intensity of the storm made every inch of forward progress up the mountain a challenge. And the pair of skis strapped to his back didn't help his momentum. The machine climbed like an animal, ripping apart the massive amounts of snow under its treads. But without a shield, its rider felt every aspect of the elements' wrath. The huge, high-speed snowflakes were already continuously pounding Chris's goggles, but flying against them at sixty mph turned the non-stop barrage into a fury of fluffy bullets. If he thought it was hard to see before, now it was damn near impossible.

Luckily, the young patroller had a good sense of the mountain to navigate up the terrain. Snowmobile protocol had him keep mostly to the edge of the runs, hugging the tree line to avoid any collision. But Chris had seen fewer people since breaking away from Phillip only minutes earlier. He didn't know if the guests were keeping inside because of the storm or if he just couldn't see them through the snow caked onto his goggles. But the mountain seemed almost completely empty save for a few stragglers stumbling downhill like those he'd seen before.

They didn't look well. Swerving and struggling to stay upright, the skiers were certainly under some form of distress. Normally, Chris would've met the people to see if they were all right. After all, it was his duty. Without a call from dispatch though, it wasn't his concern or, more importantly, his responsibility. Something strange was going on, churning a bad feeling in his gut. The storm had certainly put things into perspective, and with Sarah in trouble the thought of stopping never even entered his mind.

He'd been that way ever since hearing her name over the radio. It was a little bit of a sly move for Phil to take off without him. Technically, no two-man team was to separate for any reason. But that last call was pretty much a no-brainer. There was nothing for the patrollers to do but strap the woman to the sled, keep her warm and get her to a doctor. Meanwhile, Sarah was obviously in some type of distress. In all her years working ski school she'd never called for help before. So, almost as if they read each other's minds, Phillip quick-pitched the husband by zooming down the mountain with his wife and forcing his attention away from his partner. Some might've called it a shady move, however, the occasion called for it. Chris was usually reluctant to use the "e" word, but he thought it was safe to classify this as an emergency.

The snowmobile continued to claw its way high up the mountainside, eating through the treacherous snow conditions with ease. It didn't take long for Chris to pass the tree line and reach the top of the mountain. The ski run opened up to a great expanse of flat terrain where the snowmobile leveled off into a cruise.

Chris felt freer without the trees bearing down on top of him. But the snowfall still clouded the air, obscuring the scene in every direction. Completely surrounded by rocky peaks and a clear shot of the town in the valley below, the sight was usually a beautiful view. It was an area almost always packed with activity. Tourists stopped to take pictures with mountain photographers. Families used the spot as a meeting ground to rest and regroup. Now it was nothing more than a barren mountaintop filled in by a never-ending layer of falling snow.

Chris knew there was a chairlift around somewhere that dropped riders off on this plateau of land, a landmark for those trying to navigate the mountain. Now the giant mechanical structure was completely hidden, buried behind a dotted wall of moving white that flowed from side to side as if it were alive. Chris lifted his goggles ever so slightly, but it didn't help. With the snow and wind constantly attacking his face, Chris was barely able to keep his eyes open let alone see off into the distance.

Finding Joseph's would be difficult without a point of reference. But not impossible. Like any patroller, Chris had memorized Telluride's trail map to the point where he could recite all of the mountain's runs in alphabetical order.

He knew the building's general location and started slowly riding in that direction. From the top of the nearest chairlift Joseph's was a good five-minute traverse on skis. Obviously, the snowmobile could get there in no time, but without knowing exactly where he was headed, Chris had to restrain the urge to open the snowmobile up full throttle. He could easily miss the lodge or worse, accidentally drop off the side of a run. Hopefully, Chris could find some structure or familiar spot that could get him there quickly.

His head remained on a slow and deliberate swivel, making sure to completely survey the entire area. But nothing stood out as unique among the snow and emptiness. When no sign appeared after the first minute of putting forward, Chris had to actively fight off disappointment. Giving up hope wasn't an option. One way or another he was going to find Sarah. Even if he had to ride around in circles until the snow stopped.

The endless search for the lodge continued as Chris's eyes remained perpetually focused. They peered back and forth through the goggles, looking for any sign of something other than snow. The patroller was so zoned into his mission that when an alarm rung through the radio attached to his chest the loud ringing nearly frightened him half to death. The loud noise was a signal for an incoming call, but Chris couldn't understand why he was getting it? As far as he knew Phillip hadn't yet dropped off their last patient, and only crews on standby could receive an alert.

Curious about the call, Chris lowered his ear down by the radio to hear the dispatcher over the storm's roaring wind. "All units. All units. Chair six is down. I repeat. Chair six has collapsed."

Chris gasped from shock. That was the lift he passed at the top of the mountain if he even passed it at all. The whole structure might've gone down before he even got there. Maybe that's why he didn't see it. Because the chair wasn't there anymore.

He began to think about the lives on board. The people hurt, dead or dying as the dispatcher went on. "I know you're all busy. I don't know where anyone is anymore, but we need somebody over there. Anybody. Please."

He continued to muddle forward, but the thought of turning around crept into the back of Chris's mind. This wasn't a couple of people who didn't look well. This was a mass casualty incident. People needed help, and he was probably the only patroller even remotely close to the area.

But what if Sarah really needed him? Was he truly willing to risk sacrificing her to do his job? Could he live with himself if she was lost? These were the questions she'd been asking him that he was refusing to answer. And now he was forced to make a split-second decision in a time of crisis. When Chris told her earlier that they would talk about it later he didn't exactly have this scenario in mind.

He honestly didn't know what to do, but before he could make a decision, the falling snow suddenly parted, revealing a rapidly approaching figure right in front of the vehicle. The shock and surprise sent a surge of adrenaline through Chris's body causing his arms to jerk on the handlebars. The snowmobile quickly veered to the side, averting a head on crash but still catching a leg of the unlucky soul. The collision sent the stranger's body flipping up and over Chris's head. Not designed for such a hairpin turn, the snowmobile rocked over onto one side, slowly tipping over to its edge and leaving Chris enough time to jump off rather than being pinned under it. At the end of his leap, Chris tucked and rolled through the cushiony snow, crushing the radio on his hip and sending the skis attached to his back flying through the air.

Once his spinning body came to a stop, Chris took a deep breath to regain his senses and figure out exactly what happened. Did he really just hit someone? He wasn't going that fast. Slow enough that he should've been able to see someone approaching through the storm. But the strength of their collision didn't accurately reflect his speed. In order for them to hit as hard as they did the other person must've been running. But why?

Uninjured, Chris briefly lamented the loss of his radio before quickly scrambling to his feet, hoping and praying that the victim of their collision wasn't seriously hurt. He could barely see the turned over snowmobile through the storm but the loud roar of the motor allowed him to find it easily enough. The engine continued to run as Chris approached it, but then slowly puttered out from lying on its side.

Chris kept moving past it and soon came to the dark figure, a man, thrashing about in the snow like a wild animal. As a patroller, Chris had responded to situations like this more times than he could count. But he'd never been the one who caused it before. It was his fault and that scared the shit out of him.

Chris slowly approached, unsure as to how he should react. Although writhing around, the person wasn't saying anything, screaming or otherwise. And as he got closer, Chris noticed silence wasn't the only peculiar thing about the incident. His victim's face was ghostly white, paler even than Chris's previous patient, but the stranger looked to be full of vitality. And he was raging mad. Almost feral. Rabid even. Like a furious madman with beady eyes of anger, the stranger's arms pointlessly reached and grasped in Chris's direction trying to reach him. His teeth sneered and chomped while he rolled from side to side on his back, futilely trying to get up. It was then that Chris looked down and saw the man's leg bent backwards and twisted to the side, a crippling injury from the crash.

Chris's heart sunk deep into his chest. In all his years as a patroller he helped countless numbers of people on the mountain, but now all he could think about was the one he deformed for life. He stood there in the snow, mentally frozen and unable to act. The man would surely lose his leg and had every right to be angry.

From such a horrific injury, the man surely had to be in unbearable pain. Chris noticed his rage though didn't seem to stem from the accident. It looked as if there was some other force driving the man to anger. The patroller's training started to kick in as Chris felt the urge to begin questioning the man, though he wasn't sure if he would even be able to get a response. The victim was completely conscious and alert, but with the exception of a few animal-like snarls, had yet to say a word

And then Chris realized the weirdest part of the whole scene. The man, who looked enraged with boiling blood, laid in snow wearing nothing above his waist but a single thermal top. No hat, gloves or jacket. He still had on a pair of ski pants and boots. But other than that, the man looked as if he had just undressed.

Before Chris could think any further, a woman's scream of terror rang out from behind him. And with that horrifying noise, a shockwave of fear bolted its way through Chris's mind. He'd heard screams before. Wails of pain and agony. But this was something else. Any experience he had dealing in a crisis under pressure had vanished and was replaced by paralyzing dread. He had a feeling something wasn't right in Telluride today, and that scream confirmed it.

Like a petrified boy, Chris slowly turned to the direction of the scream, which looked like nothing but a swirling space of white snow. Completely forgetting about the ravenous man he had just hit with the snowmobile, Chris started to slowly walk forward. He was cautious and curious as to how and why the woman screamed as she did. He wanted to know the answer but was fearful of it at the same time.

Slowly but surely, the white wall of snow before him faded with every step. Little by little the gigantic wood cabin that was Joseph's came into view. First, the long, modern logs appeared protruding into the sky. Then, right in front of him Chris noticed the long rows of ski racks completely filled with equipment. And last, as he finally approached the front of the lodge, a nightmarish scene of death revealed itself within the snow. Men and women covered the entryway to the building, biting, chewing and tearing each other to pieces like deranged animals.

Chris had stopped in his tracks, still unable to comprehend the destruction. For a moment, all he could do was watch and survey the murderous scene from amidst the freezing wind, trying to make sense of the madness. A steady coating of red covered every inch of snow by the entrance, but blood continued to spurt in every direction from more sources than Chris could count. A wave of people consumed by panic poured through the doors to get outside only to be grabbed and dragged back inside by the crazed mob.

Chris remained in his trance of disbelief until screams and shouts for help echoed out from inside the building. The sounds of those helpless people snapped Chris back to his purpose. He had come here for Sarah.

Without a second thought, Chris's legs kicked into gear, bringing him head first into the insanity. He charged through the chaotic scene, weaving in and out of people being mutilated all around him. Both the victims and their attackers were too pre-occupied with their own safety or bloodlust to notice him. And now, Chris was too driven to care. With the danger Sarah was in pressed right in front of his face, the only duty he felt was to the woman he loved. He kept feeling that strength within him grow, even as he lowered his shoulder and barreled into the lodge's thick wooden front door.

**

Beth hated snowboarders. Didn't matter how old they were or how they acted off the mountain. Once they put on their baggy ski clothes, they were all the same in her book. Some might call that prejudice. But she admittedly grew up in a highbrow Utah community who thought all snowboarders were pot smoking degenerates. Now Beth was educated and far enough from ignorant to know that wasn't true. Yet a part of her still refused to look at them any other way. Which was why her current situation was so unbearable.

After leaving the office, Beth quickly rushed to the gondola, hoping to make it back into town before the storm got any worse. The ride up went smoothly enough. She was joined by a young European couple looking to have a late breakfast at the restaurant in the mid-mountain station. But when they got off she was soon joined by two young snowboarders, unshaven, unrefined and reeking of marijuana. Beth was immediately repulsed by the walking stereotypes and moved over into the corner of the gondola chair, as far away from them as she could get inside the confined space.

At first, she didn't understand why they got on the gondola. It was a standing cliché that boarders lived for weather like this. But once she really took the time to get a good look at their faces, Beth could see why they wouldn't want to take their chances out in the storm. Both of the young boarders represented the epitome of sickness. Most likely college students, the boys didn't exactly resemble the cleanest of specimens. But their complexion went far beyond acne and oily skin. Both of their faces reflected the same pale and dry fleshy tone, which looked all the more rough behind their uncontrollable shivering. They were obviously sick, no doubt with the illness that everyone was catching.

Beth tried her best not to either stare or look repulsed by the sight of them, but the boys seemed fairly uninterested in her. For most of the ride down into town, the snowboarders carried on with their own blubbering conversation. Beth was grateful they were pretty much ignoring her, but at the same time, she almost felt offended. They were two young testosterone filled juveniles, and she considered herself attractive enough to at least be noticed by them. But they simply carried on talking among themselves, almost oblivious to the girl in front of them.

Throughout the gondola's descent into town, Beth's eyes pretended to stare out the window at the endless snowfall. But her ears were completely focused on eavesdropping, wondering what could be so riveting a topic that her passengers couldn't bother to acknowledge her. At first, the conversation puttered at a snail's pace. Both boys were completely sick and neither looked to have enough energy to carry on an engaging dialogue with one another. For the most part, all they did was complain about how awful they felt.

But Beth could sense the tone in the conversation pick up as the snowboarders started to assign blame for their condition. Each one thought the other had gotten him sick. And that train of reasoning led to an escalating series of accusations and name calling that drastically increased the tension in the tiny gondola cab. When that topic of discussion was exhausted, the argument seamlessly transitioned into who was responsible for losing their friend on the mountain.

Before she knew it, Beth was in the middle of a heated shouting match that made her forced presence an awkward addition. Neither had yet to acknowledge that she was there, which, surprisingly enough, made her feel even more uncomfortable. She was also taken aback by how quickly the conversation went from dull chatter to a ferocious argument. Less than a minute ago the two boys barely looked like they had enough energy to stand let alone scream at the top of their lungs. Yet there they were, sitting side by side, pointing fingers and yelling to the point where veins were bulging through their skin.

It was only a matter of time before it all turned violent. Beth could see each boy preparing to throw fists with the serious intent to do harm. And of course, her main concern was that she was practically held captive, locked into a small, confined space with an imminent brawl. She could see them both tense up, ready to lunge at one another. This was it, she thought, just stay out of their way.

When suddenly, the gondola car bounced up and down, the sign that the cable had entered the Telluride station. A second later the door opened, and the two friends on the verge of destruction simply exited the car and walked outside.

Beth was speechless. She was convinced a war was about to break out in front of her. When out of nowhere the topic seemingly dropped and the two combatants left together as if nothing happened. Boys were strange.

She sat stupefied in the car for a moment, unable to curb her adrenaline. A gondola attendant asked if she was getting off, which snapped her out of the trance. She responded by hopping out of the car and preparing herself for the blizzard just outside the small, glass station.

Despite the ride being only thirteen minutes long, the strength of the storm was worse than when Beth jumped into the gondola back in Mountain Village. From where she stood just outside the station, the first row of shops and restaurants, located at the mouth of where the town opened up to the base of the mountain, resided about a hundred feet away. As she hurriedly scuttled over to the shelter of a cafe awning, Beth clutched the top of her coat together, scrunching her shoulders up and over her neck like a turtle trying to recede into its shell. But the futile attempt did little from stopping the wild, falling snow from penetrating its way to her skin.

She eventually made it to the sidewalk, but the cover of the building only offered a slight reprieve from the snow. Still, the shelter was better than nothing, and she took advantage of the time by preparing herself for the walk home. It also helped that she wasn't the only one out in the storm. Anywhere else besides a ski resort, people would be hiding away at home. But in Telluride, a blizzard, no matter how strong it grew, was just business as usual.

As Beth stood huddled by the building, she continually rubbed her arms together, trying to gain some semblance of warmth. Spying on the other travelers, either shopping or headed up the mountain, offered a distraction from the cold. Her mind drifted a bit while watching them, but her attention was soon pulled in by a faint scream coming from behind her.

She turned back to the gondola and through the snow saw a series of black specks rolling down the mountain. Whatever they were or wherever the scream came from, Beth couldn't tell. The black specks, which grew larger in size every second they drew closer, were still too high up on the run to decipher what they were. And she highly doubted the noise had come from the few skiers and snowboarders further down the mountain who were rapidly coming towards her.

In fact, Beth could see them all heading down way faster than they should be. It's always expected that a few riders would be bombing through the run all the way down to the bottom, but she was quite surprised to see a whole row of skiers bent over and zooming down to the mountain's base as fast as they could possibly go. The whole bizarre scene was almost like a race to the bottom.

Meanwhile, the sporadically placed specks higher up on the mountain continued to follow behind them, growing larger and larger the further down they came. Beth held a hand over her face and squinted her eyes, trying to see through the snowfall. The black dots randomly bounced and bumped their way all over the hill, and Beth curiously kept her eyes on them until the objects finally started taking shape. At first, she couldn't believe what they were. It just didn't make any sense. But once the figures entered the clearing for the final run into town, Beth couldn't deny that the mysterious shapes were in fact an army of people tumbling head over heels down the mountain.

It was truly a strange sight to behold. One which had no immediate cause, purpose, or explanation. Limbs flailed about as their bouncing bodies twisted and turned in every possible direction, dragging a sheet of loose snow along with them. All those people must've been seriously hurt and in incredible pain, that was if they were still conscious or even alive.

Beth could only imagine what kind of catastrophe happened on top of the mountain that could cause such a horrific human avalanche. But her train of thought immediately shifted when she noticed the skiers preceding them had reached the base and ceased to slow down. In fact, they all hit the flat bottom of the mountain where the gondola resided and kept on going as far as their momentum would take them. Then, once they had completely stopped, the skiers and boarders popped their boots out from their bindings and took off running towards the town, leaving their equipment behind in the snow.

Once again, Beth was dumbfounded. What the hell was going on? She grew even more confused when one of the skiers sprinting towards her at full speed kept yelling for everyone to get back and run. Beth's whole body clenched in fear at what she thought was an attack, but it quickly vanished when the man passed straight by her, never missing a step.

Beth let out a long sigh of relief. This was a strange day that only continued to get stranger. She turned back towards the mountain just as the human bowling balls reached the base. She readied her cell phone to call for help, expecting the first body to slam into the ground. But it didn't. Instead, the bulky form hit the flat mountain base and used its momentum to roll over, springing to its feet. Without missing a beat, the person started running towards the gondola station with its arms flying all around.

Within seconds, a loud scream for help yelled out from inside the glass station. And before Beth could assess the situation, the rest of the living landslide hit the mountain base one by one, following the same path as the first. Except instead of running for the station they all continued straight on towards the town.

Like many of the other pedestrians unlucky enough to be out in the street, Beth froze in place, either from fear or indecision. She wanted to run but knew it would take a moment for her body to catch up to her mind. Although it was just a few seconds, Beth wanted to make the most out of her lapse in action by surveying the mob pouring off the mountain, but there were just too many to count. They all moved so fast weaving in and out of each other like a chaotic stampede. And by the time they got close enough that Beth could make out the crazed look of deranged violence on their faces, she was able to turn around and get her feet moving as fast as they could into town.

Behind her, Beth could hear the loud shattering of glass as the first wave of fiends bombarded the storefronts within reach. She never turned around but could hear the sounds of destruction continue intermittently between screams and more shouts for help. Either curious or catching on to the chaos, people from inside the buildings came outside and soon joined in on the mass exodus from the base of the mountain. Covered in a gigantic blanket of snow that continued to fall like bullets, the town's streets turned into a flood of people fleeing in the same direction, all being chased (and in some instances overtaken) by a wild riot biting at their heels.

Beth continued to push on, never looking back or fully listening to the screams of pain echoing all around her. She needed to get to safety but didn't know where to go. For now, all she knew was that she needed to run. Somehow, some way, she needed to carry on fleeing for her life. And that was her last thought as a runner shoved her from behind, trampling her down into the thick layer of snow covering the street.

9

It was supposed to be an epic day. Storm of the century, they said. Kenny Parker didn't believe it though. He heard weathermen predict the snow-pocalypse before when it was really nothing more than a few flurries. But his friends bought into the hype and wanted to ditch class to go boarding. So with the bribe of smoking a blunt on the way, his friends threw Kenny in the car and took the long drive from Montrose to Telluride. That was four hours ago.

Now Kenny was sitting alone at the top of the last run before the trails emptied out at the base of Mountain Village's gondola. He wore his usual waterproof snowboarding shell, hat and goggles, but not the thermal underwear most people on the mountain considered a must. He just never felt the need to. Kenny had never been cold before, even in almost zero degree weather.

But now, as he sat looking down at the merging area where all the trails came together, Kenny's body was crumpled into a ball to keep itself from freezing. The whirling snow completely encompassed him, chilling his arms and legs into icicles. He'd only been sitting for a minute, but his board already had a solid layer of frost covering up to his boots.

The situation wouldn't be as bad if Kenny had his friends sitting alongside him. But somewhere amidst the heavy snowfall they all got split up. He turned left. They turned right. And now here he was, alone and cold in a blizzard trying to figure out what was going on inside Mountain Village.

Normally he would've just boarded to the bottom and waited for his friends at the lift line. But as Kenny got further down the hill, he noticed something off about the crowd of people gathered around the base. The area was usually a meeting ground for ski school and guests wanting to head up the mountain together. The falling snow did make it hard to see, but it looked as if people were running all around, chasing each other back and forth. Almost like a panic.

The whole scene was strange. So despite nearly freezing to death, Kenny plopped himself down on top of the run to figure out what was going on. He was too far away to hear anything, and the roar of the wind didn't make it any easier. All the while, other skiers and boarders whizzed past him on their way down the mountain. They didn't seem too concerned about the activity down below. Or maybe they just didn't see it.

After a few more minutes of uncontrollable shivering, Kenny convinced himself he was just being paranoid. He must've still been high. Damn that was some good weed.

Kenny summoned up the strength to force his frozen ass off of the snow. But as he rose to a standing position, a small break in the endless snowfall finally allowed him to clearly peer down to the bottom of the run. For a brief moment, the entire Mountain Village courtyard was revealed, and Kenny realized his fears were justified. Behind the ironically placed "caution" and "slow" signs, Mountain Village base was nothing short of a warzone. A portion of the crowd had turned into a mob, rioting and attacking anything in sight. Bodies, some moving and some not, littered streets and lift lines like garbage tossed to the ground. Streaks of blood painted the snow, radiating out amongst the crisp whiteness. It was an ongoing massacre, and Kenny had no desire to join it.

It also seemed he wasn't the only one. As soon as the break in the snow displayed the carnage for all to see, the skiers and boarders that had been blindly charging straight into it stopped dead in their tracks. Together with Kenny, they all stood on the side of the mountain, utterly speechless as to what they were witnessing.

But Kenny's stoned mind didn't stay harrowing on the grimly sight for long. The rapid snowfall picked up again, and he immediately began wondering, thinking, planning as to what he should do next. He couldn't go down there. He would just become another victim to the chaos. But where then? Try and traverse over to the other side of the mountain? Bypass the village and hope the town was any better? Maybe he could take off his board and hike up to the gondola's mid-mountain station. His friends weren't feeling well so that's probably where they went anyway. He could just wait out whatever this craziness was in there with them.

Kenny turned his head, hoping to see the gondola's path up to the station, when a lady skier tumbling down the mountain suddenly slammed into his legs. The collision violently locked all their limbs and equipment as one while the skier's momentum brought them over and down the mountain together. In a tangled ball, Kenny and the strange skier tumbled and spun all the way down the run, twisting and contorting each other's bodies as they fell.

When the entwined couple finally came to a stop, Kenny moaned and opened his eyes in a massive amount of pain. He was sure something was broken, but couldn't locate exactly where on his body the excruciating agony was coming from. He was lying on his back with his face covered in snow, but he still managed to look over and catch a glimpse of the skier, whose legs were still latched onto his own.

Kenny wanted to say something, but didn't know whether to curse her off or ask if she was all right. Either way, he soon realized she probably didn't have the strength for any kind of response. She was barely moving in a kind of weak twitch. Kenny wanted to push her off and start running before the crazies smelled fresh meat, but his arms were too bruised to move.

The woman then started rolling over with her head down, slowly reaching her arms up and onto Kenny's chest. Like talons, her gloveless, bare hands latched onto his jacket as the woman clawed her way up on top of him. While she slowly inched her way up his body, Kenny wondered how she was even still moving her frostbitten, mangled fingers. But somehow they continued to grasp onto him and pull the woman's head closer to his face.

Kenny curiously watched on, but remained worried as to what the skier was actually doing. She didn't say a word. No moans or groans of pain. Just continued to inch closer to him with her head down and her icicle fingers scratching up his jacket.

Just as her head was about to reach his, Kenny finally decided he wanted her off. He prepared himself to move when, in a sudden rush of energy, the woman quickly looked up, springing herself towards him. The lunge happened so fast, but in that moment Kenny caught a glimpse of the woman's pale, horrifying face. Her eyes were a dark, veiny red and her mouth was spread wide open like that of a savage creature.

Kenny had neither the time nor the readiness to act, and the woman sunk her ravenous teeth straight into the center of his face. The unsuspecting snowboarder let out a scream as his attacker chomped down even harder into his cold skin. The skier's teeth easily pierced through the flesh, digging deeper and deeper with every thrust of her jaw. Kenny continued to shrill and shout while flailing about, trying to push the woman off. But she continued to hold a firm bite onto his face, even as the blood oozed out from the wound and dripped down between her lips.

***

The time for simply listening to the radio had long since passed, and Peter was now pacing around his office with a cell phone all but glued to his ear. From the sanitation department to the fire station and everywhere in between, there were very few people who didn't get at least one phone call from Peter within the past hour.

For the most part, Telluride and Mountain Village respected and enjoyed their own autonomy. But while one could certainly function without the other, the different communities understood that they had to work together if they were to flourish. And during a crisis, which they were both finding out together, it was essential to pool their resources if they were to even survive.

So for the first time since establishing Mountain Village, Peter had taken direct command over many aspects of Telluride's emergency services. The region's personnel was just stretched too thin to handle every situation at once. At first he took the responsibility as a badge of honor, but that pride quickly evaporated as the job proved more overwhelming than he possibly imagined.

Peter removed the phone from his ear and ended the call with Marshal Walker, who just informed him that in the past hour Telluride's nine-one-one center received more calls for violent crimes than they had in the past year. It was a statistic Peter just didn't know how to comprehend, let alone react to. He was in complete and utter shock. In less than a morning his small town had literally dove into chaos.

Like a stupefied zombie, Peter strolled over to the chair behind his desk and fell back into the seat defeated. The marshal told him that he would continue to do everything he could to maintain some semblance of order, but he just didn't have enough manpower to deal with every act of violence being reported. It was hard for Walker to admit, but the small force charged with safeguarding the community would ultimately fail at their job. They were being overrun.

What started out as a serious health problem had somehow devolved into an all out attack. The amount of patients pouring into the health centers was enough cause for concern. But now a mob of violence had stretched every resource to the brink of collapse. Even the mountain's ski patrol was being swamped by turmoil. Throw in the intense blizzard that continued to pound the valley for hours and Peter was literally experiencing a perfect storm of disaster. He didn't know if it was the weather or what, but something was making people crazy. And it actually scared him.

For almost a full minute, Peter just sat in his seat, completely paralyzed by indecisive fear. What was he supposed to do? What could he do? Call in for help from Denver? Homeland Security? The National Guard? Telluride was a small town almost completely isolated from the rest of the country. How soon could they possibly get here to stop the downward spiral of anarchy?

Peter spun around in his seat to face the large window behind him. Weather forecasts indicated the rate of snowfall had actually increased in the past hour, but if that was true Peter didn't notice. All he could tell was that it was snowing like hell outside, and he couldn't see a damn thing through the glass.

Normally from his office he could see the top peak of the ski resort and a small portion of Mountain Village's shops. But now he was almost grateful that he couldn't make out the rows of buildings below. Reports coming in didn't paint a pretty picture of what the Village's courtyard had become. And a small, shameful part of Peter was glad the storm obscured the violence from his view. Otherwise, he'd have to witness firsthand his failure to save what he worked so hard to create.

And that's when the dreadful reality of the situation finally sunk in. That's when Peter Hayden remembered that he had more than just Mountain Village to watch over. He also had a family.

In a frantic panic, Peter fumbled the phone as he quickly tried to dial his wife's number. Ryan's ski school should've been over soon, and given the situation all Peter could hope for was that Sarah somehow found a safe place to hide the children until everything was over. There was nothing else he could do. But Cheryl was still at home and he needed to know she was all right.

The phone started ringing and Peter could consciously feel his heartbeat grow more intense with every second. The phone rang again. And again. And again. And Peter's rapid, intense breaths quieted down to a whisper, hoping and praying that she would answer.

A soft voice, harsh from crying, finally emerged through the speaker. "Hello?"

Peter released an exhausted sigh, and it was only then that he realized he had been holding his breath. "Cheryl honey, are you safe? Is everything all right there?"

An outburst of relief poured out of the phone. "Peter? Thank God! There's someone at our door. I don't know who it is."

And as quickly as Peter was relieved to hear his wife's voice, his entire being was overcome by fear. "What do they want?"

"I don't know. It's a man, but he hasn't said anything. He just keeps pounding on it over and over again."

Peter then started to notice a subtle noise in the background of the phone call. Almost like the random beating of a drum. "Cheryl, whatever you do, don't answer the door. Don't even try to talk to him. Just go upstairs and hide."

The background noise started to grow louder, and Peter could hear the fear in his wife's voice increase along with it. "I asked him what he wants but he didn't answer. Just keeps pounding the...no...now he's...he's kicking it, Peter! He's kicking the door!"

The thought of his wife's imminent danger unleashed a floodgate of adrenaline inside Peter's head. His heart began jumping out of his chest, almost distracting him from trying to think. He had to do something. Anything! But he was helpless to do it himself behind his office desk. He couldn't get there in time. No one could. Trying to reach Marshal Walker again or calling nine-one-one would only waste time, and what could they do anyway? This attack was just one of hundreds they had to deal with.

No. As much as he hated to admit it, there would be no one coming to save his wife. Her only chance was to run. "Cheryl, listen to me. I need you to get clothes on to go outside. A jacket. Hat. Gloves. Whatever."

The fear in her words had become too much to hide and started to take over her voice. "I...I tried calling for help but..."

"They can't do anything. You have to get out of there. Now."

She tried to speak, but the pounding had grown so loud it moved up from the background to dominate the phone call. Cheryl's voice had become just a faint echo behind the repeated thud of the man's foot against the door. "OK. OK. I'll go out the back."

The tension remained through his body, but with a planned course of action Peter at least felt more confident than he had. Cheryl's voice had left the phone and was replaced by the creaking of a closet door. Then a zipper. Good, Peter thought. She's ready to go. He heard a light tapping of feet, most likely as Cheryl moved towards the back door. Then her voice returned. "Have you heard from Ryan? I hope he's..."

Her sentence was suddenly cut off by a loud and final bang, surely the sound of the door breaking off the hinges. Peter's heart sank into his chest as the explosive noise was immediately followed by his wife's cries of despair. "God, no! Please...stop!"

He screamed her name, hoping to get a response. But the only sound on the other end was the quick rustling of a scuffle followed by a solid knock as her phone dropped to the floor. Then there was only silence and Peter's jaw fell in complete and utter disbelief.

For a moment he still held the phone up to his ear, listening intently for any sound at all. But there was nothing. She was gone. Dead or otherwise. And given the circumstances he could only assume the worst.

Peter clutched the phone at the side of his head, squeezing it with everything he had. And when that did nothing to dissolve his anger, he wound up and threw it against the wall, shattering the small device into a hundred pieces.

The action was meant to subside his anger, but all it did was force Peter to drop his head into his hands and burst into tears. He cried like he'd never cried before, and it honestly surprised him. He didn't even know he was capable of such sadness.

But the tears eventually stopped. Not because he ran out of them but because they had to. Peter was still in charge of fixing this mess and he had to take some action, any action, to make things right. That's when he realized it was time to declare a state of emergency. The next step after that was figuring out how.

***

Malcolm was at the end of his rope. Currently he sat behind the desk in his tiny, cramped office listening to Georgia go on and on about people being sick and violence across the town. She hadn't played a song for a solid hour now and just continued to take a never-ending chain of complaining callers.

Mal didn't see what the big deal was. People just get crazy in a crisis. Sure the storm was bad, working people into a frenzy, but sooner or later the weather would clear. Then the clean up would begin like nothing ever happened.

All you had to do was stay inside and lock your doors. Let the crazies be crazy and nothing would happen to you. But people aren't that smart. They want to go outside and play in the snow. Then they wonder why they're sick and people are getting violent. It's a fucking blizzard for Christ sakes. Mother nature's the most violent one of all. Hell, Malcolm wasn't feeling well himself, but you wouldn't hear him complaining. What's the point? Just suck it up and get your job done.

Which at the moment proved to be increasingly difficult for Malcolm. It would be great if Georgia focused on cheering people up. Played some good time music or something. But no. She had to keep the people focused on the doom and gloom of the day. Thinks she's Barbara fucking Walters reporting the town news like it matters.

Malcolm would've pulled her the first moment she started playing up to a scared caller. But he had no one to fall back on but himself. No other DJs. No call screeners. Not even a goddamn intern.

So there he sat, huddled into his miniscule desk in his janitor's closet of an office, leaning over a hot cup of ramen. He wasn't eating it. In fact, his stomach was in shambles. But the steam from the soup helped clear his sinuses and soothe his throat. Which he would need if he were to take over for Georgia.

He really didn't want to but damn! She's fucking killing the audience. Every caller had another pathetic sob story about being attacked. TORO had a worldwide audience now. Nobody wanted to hear about this petty local crime bullshit. What was he doing listening to her on the radio from his office anyway? He was the station's fucking manager. He should be in the sound booth controlling everything she did and everything she said. Why did she get to pick the callers? Why did she control the music? From the moment he met her Malcolm had given that hippie, punk bitch way too long a leash. And it was time to reel her in.

Malcolm stood from his desk, throwing the thermal blanket curled around his shoulders to the floor, and stormed out of his office ready to take the station over for himself.

10

Stuck in disbelief, Chris raised the goggles to the top of his head but nothing changed. He was still witnessing the same onslaught of horror and carnage he did with them on. Once one of the best lunch stops in Telluride, Joseph's had been transformed into a human slaughterhouse.

With his jaw dropped in shock, Chris's head stared straight ahead, but his eyes darted around the room catching glimpses of the anarchy. Giant pools of bodies and blood littered the floor as a pack of wild guests, just as crazed as the ones outside, led a chaotic massacre of defenseless men, women, and children. Without any sense, rhyme or reason to the madness, the ravenous group threw punches and kicks around freely at any "normal" person that moved. There was biting and clawing, pushing and slamming, anything and everything that could be done to cause as much death and destruction to the world around them. Screams, shouts, and cries for help rang out from every corner of the lodge. And one in particular grabbed Chris's attention enough for him to spring into action.

His legs immediately started moving in the direction of the familiar voice. Turned over tables and chairs acted as obstacles for him to leap over and maneuver around. A wide assortment of food; ribs, hamburgers, hotdogs and pizza, had been flung around the room adding to the mess. But like a man on a mission, Chris navigated the maze of crazed attackers, plowing through them with his shoulder strong and his head down in determination.

Guided by his girlfriend's screams, Chris found a girl pinning Sarah into a wall at the corner of the lodge. Dressed in a Joseph's employee outfit, the girl looked to be jerking her arm back and forth on top of Sarah. And it wasn't until he got within reach that Chris noticed the metal fork clutched tightly in the girl's hand.

He lunged towards the attacker, grabbing her arm and stopping her from stabbing Sarah again. The girl snarled from primitive frustration, trying over and over to break free from Chris's grasp. But the patroller held on tight while wrestling the girl off of Sarah.

As he did, Chris quickly looked up and caught a glimpse of his girlfriend. But the appalling sight of her sent a sudden shiver down his spine. Covered in cuts and bruises, her face had swollen up to twice its normal size. Beneath her tattered and torn blood-soaked shirt, a series of small yet deep punctures in her chest oozed a crimson red.

Chris gasped on instinct, causing him to balk from fighting the girl. And the momentary distraction allowed her the opportunity to throw herself back, catching Chris off guard and sending them flying backwards into a cushy pile of bodies. Without the girl holding her up, Sarah was too weak to stand and slid down the wall to the floor.

Lying on his back, Chris still held tight onto the crazed girl as she flailed around on top of him. Writhing around like a fish out of water, the girl continued to jerk her arms in every direction, hoping to wriggle free. Chris struggled to keep her contained and eventually tossed her to the side.

She hit the ground, immediately springing back up and charging at him, fork in hand ready to strike. Shocked and surprised by the young girl's ferocity, Chris just barely raised his arms in time to catch her as she dove on top of him.

Hissing and growling like an animal, the girl put all her strength into her arm, trying to force it down and through Chris's block. On the other end of the struggle, Chris pressed hard against the girl's attack but was taken by surprise at her strength and determination. Under normal circumstances, he would've never questioned how easily he could overpower a teenage girl. Yet here he found himself, barely able to defend his own life against some crazed girl's attempt to kill him with a fork.

Chris looked over at her hand and saw the small metal object protruding out from within it. Its tiny prongs were barely sharp enough to pierce his skin. But when bearing down on top of his face, Chris would've sworn the dull weapon magnified to the size of a pitchfork ready to impale his head on its spikes.

It wasn't, though. It was a stupid kitchen utensil. And this wasn't a raving serial killer. She was just some local youngster on steroids. One who just brutally attacked the woman he loved. And he wasn't going to put up with her bullshit anymore.

Still fighting on his back, Chris reached over to grab the girl's hand, fork and all, and twisted her over, snapping her wrist while slamming her into the floor. The fork dropped free, and Chris quickly grabbed it, transitioning into his own onslaught of attacks, stabbing the girl repeatedly wherever his arm desired. Up and down like a fluid machine, the tiny fork poked holes in the girl's chest, cheeks, ribs, throat and nose. Everywhere Chris could land a strike, over and over again until her ravenous wailing simmered down to a murmur.

Whatever small semblance of life she had left finally puttered out. And even then, Chris continued to drive the fork into her body several more times before stopping and surveying the corpse he had created.

When the realization of her murder eventually set in, Chris's attention drifted back over to the wall, where Sarah rested peacefully with her eyes closed.

While the massacre still raged on all over the lodge, Chris quickly scampered on his hands and knees over to his battered girlfriend. "Damn it, Sarah. You OK?"

Ignoring his question, she struggled to slit open her eyes and peer over at the dead girl's body behind him. "She...she was a good kid."

"Yeah. A fucking honor student. Come on. Let's go."

He carefully wrapped his arm under hers and gently began to lift her up, but Sarah suddenly objected as a surge of pain shot through her body. "No-no-no! I can't."

"What's wrong?"

"It hurts...too much."

Chris could feel his teeth clench together and pointlessly punched the floor, releasing his frustration. "No! Do you see what's going on here? They'll kill you."

"I don't deserve to live."

"What are you talking about?"

Still struggling to open her swollen lips, Sarah was barely able to speak through the pain. "I couldn't...protect...them all."

At first, Chris was utterly confused and thought she was just rambling from the stress. But then he noticed that there was something different about the graveyard in this corner of the room. When he first arrived, Chris's mind was so zoned in on finding his girlfriend that he only took a brief survey of his surroundings. He hopped over and passed by so many bodies to get to her that he didn't give a second thought to the ones around him.

After hearing Sarah's words though, he finally took the time to look at the corpses littering their isolated corner of the room. Children. Small bodies covered in blood and ripped clothes. Bite marks and stab wounds dotted their tiny frames to the point of mutilation. And if his own body wasn't surging with adrenaline, Chris wasn't sure that it wouldn't completely collapse from the heartbreaking scene.

Pushing his revulsion aside, Chris then turned back to Sarah just in time to see her mumble again. "Save...Ryan."

And upon that final word leaving her mouth, the small slats in Sarah's eyes shut, and her limp body slumped over towards the floor.

Chris reactively caught her falling shoulders but was unable to do anything more. He just stayed still, holding her, trying to process the reality that she was gone. Then, with his mind slowly reacting to the traumatic loss, he carefully leaned her over and laid her body onto the floor.

Once she was down, Chris continued to stare at her, holding back a wave of tears that wanted to explode from his eyes. He could hear the violence around him slowing down. The screams and shouts from the dying went silent one by one. Chris knew it was only a matter of time before they turned their attention towards him. But now it didn't matter. They could take him away for all he cared. Rip him limb from limb until he was nothing but a bleeding stump on the floor. Because that's all he felt like: a small man who never committed to the life he truly wanted.

The growls and roars of the feral mob around him continued, but an odd noise stood out from within the chaos. A small cry faint enough to be a whimper could be heard at Chris's side. And the grief-stricken patroller was curious enough to look over for its source.

What he found was a young boy, the same age as the bodies around him, hiding underneath a turned over table. In contrast to the squirts of blood covering Chris's face, the boy's cheeks were drenched in tiny tears. Judging by the stern look on his fearful expression, he was obviously trying to hold them back, but his attempts were proving unsuccessful as they continued to roll down to his chin.

Through his anger and anguish, Chris remembered Sarah's final words and called out to the boy. "Ryan?"

The young child's face curiously lit up upon hearing his name but was still reluctant to move. For a moment, Chris just sat staring at him, unsure as to what he should do. Only seconds earlier he was ready to die alongside the woman he loved. Even if he wanted to live, how could he escape this madness? In less than a minute the crazed savages would mark him as their newest prey.

But this boy was a part of Sarah's soul. Chris knew just how much she loved her students. Caring for them was her life, and it was a life she wanted to share with him. All that was over now. But as long as one of the children she cared so much for was still alive her death had meaning. He would get this boy home...no matter what.

Chris held out his hand, further calling for Ryan to join him. "Come on. I want to help you."

The boy didn't move, but Chris could see the gears in his head moving as he spoke. "Are...are you Sarah's boyfriend?"

Chris nodded his head with a smile. "Yeah. I'm Chris. She wanted me to help you. But we gotta go now."

Once again, Chris could tell the boy was thinking intensely, most likely weighing his chances of escape. So Chris took the initiative and began searching for options. It only took one spin around for him to see the closed window behind him. Chris leaned over and opened the window, immediately being met by a face full of windy snow. But he quickly turned back, signaling for the boy to move. "Out. Now!"

Ryan darted out from under the table, but his sudden movements caught the mob's attention. As one cohesive yet disorganized unit, the crazed attackers charged towards the boy from across the room. Ryan was ready to jump out the window when he briefly glanced down at Sarah's beaten body. Chris saw the boy's hesitation and quickly lifted him up and out into the storm.

He was about to climb out himself, when he noticed the boy's thermal shirt already covered in snow. In a frantic panic, Chris swiftly scattered the area and found a loose jacket and hat under a nearby body. He jerked the clothing free, causing the body to roll over, and then dove towards the window.

His upper body made it through when he suddenly stopped in mid-air. Chris tried to lift himself out, but a tight hand held onto his ankle, pulling him back inside. Still shivering from the bitter cold, Ryan grabbed onto the back of Chris's jacket, trying desperately to bring him outside. Chris could feel more of the crazies inside trying to grab hold of him but kicked his legs around to keep them from latching on. Eventually, one of those kicks connected, and Chris could feel a hard head rock back under the sole of his ski boot.

Now free, Chris's momentum took him outside and on top of Ryan into the packed snow surrounding the cabin. With his heart still racing, Chris quickly sprang to his feet, immediately shutting the window behind him. He then shook off the snowy clothes still clutched in his hands and saw Ryan had a tough time standing in the powder up to his chest.

Feeling his troubles, Chris lifted the shivering boy from the ground and quickly brushed him off before handing over the jacket and hat. "Here. Put these on."

After dropping the hat on his head, Ryan slipped his arms through the jacket two sizes too big and struggled to zip it up with the long sleeves covering his hands. "What if they come after us?"

"Let's hope they're not that smart. Follow me."

Chris took off around the building, lifting his legs up and over the high snowfield to run. He kept moving past the side of the lodge and peeked around the corner to the front entrance. Any of the wild guests he encountered on his way in had long since gone, leaving only freshly snow-covered bodies in their wake.

Chris remained still and heard the faint commotion of movement inside the cabin. A second later, the front door to Joseph's burst open and the large mob from inside blitzed into the snowstorm. Without purpose or intentions, the crazed fiends scattered in every direction, running straight through the blizzard to no place in particular.

Chris waited by the corner for a moment until the mad dash had ended and all the psychos disappeared into the falling snow. He then turned back around to instruct the boy, but Ryan was several steps behind him, still struggling to wade through the snow up to his waist. Chris let out a sigh of frustration, not so much towards the kid but at his own failure to help him. The patroller then took a step back and reached for the boy.

After grabbing him by the baggy jacket, Chris swung him around and placed him onto his back. "Hold on, Ryan. OK? We're going to make a break for it."

He could feel the boy bury his face into the back of his jacket, either to shield himself from the cold snow or to refrain from witnessing their daring escape. Chris assumed it was probably just a combination of both and reassured him anyway. "We're going to be fine. Just take a deep breath and hold on. I'm going to get us out of here."

Chris prepared to take off into the snowstorm when he heard Ryan mumble out from under his muffled mouth. "Just like Austin Cage."

An awkward smile formed under Chris's gaiter. He contemplated responding to the boy's remark. Then realized it wasn't a question and wasted no time bolting off straight into the storm.

Through the whirling and whizzing of the wild snow, Chris couldn't tell if he was headed in the right direction but figured that moving in a straight line from Joseph's entrance was as good a path as any. The freshly fallen snow was still high up on his legs, but the often traveled mountaintop was compact and not as deep as the no man's land behind the restaurant. Chris's legs ran through it with ease, and before he knew it, came across the incapacitated man he hit with his snowmobile.

The accident didn't happen that long ago, but already the man, barely visible through a mound of snow, was showing obvious signs of long-term exposure to the cold. His face looked even rougher than before, and the pallor of his skin dropped to the same shade as the snow.

But even though he moved as if his depleted energy was running out, Chris could still see the same vivid hate and murderous rage within his eyes. The man's vicious growls had gasped out to a mere whimper, and Ryan clutched harder around Chris's neck at the sound, even with his eyes still buried tight into the jacket.

Where once he felt utter and complete guilt at the man's injury, Chris now barely gave him a second thought as he passed. He still didn't know what affliction had created such violence but felt no remorse for the inhuman creature he crippled into the snow. Chris only slowed down enough to acknowledge the dying man as a landmark on his journey. It meant his means of escape was nearby.

Chris continued to tread through the snow carefully, his eyes moving back and forth in search of a large black object. He stopped for a moment and spun around in a complete circle, but all he saw was white. Even the injured man was now completely hidden from view. But then, out in the field, Chris spotted a small black rod protruding from the snow. He ran out to it without delay and saw the snowmobile on its side with the rubber handlebar sticking up like a marker. Chris started brushing off the flakes from the seat and dashboard, but then spotted a puddle of fuel burning a hole in the snow below, an obvious sign that the accident left the vehicle inoperable.

Chris slammed the snowmobile's seat in frustration. "Shit!" He then briefly looked back over his shoulder at Ryan still holding on. "Sorry, kid. Guess we need another ride."

Rather than waste time trying to repair the snowmobile, Chris popped up and looked around for another way down the mountain. But after a complete three sixty, he continued to see nothing.

That's when he felt Ryan's arm leave his neck and point over to their side. "What's that?"

Chris turned his head and, only after squinting to focus, spotted a bright orange color emanating from under the snow. It took a moment for the sight to process, but the patroller soon realized he was seeing the reflector of his ski bindings.

Another smile worked its way onto his face as he rubbed Ryan's arm, which returned to its spot around his neck. "Nice work. Looks like I'll really be Austin Cage now."

Chris ran over to the shimmering orange spot of snow and began digging with both hands. He soon pulled out one full ski but immediately resumed his search for the other. It only took a moment for him to spot it several feet away further into the storm. He, once again, trotted over to it, but a commotion from behind them grabbed Ryan's attention.

While Chris dug the second ski out and set it up alongside the other, Ryan peeked over his shoulder to see the outline of a figure running towards them wildly through the falling snow. "Ummm...Chris?"

The patroller didn't have to turn around to know what the boy was seeing. At the same time both frantic and calm, Chris kicked the top of the binding, knocking loose the snow from his boots before carefully clicking them into the skis. It was an action he'd done a thousand times before but never with his life in danger. Chris found himself moving slower than normal, making doubly sure his boots were secure. Otherwise, he'd have to waste time doing it again.

Rather than look away, Ryan continued to watch the running figure grow larger and larger as it came into focus. "Can we leave now?"

And with that said, Chris pushed off with his skis down the flat stretch of mountaintop. At first, he moved even slower than he did on foot, his pursuer gaining ground with every step.

But Chris continued to push off through the snow, alternating between skis. Right leg. Left leg. Right leg. Left leg. His speed gradually increased just as the snowy plain started to tilt downhill. With his momentum picking up, Chris stopped pushing off and leaned forward down the mountain.

Having long since closed his eyes back into Chris's jacket, Ryan could actually feel the person at their heels reach for his back and barely miss grasping onto his arm. And with that failed attempt, their pursuer tumbled to the ground, rolling downhill in a small avalanche of snow.

Chris continued moving forward, picking up speed as the plain dipped further and further down to an incline. A barrage of snow pummeled his shielded face, limiting his visibility to a thin slice through the goggles. It wasn't a straight downhill just yet, but the faster they went, the tighter Ryan's grip grew around his neck.

For a moment, Chris was distracted from his path down the mountain by checking to make sure the boy was secure. He was then shocked when he turned back around and saw another crazed lady running at them through the snow.

Reacting on pure skier's instinct, Chris veered to the side, narrowly missing a swipe of the wild woman's bare hand. Just as he thought himself safe, another attacker came from the side. And another. And another. Chris quickly realized he found himself amidst a pack of the mob that had frantically taken off from Joseph's.

One by one, Chris veered and dodged to avoid every fiend's attempt to grab or knock them over. Through the cloud of falling snow, their pursuers seemed to randomly appear left and right all over the traverse. Chris could still feel Ryan's head buried into the back of his neck, the boy's grasp growing tighter and tighter with every turn away from danger.

Eventually, the sloped mountaintop dropped off completely, and Chris passed the tree line, entering into a downhill run. The closest pursuers continued to follow him, tripping over the steep slope and falling head over heels down the mountainside. Some of the mindless fiends in front of them had already taken the plunge and were struggling to stay on their feet as they plummeted downhill.

As if in a moving racecourse, Chris leaned further over, gaining speed as he weaved in and out of the tumbling obstacles. The expert skier floated atop the freshly packed snow like a cloud, gliding past his disheveled attackers with grace and speed. He then finally broke free from the pack and darted straight downward, taking refuge into the dense woods on the side of the run.

**

"We're upstairs in the bedroom but...but I can hear them down in the kitchen. They're tearing the house apart."

Georgia took a deep breath, trying to absorb another heart-wrenching account of the brutal violence around Telluride. The police had been all but useless to stop the chaos. So instead of dialing nine-one-one, those in need had been picking up the phone and calling the radio station.

Why? Georgia didn't know exactly. Maybe in a panic people turned to an easily remembered number they've heard many times before. Or perhaps a sense of impending doom made them want to broadcast their thoughts to as wide an audience as they could.

Either way didn't matter to Georgia. It was obvious something was wrong in her town. And for whatever reason, she had fallen into the role of reporting it to the world. But it was a task that had slowly worn her down. What started off as a few people calling in about isolated incidents had turned into a full-blown catastrophe. And with each call getting more depressing than the last, Georgia felt more and more helpless.

There was no one to turn to. No one to call for help. She felt secure herself, tucked away in a small locked building on the outskirts of town. But for the others, there was nothing for her to do but take their calls and document their stories.

With the last frightened caller still on the line, Georgia swallowed deeply, trying her best to keep her own fear contained. "I think it's best if we hang up now. You should keep quiet."

The caller responded with a soft whisper that sounded like a thank you, but Georgia couldn't tell. What she did hear was the loud click as the phone hung up soon after.

A silence filled the air, usually the cue for a radio host to say something. But Georgia remained quiet for a moment, her thoughts stuck on the previous caller's family as she privately wished them luck.

A few more seconds passed, and Georgia took her time with a deep sigh before speaking. "This isn't getting any easier, folks. And it sure doesn't seem to be slowing down. But as long as we're on the air I'll be taking all the calls I can."

She then looked over to the caller ID screen, which displayed the information for every phone number coming in. The monitor was completely lit up, flashing names and numbers non-stop like a roulette. The station had never seen this amount of phone traffic before, and without a screener Georgia couldn't place anyone on hold. Fielding calls as they came in was the best system she had. Good thing there was no shortage of them...or maybe that was a bad thing.

Georgia contemplated which caller to choose next. Usually, she picked at random, not wanting to play favorites to anybody she might've known. But while scanning the list a name of interest popped out at her: Mountain Village Hall. Who it was at the office or why they would be calling she couldn't know for sure.

But it made her curious enough to pick up the line. "All right, TORO listeners. We have an interesting caller next from Mountain Village's government office. Hello, can you hear me?"

"Yes. Yes, I can."

It was a man's voice. Georgia didn't recognize it. Then again, she didn't know anybody who worked in the Telluride government, so it wasn't surprising. "Hi, sir. Can you tell us your name?"

"My name is Peter Hayden. I was the financier behind Mountain Village's construction and have held the office of Village Manager since its founding."

Georgia was taken aback for a moment. Next to the Mayor of Telluride, this man was the second highest government official in the area. But she didn't know what surprised her more: whether he actually called into the station or whether he called in from his office and not some isolated safe house made especially for the rich and famous. "Mr. Hayden, thanks so much for calling in. I hope you're safe and that maybe you have some official announcement for us?"

"I do."

Georgia could hear strain in the man's voice. She couldn't imagine what he'd possibly been through in the last couple hours but could actually feel the man's stress oozing through the phone as he continued on. "As most of you know, the massive blizzard which hit our town has been the least of our problems. Since this morning, a health crisis has plagued the region and was soon followed by an unprecedented wave of violence. It all happened so fast I couldn't possibly give you an explanation. And I'm sorry to say our law enforcement and emergency services have been insufficient to handle the panic.

"That said, I've spoken with the mayor and together we've declared an official state of emergency. As we speak, he's on the phone with the governor requesting any and all assistance available to us. Military and medical personnel will be arriving shortly. If you're listening to this broadcast, all I ask is that you please stay calm and take shelter. Help is on its..."

The last word of Mr. Hayden's sentence was cut off as the sound room window shattered into a million pieces in front of Georgia. Shards of sharp glass flew through the air to the other side of the room, showering the girl's face and body as she toppled over in her seat.

In the sudden chaos, Georgia looked up to see Malcolm flying through the window straight at her. Sparks shot out from the trampled control room panel behind him as he used it as a springboard to propel himself forward. Her boss was now soaring through the air, tangling his body into the microphone as he fell down on top of his DJ.

Reacting on instinct, Georgia immediately kicked and clawed her boss away as she got to her feet. Confused and disoriented, she took a quick survey of Malcolm's face and saw nothing but animal rage. His eyes, bloodshot and bulging from his skull, represented a crazed anger that was further amplified by the snarling sneer in his mouth. It was an appearance that'd been described to Georgia many times over the past hour but that she'd yet to see in person for herself.

Regardless of the adrenaline pouring through her, Georgia wanted to stop and think for a moment. Maybe talk to Malcolm. Ask him what happened to make him like this. But she had heard this story enough times to know there was no point. Regardless of their friendship, Malcolm West wouldn't stop his assault until she was dead. And there was nothing for her to do but hide.

The crazed attacker scrambled to get off the floor, cutting his hands on the shards of glass spread under him. Georgia wasted no time getting to the door, but she could feel Malcolm right behind her. Without form or thought, he threw himself forward, slamming his body into the radio equipment standing between him and the exit.

As she ran down the hall, Georgia could hear Malcolm destroying everything in the room that stood in his way. She stopped for a moment, listening to the utter and complete destruction taking place behind her. And that's when she realized running was pointless. Where would she go that he couldn't find her? How could she escape someone so determined to catch her? Over and over she'd taken calls from people doing just that, and all it did was leave them waiting helplessly in fear. She wouldn't allow herself to be put in the same position. She had to fight.

But Georgia's spike in bravery was interrupted by an attack from behind. A strong force slammed into her back, tackling her to the ground. Georgia managed to spin around to her back and once again found Malcolm on top of her, gnashing his teeth in her face.

She'd been distracted, allowing Malcolm time to climb back

through the control room window and enter the hall from the other side. But Georgia couldn't think about that now. She literally had her hands full trying to keep Malcolm's face back and away from her own. As he continued to push himself closer, her boss swiped repeatedly at her arms and face, scratching and clawing shards of skin with his fingernails. Georgia screamed from the pain but never stopped pressing back against the maddened fiend on top of her.

She finally found an opening in Malcolm's attacks to scrunch her knees up and kick him away. The large man lifted off of Georgia's body just long enough for her to pop up off the floor. But he stood just as fast and lunged forward again, quickly grabbing the girl from behind and slamming her into the wall. Georgia had just enough time to brace herself for the impact and remained tense as Malcolm relentlessly dragged her down the hallway, slamming her body back and forth as he walked.

Finally, Malcolm spun around once more and flung Georgia's body through a door, breaking it off its hinges and sending her falling into the station's small server room. No bigger than a closet, the room's walls were lined with towers of computers acting as the controls for the radio's broadcasting network. The dark room was illuminated by a series of colorful lights flashing from the system, and Georgia peered up from the darkness to see Malcolm's big figure leering through the doorway. The light from the hall shined bright behind him, but the random green and red flashes from inside the server room lit up his menacing face like a horror movie.

While looking up at the man who desperately wanted to hurt her, Georgia assumed she would be afraid. After all, her life was in danger of ending at any moment. Fear would be the natural reaction. But surprisingly, she wasn't. There was an eerie calm that came over her, along with a strange feeling of remorse. Because although she had no other choice in the matter, Georgia knew she was going to kill her friend. She'd never killed anyone before, and under normal circumstances, no person would ever assume someone of her size could beat an individual as big as Malcolm in a physical confrontation. But Georgia took pride from proving people wrong. She'd been doing it her whole life. And regardless of how fucked up this situation might've been, somehow, someway, she was still going to win.

One more time she sprung to her feet, triggering Malcolm to charge at her full speed. She planted her feet, hoping to stop him head on. But Malcolm's brute force plowed straight through her, grabbing her by the shoulders and slamming her against the tower at the back wall of the room.

Georgia's head snapped back, hitting the hard case of the server. Disoriented from the blow, she dropped her arms, letting her guard down for Malcolm to sink his teeth into her neck. A sharp pain radiated out from the wound, bringing Georgia back from her daze. She then let out a tormented scream of agony as she pounded her fists into her attacker's back. But it was no use. Malcolm dug his jaw deeper and deeper into her neck, refusing to let go.

Finally finding a rage of her own, Georgia grabbed onto the sides of Malcolm's head while pulling herself away from him. The hold he had onto her neck was too tight, but Georgia dug down deep for the strength to break free from his grasp, ripping and tearing her own flesh still clutched between his teeth. With blood seeping out onto her shoulder, Georgia's skin stretched to its limits until it finally broke under the stress, releasing her from his mouth.

In a moment of freedom, Georgia quickly turned around and grabbed onto the tower behind her. She began rocking the thick metal frame back and forth in an attempt to tip it over, but Malcolm resumed his assault by wrapping his arms around her body and biting down on her neck once more. Again, blood oozed out from Malcolm's lips, but Georgia was now numb to the pain and ignored it while resuming to uproot the heavy tower.

With Malcolm's strong arms squeezing from behind, Georgia lifted both legs and started pressing them against the tower. It continued to rock back and forth, swaying a little further with every kick. Georgia ground her teeth, still blocking out the pain from her neck until she finally pushed off as hard as she could, sending her and Malcolm falling backwards to the server room floor.

The force of hitting the hard tile stunned Malcolm for a moment, releasing his hold from Georgia's neck. While the fall took its toll on her as well, Malcolm's body cushioned her from the worst of the blow. She managed to stay aware enough to notice the tower in front of them finally teetering to its edge. The lumbering stack of metal slowly leaned further and further until it eventually tipped over, beginning its descent towards the floor.

With the tower quickly dropping towards her, Georgia rolled off of Malcolm just in time to narrowly miss being crushed under it. She didn't see the tower land but assumed from the loud crunch of bone and flesh that it fell right on top of her attacker, killing him instantly.

For the moment, Georgia felt content to lay still with her face buried into the ground. The lack of movement next to her meant that for the time being she could relax, not that she had the strength to move anyway.

Without ever lifting her head, Georgia used whatever energy she had left to say a small goodbye to the friend laying dead underneath the server next to her. And then she let out an exhausted sigh, closing her eyes and fading asleep on the cold floor of the room.

11

The Telluride Regional Airport was famous for a lot of reasons. One being that it was the highest commercial airport in the country. At over nine thousand feet above sea level, inexperienced pilots often dreaded navigating the mountainous terrain in the surrounding area. To make matters worse, beyond the airport's single runway waited a thousand foot drop straight down off a cliff. So when taking off, pilots had only one of two options: fly or plummet to their deaths.

For these reasons, many of the flying conditions for TEX were limited. The weather had to be pristine and the plane had to have a full tank of gas when taking off to fight against the altitude. As a forty-year veteran of the skies, Captain Eric Hitchens knew these restrictions all too well. But still simply yes'd his boss to death rather than trying to argue with him over the phone.

So for the past hour the captain sat looking out the window and waiting. The falling snow had piled up to several feet all around the airport's small terminal building, which only consisted of a single check-in counter and a one-man security detail. Several small planes peacefully sat just outside the building off to the side of the runway, many of them already buried under the snow.

Minus a few stranded travelers and pilots chatting behind him, Captain Hitchens enjoyed the peaceful whistling of the wind outside. It was a sound he usually only heard alongside a loud jet engine. He would like to have shared the moment with his co-pilot Janet Thorn, but she opted to wait out the storm being social with the others.

Although her senior by several decades, Eric actually enjoyed Ms. Thorn's company. As a professional pilot, he missed a great deal of his own daughter's childhood. He was constantly in the sky working and even now still rarely found time to visit his grandchildren. But Eric also felt he was making up for his shortfalls as a father by being something of a mentor to Janet. Piloting came natural to her, but she was still learning the delicate nuances of privatized aviation. And Captain Hitchens took pride in showing her the ropes.

Just as his reminiscing began, Eric's nostalgic memories were interrupted by the faint grumble of a diesel engine out in the storm. He slowly stood from his seat and moved closer to the window. The only road that led to the terminal winded down and around the entire airport, disappearing from view underneath the mountain it rested on. The area was technically outside the town limits and primarily filled with dirt roads. But upon its opening, the first thing the airport did was pave a main route from the terminal straight into Telluride seven miles away. However, that was all meaningless now with several feet of snow built up on top of the road.

Unless of course, you had your own personal industrial sized snowplow to bring you wherever you wanted. And that's exactly the noise Eric was hearing. It continued to grow louder until the bright yellow machine eventually peered over the ridge and into view. At fifteen feet high, the overbearing machine looked like it belonged on a construction site rather than the road. It did, however, look more at home when it revealed the Town of Telluride seal on the side of its body as it parked.

There was little doubt in Eric's mind that his boss was inside the vehicle, but he couldn't imagine how he wrangled a town-owned snowplow to act as his own personal chauffeur.

That was until Scott Brooks jumped out of the passenger seat, throwing a wad of money back into the cab. Without a band holding them together, the green bills scattered every which way in the air. And Brooks reached back inside, carefully pulling someone out with him.

Captain Hitchens couldn't tell who Mr. Brooks had under his arm as he hurried them both inside through the snow. The mystery guest had his head down and shuffled his feet as though he was struggling to walk. The man was hunched over, forcing Scott to help carry him to the terminal. And it was only when they got close enough for the captain to see the man's large physical size that he realized it was Charlie Young, his boss' driver and bodyguard.

Eric opened the door just in time for the two men to pile inside and flop down on the couch the captain had been sitting on. Despite two new arrivals, the commotion at the back of the building never missed a beat, but Captain Hitchens was almost disturbed by Charlie's appearance.

Beads of sweat completely drenched his face and he looked exhausted from an incredible amount of pain. He relaxed his body and sunk into the couch, completely drained from ill fatigue. Mr. Brooks then did the same, but he was probably just tired from having dragged the large man through several feet of snow.

The sound of the snowplow shifting into gear rung out before the machine backed down the mountain. But Captain Hitchens ignored it as he carefully surveyed the two men before him, both of whom appeared as if they had just escaped a warzone. "Are you all right?"

Mr. Brooks answered the pilot in between his heavy breaths. "Does it look like we're fucking all right?"

After years of working for him, Eric still felt uncomfortable by his boss' attitude but hid it well behind a face of concern. "What happened?"

Scott sat up in his seat and leaned forward, staring at Eric with a look of frustrated disbelief. "You don't know what's going on out there? I thought you heard me on the radio?"

"No. We don't have one in the building."

Brooks jumped off the couch, throwing his hands in the air and stomping around the room in a frenzy. "Holy shit blizzard! It's like a wintery Vietnam down there. White Charlies jumping out of snow banks and everything."

The group in the back of the terminal stopped their conversation, all turning one by one to face the strange, loud man. Only one of them, a young female pilot with short black hair, recognized him. She let out a sigh before leaving the group to join her boss on the other side of the building.

Her movement grabbed Scott's attention, and he turned to see the young woman approaching him. "Good. The female you is ready. Now let's go. Cause' we gotta get the fuck outta here."

Janet answered her boss just as she reached the couch. "We can't leave."

"What're you talking about?"

Ms. Thorn opened her mouth to speak, but Eric quickly cut in to divert their boss' frustration onto him. "That's what I wanted to tell you. We can't take off in this storm?"

"You're shitting me, right? We've left in blizzards before."

The captain shook his head in response. "Not from this airport."

Once again resuming his eccentric tantrum, Brooks threw his arms around and pointed out the window towards the runway covered in snow. "Bullshit. I own the fucking plane. If I want it to fly it better goddamn fly. So grab your wings and let's go!"

As a typical bully, Scott Brooks stomped passed his pilot and over to the runway door. But this was one time Captain Hitchens wouldn't give in to his cocky boss' demands. He stood his ground and shouted out to Mr. Brooks, who was already on the other side of the building. "We'll crash."

Scott stopped in his tracks and remained still for a moment before slowly turning around. He then silently stared back at the captain while everyone in the room curiously kept their eyes on him. Even Charlie Young, still weak and covered in sweat, had sat up and peeked over the back of the couch, eagerly awaiting his response.

But when the egotist failed to speak, Captain Hitchens continued on. "Not maybe. Not possibly. Not even most likely. If we try to take off from this airport in this storm: We. Will. Crash. Guaranteed. It's as simple as that."

The eyes in the room shifted back to Scott, waiting for him to blow up in a tantrum of rage. But after a few moments of silence, the renowned hothead simply took a deep breath and calmly said his response. "Well... fuck."

***

In a million years, Marshal Travis Walker never thought he'd be in a situation like this. Standing in the middle of a snow covered Telluride street, the marshal carefully aimed his service pistol at the voracious mob that continued to press deeper into town. He fired sparingly, making sure each shot hit its mark. It wasn't that ammunition was limited. In a Western mountain town like Telluride it wouldn't be hard to find more guns and ammo than there were people to use them. But reloading took time. A scarce commodity when a horde of crazed skiers was charging straight at you.

Most of the possessed attackers were resort guests coming from the direction of the mountain. Strangers Travis had no connection to. The majority of the residents that were causing trouble got locked up early on during the crime wave. But every once in a while the familiar face of a local stood out amidst the current firefight. When it did, pulling the trigger pained the marshal straight to his core. Of course, he didn't want to kill anybody. But the time for soft approaches to the violence was gone.

For hours, he watched the situation in town deteriorate to the point of chaos. When the nine-one-one calls first started rolling in, many simply attributed the spike in crime to the storm. But when his men and resources were rapidly being overwhelmed, Travis had to admit the craziness was caused by something else entirely.

He didn't know what plague of insanity had swept across the town to create such horrors, but it was a mess of mass hysteria unlike anything he'd ever seen. He tried reasoning with them. He tried arresting them. He even tried what little riot control equipment he had at his disposal. But nothing worked. They never stopped. Never rested. And it quickly became apparent that the violence wouldn't end until everyone was dead.

The only saving grace to Marshal Walker's decision was that he wasn't alone. Standing alongside him was a small battalion of men and women he currently commanded in what had basically become a warzone. A strange mixture of police and locals, each one held a firearm with reluctant conviction at the crazed crowd barreling towards them.

Like the marshal, not one of them wanted to be there, aiming weapons at their fellow Man. But also like the marshal, they had come to the same unfortunate conclusion that taking up arms was their only option. This wasn't about keeping the peace anymore. They were fighting for survival.

With the visibility from the storm continuing to deteriorate, their eyes could only see so far through the street before it vanished within a falling blanket of white snowflakes. They kept their eyes peered into the storm and waited for their attackers to suddenly burst into view from what seemed like nothingness. Only a few of their foes were in sight at a time, but the stream of crazed aggressors was endless, charging at them without fear or remorse. One after another, the gunmen fired at the immediate threats, always knowing that behind those charging at them was a whole crowd waiting for their turn.

The marshal continued to shoot, carefully putting down the savage fiends close enough that he could see the red strain in their eyes. He was locked into a steady rhythm. Aim. Fire. Breathe. Aim. Fire. Breathe.

Until he pulled the trigger back only to hear the click of an empty chamber.

For an instant, the marshal was disappointed in himself for not keeping track of the bullets in his clip. Then realized this was the first real situation of combat he'd ever seen and was just glad he wasn't throwing up in front of the stone cold locals who'd been firing alongside him without ever batting an eye.

Travis reached for a spare clip, but his sudden lapse in battle discipline grew, causing him to look around at his surroundings in a surreal state of awe. Besides the blizzard that had somehow transformed the area into an Arctic outpost, the entire scene held an eerie resemblance to a shootout of the old Wild West. With Telluride's stylized 1800's architecture looming on both sides, the neighborhood already embodied the feel of cowboy lawlessness.

But it seemed as if the marshal was the only one transfixed by the outlaw-like scenery. In a standoff against an incredibly driven enemy, the other brave shooters stood their ground firm in the middle of the street, while others took cover behind cars buried under mountains of powder. The plows had long abandoned their duties, leaving the roads and bodies scattered throughout to be overrun by falling snow. With the exception of the sporadic trails of bright, crimson blood sprayed randomly across the street, Travis felt trapped in a deep sea of white.

And just as he could feel the overwhelming crush of panic start to settle into his chest, the marshal remembered the endless wave of psychotic tourists charging at him and snapped back to reality.

But as Travis lifted his pistol to aim, he saw a lot more of his enemy than he had only moments earlier. He immediately started firing but found that the time he waited in between shots was becoming less and less to the point where he was forced to pull the trigger as fast as he could. The fearless mob steadily increased their numbers, pushing closer and closer to their targets as evident by the trail of bodies marking their forward advance.

After a quick glance to his left and right, Travis could sense his fellow gunmen growing frustrated by the never-ending onslaught. They were stuck in a losing pace, and it was only a matter of time before their line was completely overrun.

As if his short moment of distress never happened, Marshal Walker assumed his role as leader and barked out orders over the storm's roaring wind. "There's too many! Fall back!"

Keeping their weapons aimed at the horde ahead, every shooter started backing away. Those few in the street moved in a straight line while the rest emerged from their cover to join them. Together in a tight-knit unit, the men and women moved back into an intersection towards the center of town, continuing to fire as the frenzied pack pressed on. The group was strong and cohesive, locked into a steady retreat while defending the threat ahead of them.

But their stoic concentration was shattered when a scream rang out from within their ranks. Travis, along with the others, turned to face the noise and found one of their own on the ground with a crazed old woman digging her nails into his face. The gruesome scene caught the makeshift militia by surprise, causing them all to stop in shock.

Their firm line in the intersection dissolved, and Travis couldn't tell where the loud shot came from that blasted the old woman's face into a hundred pieces. He looked up and realized the old woman had come from behind them, a local they missed during their roundup. The marshal opened his mouth to regroup his troops, but by then it was too late.

Distracted by the attack from behind, the stampede from the front overwhelmed the group, jumping on and tackling the unsuspecting men and women to the ground. Most of the gunmen still on their feet scattered throughout the intersection, screaming and shouting for help as they disappeared into the storm. Only a few remaining soldiers, the marshal included, stood their ground, randomly firing as the barrage of fiends continued from every direction. Spinning in circles alongside the other disoriented fighters, Travis frantically aimed his gun with both hands, instinctively pulling the trigger at almost anything that moved.

With every loud bang, another would-be attacker dropped into the bed of snow covering their feet. But Travis knew it was only a matter of seconds before he ran out of bullets again, and this time he wouldn't have the chance to reload.

He continued to wave his gun back and forth when a loud roar of a truck struck through the cold air like thunder. Breaking from the mob around them, Travis's eyes did a quick scan of the area and found nothing but snow down the unplowed street. The grumble of a large engine continued to grow louder until the others broke from firing to curiously look around as well. However, none of their attackers balked at the noise and continued their forward charge like nothing had changed. And if they didn't stop, neither could Travis.

He lifted his gun to fire when a searing bright high beam pierced the thick veil of snowfall, shining light on the warzone like an angel from above. Only this savior came from Travis's side, and revealed itself to be a large diesel pickup as it broke through the wall of snow.

Upon entering the intersection, the truck slammed on its brakes, sliding and skidding across the snow covered streets like a missile. Sensing the large metal object barreling towards them, Travis and his local warriors broke free from their combat long enough to dive out of the way just as the truck reached the battlefield, running over and sending a few of their crazed assailants flying through the air. As soon as the truck nailed its targets the vehicle came to a stop, almost as if it were aimed to precision. And not a second later, Nellie Sheridan emerged from the driver's seat followed by her husband, Bill.

The old couple came ready and equipped, each holding a shotgun in hand and a rifle wrapped around their backs. Travis was shocked at how the senior citizens entered the battlefield. But besides the two large weapons easily noticeable on each of their persons, the marshal also happened to spot several smaller handguns secured in a series of holsters outfitting their thick winter clothing.

Without a welcome or introduction, Nellie and Bill aimed and fired at the mob, which had already run either around or over their parked pickup truck. And as the fighting commenced, Travis and his crew jumped back into the fray, shooting alongside the elderly couple.

Together, they all continued their organized retreat through the town, carefully backpedaling while keeping the enemy advance at bay. A few shots later and Travis's pistol clip emptied as he predicted, only now the much-needed cavalry gave him time to reload. But while looking up through the riot before him, Travis knew they couldn't keep up their current pace of attack.

He turned to Nellie and screamed over the wind and constant gunfire. "There's too many!"

Travis could see Nellie think for a moment and then she spoke, fitting words in between rounds of fire. "Where…can we…hold up?"

Without a second thought, only one place popped into the marshal's mind. "The Town Hall. Let's go!"

He didn't know if Mrs. Sheridan agreed with the choice but there wasn't time for debate. Marshal Walker turned and started running down the street towards the large brick building at the edge of town. He never looked back but could hear the repeated thud of footsteps pounding in the snow directly behind him. Travis hoped and prayed that it wasn't someone about to pounce onto his back but knew he would find out soon enough once he reached the heavy front door of the town's government office.

After scaling the short, slippery steps, Travis pulled back on the door's handle and was immediately swamped from behind by his fellow gunmen. He held the door open while the small group poured inside. As they did, Travis gave a quick look back and saw the ferocious mob had reached the bottom of the steps. Without delay, he spun around the door, quickly slamming it shut and flipping the lock down all in one motion.

12

Chris immediately found that the trees offered a considerable amount of shelter from the storm. The area wasn't technically out of bounds for guests, but the woods were too dense to act as a normal run. It was mainly skied by experts, locals mostly, who used it as a shortcut to get to the other face of the mountain. And now Chris reaped the benefit of the close quarters by not being harassed by a perpetual hive of snow.

Unfortunately, that blessing also made his ride all the more dangerous. Moving at speeds faster than he actually felt comfortable, Chris weaved in and out of the thick tree trunks, repeatedly ducking under a never-ending line of branches and leaves. Twigs and pinecones, as well as other debris from the foliage, littered the ground making the ride that much bumpier.

The snow in this area was packed and hard from days of sitting still under the mountain's freezing temperatures. But that didn't stop Chris from seamlessly speeding through the wooded obstacle course, guiding his large skis around the trees and rocks with uncanny precision. He didn't know if any of his barbaric pursuers happened to be chasing him, but he damn sure wasn't giving them the chance to catch up.

Ironically enough, Ryan had felt the change of scenery as a step toward safety and loosened his grip around Chris's neck. The patroller was a little shocked to glance back and see Ryan's eyes open, perfectly aware of the harrowing terrain passing them by. Responding to the boy's demeanor, Chris opted to slow his pace and began carefully navigating the trees with a bit more caution.

When it finally became apparent that nothing was following them, Chris stopped and leaned forward onto a tree to catch his breath. Thoughts of Sarah's dying face tried to creep their way into his mind, but he fought them off, choosing to focus on the rattled nerves still surging through his body.

Uneasiness forced Chris to look back through the forest just to be certain. Only a few flurries made their way down passed the canopy of trees, and without the heavy snowfall clouding the air, Chris could see all the way back through the path he had taken to the open run still being attacked by the storm. It only took a moment for Chris's breathing to relax, but he remained still, waiting for his mind to catch up.

While they rested, Ryan's comfort zone expanded and lifted his head from Chris's back to look around at their surroundings. "Where are we going?"

"We need to get down somehow. Mountain Village is closer than town, and these trees open up to a glade near Chair six that will take us there."

Chris's head turned back around to scope out his route when he heard a strange noise up against his ear. It took a moment for him to figure out the sound was actually Ryan's teeth clattering together. Chris didn't know if the boy was cold or scared, but either way, he admitted to himself that he needed to show the boy a little more compassion.

Chris grabbed the baggy arm of the boy's jacket and swung him around, placing him down between two trees uphill from where he was standing. "How you doin', Ryan? You OK?"

Since leaving Joseph's, this was the first time they stopped to think, giving the boy's fears a chance to catch up with him. And despite all his bravery, Ryan's eyes started to fill with tears. Chris could see him trying to hold them back, but it was only a matter of time before the young child gave in to his sadness.

Chris reactively felt himself growing frustrated by his new role as babysitter. Besides the blizzard and mountain-wide epidemic, he was currently cut off from any kind of communication. The resort was in the middle of a crisis, and trying to wipe away some kid's tears was the last thing on his mind.

But then, after working through the rising fury in his heart, Chris found the true source of his anger and confronted it by repeating the truth: Sarah was gone and she wasn't coming back. It wasn't this boy's fault. In fact, saving him was Sarah's dying wish. And as a patroller, that was a job he felt more than capable of accomplishing.

Chris examined the boy, whose neck seemed to be retreating inside the oversized jacket, and spoke with a ski patroller's tone of concern. "Are you cold?"

"My fingers...a little."

Ryan lifted his arms and poking out through the large jacket's sleeves were the tips of his tiny, bare fingers, shivering and red. Now with a patient in front of him, Chris's mind snapped into gear as he pulled the long sleeves over the boy's hand and began gently blowing into them.

He then rolled the sleeve up and held Ryan's hands into his chest, shielding them from the cold. "Look. I know you're probably scared. To be honest, so am I. But I'm going to get you home. I promise."

Ryan took a deep breath, absorbing his protector's words for a moment before speaking. "What's going on? Why did everyone go crazy?"

"I don't know. And I'm sorry you had to see all that stuff. But we can't think about it now. Just gotta keep moving."

Chris then moved his hands over to Ryan's shoulders and held the boy tight while staring deeply into his eyes. "I need you to be strong and watch my back. Like a partner. Think you can do that?"

Ryan swallowed deeply while lifting his chin stern and proud. He then gave a firm nod and smiled. "You can count on me."

Chris smiled in return and bent his shoulder down to Ryan's level. "Jump on."

Ryan got himself resituated onto Chris's back, and the two continued on through the densely packed trees.

Their pace had slowed considerably since they first entered the woods. Enough so that Chris technically wasn't even skiing anymore. He simply pushed off as he swung his body around from tree to tree, periodically forcing himself to almost step through the frozen snow because he lacked the momentum.

It didn't take long before the forest opened up slightly into a peacefully serene ski run amidst the trees. The wooded area still had plenty of pines scattered throughout, but the space was more expansive than the closely packed route they just emerged from.

A trickle of snowfall made its way down through the tree canopy and sprinkled enough to create a fresh foot of snow down on the slope. It was more than where they were but still considerably less than the blizzard raging in the open air. The trail was obviously a designated run listed on the map which Chris had long since memorized, and he sought it out as the perfect pipeline to bring them down the mountain shielded from both the storm and any unwelcome stragglers.

Before dropping down into the run, Chris gave a gleeful smile at the fresh untouched snow before him. He then took a deep breath and gave Ryan a slight nod as he bent his knees preparing to embark. With the grace of an Olympian, Chris pushed off and soared straight, building up a healthy speed right out of the gate.

Moving at a brisk yet steady pace, Chris weaved carelessly through the spread out trees. The skiable landscape was far smoother on his legs than the rough rocks and untreated terrain from before. After the first couple turns, Chris actually found himself enjoying the ride down. The hidden run naturally acted as an isolated safe haven from the blizzard, and the snowfall that did make it through covered the ground in several inches of powder, allowing Chris to glide down the hill as if it were a cloud. For a moment, the patroller seemed lost in his own world, transported away from the nightmare of the past hour to a simpler time skiing as a kid on the small mountains of the Catskills back East.

He was so enthralled into the ride that he barely noticed the slim figure staggering out from the woods below them on the opposite side of the run. Reacting purely on instinct, Chris skidded to an immediate halt and just stared the person down. Ryan's head popped up from the sudden stop and looked in the same direction. The boy then let out an audible gasp right into Chris's ear.

He didn't quite share the boy's fear but was admittedly wary about seeing another human being. Whoever it was looked to be frantically scampering as fast as they could, tripping and clawing their way forward in the process. Chris couldn't tell from a distance if the person was deranged or just panicked. And after narrowly escaping a murderous mob, he wasn't taking any chances.

He bent down, lowering Ryan off of his shoulders and plopping him into the snow. "Wait here."

Without protest, the boy sat up from his seat in the snow and watched as his protector slowly skied over to the figure. As he drew closer, the mystery person came into focus as a young teenage girl fleeing for her life. From the look of panic screaming across her face, Chris could tell she wasn't so much running towards him as she was running, or more precisely, limping away. The girl fled in such distress that it was hard to notice, but Chris's medical eye caught onto an injured leg that kept her from continuously running on her feet.

Still uneasy about the previous attack, the patroller continued to approach the scene with caution. Upon finally reaching what he considered a safe distance to evaluate the situation, Chris came to a stop and called out to the girl. "Hello. Are you OK?"

Her response came with a strain in her voice that developed after a bout of heavy crying. "Help…please!"

Hearing words further relaxed Chris towards her innocence. Of the many psychotic ravagers he encountered, none of them had spoken. It was a good sign that he had actually found another survivor who could use his help.

But no sooner after realizing that, Chris spotted what she was actually running from. Up into the woods behind her emerged a man running towards the girl at a dead sprint. Chris saw the man flailing his arms and grasping ferociously in front of him, recognizing it as the same form as that of the crazed tormentors that chased him from Joseph's.

Chris's eyes immediately shot open, and his muscles kicked into gear, hopping from his position straight into a downhill dash.

Seeing the patroller in his red jacket coming towards her, the girl's face lit up with a joy of salvation. But as Chris approached, bent over, and picked up speed, he showed no signs of slowing down. In fact, he wasn't even looking in her direction. His attention was focused towards her attacker, who had continued his sprint through the trees and was a step away from diving head first for his prey.

Hoping for a miracle, the girl made a weak attempt to reach out for her rescuer. But her arm fell short of grabbing onto Chris's jacket as he passed her by.

Instead, his collision course with her pursuer ended with a bang as he lowered his shoulder and crashed straight into the man's chest. Chris's momentum sent the couple flying back, tumbling through the snow head over heels down the mountain. Entwined as one with his foe, Chris's awkward contact with the ground caused his ski bindings to release, sending his two skis soaring in opposite directions. The pair of twisted adversaries bounced once through the lush powder covering the ground before flipping over again and making hard contact with one of the run's many trees.

The couple broke apart and landed separately, but only one of them showed signs of trauma from the incident. Chris let out a scream and sporadic grunts of pain while his counterpart only responded to the crash by slowly staggering to his feet.

Chris looked back up the mountain to see the speechless girl watching on, her jaw dropped open in a state of shock. Further up, Chris also saw Ryan sliding down the slope on his backside, carefully using his ski boots to control his speed.

With a renewed sense of courage, the boy fearlessly continued his descent, passing by the unsuspecting girl with a wave. "Hi there."

He continued on ahead of her and approached the scene without slowing down.

Chris, still struggling with the pain, reached his arm out towards the boy, signaling him to keep back. "Ryan, no! Stay up there!"

Ryan spread his legs, dug his boots into the ground and pointed behind Chris. "Don't look at me! Watch him!"

Confused, the patroller looked backwards to see the man back on his feet and lunging down at him. With a snarl of a look burned into his face, the man grabbed Chris by the coat and lifted him up off the ground with ease. Then, as if he was playing with a ragdoll, the raged man twisted his body around and slammed Chris's back into the tree they previously hit.

Chris, once again, roared in pain but regained his senses enough to shoot his hands out and stop the crazed man from digging his gnashing teeth into his face. The man fought back, and Chris could feel the strength in his own arms slowly giving out. He couldn't hold his attacker back forever.

In a last ditch effort, Chris lifted his legs up and kicked them out, breaking the man's hold from his jacket. The stranger quickly recovered though and lunged again, only this time, Chris was ready enough to duck and scramble through the deep, powdery snow away from him. But the attacker was relentless, his face sneering back at Chris with a visage of pure hatred. The man lunged again. And again. Each time Chris frantically dodging away, coming within inches of falling back into the man's grasp.

Chris could feel fatigue catching up with him. The cold air burned his lungs, and his muscles screamed out to rest. He fought the urge to give in when he heard his name called out from above. It was Ryan. He had, once again, made his way down the mountain and, this time, held Chris's bright orange ski in his hands.

Without another word between them, Ryan tossed Chris the weapon, who instantly turned around and met the ferocious man's next lunge with a hard ski to the abdomen. He stumbled back, creating enough space between the two of them for Chris to wind the ski up and hit his attacker square in the temple. The man rocked to the side, dazed but not down. Chris quickly wound up and struck again to the other side. The man staggered back once more and, this time, dropped into the snow.

Without any other thought coursing through his mind, Chris lifted the ski over his head and smacked it down hard upon his enemy. He then lifted it up and brought it down again and again, repeatedly whacking the flat fiberglass of the ski across the man's body. Each time he felt his muscles burn uncontrollably, but he ignored it and fought through the pain until he finally lifted the ski above his head and drove it downward, spiking the curved tip through the man's body like a spear.

Blood oozed out from within the man's ski coat, and, for a moment, Chris left his hands on the unlikely weapon while catching his breath. His mind raced with strange thoughts of guilt and remorse. After the girl in Joseph's, this was now the second human being he had killed with his own hands. Hands he had dedicated to helping people and saving lives. But his life was in danger. What else could he have done? The man was going to kill that girl...the girl!

Chris's body spun around, and he quickly climbed up the run on his hands and knees. His attention was focused on the girl, who still sat speechless, but he placed a brief hand of gratitude on Ryan's shoulder as he passed him by. "Thanks for the assist."

Chris caught a brief glimpse of Ryan's smile as the boy turned his body and followed him uphill. Together they reached the traumatized girl, who in a trance stared past them at the lifeless body down by the tree. Chris removed his gloves and slowly brought his bare yet comforting hands to the girl's face. "Hey. Look at me."

Her eyes moved over and met with her rescuer's, but she still retained the same blank expression as he questioned her. "I'm Chris. Can you tell me your name?"

She barely spread apart her trembling lips to speak. "St… Stephanie."

Chris nodded his head and formed a smile of his own. "Good. What happened? How did you get here?"

"My brother…he went crazy on the chairlift. I had to jump and then it just…it fell over. The whole thing fell over."

"You jumped off the chair?"

The girl gave a slow and steady nod as a response. It was then that Chris remembered the call from dispatch. Chair six went down, and the mention of her brother had confirmed Chris's fears. Whatever happened at Joseph's wasn't an isolated incident. These wild, ravenous things were everywhere. It was a miracle the girl was still alive.

Remembering her injury, Chris shifted his attention down to her leg, carefully examining it through her snow pants. As he did, Ryan waved, staring at the girl with a shy smile. "Hi. I'm Ryan."

Her blank stare moved over to him with the same emotionless expression, but that didn't deter the boy from continuing his gleeful smirk.

A moment later, Chris looked back, ending the awkward greeting. "It's just a contusion. You're lucky it's snowing as hard as it is. Must have broken your fall."

The girl swallowed at the news, and her eyes, once again, shifted past the patroller to look downhill. Chris noticed her gaze wasn't focused on him and followed it down to see the corpse with the impaled ski still sticking out from its chest. "You know him?"

He looked back at the girl, who didn't falter or break her concentrated stare. Her eyes remained locked forward on the dead body for several silent moments before her trembling lips opened again and muttered just under her breath. "He…he's my dad."

Chris's heart immediately sank into his chest. Now he was just as speechless as the girl, unable to give her any words of comfort or condolence. But what was he supposed to do? The man was going to kill her. That much was certain. But does that make the pain he caused any more bearable?

Ryan's cheery smile had suddenly vanished from his face, opting to lower his eyes shamefully rather than make eye contact with the shell-shocked girl. Chris continued to look at her blank expression but didn't say a thing. There was nothing to say. He just sat silently looking at her, waiting for a response.

Her eyes remained staring at the body when Chris could see them slowly start to quiver. Little by little, small flutters in her eyelids gave birth to tears until the girl's face gave way to an avalanche of sadness. The emotional grief rocked her body and she fell forward into the patroller's arms. He instinctively opened them to catch the weeping girl but didn't have any clue as to what he should do next. How does one console the daughter of the man you just murdered? You don't. Regardless of the situation, there were no words worth mentioning. So he simply wrapped his arms around her and let the girl cry into his shoulder as the flurries from the blizzard raging outside the forest continued to slowly find their way down on top of them.

PART II
WHITEOUT

13

Like any ski resort, Telluride considers winter its busiest season. But it's during the spring and summer months when the mountain reveals itself as the beautiful paradise it is.

The snow slowly melts and enters into a series of continuous streams that cut through trees reborn under spring sunshine. Crystal clear water trickles its way down the mountainside, glistening over giant rocks, tiny pebbles and gravel trails in its path. The flowing rivers and whistling wind merge together to form a soothing backdrop for the rhythmic music of the region's chirping birds.

For several months out of the year, a zoo of wildlife claims the mountain's snowless trails as their own. Deer, beavers, coyotes and bears endlessly roam the pastures of Telluride's rolling hills. Fearless and enduring eagles of American legend soar gracefully overtop wandering hikers and tourists. Warmed by a burning sun, the thin summer air fills those who breathe it in with a crisp rush of pure vitality.

Bright flowers unlike any on Earth bloom and flourish, covering the mountain's steep stretches of land with life and color. Lush meadows of green fill the canyon's entrance and greet the valley's visitors with tall grass swaying to the breeze. A large sun, strong and proud, reigns overhead amidst an eternal sheet of cloudless blue sky. And from the top of the mountain, one could see the Rockies's tall, roaring peaks vanish into the horizon from every direction.

Although not as busy, Telluride still sees visitors during this majestic unthawing. It's impossible to keep such unrefined beauty a secret. Perfect for a postcard, the quaint, old mining town represents the epitome of nostalgic relaxation. A glorious utopia of wilderness and nature.

But this so-called "offseason" produces a different aura in the atmosphere than the frigid cold of the ski months. A warmth that resonates not just from the summer air but from being engulfed by the raw magnificence of such an alluring valley. It's lively. Jubilant. And above all, free from the peace of death that follows in winter's wake.

***

Georgia woke to a strong taste of bitter building against her lips. Next she felt a hard, cold surface pressing against her face. The young DJ wondered why her head wasn't snuggled comfortably in between her pillows. And then, when she finally opened her eyes, Georgia saw that

Malcolm's body, crushed beneath the heavy frame of the computer server, started to ooze a pool of blood, which had made its way into her mouth.

She quickly pressed off the tile floor, repeatedly spitting a mixture of blood and saliva off her tongue. After a few quick, nervous breaths of panic, the terrified girl slowed her breathing and calmed her nerves. The immediate danger that forced her into this situation had receded, and she was finally safe. At least for the moment.

With that realization, she summed up the courage to slowly look over to Malcolm's lifeless body. Or at least what was left of it. Over the pool of blood that had settled into the floor was a hand that looked strangely propped up at an awkward angle. Following the hand's arm back to its body, Georgia could barely see the shoulder it was connected to. Whatever remained of Malcolm's torso and head (if they were even intact) was hidden beneath the massive steel frame of the computer server.

The frightened girl let out a sorrowful gasp at the grizzly sight, but she couldn't put a finger on the exact emotion it came from. Was it that her friend was dead? The gruesome nature of his death? Or the fact that she was the one who caused it?

Whatever the reason, it didn't matter now. The immediate threat was gone, but as the unofficial reporter of the epidemic, Georgia knew all too well what was waiting for her outside the station's walls. She had no idea how long she was passed out for or if the storm outside had finally let up. Regardless of the answer, the first thing she needed to do was get up and out of the server room.

With the dull, metallic taste of blood still lingering in her mouth, Georgia cautiously stood to her feet. Achy muscles and other physical reminders of the fight lingered across her body, and a dizzy head forced her arms out to keep the battered girl from falling over. Once her balance was stable, Georgia started moving towards the door by taking small steps and cradling her bruised sides. Without ever missing a beat, the punk DJ entered the doorway and kept on going while making a conscious effort not to look back into the room.

She'd been up and down the TORO building a thousand times before, but Georgia never recalled the halls to feel as long and narrow as they did in that moment. Each step shot a small ounce of pain through her body, and it seemed as if the hallway physically grew another foot every time she suffered the ache. Georgia wasn't sure if she was experiencing some type of hallucination. Perhaps it was a side effect of banging her head during the struggle with Malcolm. Or maybe a surge of hopelessness had showered her with dread. Either way, stopping wasn't an option.

Georgia continued to move through the halls, focusing all her strength on every step forward. Simply putting one foot in front of the other became a tiring event and required more energy than she thought possible.

For a good portion of the journey her eyes were closed, relying solely on the closest wall for guidance. While moving on autopilot around corners, Georgia's attention was so spent on staying upright that she couldn't tell how long she'd been walking. Without realizing how close she was to it, the distraught girl physically bumped into the front door of the building but felt nervous about her imminent escape. She had to get out because staying inside the radio station wasn't an option. That much was obvious. But she could only imagine what kind of wintery hell would be waiting for her on the other side.

With her body almost paralyzed in fear, Georgia had to force herself to turn the handle and push it forward. The door was only open a sliver when a strong light pierced through the crack and blinded her in the face. Using her other hand to shield her eyes, Georgia finished opening the door with her shoulder and burst through into the cold mountain air.

She took a step forward out of the one-story brick building and her foot immediately sunk down deep into more than a foot of snow. Georgia released the heavy, metal door and it slammed itself shut, leaving the young girl alone and in awe of the sight around her.

The dark clouds that were gathering overhead when she arrived at work had vanished. The only thing left above her head was a crystal clear plain of blue sky. The sun stood alone, shining bright and strong as if it had been reborn. The tumultuous wind that ruled the air only hours earlier was gone, replaced by a serene and still atmosphere of clean mountain air. But what shocked her the most was the snowy aftermath the blizzard left behind.

From the TORO building's far corner of the valley, Georgia could usually see all of Telluride, but now the only thing visible in every direction was a pristine sheet of white. The onslaught of the storm had completely buried every surface in its path. The entire canyon from the street to the mountainside was covered in snow. Every house, car, and roof. Every tree, sidewalk, and porch. Not an inch was left untouched by the soft glisten of the Rockies's white powder.

It seemed that the storm had left town just as quick as it came in and was replaced by the clearest day Telluride had seen in months. The only thing missing from the scene was any sign of movement. Every way Georgia looked there was not a single person, ravenous or otherwise, in sight. The entire town of Telluride had been transformed into a barren snowfield completely devoid of life.

Where was the infected mob? Where were the police? Where were the survivors? Or more importantly…were there any to begin with?

These were just some of the questions racing through Georgia's mind as she bore witness to the sunny winter wonderland before her. But the most pressing one of all, (and by far the most difficult to answer), was what the hell was she going to do now?

***

An hour had passed since Chris and the two children under his protection emerged from an equipment shack tucked in the middle of the glade. He considered them children in his mind but could already tell the girl would've resented the label. Stephanie represented the stereotypical teenager in today's society that was always so quick to grow up. When in reality she was really just a scared kid who had just lost her whole family in the blink of an eye.

She seemed like a catatonic zombie herself as the three of them carefully slid down through the forest. Without skis or any other way to get down the mountain, they were forced to either walk through whatever flat terrain they could find or slowly slide down on their backs. They had to be careful not to pick up too much speed or step where they weren't supposed to. There were a million ways one mistake could prove fatal. And Chris was concerned enough about running into a pack of crazed, homicidal skiers that it would be a shame meeting their ends at the hands of the mountain itself.

It certainly helped that the storm had ended. Chris was worried they might've been snowed in at the shack for days. But when the wind died and the snowfall stopped, the three of them emerged outside into a sparkling white room. The snowy branches of trees blended together into seamless walls of white while the crisp sky above shined as a bright blue ceiling. It was a majestic and mystifying experience. The kids were certainly amazed by it. But Chris was quick to shake off his wonder knowing full well how dangerous the tranquil scene could be.

Now they were all cautiously making their way down the mountain, being extra sure not to move too fast or disrupt the loose snow accumulated all around them. Chris led the group, mainly keeping the three of them inside the glade. He had a general idea of where they were going, but the blanket of snow draped in every direction made navigating through the woods all the more difficult. For now, just moving down at a slow yet steady pace seemed like the best option.

Besides the ruffling of their baggy winter clothing, the air was quiet. There was no wind or synchronized chirping of birds to fill the silence. But awkward tension between them continually forced young Ryan to do all he could to generate noise by talking. "So, this is the zombie apocalypse, huh? I wonder if it's like this across the country. Or around the world even."

Stephanie had yet to say a single word during their journey, but Chris gave her the opportunity to respond anyway. When she didn't, he chimed in so the boy wouldn't feel neglected. "I don't know."

"You're telling me you're not the least bit curious as to how this happened? Is it an old school 'dead come back to life' kind of thing? Or maybe a military experiment?"

Ryan spoke with a nervous enthusiasm, and Chris did his best to interact with the boy while at the same time trying to discourage his thinking. "Right now all I care about is getting us off this mountain."

But Ryan ignored the ski patroller's disinterest by delving deeper into the topic. "Come on! How can you not think about it? I bet it's a virus, though. In the movies it usually is. Especially since they were running, ya know? Not the slow-walking, living dead kind."

Chris was getting ready to respond when Stephanie suddenly stopped in her tracks and snapped at the boy. "You think this is funny?! Like it's some big joke?!"

Fearfully caught by surprise, Ryan's shoulders backed away from the girl, and Chris quickly took a step in between them. "Whoa. Calm down."

But Stephanie's bottled anger continued to flow out of her. "My family is dead. My whole family! And he's acting as if it's some kind of game."

Stephanie waited for Chris to respond, but he simply stared at her, allowing the girl time to take several deep breaths and calm her frustration.

Once the fuel for her outburst had passed, Chris gave the startled boy behind him a quick glance. "Ryan, go on and scout ahead. Not too far, though. Just give us a minute."

Without saying a word, Ryan simply turned and continued on down through the trees. Chris was half surprised the boy didn't put up a fight to stay and gave him credit for understanding the situation. But Stephanie wasn't so willing to let it go. "You're defending him?"

After waiting for Ryan to disappear out of earshot, Chris turned to the girl and put on his most calming ski patrol voice. "I'm not defending anyone. He's a kid. Just a scared little boy who saw an entire room full of people get slaughtered in front of him. Including my girlfriend. Someone he's known for years."

With the reality of the situation placed in front of her, Stephanie's puffed out chest deflated and she took another deep breath to relax.

Then, after seeing her sigh, Chris continued on. "He's in shock. We all are. And we're all going to deal with it in our own way. You want to get angry? That's fine. But get angry at me. Not him. OK?"

The girl stared back at Chris and refused to nod her head in agreement. She didn't want to concede to him, but the humbled look in her eyes made it obvious to Chris that she got the message.

It was an odd moment for both of them, and Chris didn't know exactly how to respond. He was never the best at cooling emotions. He always deferred that job to Sarah. But here he was: physically watching a teenage girl come to terms with a devastating tragedy right in front of his eyes.

He thought about what to do next but then gave way to a strange instinct inside of him. "Come here."

He held out his arms and Stephanie took a single step forward into them. It was the second time that day he consoled the girl, and it still felt just as awkward. But regardless, he could tell by the tightness in her arms as she pulled herself into his chest that it was the right thing to do.

They remained still for a few seconds before Ryan's voice interrupted their moment. "Ummm...guys?"

Stephanie and Chris then let go of one another and turned to see the boy positioned down a steep drop at the edge of the woods. "I think I found something."

They both slid down to the boy on their backsides before trudging through the snow to look out through the trees. Once they reached Ryan's position, the two of them pushed the snow covered evergreen branches away from their faces and peered out into the open space that was obviously a ski run. The blizzard had covered every inch of the trail with more than a foot of powder, and the entire mountainside was nothing but an immaculate white carpet free from blemishes.

But after silently staring at the scene for a few seconds, Chris noticed something strange. The trail wasn't uniform. Patches of snow rolled up into large scattered hills around the area. The mountain seemed to have jagged sand dunes like welts to its skin.

And then he saw it. Buried amidst the powder was a steel rod poking out through the snow. After the first one was spotted, Chris began noticing more and more. Until he finally realized where he was on the mountain and what should be standing before them: a chairlift.

The realization that dawned on him revealed the entire scene for what it was. The ski trail had hidden a gigantic metal wreckage of gears and cables beneath its snow. Like a relic from some post-apocalyptic nuclear winter, remnants of the chairlift randomly protruded out as artifacts of its glory. What was once a towering hi-speed marvel of engineering had now become nothing more than icy ruins of the past.

Chris started to slowly approach the site, and only after taking the first step forward did the children follow suit. He tried to focus in on the chairlift's remains as a whole, but he then began to notice the most disturbing aspect of all. Poking out through the mountain's cold husk were body parts frozen beneath the snow. Ski boots, helmets and gloves still attached to their owners were scattered across the trail like a minefield. Pain filled faces covered in ice stared up at him, still stuck in an expression calling out for help.

It was an horrific scene to be sure, but Chris was actually surprised that there weren't more bodies in front of him. Were the bulk of the victims simply buried deeper underneath the snow? Or did they rise from their cold graves to run off across the mountainside?

Either answer frightened him, and he could see his two young companions silently coming to the same conclusion. Ryan was physically shaken by the cold graveyard, and Stephanie was understandably speechless. After all, there was a good chance her mother and brother were still under there. Chris half expected the teenager to either frantically run around searching for them or break down into tears. But was surprised when she didn't do either.

Instead, the girl stood stoically strong, staring up at the collapsed chairlift like a warrior after a battlefield. She didn't cry. She didn't scream. She didn't even get angry. She simply took a deep breath, and from the look in her eyes, Chris could tell she had finally accepted that her family was gone.

14

Dr. Anna Morris never dreamed that she would ever have so many patients at once. From her position at the main doors, she looked out over the gymnasium floor, which had been converted into a makeshift medical center. Fold out beds and stretchers were evenly placed in rows up and down the basketball court like a scene from some disaster movie, and there were bodies resting on top of each and every one. As one of the main trauma doctors stationed at the ski resort, Anna had of course practiced and prepared for such an occasion. But she never anticipated anything like this.

When the town's actual medical center started getting overwhelmed it began differing people to the high school, where Anna was in charge of setting up the temporary facility. It quickly filled with people, mostly those who couldn't make it through the blizzard to the medical center on the other side of town. When the storm first began, many of those admitted to the permanent medical center came in with flu-like symptoms. But Anna found it strange that the majority of patients coming to the high school had trauma injuries instead. She heard rumors about crazed attackers and violent mobs but didn't believe them to be true...until the medical center was overrun.

One by one the sick patients over there started to become hostile, attacking everyone and everything in sight. Anna was on the phone with a young female receptionist when it happened, but there was nothing she could do. The scared girl begged and pleaded for help, but her voice was drowned out by screams of agony bellowing from the background. Anna was frozen in place, listening to the call with paralyzing fear. The whole incident only lasted a minute, but to Anna it felt like a lifetime before the phone finally clicked to silence, forever cutting her off from the medical center she worked so hard at for years.

It immediately became clear to the doctor that she was dealing with some kind of illness but had no idea what. No virus or bacteria could spread this fast or cause such mind-numbing violence in its victims. Regardless of the why, the what was obvious. And she needed to act.

Dr. Morris took the few non-trauma patients she had under her care and separated them from the general population. There was no denying what was going on, and so she was relieved when the sick patients agreed to voluntarily move themselves into separate classrooms around the school. The rooms were then locked and checked on regularly by nurses, who still gave the quarantined patients whatever treatment they needed.

Anna had yet to actually see any of her patients turn into maniacal freaks (or anyone for that matter), but she wasn't taking any chances. Based on what happened at the medical center and the few callers she heard on the radio (which coincidentally had also gone silent), Anna prepared for the worst.

Luckily, she didn't have much family in Telluride to worry about or distract her from the crisis at hand. Her kids were all grown up with families of their own across the country. The only other person she truly cared about was her husband Tom, but Anna was wise enough to get him over to the high school when the decision to set up shop there was first made. He was now helping out around the gym as a volunteer, passing out water and snacks to those who needed them.

The high school gym had been turned into a little refugee camp, and Anna was already pushing her small staff of nurses and volunteers to their limits. Supplies were running low, and she didn't know how long they could hold out.

When the blizzard ended she half expected a wave of new patients to storm through the door and was almost glad when they didn't. Either nobody else in town was hurt or they were too terrified to leave their homes. Anna also knew there was a third possibility: that everyone was dead, but at the same time, she refused to believe in such hopelessness.

The Village Manager on the radio said that help was on its way, but who knew how long that would be. The weather broke and so far her makeshift clinic, which was located at the front edge of town, had been free from any attack. But the speed at which this epidemic grew didn't bode well for her future. Unfortunately, quarantine had been her only option. For now, the best thing she could hope for was to toughen it out and assume she would be stuck in this gymnasium for the long haul.

"What are you talking about?"

Anna's runaway thoughts were abruptly interrupted by a fellow doctor's concerned voice as he conversed with a young nurse. They stood several feet over to Anna's side and she opened her ears to listen in to their conversation.

"Some of the patients on the main floor…they're…" The nurse was nervously fiddling her fingers and clenching her teeth as if holding something inside she was reluctant to share. "…they're starting to…well…"

The doctor looked down at the girl with a stern yet compassionate expression. "We don't have time for tiptoeing. Just tell me."

"They're spiking fevers. I think they're getting sick."

Anna immediately felt a lump grow in her throat. She was expecting some of the physical injuries to get worse but not for those patients to fall ill. She thought she acted quickly enough by separating them from the others. She thought she had the situation under control. And maybe she still did. After all, an elevated temperature could just be an infection or any of a million other things. It didn't necessarily mean the outbreak was spreading through her ragtag clinic.

Without waiting to hear the rest of the nurse's report, Dr. Morris stepped forward and entered into the temporary infirmary she'd created. As she walked up and down the aisles of beds, Anna could visibly make out the ones who were starting to feel ill. Severe surges of chills randomly shot up through their bodies, physically shaking the beds off the floor. Beads of sweat formed around their foreheads as they clutched blankets tight to their chests. There were only a handful starting to show symptoms, but Anna didn't have to physically examine them to realize what was happening.

She could deny it all she wanted. That wouldn't make it any less true. She could also try to contain the sickness like she did before, walk every one of them down to their respective classrooms and lock them away like lepers before they got worse. But the doctor wasn't convinced it would help. Slowly but surely, they would all progressively get worse, until one by one her patients would burst into a whirlwind of violent rage.

Anna knew she had to do something, but it was all happening so fast. One after another the weathered doctor was being hit by a series of crises without having a chance to think in between them. Her mind was running on overdrive trying to find a solution. All it could come up with, though, was a sludge of pity and desperation. She had hoped that Telluride's troubles left with the storm which brought them. But as expected, that prayer was slowly being shattered.

∗∗∗

It was absolutely surreal for Peter walking back through Mountain Village. The route was one he'd taken a million times before, but he never experienced it quite like this. The blizzard had drenched every building with a fluffy buildup of powder. It almost seemed as if the whole village was made of snow, a replica of Santa Clause's North Pole workshop.

One key luxury of Mountain Village was its heated sidewalks that quickly melted any snow that fell upon its surface. The clear path made the tranquil atmosphere that much more peaceful and majestic, like that of a fairytale gingerbread house. Tourists and locals alike could hardly resist the romantic urge to stroll about aimlessly. But now there was nothing. No pedestrians walking through the courtyard. No skiers zooming down the mountain. Not even a single member of the frantic mob that wreaked havoc up and down the village square.

Besides a bright blue sky, the only thing Peter could see on the mountain was an ocean of white and the occasional limb that poked out through the snow from a body buried beneath it. It was almost a blissfully serene setting. Except for the reminders of blood and death that laid just underneath the surface.

The heated walkway was a different story. Without any snow to cover them up, the bodies were clearly visible all throughout the village. Some mangled. Others mutilated. Most just bloody. Disturbing artifacts of a tragic massacre that was only hours old.

Peter himself felt like a zombie, walking stupefied in a comatose state of shock. How could this happen? Why wasn't he prepared? And most importantly, what happens next?

Only questions plagued Peter's mind, and he didn't bother thinking of the answers. For now, he was content to wander on through the village. No longer blocked by tumultuous storm clouds, the sun was free to warm the winter air to a comfortable coolness. And so Peter felt fine enough making the long walk down the road all the way back home.

It was a journey he'd made once or twice before simply for the heck of it. He considered this mountain his and felt obligated to at least know what a walk home from work was like. It was tough, no doubt, as was any hike at nine thousand feet. But at least it was downhill.

The sidewalks didn't extend past the village properly, though, and so Peter was forced to trudge through the foot of snow covering the street. Of course, he would've preferred taking his car. But without a snowplow to clear the way, the blizzard's dump would make it difficult for even his SUV to get through.

Not that Peter was fit enough to get behind the wheel anyway. As soon as he saw the storm break he left his office and walked straight outside as if in some sort of trance.

The thought of survivors in the buildings nearby only briefly crossed his mind. He couldn't help them when it mattered. What could he possibly do now? They were probably safer where they were anyway. Either hiding in a closet or under some stranger's desk. Peter knew he should've followed suit. Going outside was probably going to get him killed. But then again, that was another thought which he didn't bother focusing on for more than a moment.

Peter was being drawn back to his house like a beacon calling him home. Passed the gondola's base, passed all the ski trails and the parking lot built behind the lowest lift on this side of the resort, Peter had continued on down the windy road that flowed in and out with the rolling hills of the mountainside. One by one, he passed by the million dollar log cabins and mansions that now looked like nothing more than giant igloos.

It was a long and tiring trek that left Peter dying for a drink. Several times he dug his bare hands into the fresh snow and threw the cold powder into his mouth, but the frozen water was barely enough to quench his thirst. His fancy, expensive snow boots had become saturated and wet only minutes into the journey. And despite being so close to the sun, prolonged exposure to the chilly mountain air left his bare hands and face sensitive and rough.

But when he finally made it over the last hill and his sprawling house came into view, every ounce of pain and discomfort vanished from his mind. Seeing his front door swung wide open made Peter eager to get inside. However, his body wasn't willing to increase its pace. So he kept on moving at the same speed, pushing his feet forward through the dense snow with all his might.

The house was only a hundred yards away, but it seemed like it took longer to travel that short distance than the whole trip itself. As Peter approached the front stoop, he could see the sheet of snow covering the porch had continued on inside. With the front door open, the windy blizzard had ferociously blown snow into the house. Upon crossing the threshold inside, Peter could see the trail of snow lead into the kitchen and then slowly dissipate when it reached as far in as the wind could take it. He cautiously followed the white road through the house until it stopped, where his wife's desecrated body rested peacefully at the end of the snowy path.

Rachel's skin was half way between its natural flush pink and the dull blankness of a white sheet. Her eyes were still wide open, stuck staring off at nothing in particular. Her clothes were ripped, tattered, and torn, but aside from a large supply of ravishing scratch marks, there were no signs her body was sexually violated. In between several large gashes, her arms, legs and torso were covered in random cuts and scrapes. It was obvious she had suffered by the dried blood covering her clothes and skin, but the multitude of wounds were now frozen over by the icy chill running through the house.

Peter stood over the body and stared at her lifeless face. Even under such horrific conditions, he was still captivated by her beauty. Her lush hair lay scattered and spread out over her head. Memories of its smell and touch flooded Peter's mind, and the euphoric fantasy took him away from the nightmare around him. The pleasant daydream distorted any perception of time, and Peter was all too willing to succumb to the delusion. He closed his eyes, completely unaware if minutes or hours were passing him by.

But the sweet hallucination ended abruptly when a voice called out to him from behind. "Hello? Anybody home?"

Peter's adrenaline suddenly spiked. He turned around ready to be assaulted but quickly realized that a raving lunatic wouldn't announce his presence. The sound of slow footsteps squishing into the snow grew louder until an oddly familiar man came into view.

His eyes immediately shot down to the body on the floor as a mixture of shock and sympathy grew across his face. "Oh, God. I'm so sorry."

Peter didn't respond. He simply walked around Rachel and went deeper into the kitchen while the man continued on. "When I saw you walking by I thought maybe you could use some help. I live next door and never got a chance to introduce myself."

Before the man had a chance to go on, Peter chimed in as he proceeded to search through the cabinets. "I know who you are: the world famous Austin Cage. My son loves your movies."

Upon hearing that his neighbor was a fan, Austin's face slightly lifted from its depressing look. "That's great. Maybe I can get him an autograph or some free stuff."

After finally finding what he was looking for, Peter pulled out and examined a large serrated knife from the cabinet. "That would be nice. If he's even still alive."

He didn't know how the actor would react upon seeing the blade, but Peter wasn't surprised when the large movie star gulped in fear. "What... what are going to do with that?"

"I'm sure you're aware of the mayhem that's erupting throughout the town, Mr. Cage."

"Yeah. Of course. But what does that..?"

Peter then moved through the open kitchen back to his wife's body. "I haven't seen all your movies, so forgive me if I'm wrong, but I don't think you've ever starred in a zombie film."

Austin remained silent as Peter approached his wife and knelt down by her side. "Well, Ryan, that's my boy, he makes me watch them all the time. So while I really don't know what the hell is going on around here, the word 'zombie' certainly comes to mind."

Tears began to build under the lids of Peter's eyes, and Austin could see him clutching the knife at his side tighter than an emotional man should be. "And if there's one thing I know about zombies, Mr. Cage, it's that they come back to life."

In a fluid wave of motion, Peter lifted the knife in the air and repeatedly slammed it down and into his wife's body. Although consistent, the stabbing action was sporadic and random, dropping the sharp tip all throughout her neck, stomach and chest. Over and over again, the blade alternated between making a squishy and crunching noise when bloodlessly sliding through the dead woman's frozen flesh.

Austin stood by speechless and unable to move as he watched tears burst from Peter's eyes. But he didn't cry or weep. He didn't even make a sound as he continually jabbed the knife into his wife's corpse for a full minute.

Finally, Peter raised the weapon up and moved it forward, thrusting the knife one last time directly into the center of her head. Once it was secure into Rachel's skull, Peter released the handle and let out a long breath that he'd been holding in.

For a moment, Peter remained in that position until his shoulders and body eventually relaxed back onto his knees. He then took several more deep and much needed sighs before turning to Austin with a blank, emotionless expression on his tear-ridden face. "I'm Peter, by the way."

15

People will do just about anything for money. That was the premise for which Scott Brooks had built his fortune. Over the years that notion had been refined. Now he believed there to be a direct correlation between what people would do for money and how much they currently had. And it was a well-known fact that a pilot's bank account was usually bare.

Scott always found it interesting that a profession which was once so highly revered could have fallen so far. Pilots used to be treated like rock stars. Now most of them barely made a living. Except for his, of course.

Scott understood just how important air travel (or more precisely, private air travel) was to his operation. The ability to not only travel large distances in a short amount of time but to do it at the drop of a hat was invaluable. And he rewarded his employees handsomely for providing that luxury. Captain Hitchens was one of the most well paid pilots in the country. And his protégé, Janet Thorn, made more than enough money for someone her age.

So it hardly came as a surprise to Scott when they didn't take him up on the offer he made to the others. Why would they want to shovel out the runway when they could sit comfortably in the cockpit doing their pre-flight checks? They left that job to the other grounded pilots and airport workers who were seeing their opportunities for employment dwindle before their eyes.

Scott's excitement erupted when the storm finally let up and the sun burst through the clouds. He was ready to leave that moment. Then his captain reminded him that the airport was still covered in snow, preventing them from taking off. The series of loud curse words and expletives that followed had left the entire airport speechless.

When his pointless and vulgar rant finally ended, Scott collected himself enough to formulate some sort of a plan to get in the air before nightfall. By applying his philosophy on life, Scott took advantage of the financial troubles of the people around him. He lifted his arms in the air and offered a year's salary to anyone who helped get his plane off the ground in the next hour. Most of the onlookers immediately grabbed every shovel they could find and ran outside. The few who didn't, waited a minute before realizing that their odds of success increased with the amount of people who were helping. They soon joined in and before he knew it, Scott Brooks had a snow shoveling army at his disposal.

Those who could operate the airport's small snowplows were busy clearing off the runway while the rest worked on shoveling a path out of the hangar. It was an impressive and captivating swarm of activity. So much so that an hour had come and gone without Scott even realizing.

He was leisurely finishing up a stale donut and coffee when he finally looked outside and noticed the storm clouds had completely vanished from the clear blue sky. Below it, his peons were still frantically working away to meet their deadline. Their job was rough, sloppy and by no means presentable, but it seemed as if enough snow had been cleared to make the plane's takeoff possible. And that was all Scott Brooks needed to know.

The whole time this was happening, Charlie had been resting peacefully on the couch, and Scott had no qualms about waking him up. "Come on, big boy. Time to go."

Scott tried pulling his bodyguard up but realistically had no chance of lifting the large man to his feet. Instead, the incessant nagging was effective at waking him up. "We ready?"

"Yeah. The champagne and caviar are waiting. Let's go."

Charlie took his time rolling up and off the couch before stumbling to his feet. Scott positioned himself under his bodyguard's arm, and together they began the long trek outside and towards the plane already parked just outside the hangar.

When they emerged from the building, all the workers stopped simultaneously and turned in anticipation. Scott knew they had been nervously watching the clock and were aware of the passed deadline. Whether or not they would still be getting paid was at the mercy of their temporary employer.

With Charlie's arm wrapped around his shoulder, Scott was struggling to support his bodyguard. None of the onlookers said anything, though. They simply watched as the two men slowly made their way down the path that had been shoveled and salted for them.

It wasn't until they were about half way to their destination that Scott finally spoke out loud enough to project his voice across the runway. "Sorry, everybody. Time's up. Looks like this pizza's free. Thanks for the help, though."

Nobody moved. They all remained still. And as he continued on his way, Scott wondered whether the crowd would soon turn ugly. He was especially concerned about a line worker who stood next to the private plane's open door.

The man was holding a shovel and didn't appear too appreciative of the fact that he wasn't getting paid. Being that he was the closest person out of everyone to the action, the disgruntled man become the group's de facto union leader, and his reaction would dictate how the situation would end.

Scott assumed it was a fifty-fifty chance that his face would soon be meeting the flat side of that shovel. But he caught the man off guard when he stopped at the first step up to the plane and winked at him with a large, unimposing smile. "I'm just kidding. Call my office. They'll take care of each and every one of ya."

He then reached into his jacket, pulled out a business card and tucked it up into the man's hat, who stood there bewildered and confused by what just happened. Before the man had a chance to respond, Scott continued on up into the plane where Captain Hitchens shut the door behind him, sealing them off from the outside world.

After plopping Charlie down in a rear-facing seat, Scott turned and followed the captain into the jet's small cockpit. "All right! Let's fire this puppy up and get outta here."

Captain Hitchens sat down in his left seat and worked in sync with his co-pilot, Janet, who was finishing her pre-flight checks. "I want to state for the record, Mr. Brooks, that what we're doing here isn't exactly legal."

"Yeah. I'll tell them to put the handcuffs on me as soon as we land."

In the middle of fixing a dial, Janet's head suddenly reared back and unleashed a giant sneeze into her forearm. Scott's arms instinctively shot up, and he looked on disgusted as the girl recovered from the sneeze. "What the hell was that?"

She sniffled while reaching for a tissue under her seat. "Sorry. This cold came out of nowhere."

Scott rolled his eyes as he turned around and left the cockpit. "Well, if you're going to hurl at least make it to the bathroom. Jet fuel's expensive enough. Don't need to pay to have this thing disinfected, too."

He sat down in the seat opposite Charlie just in time to hear the plane's loud engines roar on either side of them. The fatigued bodyguard sat reclined with his buttoned up shirt drenched from sweat profusely dripping off his face.

Scott failed to notice that, though, as he relaxed back and sighed deeply. "Damn, I forgot to order catering. Think I can get that guy with the shovel to make us some sandwiches real quick?"

Charlie declined to look amused from his slouched position. "Everything has to be a joke to you, doesn't it?"

The rumble of the engines grew louder, and Scott's body shook with the motion of the plane beginning to roll forward onto the runway. "If I didn't laugh then I'd have to cry."

Rolling and lunging his body forward, Charlie struggled to sit up in the seat. "Maybe you could use some humility."

"What are you, my therapist now? I pay you to look scary. Not give me advice."

As their conversation heated up, the plane continued to slowly putter towards the back of the runway. "Money. It's always about the money with you. Never about the people you give it to."

Scott's eyes drifted out the window to see the horde of workers who helped clear the snow for him standing idly by. "Exactly. And if you want to keep being one of those people then it'll behoove you to shut the fuck up."

"No! You shut the fuck up!"

Having finally reached the beginning of the runway, the plane began to turn around and face out towards the valley's entrance. "Relax, Charlie. I'm kidding. Don't get so stressed out. You need to take it easy."

"Why? Because you know what's best for me?"

Despite trying his best to listen to his employee, Scott's concentration on Charlie was broken by a loud exchange between Janet and Eric in the cockpit. The engine revved up, and so Scott assumed they were just doing their final checks before takeoff. But the two pilots were louder than normal and drew his attention. "What's with the commotion up there?"

Whatever it was didn't stop the plane from starting its takeoff. The jet rumbled forward, slowly gaining speed down the runway.

But Charlie was too focused in on Scott to take notice. "Don't worry about them! Worry about me! Because I'm the only one who gives a damn about you. I used to think you actually cared about me the same way. But I'm just a goon to you, aren't I? Another tool you use up and throw away. Well, I've had enough of your...!"

"Ahhhhh!"

After a loud scream from the cockpit, the plane suddenly jerked left then right, continuing its speedy approach down the runway. With the ground bumping and swerving, Scott struggled to stand out of his seat and look towards the front of the plane.

But he eventually managed to peek over Charlie's shoulder and see Janet lunged on top of the avionics with her jaw latched firmly onto Captain Hitchens's throat. "Well, this can't be good."

Scott pushed off his seat and quickly propelled himself forward into the cockpit. He grabbed onto Janet, futilely trying to pull her grasp free from the captain. "Let go, you crazy bitch!"

She flailed her limbs around like a fish out of water, all the while her teeth were still firmly secure into her mentor's neck. Scott continued to tug and pull, but it soon became clear by the blank expression on Eric's face and the streams of blood squirting from Janet's mouth that there was no hope in saving him.

That thought was immediately followed by his attention moving over to the end of the runway rapidly approaching through the windshield. "Not good indeed."

Fighting and pushing his way up and over Janet's bloodthirsty delirium, Scott frantically reached for anything remotely resembling the plane's controls. Even with her clawing at his neck and face, he still managed to grab and pull back on the throttle. But it was too late.

The plane dipped down the embankment at the end of the runway and came up the other side, plowing through the fence beyond it. The bloody mess of people Scott found himself entwined in bounced and spun around the cockpit on the jet's bumpy journey through the snowy plateau.

Then, in one frozen moment of time, Scott could see a clear view through the windshield as the nose of the plane dipped over the cliff edge and plunged straight down towards the rocky canyon below.

***

Patience was never Nellie's strong suit. She was always a person of action. A real take charge kind of girl. Which was why the last couple hours had been so hard for her.

It wasn't that she had just narrowly escaped an attack by a pack of raving lunatics. That's something she could deal with (or at least the adrenaline made it bearable). It was the waiting afterwards that got under her skin. The irritating silence that filled the air between her and the other four people in the room. Even her husband had little to say following their escape.

A few options were discussed between her and the marshal. Should they fight the creatures head on, search for others that needed help, or simply try to assess the situation from afar? But before they could make a decision, the first thing on their list was allowing the storm to pass.

It was obvious that their attackers had the advantage out in the blizzard. For about twenty minutes after the attack, the fiends outside the building continued to pound on the door. Then it went silent and appeared as if every one of them moved on. But the mob could've still been out there. So the survivors had to wait until the skies cleared before heading back outside.

Eager to fight, Nellie reluctantly agreed to what she knew was their only option. In the meantime, though, she did the only thing she could think of to take her mind off the anticipation: counting ammunition.

Unfortunately, there wasn't much to count. There were only so many places one could store extra ammo on their person while still being able to run for their life. Her and Bill managed to carry on them a decent amount of small firearm rounds, but anything larger was left in the truck.

She also managed to find a spare box of handgun bullets in the Town Hall's guard post. It was locked, of course. But given the circumstances, Nellie had no issues breaking it open.

As expected, the marshal and whatever posse he had left were slim pickings in the ammunitions department. They put up a tiny fight when Nellie tried to collect it from them, but there was no denying that she was right to take an inventory of what they had left.

Their supply turned out to be adequate. Nothing they could go to war with (especially with the firepower currently available to them), but there were enough guns and ammo to comfortably fend off an attack or two. Nellie then decided not to speculate beyond that.

When the silence persisted after double and triple checking their munitions, Nellie moved on to double and triple checking their weaponry. She had collected eight handguns from everyone: five pistols and three revolvers. More than enough to go around.

After she made sure each was in decent enough shape to operate, Nellie returned the guns to their owners. Besides Marshal Walker, Mrs. Sheridan wasn't familiar with the other two people in the room. One was an older man around the same age as her husband and the other a middle-aged woman that could have easily been her daughter. Nellie hadn't seen them before but could tell they were locals. Mostly because the marshal wouldn't have recruited them had they been tourists.

If they were, though, Nellie assumed they would think she was some type of hillbilly gun nut who could take apart and reassemble a rifle in her sleep. But she really wasn't. She just enjoyed hunting with her dad and brothers as much as the next tomboy. Firing a weapon was practically a rite of passage when growing up on a Colorado ranch. And now her country bumpkin pastimes were starting to come in handy.

It was on that thought Nellie realized she was running out of things to preoccupy her mind. Nostalgia was never her strong suit, and her nervous energy was starting to get the best of her. Which was why she secretly contained her appreciation when she spotted Marshal Walker approaching the corner office she had taken up shop in.

The marshal didn't look too happy (not that anyone would in this situation), but she braced herself for a rough conversation as he walked through the door. "Storm's cleared up completely."

When put into context, Nellie knew Travis was just breaking the ice between them with small talk about the weather. But she simply went along with it for now. "Good. Now we have a couple more hours of daylight. What about those things outside?"

"Haven't seen them since they stopped attacking the door. What do you think we should do next?"

Seeing an opportunity to exit the conversation, Nellie started to make her way past Travis and out of the office. "Right now I'm gonna take a look outside."

But Travis leaned over slightly to block her path with his shoulder. "Be honest with me, Nellie. Did you know this was going to happen?"

And just like that, the small talk was over. She knew a serious conversation was coming, but Nellie was still surprised by the question. "What are you talking about?"

"You and Bill arrived to the fight pretty prepared. Seemed like you were expecting things to be this bad."

She did admit that their timing was impeccable, but Travis was still poking at a big accusation. Fortunately, she didn't have to say anything other than the truth. "We ran into one of those things up at the ranch. When the girl on the radio went silent we figured it was time to lend a hand."

However, the marshal remained unconvinced. "Lend a hand? You two stormed into town like it was Normandy."

"What do you want me to say?"

"The mine. It's got something to do with this, doesn't it? That's why you were always trying to close it. Because your brother…"

She could see where the conversation was going, and Nellie acted quickly to get ahead of it. "I had suspicions. Nothing more."

"Suspicions? Come on, Nellie. People are dead! You didn't think..?"

Nellie wanted to cut him off again, but Travis suddenly stopped his own sentence, replacing it with a grave look of shock. His gaze quickly fixated past Nellie, and she turned around to see what he was looking at, which immediately became apparent.

Through the office window, the two of them watched in silence as a small jet tumbled over the edge of the airport's cliffs in the distance. The plane spun over once on its way down before smashing into the rocks against the backdrop of a snow drenched canyon wall.

Nellie was surprised the whole jet didn't go up in flames. But that didn't stop her from storming out of the room ready for action. "Bill, we're moving."

Her husband had been resting his eyes against the far wall and shot them open confused. "Wha…what's going on?"

"A plane crashed at the airport. We have to check it out."

But Travis yelled out to her from the office before she could reach the front door. "We don't have to do anything. They're probably dead."

Right before the Town Hall's giant wooden doors, Nellie stopped, took a deep breath, and waited a moment before turning around with a blank expression. "You want to know why I charged in to save you, Travis? Because you needed help. Not because I knew this was going to happen. Not because I've been sitting on the ranch hording my guns with a copy of the second amendment framed on the wall. It's because I knew there were people in trouble, and I didn't think twice about it.

"Is this a stupid idea? Probably. Are there people around here who need help, too? More than likely. But I'm tired of sitting here doing nothing. And this is a problem that happened in front of my eyes that I could do something about right now. So I'm not gonna think about it. I'm just going to go. With or without you."

Travis thought for a moment before taking a glance at the remaining members of his pitiful militia, who actually had on them a similar face to Nellie's. They too were tired of waiting and needed to take action, regardless of what that action was. A plane crash was as good a time as any.

So, Travis turned his attention back to Nellie and nodded his head in agreement. "Then let's go."

16

The snow was a lot deeper than Georgia thought it would be. She knew she was in for trouble when her first step forward required more effort than any she had taken before in her life. And the next wasn't any easier.

So far her journey into town from the TORO station had consisted of about twenty minutes worth of awkward walking and only five small blocks worth of travel. Under different circumstances, she might've considered the experience moving. Relaxing. Spiritual even.

She was completely alone and Telluride had literally become a snowed in ghost town. So far she hadn't seen another soul, crazy or otherwise. And she didn't know whether to take that as a good thing or bad. Sure, finding someone of sane mind would be reassuring. But for now, she was happy just not being attacked by a raging lunatic.

As she continued to move forward, Georgia tried to look for signs of life around the town. Maybe she could spot footprints of someone who passed by. Or perhaps a car that had been cleaned off by a driver hoping to get it started. But nothing. Not even a curious spectator peeking out through a window. Those, at least, that weren't completely blocked off by snow.

Telluride had seen several large storms in the time Georgia had lived there. Larger even than the one from this morning. But it wasn't the amount of snowfall which crippled the town. It was how quickly it accumulated. In the past, Telluride had seen several feet of powder spread out over the course of a day. But this storm only lasted for hours and managed to dump as much as it could before vanishing into the sky. For this reason, coupled with the fact that a mob of raging zombies disrupted snow removal, Georgia was forced to trudge along through the streets as if she were on an Arctic expedition.

Luckily, the snow was as soft and fluffy as fresh Rocky Mountain powder could get. With little effort Georgia was able to wade her legs through it, pushing the snow aside as if it were piles of feathers. The small girl gave a silent prayer that the flurries hadn't been turned to thick, heavy slush. Otherwise, she might've not had the strength to go on.

Her battle with Malcolm did a number on her, and it was a struggle just getting out of the station. But luckily again, the shining sun, when combined with the crisp coolness of the fresh mountain air, had rejuvenated her with new life. Of course, she expected winter to be cold at nine thousand feet, but the air was brisk rather than freezing.

It also helped that the blizzard used up all its wind and there was not a breeze left in the valley. If there had been, Georgia would've once again been in trouble. She was walking down the snow-covered street still wearing the same baggy sweatshirt she had on for the radio show. No hat, gloves or jacket. But it'll work, at least until she found help…if she found help.

During her rambling thoughts, Georgia continued to scan every neighborhood she passed, still hoping for any sign of life. But there was nothing, and she was just about ready to give up hope.

Suddenly, the snow next to her exploded up into the air as a figure burst out from within it. The cold powder shot into her face, and Georgia reflexively put her arms up as a shield. Without time to react, she immediately saw an old man behind the snow as he lunged towards her.

After being hit by his tackle, Georgia fell back and sunk straight down into the snow with the man right on top of her. She put her arms up to keep the man away but quickly felt trapped and cramped in the narrow space she found herself in. Submerged in the snow, Georgia realized she was stuck in a bright white coffin with her attacker as the ceiling.

The whole incident developed in a matter of seconds, but even struck by fear, Georgia found it odd that she took the time to notice her attacker's face. She had heard countless tales of people turning into murderous fiends from her callers and even experienced it first hand with Malcolm. But this man looked different. His face didn't look crazed or ravenous. In fact, it was covered in a layer of blood that was still oozing from his ears and eyes. The man wasn't ferocious. He was in pain.

But either way, Georgia was still at the receiving end of his assault and had to act. She struggled for a moment in her confined environment, trying to get in a position to retaliate. But every futile attempt at movement only made it easy for her brutish attacker to pin her down.

Georgia could feel the strength in her arms starting to sap and her will along with it. Then she noticed the rivers of blood flowing down the man's face were beginning to pool into droplets off his cheeks. The droplets drooped lower with every passing moment, and Georgia knew it was only a matter of time before they broke free and fell towards her.

The immediate thought of her skin being covered in the man's blood freaked Georgia into action. A spike of adrenaline surged through her, giving the girl just enough force to overwhelm the man and toss him into the snow to their side.

Her lumbering attacker awkwardly sunk face first into the powder and struggled to get back up. Georgia wasn't very quick to sit up either but still beat the man to her feet and proceeded to stomp down onto the back of his head. He wasn't moving very fast to begin with, but after every one of the DJ's ferocious kicks his attempts to stand became slower and slower.

Once she realized his movements had ceased completely, Georgia stopped as well and took the opportunity to catch her breath while staring at the man's motionless body pressed down deep into the snow. She had stomped him so quick and fast she couldn't tell exactly what was going on beneath him. Had she really crushed the man's head down into the street? Or merely squished him deeper into a firmly packed pillow of snow. Either way, he stopped moving. So the result was good enough for her.

It was time to move again, but when she tried to turn around, Georgia's legs gave out from under her. She only managed one step forward before her body collapsed into the fluffy cloud of snow. That's when she realized every other time was a fluke and now it was official: she was all out of energy.

Within a different context Georgia might've met her current situation with laughter, but now she just couldn't bring herself to chuckle.

She contemplated what would happen in the next couple hours if she couldn't move. She also noted to herself how ironic it would be if she died in that very spot, only several feet from where she saved her own life by fighting off a crazed lunatic.

Of course, she didn't want it to end like that. But Georgia had to accept that her death was a strong possibility. She was too weak and battered to move before being jumped on by a hidden maniac. Now she couldn't even feel the loose snow that was beginning to fall in, burying her underneath the powder. It would've been so easy to just close her eyes and drift off to sleep. The air was so still and quiet. Not a sound for miles.

Georgia began focusing into the absolute silence when she noticed it wasn't there. In the distance behind her she could hear the faint patter of footsteps trudging through the snow. A lot of them, in fact.

Her first instinct was to cheer. She was finally getting saved. But then she realized it could've just as easily been a group of those things ready to rip her head off. A sudden burst of fear sent a shiver down the girl's spine. Then, after accepting her fate, Georgia concluded that no matter who it was, at least she wasn't going to die bored.

After a full minute, the patter of feet continued to grow louder without Georgia knowing who or what was behind her. Then it suddenly stopped all at once and was soon replaced by several slams and clicks.

They were distinct sounds, and Georgia had lived out West long enough to know the noise a truck's door made when it shut.

They were people! A couple of them. And they had a car!

Georgia took a deep breath to scream as loud as her little lungs would allow. She then prepared to shout when the loud grumble of a diesel engine overpowered her weak cry for help. She tried again but couldn't even hear the sound of her own voice.

A moment later the roar of the engine gave way to the sound of snow tires eating their path through the street. She could hear the truck fade off into the distance, well on its way to wherever it was headed. And now, Georgia realized, it really was time to take a nap.

***

It had only been a little over an hour since Austin Cage met Peter Hayden, and already he felt they had been on quite a journey together. Before buying a vacation home in Telluride, Austin had briefly heard about the man who ostensibly ran Mountain Village. Mr. Hayden had been described to him as friendly, accommodating and very approachable. Three qualities Austin wouldn't relate to the barbaric display he witnessed upon walking into the Hayden's kitchen.

But to be fair, calling the last twelve hours of Peter's life dire would be an understatement. If there was one thing he took out of the roles he played as an action hero, Austin knew all too well that normal men were certainly capable of extraordinary acts in times of stress. In this case, that meant a husband brutally mutilating his wife to prevent her from turning into a zombie. Austin even had to admit it was kind of romantic, in an insane, end of the world kind of way.

Once the act was over, it took a while before Peter was ready to move again, and given what had just happened, Austin was more than happy to let him have all the time he needed. Once Peter was up and moving, though, he seemed to be back to his old self (or at least what Austin assumed to be his old self). The man went rummaging through his house for anything that could be of use in the situation they found themselves in. Flashlights. Canned food. Extra clothing. Pretty much the post-Apocalypse necessities.

Austin helped Peter pack everything they found in a bag, but there was something disconcerting about him. It wasn't that he was acting strange or anything. In fact, he was acting fairly normal. Too normal for a man who had just lost his wife and watched his entire town dive head first into madness. And that's what seemed off about Peter. That it only took a few moments for him to move on past his grief and look ahead. A part of Austin actually admired the quality, but a different part of him was curious what kind of man could write off such a tragedy so quickly.

Regardless of the answer, Austin followed Peter's lead to head up the mountain and into the village proper. Peter had just come down that way to search for his wife, and after what he found, there wasn't much reason for him to stick around.

The uphill hike was both daunting and treacherous due to the amount of snow they had to overcome. Even having the physique that his Hollywood career demanded, Austin didn't think they would have been able to make the journey if not for the path Peter carved on his way down.

The only time the couple veered off course was when they came across a house on their way. Alternating turns, they each knocked on every front door they passed, searching for survivors. There weren't really that many houses, though. The sprawling acres of real estate that the mansions stood on prevented them from having close neighbors. And to their surprise, the heroic duo actually managed to find several mothers, fathers, and children too scared to leave their homes on their own. Before he knew it, Austin had himself a small caravan of families under his protection. The only shame about it was that not all those families were whole.

Unfortunately, they weren't able to check on the houses off the main road. Neither of them (nor any of the strays they picked up along the way) had the energy to go door to door on foot to every mansion sprawled out across the mountain. They both knew there was always a chance people could've been alive up there. But it just wasn't an option. Searching every house would've taken them hours. Time that was better spent getting to shelter back at Peter's office.

Looking back on what they had accomplished in such a short period of time, Austin was actually impressed. It was a far cry from being air lifted to safety. But there was definitely a feeling of achievement as the group approached Mountain Village courtyard. Even after their fearless leader gave the group a fair warning about the corpses they were sure to encounter along the way.

With that announcement, Austin once again felt concerned about Peter's lack of emotion. He led the whole crew, bag in hand, barely looking back to check and see if everyone was all right. Austin didn't have to, though, seeing as how he brought up the rear. By his count, there were two other men, three women, and five children. To the famous movie star, the whole scene played out in his mind like a refugee convoy on a wintery Oregon Trail.

Finally, Peter's cold bedside manner got too much for Austin, and he hurried up to the front of the pack. For several steps, Austin waited for Peter to initiate some kind of conversation, but the man kept his dead stare forward, never wavering from his determined path.

Eventually, though, Austin spoke up when the silence got too much for him. "So, what's the plan?"

"We set up camp in my office."

Austin rolled his eyes after receiving the information, which he already knew. "Then what?"

"Search the village for more survivors. Maybe head into town."

As a movie star, it felt weird for Austin to be the one purposefully engaging a stranger in a conversation. Usually, it was the other way around, but it was the only way he could figure out what was going on inside Peter's head. "Ok, but then what? There has to be something more than just seeing who's still alive?"

Even though he didn't look in his direction, Austin could tell Peter was slightly perturbed by the questioning. "For someone who's dealt with a lot of fictional crises, you seem to ask a lot of questions when you've finally found yourself in a real one."

"Hey! When I bought a vacation home here I didn't exactly read the emergency manual on zombie outbreaks."

Austin's voice rose a little louder than he wanted it to, and he glanced back to see the crowd following him growing slightly nervous. The actor then turned back to continue the conversation with a much softer tone. "Look, I'm not a real hero. I'm actually pretty scared, and I don't even have a family here like you or these people behind me. So I can't imagine what you're going through but…"

Austin was doing his best to try and have a sentimental moment with Peter, but the man suddenly stopped walking out of nowhere. Following their leader, the entire group stopped with him, and Austin could hear confused chatter from the people behind him. They, just like he, were curious as to why they stopped. But when he looked at Peter all he saw was a man wrecked with emotion. He was staring ahead, locked in a puzzled trance. And for a second, Austin actually believed he had gotten through to Peter on an emotional level.

That was until he saw the man squinting his eyes as if he was trying to see something in the distance. Austin looked in the same direction, but it wasn't until he squinted himself that he saw what Peter had noticed.

Past the long rows of condos stretching before them was the end of Mountain Village's cobblestone pathway. And just beyond it was the bottom of several ski trails that funneled into the gondola station. Focusing in on that building, Austin could actually see two figures moving towards them. They looked to be approaching quickly, or as quickly as someone could while wading through a foot of snow.

A brief series of scenarios rushed through Austin's head. Were they more survivors? People here to help them? Or perhaps more zombies? Peter didn't seem worried, though. In fact, he still had the same, strange expression of emotional inquisitiveness. Why did he look so weird?

Austin turned back to further inspect the silhouettes and saw that one actually had an odd shape around his chest. Almost like he was carrying something. He, once again, quickly pondered a list of scenarios in his mind, but Peter, almost on the verge of tears, interrupted his thought process with a single word that explained his demeanor. "Ryan?"

***

"Are we...are we there yet?"

Stephanie didn't know the answer to Ryan's question. But even if she did, she wasn't sure if she would have the strength of will to tell him. It was hard enough watching his condition rapidly deteriorate on their way down the mountain. She didn't want to also be the one filling him with hope...or despair.

From about half way between the peak and Mountain Village, Stephanie had followed Chris down the easiest route the patroller could think of. Granted, no mountainous terrain was considered safe to traverse on foot after a snowstorm. But the teenage girl was surprised at how resilient she had become. Her and Ryan both. Surely it had to be difficult for the boy. The snow was much higher on someone so low to the ground. But he did a decent job keeping up...at least in the beginning.

First he started complaining about being thirsty. But then again, they all were. It was expected when performing rigorous physical activity at high altitudes. Especially for a little kid. But Stephanie noticed something was definitely wrong when she looked over every so often and could see the boy's face growing whiter by the second.

Chris noticed it, too, and Ryan wasn't stupid. He could feel himself getting sick out of nowhere. And as an avid zombie enthusiast, he knew all too well what was happening. They all did. Which was why Chris eventually scooped up Ryan into his arms and took off down the mountain.

Stephanie did her best to keep up in her clunky ski boots, but it wasn't until they reached the gondola base that she got close enough to see Ryan visibly shaking in Chris's arms. The boy was pale white with a thick layer of mucus bubbling under his runny nose. The patroller was squeezing the baggy jacket around him like a blanket. By the way Ryan's eyes kept fluttering closed, though, his chills got to the point where no amount of body heat could warm him.

With Ryan secured tightly in his arms, Chris began trudging through the snow towards Mountain Village's courtyard. The boy must've felt them pick up the pace because that's when he asked his question, which Stephanie refused to answer.

But with the ski patroller inside him cranked to full gear, Chris couldn't resist trying to comfort the terrified child. "Soon, Ryan. Soon."

"I'm...scared." It was only two words, but his trembling lips made it hard for the little one to speak.

Chris, on the other hand, spoke strong and with conviction, fueled by a need to save those in his care. "Don't worry. There's gotta be something that can stop this. Fluids. Sedatives. You're not going to turn into one of those things. I promise."

"Don't...promise. I don't want you...to break it."

After finally reaching the village's cobblestone walkway, Stephanie and Chris stuttered at the bloody sight of sporadic bodies sprawled out before them. It was only a moment, though, before Chris continued their trek to the ski patrol outpost on the other side of the courtyard. "That's not an option. I promised Sarah I would take you home and..."

"I said don't promise!"

The boy's voice suddenly snapped out of its weak cocoon and became a booming force of rage. So much so that Chris had stopped moving in the center of the courtyard. He looked shocked and surprised. Who wouldn't be? But Stephanie wasn't.

She recognized the boy's sudden spike in anger and knew all too well what was coming next. "He's getting angry. Get rid of him."

"Yeah! Just get rid of me! We all know you want to."

But Chris held onto him, tighter than he had before. "No. This can't be happening."

Caught between wanting to help and procuring her own safety, Stephanie froze with inaction. "It's too late. He's a time bomb. Just..."

"Ryan!"

To her surprise, Stephanie looked up to see a man running towards them. He was already so close and looked frantic with his eyes locked firmly onto the boy. Chris didn't know how to react and remained still as the man reached for him.

But Stephanie quickly yelled out when she foresaw the terror about to unfold. "Wait!'

All at once, Ryan suddenly burst out from within Chris's arms. His legs pushed hard off the patroller's chest as he lunged at the surprised man, who stopped dead in his tracks. The baggy jacket, ripped right off the boy's body, was still held firm in the clutches of Chris's hands. He, too, was shocked and stood speechless as Ryan ferociously latched onto the man's face.

Together they fell backwards onto the hard courtyard ground and the man began horrifically screaming as Ryan scratched, clawed and bit like a rabid animal. The shrieks of pain immediately snapped Stephanie and Chris into action, but that still wasn't quick enough to stop the boy's attacks.

They both grabbed onto Ryan's flailing arms to pull him back. As he was lifted into the air, his legs kicked and squirmed until his body was free from their hold. He dropped hard at their feet where Chris and Stephanie once again tried to smother him down. But the boy nimbly squirmed away and tried to flee deeper into Mountain Village.

Despite a ravenous energy fueling him forward, he only got several steps into the surrounding area before more survivors, presumably from the man's group, managed to cut him off.

Discouraged by the outnumbered fight ahead of him, Ryan actually stopped and took a look around, sizing up his situation with intense, devilish eyes. Chris and Stephanie circled around him to cover the boy from every direction. She was even surprised to see the injured man on the ground slowly get up and do the same.

His face was torn and bleeding but there was an undeniable anguish in his eyes as he approached his attacker. He soon stopped and stared at the boy with a look of devastating loss. A look Stephanie could relate to. A look she understood. That's when she knew the deranged, bloodthirsty boy she had actually grown fond of was the man's son. And she refused to prolong the death of another family any longer.

Ryan still stood in the same position, gnashing his teeth at the people around him. He was trapped but still a wild, dangerous beast. He could sense the fear in the men, women, and children before him. He felt their bodies tremble at his crazed appearance.

But was caught off guard by a voice from behind. "Hey, Ryan."

The small boy turned around and was suddenly struck in the mouth by a bare fist that dropped him to the pavement. Stephanie immediately saw the boy's eyes flutter shut from the knockout punch she delivered and stood over his unconscious body for another moment just to be sure.

The whole standoff ended as quickly as it developed, and Stephanie was a bit taken aback by both the how and why of what happened. She didn't expect to be able to sneak up on the boy without him noticing, let alone deliver a punch (the first one in her entire life) that would knock him out cold. Then again, she did hit a little boy, so she told herself it wasn't that impressive.

As far as the why, Stephanie also had no answer. Her body moved on autopilot from the moment she stepped forward to when Ryan lay flat on the walkway with a bloody nose. It wasn't until she looked up and caught a glimpse of the man's battered face that she was reminded of the pain she experienced only hours earlier. Reminded of what she felt seeing her own father and brother, a boy not much older than Ryan, becoming those things. Terrorized by crippling emotion, she was unable to act then, like he was unable to act now. And the teenage girl realized why she did what she had. Because she knew someone had to ease his pain. Why shouldn't it have been her?

But the sentiment was soon lost when Stephanie's eyes drifted from the man and quickly recognized one of the strangers gathered speechless around her. "Hey! Aren't you Austin Cage?"

17

The Sheridans owned one hell of a truck. That was the only thought going through Marshal Walker's mind as Nellie gripped the wheel with a fierce determination. He was concerned that the thick layer of snow covering the town's unplowed roads would've been a problem. But like the expert driver she was, Mrs. Sheridan alternately shifted gears and toyed with the gas just enough so that the Ford's four-wheel drive ate up the snow without overheating.

It was a skill Travis was admittedly shocked that she had. He assumed Billy would've been the one to jump behind the wheel, but after leaving the Town Hall, Nellie never stopped for a moment to let anyone other than herself into the driver's seat. Knowing better than to challenge his wife, Billy instinctively headed for the passenger side door.

Now that their journey to the plane's crash site was well underway, Travis sat comfortably in the Super Duty's roomy back seat in between Molly and Hunter on his left and right respectively. As he took a quick glance at his two companions, both of whom focused intently out their windows, the marshal experienced a quick flashback to when he recruited them for his little posse.

The chaos of the storm created such a panic that he was looking for anyone with a familiar face that could hold a gun. Despite his age, Hunter was an obvious choice to help. But Travis was surprised when Molly stepped forward and volunteered. He would've expected the schoolteacher to be at home, riding out the horror with her husband and kids. That's when he learned that there was no longer anyone alive for her to be home with. And then, with that grim clarity staring him in the face, her decision made sense.

Even though the memories were just hours old, that moment was still a hazy blur in Travis's mind, almost as if the adrenaline had repressed all evidence of the event. Remembering it only brought back painful dread.

And although the nightmare wasn't over, he was still grateful when Nellie distracted him by breaking the silence from her driver's seat. "When we get out, William, Travis and I will check the plane while you two watch our backs."

Her speech was short and succinct, and Marshal Walker saw it as a perfect opportunity to familiarize the group with each other. "Oh! I forgot to introduce you guys. Bill and Nellie, this is Hunter Simpson and Molly Pullman. They're both…"

But Mrs. Sheridan abruptly cut him off in the same cold tone she used to lay out her plan. "I don't need to know their names. I just need to know if they can shoot."

Already on edge from hours of fear and tragedy, Molly was the first to snap back. "I didn't learn on the famous Sheridan ranch, but I'll have no problem shooting you in the back of the head for being so bossy all the time."

And Nellie responded with her patented dry sarcasm that always seemed odd coming from a woman her age. "From this close? Now that would be an impressive display of marksmanship."

Molly wanted to go back and forth with her, but she looked to Hunter, who then opted for a more diplomatic approach. "Don't worry about us. We're still alive, aren't we?"

For the first time since the tense conversation began, Nellie finally peeked over her shoulder at the three passengers in the back seat. "Congratulations. Now let's keep it that way."

Travis debated with himself on whether or not he should intervene. He was the marshal, after all. It was his job to lead in situations like this. But there was a finality to Nellie's comment that he didn't want to tamper with. What could he possibly say to make the situation any better? And so he sat back in his seat and watched through the windshield as they passed the outskirts of town.

It was amazing how Nellie could even stay on the road let alone drive through the snow. As far as he could tell, Travis saw nothing more than a sheet of white across the countryside. But as the truck tore through the deep snow in its path, it was obvious that the driver could've probably reached their destination blindfolded. That's what spending your whole life traveling the same ten square miles would do to you.

Eventually, the truck approached the driveway leading up to the airport, which was located higher up against the valley wall. But instead of turning down it, Nellie kept going straight, hugging the edge of the road near the mountainside. It wasn't long before the party came across the wreckage of a small plane nestled into the boulders at the base of the rock wall, and Nellie pulled the truck up as far as it could go without getting stuck in the jagged terrain.

As soon as she threw the vehicle in park, all four doors of the truck flew open, and Nellie immediately turned around to see what the two strangers she had taken along with her would do. Travis could see she half expected them to stand around moping while holding their guns like they were in some kind of action movie.

But she was pleasantly surprised when they hopped in the back of the pickup and started clearing out the snow in case they needed the extra room. That's when the marshal gave her a quick glance that justified his faith in them. And Nellie was happy to have been proven wrong.

Turning their attention back towards their mission, Travis and Nellie quickly caught up to Bill, who was already trudging through the knee-high snow on his way towards the wreckage. The marshal was certainly telling his body to run, but the only way he could move forward was by lifting his legs up and over the dense sea of snow. All three of them moved forward at practically a snail's pace and were completely exhausted by the time they reached the crash.

The plane wasn't big. Definitely some form of private jet. But then again, large commercial airlines weren't allowed to fly into TEX anyway. It was hard to tell what was what from the crumpled debris and twisted metal sprawled out across the area, but it appeared as if the plane crumpled in on itself upon hitting the ground. The most recognizable part of the ruins was the nose of the aircraft, where the broken windshield gave a clear view inside the fuselage.

After climbing over the rocks and carefully scaling the secure portions of the plane, Travis peered into the cockpit and found a mangled scene of bloody body parts interwoven between the destroyed avionics. Upon approaching the disaster, Marshal Walker knew the inside of the plane wouldn't be pretty, but even after everything that had happened, the marshal still had to swallow down a rancid sickness creeping its way up into his throat.

Besides the broken bits of plane crisscrossing every which way, Travis immediately saw the battered faces of a man and woman, each covered in blood and bruises. Where the rest of their bodies were was a whole other question, but Travis could definitely tell who was the aggressor of the two. Contrary to the man's fear riddled expression, the younger female had the same frozen stare of bloodthirsty horror that the marshal knew all too well.

It was a depressing scene that made the trip seem pointless, but Travis performed his duty anyway with a quick shout through the windshield. "Hello? Anybody alive?"

"Oh, fuck."

The profane response caught Travis by surprise, but his face lit up at the prospect of survivors. "Hey! Where are you? We're here to help."

Movements started to take shape from within the darkness of the plane, and a man in a ripped suit covered in cuts and scrapes began climbing his way through the obstacle course of wreckage. "I figured as much. I was rather hoping no one showed up, though. Then I would actually have an excuse to just lay there and die."

The bruised stranger started crawling his way through the gory cockpit, and Travis finally got a good look at him as the mountain sunlight lit up his face. "I know you. Brooks, right? You're that rich asshole I keep getting drunk and disorderly complaints about."

On his hands and knees, Scott squirmed his way through the broken glass of the windshield before struggling to his feet. "That's what you call it. I call it drunk and having a good time."

Upon first hearing the commotion, Bill immediately stopped his own search of the debris field and joined the rescue. "Are there any other survivors?"

Finally able to stand straight up, Scott took the opportunity to brush himself off. "Fortunately, no. Otherwise, I think my body would be halfway digested by now."

Without a second to pause, Mr. Sheridan continued his interrogation. "What happened?"

And without a second to think, Mr. Brooks dryly answered the man's question. "The plane crashed."

"Care to elaborate?"

"My one pilot bit my other pilot and then we no fly. Comprende?"

Travis knew better than to get between them. He'd seen first-hand what a roundabout conversation with Scott Brooks looked like. But the two men continued to stare, both obviously annoyed with each other.

Until Nellie, who'd been silently observing from the base of the rocks, called out for them to move. "It doesn't matter. Let's get him back to the truck and head into town."

Travis and Bill started to move back down to her when Scott quickly sidestepped in front of them. "No-no-no. There's other planes up there and pilots to fly them."

Travis admitted to himself that it didn't seem like an unreasonable request, but Bill didn't look convinced. "You're going to try again? Even after what happened?"

"Hell yeah. With nobody plowing the roads that runaway is our only chance of getting out of here alive."

While he was talking, a faint scratching noise began grabbing Travis's attention. He seemed to be the only one to notice and glanced up to see the spinning blade of a plane's prop bearing down on top of them. "Look out!"

A quick kick of adrenaline surged through Travis's body, causing his instinct to dive forward and tackle both men in front of him off the rocks. They quickly plummeted down into the bed of snow below just as a small four-seater plunged into the previous plane's remains. In an instant, the aircraft crumpled and tore itself apart against the rocks and wreckage, creating a carnage of spinning debris.

Even with his head buried into the mound of snow, Travis could hear the deafening screech of twisted metal shearing itself to shreds. When the loud destruction finally ceased, the marshal, as well as the three others entombed in the snow next to him, looked up to take witness of the plane graveyard sprawled across the landscape.

They just sat there silently for a solid minute, taking in the scene for all its beautiful devastation, until Scott Brooks finally chimed in with his trademark words of wisdom. "God must fucking hate me."

***

In the context of the current crisis, Peter's office was relatively the safest place in Mountain Village. The only way to access it was through a series of stairs and winding turns that a pack of wild, murderous savages wouldn't bother navigating. At least, the survivors planning to hide there hoped they wouldn't.

Inside the building they also found several of Peter's employees who waited to head home in the blizzard only to be met head on by a massacre. Needless to say, they went back inside and hid until Peter and his band of survivors discovered them upon his return. They were, of course, grateful to see him. But equally shocked (and somewhat appalled) when they saw him carrying his unconscious son in his arms.

With a bloody nose and pale white skin, it was obvious the boy had undergone the same transformation as the other raving lunatics. His legs and arms were bound together by a thin rope, but that didn't make the sight any less frightening. These things exhibited increased strength and a brutal ferociousness. Did they really think they could capture and hold a live one as a prisoner? Also, what was the point? Could they even be cured?

These were just some of the concerns raised between Peter's employees as well as the survivors he saved along the way. But the man had just been attacked by his son, and nobody was going to question his decision to hold onto some shred of hope that Ryan could somehow be saved. After all, he was just a boy. Homicidal creature or not, how hard could he be to restrain?

The patroller, who Peter quickly deduced as Sarah's boyfriend, kept Ryan sedated with meds he found at the village base camp. Whether or not they would work for an extended period of time was a different story.

Besides his status as Sarah's boyfriend, Peter also figured out the turn of events that led Ryan into Chris's care. He contemplated offering the young man his condolences but didn't see the point. People were telling him they were sorry about Rachel's death, and their sympathies didn't make any difference. The danger that killed her was still very real, and the adrenaline inside him made it impossible to mourn.

That thought led Peter to his next concern: where the hell did the danger go? There were dozens of those things in the courtyard alone. Surely, no one stopped them. And Peter couldn't believe that they would be killed by the storm. So then what happened to them? It was a question that needed to be answered. But for now, he was content simply accepting the current calm for what it was, even though he knew it was most likely temporary.

Resuming his role as Village Manager, Peter's first order of business was getting back on the phone. His first call was to the mayor's office. No answer. Next he tried Marshal Walker. No answer there either. Finally, he called the medical center but was met by a generic out of service message on the other end of the line, which Peter didn't know how to respond to. The building was a twenty-four-hour health facility. How could their phones be out?

Peter remained speechless for a moment before trying one last number, which he wasn't even authorized to dial. The ringer sounded three times before being replaced by a man's curious "hello?" Peter gasped a sigh of relief upon hearing the man's voice and went on to introduce himself.

After giving a brief scolding for being called on his personal number, the governor informed Peter that troops were mobilizing but having transportation issues because of the storm. Peter was then instructed to stay put and wait for the cavalry. It was absolutely the right move to make, but Peter knew that he wouldn't be able to.

He needed to know what was going on down in the town. Was everyone there dead? Or were they just busy handling the situation? Of course, Peter wanted to believe everyone in Telluride was safe but reserved his hope for a blessing. That maybe the survivors down there found a way to change people back. It was an unlikely possibility that he refused to dwell on for more than an instant. But he wasn't ignorant to the fact that his desire for a miracle was the driving force behind him wanting to go down there and find out for himself.

A short time later, Peter was entering the gondola's base along with Chris and the girl who punched his son. He needed someone to go with him and a ski patroller was the obvious choice. Unfortunately, the girl he arrived with was now attached at Chris's hip and wanted to come along.

Not that Peter held a grudge against her. In fact, he was grateful. But what could a teenage girl possibly do but slow them down?

He would've preferred to have taken Mr. Cage, but someone needed to watch over Ryan. And in a sad, morbid kind of way, Peter got a little bit of an ironic joy out of knowing that his son got to spend time with one of his favorite movie stars, even under such depressing circumstances.

The first problem the group encountered was restarting the gondola. They didn't know when, but it obviously shut down at some point during the hysteria of the storm. As the only one even remotely familiar with the equipment, Chris walked off toward the control booth, and Peter could see Stephanie out the corner of his eye searching for a place to sit.

She finally found a bench back by the entrance but only took a single step towards it when Peter grabbed her attention. "It's Stephanie, right?"

The surprised girl looked up in shock that the man had spoken to her. Rather than speak, though, she answered by simply nodding her head.

Peter then went on. "Thank you for doing what you did with my son. It was a scary situation, and unfortunately...I was unable to..."

Peter searched for the words to finish his thought, but Stephanie, once again, silently responded with a quiet smile that fulfilled their exchange. When she didn't immediately speak, Peter turned back around to face forward.

That's when he finally heard Stephanie's soft, fragile voice. "Mr. Cage told me about your wife. I'm sorry."

Her words caused him to breathe deeply, but his eyes remained fixated ahead. Peter could feel the girl still looking at him, waiting for him to respond just as he had done to her. But instead of letting the subject die, Stephanie followed up. "He said you did stuff to keep her from changing. Brutal stuff. Like it was nothing. Didn't affect you at all."

Peter wanted to take another deep breath but forced himself to keep it in, which caused him to swallow hard instead. He still refused to look at her, but that didn't stop the girl from continuing on. "But then with Ryan you just stood there. I could see you were emotional. Who wouldn't be? And if..."

Finally fed up, Peter snapped back at the girl with a stern tone he usually used only as Village Manager. "I said thank you. Can we just..?"

But the girl's timid appearance, hardened by recent events, was unphased by the man's booming voice. She cut him off with a strong willed tone of her own. "I did the same thing."

Her confession caught Peter off guard. He didn't know how to respond. So after seeing that her words had fully been absorbed, Stephanie began her story. "I had a brother. Little older than Ryan, but a lot alike. Mainly in that they both annoyed me. He got sick, too. Right next to me, in fact. I didn't know what was happening with him so I couldn't do anything even if I wanted to."

"Look, I'm sorry that..."

"My dad was a different story, though. We were stuck together on the mountain. Mom and Joey were dead. It was just us. And I wanted him to be OK. I told myself he was. That Joey was different. That what happened to my brother couldn't happen to him. Until...it did."

Peter never spoke, but his eyes remained fixated on the young girl. And that was all she needed to sense his thoughts and respond. "You told everyone that we were going to check on the town, but I know why you really wanted to go."

Stuck half way between shame and desperation, Peter lowered his head and felt a caring hand placed on his shoulder accompanied by Stephanie's soft voice. "We're going to find a way to help him."

He looked back up and could feel his opinion of the girl shift in his mind. Their trip had only barely begun, and already she had proven her strength and usefulness.

They each shared a warm smile that was quickly interrupted by Chris's exclamation of joy from inside the control booth. "Found it!"

The giant gears and cables above their heads began spinning and clunking in motion. A second later, the nearest gondola car swiveled around with the doors open, and the two unlikely friends jumped inside.

18

Dr. Morris quickly realized she wasn't cut out for winter pioneering.

After coming to the depressing realization that her makeshift clinic could at any moment turn into a bloodbath, Anna knew something had to be done. Any option she came up with was either impractical or impossible. She finally decided to treat her patients with a wide array of medicine and antibiotics in the hope that something combated the disease. Of course, loading up a sick person with a concoction of drugs was never a good idea. But then again, neither was letting them turn into murderers.

The worst part of the plan, though, was that Dr. Morris didn't even know if it would work. Her futile attempts to delay the massacre waiting to happen could all be for nothing. To make matters worse, she didn't even have those drugs available to her. And unfortunately, the only place that did was the pharmacy located at the center of town.

So that's where Anna currently found herself: decked out in a winter coat, hat, and boots, trekking through the snow doused streets of Telluride like an explorer on an Arctic expedition. Every step she took required more effort than the last.

She was making her way along the sidewalk towards the center of town, but the doctor felt like she was lost out in some remote part of the mountains. Snow covered absolutely everything in sight, effectively turning this small canyon of civilization back over to the surrounding wilderness it once belonged to.

Sure, the landscape was beautiful. Where else could one find such a desolate ghost town engulfed by whiteness? But the horror and tragedy that it took to create such a scene was too high a cost.

Not that she witnessed any of it firsthand. She only knew about what happened from the radio. And judging by some of the calls that came in, the streets seemed like some kind of warzone. A warzone which Anna saw very little evidence of.

Some storefront windows were cracked and cars had been abandoned out in the middle of the road. But Dr. Morris saw none of the crazed looters that were reportedly tearing through the streets, destroying everything in sight.

The air was quiet. Stagnant. And the snow had been untouched by any wandering footprints.

Then again, Anna would be lying to herself if she didn't notice every so often tiny bits of limbs sticking out through the snow-covered streets. That was one of the reasons why she decided to stay on the sidewalks. To avoid the occasional frozen foot or hand that was a grim reminder of her failure to save every life she could from the gruesome destruction.

But at the same time, the doctor had to peek over and force herself to acknowledge the bodies. That this struggle was real. People died here. Cold and in pain. And she had to use that horrible truth as a reminder as to why she couldn't let it happen again.

In reality, though, it wasn't really that hard of a thing to demand of herself. Her trip was slow and boring enough that her wandering eyes eventually made their way over to the street anyway. Anna's gaze would occasionally veer off and notice another body without even realizing she was doing it.

This time it happened to be the back of a woman's coat just barely visible through the snow. Dr. Morris gave her usual sigh of pity and remorse before planning to turn her line of sight back around. However, her head wouldn't move, almost as if it noticed something before she did. It took Anna a few more seconds of staring in the same direction, but she eventually realized what had caught her eye: the woman's back was moving.

In an instinctual panic, Dr. Morris frantically began wading through the snow in an attempt to reach her. Any caution and hesitance she had about hiking through the snow were gone, replaced by her convictional need to help someone in trouble. The woman's movements were faint, but they were enough to give Anna hope that something could be done.

Upon reaching her new patient, Dr. Morris removed her bare hands from the comfort of their pockets and began digging around the woman's body. Anna noticed that a small cave-in of snow around the stranger's head had allowed a tiny pathway for air to reach her face. An unlikely yet miraculous accident that prevented the young woman from suffocating.

Once enough snow had been cleared, Anna checked for a faint pulse before quickly examining the rest of her faced-down body. Except for a minor bruise on the back of her head, the woman appeared in decent enough shape. Cold and unconscious but physically fine. Probably left for dead among the other corpses littering the streets beneath the snow.

After making sure there weren't any broken bones, Anna flipped the woman over and began carefully slapping her pale, white cheeks. The repetitive taps grew increasingly harder and faster until the doctor became concerned that she was going to leave a bruise. She contemplated stopping when she suddenly got the first eye flutter from her otherwise hypothermic patient.

Anna stopped for a moment to give the woman's brain time to catch up with the trauma. Then, all at once, the woman gasped out in panic as her eyes shot open with fear. With her last panicky memories coming back to her, the woman's eyes began darting all around.

And it took several whole seconds of Anna holding her shoulders for the woman to calm down. "Relax! Easy now. You're OK. You're safe."

Finally settling in, the woman laid back down into the snow, anxiously catching her breath. Her eyes continued to glance in every direction but much slower than before.

And once she was able to fully process the situation, the woman looked over to the savior sitting next to her. "What happened?"

With the pain from her injury setting in, the woman began rubbing the back of her head as Anna went on to explain her diagnosis. "I'm guessing that blow to the head knocked you out. You seem fine but lucky. If I didn't find you then you probably wouldn't have lasted the night."

"And you are?"

"Dr. Anna Morris. I'm on my way to pick up some drugs from the pharmacy. I assume you'll want to tag along?"

Finally realizing just how lucky she was, the woman looked up to the doctor with the friendliest of smiles. "Sure. I could use some drugs."

Anna then returned the joke with a laugh of her own. "I would have to write you a prescription first."

"Of course. Just make it out to Elizabeth McCabe."

***

The gondola ride up was silent. Probably because Peter, Stephanie and Chris knew it was the one place they could let their guard down without fear of being attacked. No maniac was going to bust through the door of the small gondola cab while it was suspended forty feet in the air. So the three unlikely companions took the opportunity to truly relax without a conversation to distract them.

For five minutes the cab transformed into a nap area, each one of its passengers giving way to their fatigue. Despite all efforts to resist, their eyes grew heavy with every passing second. And the trip up from Mountain Village was spent with the three passengers dozing in and out of consciousness.

That all ended when the gondola hit a series of quick, consecutive bumps, signaling that the cab transferred onto the track inside the mid-mountain station. The car's shaking motion jolted all three of its riders back to alertness, each one propping themselves up off their seats as if they needed to be immediately aware of their surroundings. But once the gondola doors opened, the cab began its long, slow and rather uneventful trip through the station.

Much larger than the stations located in either Mountain Village or Telluride proper, the mid-mountain station acted as more than just a halfway point between the two. It served as a full-scale base and recreation center for the resort's guests.

Because of that fact, Chris was not too happy spending more time there than he had to. "I don't like this. We're just sitting here in a confined space with the doors open."

While looking around at the empty yet, expansive gondola station, it seemed as if Peter shared Chris's concern but was pragmatic with the group's decision making. "Well, what would you have us do? Get out, run to the other side, and jump in another cab closer to the exit?"

The otherwise sarcastic comment lit a spark of inspiration on Chris's face, one which both Stephanie and Peter took notice of. A moment later Chris darted his body out of its seat and in the direction of the gondola's open door.

He was barely outside the cab when he heard Stephanie ready herself to get up as well. "I guess that was a yes."

Without waiting for his companions to follow, Chris began his swift jog towards the other end of the station. He wanted to keep his eyes ahead. To remain focused on the task. But as he approached the halfway mark, something at the side of the station grabbed his attention.

At first, it was a noise. Perhaps the light tapping of footsteps. Loud enough that he could hear them but too soft for the others to notice from their position back at the cab. Chris stopped as soon as he heard it but fought the urge to look. He knew no good could come from his curiosity, but it eventually became too much to resist.

Chris turned his head just in time to see a male figure disappear down into the stairwell. But before the man entered the darkness, Chris caught enough glimpse of his face to see the old, wrinkled features of his ski patrol partner.

Chris couldn't tell exactly what his first reaction was upon spotting him. Relief. Worry. Shock. Fear. Truthfully he hadn't thought about Phil since he took off down the mountain with their patient in the sled behind him. When they parted ways, Chris told himself he was going to check in and make sure his partner got down safely, but he never got the chance to, for obvious reasons.

In the instant it took Phil to disappear down the stairs, Chris had to once again fight his prodding curiosity. He knew he shouldn't chase after him. The chances of his partner being himself were slim. Why else would he simply stroll downstairs like the mountain wasn't in a crisis? Or why would he take shelter in the station at all? But when it came time for him to make a decision, years of brotherhood and loyalty overcame every logical bone in Chris's body. His partner was down there. Probably infected as one of those things. But "probably" wasn't good enough. He needed to know.

Just as Stephanie and Peter reached his side, Chris started walking in the direction of the stairwell. For a moment, they both just stood there watching in disbelief, almost confused that the hardened ski patroller started wandering deeper into the station. There was an awkward silence between them as if they were both hoping Chris would just turn back on his own accord, but when he didn't, Stephanie was the one to verbalize her bewilderment. "Does he realize that is the exact opposite of what we were planning to do?"

Her pointless question was immediately followed by Peter yelling out to Chris as the patroller continued to approach the stairwell. "What are you doing?"

He responded midstride, without ever looking back over his shoulder. "I thought I saw something. Just gimme a minute."

As Chris continued his walk towards the stairwell he didn't hear any more discussion from the two behind him, but he didn't hear any more footsteps either. They must've been staring at each other, silently deciding whether to ditch him, join him, or simply wait for him to return (if he returned at all). After several seconds, though, just as Chris reached the top of the stairs, he heard the combined clatter of snow and ski boots hitting the floor as Steph and Peter jogged in his direction.

They eventually caught up to him halfway through the stairwell, and together the group emerged into the hallway of the station's lower level. Moving across the speckled carpet floor, Stephanie was the only one to browse through the old framed photographs hanging on the walls. She wanted to stop and read the captions under each one, but Chris and Peter, both of whom had traversed the station more times than they could count, had no interest in slowing down their pace for her. So she was forced to quickly scan the aged black and white photos that depicted the mountain's history.

The first few pictures were of nineteenth-century miners and their families stoically posing in front of their settlement. But gradually, the photos shifted into color and showed old time skiers in one-piece snowsuits, happily christening the resort during its early years. It was a visual story of rebirth that Stephanie unexpectedly found herself getting sucked into. Until, of course, she reached the end of the hall where it opened up into the fine dining restaurant nestled at the bottom of the station.

The restaurant's entrance was located on a hostess deck above the main dining floor and opposite a long wall of windows that allowed the powerful sun to beam light all along the room. Situated on a well-designed perch in the mountainside, the restaurant's view offered one that justified the menu's steep price tag. Through the glass, lunch patrons could casually gaze out upon a pristine row of Rocky Mountain peaks that pierced into the clear blue skyline.

It was a breathtaking view, indeed. But Chris, Peter and Stephanie were more awestruck by the large crowd of belligerent people wandering around the dining room floor. Made up of all different ages, sexes, and races, the gathering was a strange sight as its attendees continuously grumbled and moaned while walking around the restaurant's tables and chairs. There was no talking, stopping or communication of any kind. In fact, it wasn't until the trio looked closer that they noticed the people's dumbfounded faces were covered in red.

Each one wanted to move forward and get a closer look at the floor below them. But they had yet to be spotted, and none of them wanted to be the first to alert the strange, zombie-like people to their presence.

For almost a full minute they all stood there watching the overcrowded group drift about without any rhyme or reason until Stephanie ended the silence. "What are they doing?"

With Peter too concentrated to answer, Chris responded to the girl's question. "I don't know."

Still not satisfied, Steph posed a follow up. "They kinda look infected, but why aren't they all crazy like the others?"

And once again, Chris was the one to offer a response. "If I knew that I would've answered your first question."

Finally deciding to join the discussion, Peter offered a more specific topic of conversation. "I'm more concerned about what's on their faces."

Feeling that it was his responsibility to address all inquiries, Chris squinted his eyes to try and focus in on the crowd below. "It looks like…is that…blood?"

And as soon as he uttered the last word, a louder, more hostile version of the zombie moan pulled the group's attention back behind them.

They all turned together and were instantly met by an old, bearded man whose twisted, pain-filled face was completely covered in the blood oozing from his eyes, nose, and mouth. To Stephanie and Peter, the horrific man before them was just another victim of the mysterious terror plaguing the mountain, but Chris immediately recognized him as Phillip O'Neill.

His former partner was so close that by the time Chris turned around Phil was practically on top of him, pushing him down to the ground. Caught off guard by the sudden attack, they both fell hard to the floor, and before he knew what was going on, Chris was frantically fighting to keep Phil's bloody face away from his own.

The whole incident happened so fast that neither Stephanie nor Peter had time to form an emotion. As soon as they saw their companion go down, the odd pair was already pulling at the crazed ski patroller pinning Chris to the ground.

With his mouth wide open, desperately trying to latch his teeth onto Chris's face, Phil continued to let out a loud groan, which bubbled from the large quantities of loose blood dripping into his mouth. His noisy grunts only added to the loud racket caused by the struggle. And it wasn't long before the fight caught the attention of the horde roaming aimlessly around the restaurant floor.

First it was just one curious busboy, turning to the restaurant's entrance with a slightly confused look on his bloody, emotionless face. Then it was a female skier, who also turned to the noise with the same blank expression. One by one the loud struggle grabbed the attention of every zombified guest, and they all began a brisk, lumbering walk in the direction of the commotion.

"Get him off me!" Chris screamed over and over again while Stephanie and Peter continued to pull at his assailant's arms and legs. But Phil frantically flailed his limbs about, squirming around while continuing his pursuit of Chris's flesh.

Amidst the skirmish, Stephanie's eyes glanced up to see the blundering horde moving towards them like a clumsy, disorganized wave. At first, she was slightly intrigued that they weren't running like the ravenous monsters she'd met earlier, but the danger was still very real and far outweighed her curiosity. "We gotta leave. Now!"

With his hands already wrapped around Phil's head, the exclamation in Stephanie's voice prompted Chris to quickly jam his thumbs into his attacker's eye sockets. It was an unnatural feeling, voluntarily forcing his fingers to penetrate the soft, mushy tissue of Phil's eyeballs. And it did nothing but add to the waterfall of blood already pouring down onto Chris's face. But the attack caused Phil to let out a strange, animal-like shrill as his body slowly went limp.

For Chris, it felt just as physically awkward removing his fingers from Phil's eye sockets as it did sending them in. But that was nothing to the emotional anguish he experienced having killed the man who taught him so much. Chris knew he had no choice, and technically, Phil might've already been dead.

But it didn't hurt any less as he pushed the bloody corpse off him and onto the restaurant floor. "Sorry, old friend. Goodbye."

Now free from the body pinning him down, Peter and Stephanie began pulling at Chris to stand up. But the heartbroken ski patroller wasn't nearly moving as fast as they hoped, and Peter let him know it. "Pull yourself together! Come on!"

With his eyes still stuck on Phil's lifeless body, Chris started to look up and saw the advancing horde was a lot closer (and larger) than he thought. The immediate danger pumped adrenaline throughout his body, shocking his system back into action and causing him to scramble to his feet.

Once Steph and Peter realized their partner finally summed up a sense of urgency, they all took off together, backtracking their way through the station. In his light and less cumbersome footwear, Peter led the pack while Stephanie and Chris trailed behind, struggling to run and climb the stairs in their bulky ski boots.

But even with their awkward pace, Chris still managed to take several quick glances behind them and see that their pursuers were struggling to keep up. The mob's brisk, uncoordinated walk caused several of the stupefied zombies to trip over one another as they bumped and blundered their way down the hall. Like Stephanie before him, Chris most definitely noticed a change in these fiends from the others. But also like Stephanie, he didn't stop to further investigate his curiosity.

Once they reached the top of the stairs, the group entered back into the station's gondola dock and it wasn't the same desolate place they were in before. The commotion they caused had spread throughout the building, attracting more of the delirious, bleeding madmen up from other stairwells on either side of them. The floor was quickly filling up with the bumbling zombies converging on the center of the room.

Although they didn't expect to see more of the horde in front of them, the fleeing survivors never stopped to question where they all came from. They continued on their path, passing through the two slow lines of gondola cars moving in either direction.

With the blundering mess of clumsy zombies on their trail, the group headed for the gondola car closest to the Telluride side of the station. As soon as they reached it, the three of them dove inside the still open cab, hoping they were finally safe. But when the door didn't close behind them and the cab still continued its slow crawl towards the exit, they realized their dramatic escape didn't go exactly as they planned.

Their quick pants for air suddenly stopped as they all turned back around to see the zombie horde quickly approaching them. The two adults kept their eyes out the window, but Stephanie saw fit to express her frustration. "Great. Now we're in the very situation we were trying to avoid. I hope you're happy."

Leading the pack outside the cab was a large woman in a ski suit, and even through a deranged, bloody face, Chris still recognized her as the patient Phillip took down the mountain on his stretcher. At the sight of her, the young ski patroller wanted to feel hatred, but she came around the gondola car so quickly he didn't have time to draw upon the emotion.

The large woman, crazed and covered in blood, stuck her right arm and head through the door, swiping at the passengers pressed up against the back wall of the cab. When it became clear that her prey were just out of reach, the woman tried to enter the moving gondola car completely. But just as she started to pull her body inside, the cab's automatic doors began to close.

Completely oblivious of her surroundings, the demented woman gave another long reach into the car when the doors firmly sealed against her chest. Suddenly aware of her predicament, the large woman became as frantic as her humdrum disposition would allow as her body slowly dragged against the station floor.

A second later, the gondola hit another series of consecutive bumps, just as it did upon the group's arrival, and then departed the station along the cable down to the town below. Her body still pinned between the gondola's doors, the blood-soaked woman hung suspended in mid-air high above the mountainside.

With the gondola car steadily descending into town, she kicked her feet around hopelessly while continuing to moan and swipe at the people in front of her. Even under the circumstances though, the sick stranger wasn't so much asking for help but desperately trying to complete her hunt in what little moments she had left. The only difference now was that the once cornered passengers were no longer backing away from her in fear but looking on at the helpless woman with a morbid sense of fascination.

When the pitiful sight became too much to bear, Chris finally leaned off the gondola's back wall and began repeatedly kicking the top of the woman's head, forcing her back through the doors inch by inch. First her shoulders poked through. Then her neck. Until a final hard blow drove the woman's head straight through the opening, sending her plummeting down to the mountain below.

In what little time the gondola doors remained open before finally closing behind her, Chris expected to hear some type of scream from the falling woman. Or perhaps even some kind of animal-like shriek or cry. But there was only silence. Almost as if the human being had been transformed into a creature ignorant of death.

With the adrenaline in his system starting to putter out, Chris fell back onto the gondola's seat and stared off through the window at nothing in particular. He remained in that position for about a minute when Stephanie randomly broke the still silence in the air. "Was the food there any good?"

The odd thought slowly permeated its way into Peter's brain until he ultimately turned to her, almost offended that she would ask such an inappropriate question. "What?!"

But instead of being hurt by Peter's tone, Stephanie responded as plainly as she could. "My family had reservations."

And with that said, Peter slumped back down in his seat, allowing the stale silence to once again fill the gondola.

19

It had only been ten minutes and Bill already wanted to throw their new guest overboard. The man named Scott Brooks was just about the very reason he and Nellie tried to stay out of town as much as possible. Well, not him specifically. But his kind: rich city folk who felt entitled to this little corner of nature's paradise.

Not that their presence was a complete burden. Telluride certainly wouldn't be flourishing the way it had been without their money. But why did they have to be so loud?

Bill was experiencing firsthand what Travis Walker had known for quite some time: Mr. Brooks was an asshole. With their new passenger firmly planted in the middle of them, the three amigos sat together in the bed of the pickup as Nellie drove the truck back into town.

Just to make sure it wasn't a viable option (and to get their new arrival to shut up about it), she drove up to the airport and passed the tarmac. Luckily, the steepest part of the road up to the terminal was plowed not too long ago, a feat which Mr. Brooks for some reason took credit for. Bill suspected he was lying, though.

Unfortunately, the rest of the runway wasn't as favorable. It was heavily shoveled and plowed, another task Scott said he was responsible for arranging. But the clear pavement was now covered in blood, bodies and crashed airplanes.

Bill briefly wondered how the plague could infect this far corner of the valley, which, as far as he could tell, was spared from an attack during the storm. Scott Brooks wasn't surprised about it, though. And so Bill refrained from inquiring.

But that didn't stop Brooks from rambling on about everything else. First he began by championing his will to survive (while offering a brief eulogy for his bodyguard and pilots). He then moved on to criticize the town's handling of the crisis. The marshal was wisely silent when Scott began bashing the police's failure to subdue the lunatics. And it was only when the truck crossed over into town that he began actively challenging the group's plan to return to Telluride.

Bill was actually surprised it had taken him that long to speak up about it, but when he did, Mr. Brooks proved that he was indeed a very opinionated person. "I don't get it. Why are we going back to the place filled with homicidal maniacs?"

Both of the other men in the back of the pickup had enough of their companion's bickering, but Marshal Walker, the younger of the two, sacrificed himself by engaging Brooks in conversation. "Montrose is over an hour away and we have no way of knowing what the roads are like. There's a good chance we'd get stuck on them in the middle of the night."

"Yeah. A chance I'd be willing to take."

Upon realizing that humoring the man was pointless, Travis let out an exhausted sigh while leaning back against the cab. "Great. When we get back you can find a vehicle, dig it out of the snow, and hit the road."

Like a proud father, Scott reached over and slapped the side of the truck. "No way. I'm taking this tank, baby. How much you want for it?"

The marshal just shook his head. "It's not mine to sell."

"Fine. Point me in the direction of the owner."

Marshal Walker barely looked up to give a slight nod in Bill's direction. Brooks then wasted no time relocating his obnoxious charm to its new target. "All right, Buffalo Bill. What're these set of wheels gonna cost me? Name your price."

The old man let out a short chuckle to himself at how quickly the conversation shifted. "My price? Mister, if you don't say another word for the rest of the trip then nothing would make me happier than watching you drive this truck away from me."

With a sly smile stretched across his face, Scott slapped Mr. Sheridan on the back as if they were nothing more than old friends. "And what do ya know. The sooner you hand over the keys the sooner our time together can end."

Bypassing the man between them, Bill leaned forward to make eye contact directly with Travis, completely ignoring Scott's seemingly unlimited confidence. "Man doesn't seem to understand the concept of a deal, Marshal."

Travis kept his laughter to himself, but Bill could tell that even Mr. Brooks was amused by the comment. The man displayed an odd grimace with a slightly menacing smirk, almost as if he took pity on the old man for not accepting his offer. Bill couldn't understand why, but then again, he didn't much care to. As the two of them continued to silently stare at one another following their short-lived business negotiation, Bill decided to amend his earlier conclusion: Scott Brooks wasn't just an asshole. He was a devious one.

The look between them persisted for several more seconds until it was broken off by a sudden jerk of the truck. The brakes quickly locked up, causing the wheels to slide on the snow before coming to a complete stop several feet later.

Bill looked around and soon realized they were nowhere near the Town Hall. He then stood up and peeked over the truck to see the gondola in full motion. "Was that thing on when we left?"

He looked over at the two men next to him. Their attention, however, was not focused up ahead but on the ground in front of the truck. Bill followed their eyes and caught sight of a girl with purple hair lying face down in the middle of the snowy street. His first reaction to jump out of the bed was matched by the marshal, and Nellie did the same from her driver's seat.

Brooks was expectedly clueless as to what was going on, but Bill was glad to see Hunter and Molly resume their roles as lookouts as he and the others ran to the girl's side. Before they even bent down next to her Marshal Walker already had the girl identified. "It's Georgia Croft. She works at the radio station."

The Sheridans didn't bother much with local radio, which was why they just looked at each other clueless. But for those who lived in town, a local DJ with purple hair was hard to miss, especially for a marshal.

Not knowing who she was, though, didn't stop Bill from reaching down and feeling the girl's neck above a raw piece of flesh. "She's cold, but there's a pulse."

"Of course, I'm cold. I've been lying in snow."

Bill nearly fell backwards when the girl spoke, and it took him a moment to shake off his fright. Neither Nellie nor Travis, who weren't nearly as close to the girl when she uttered the words, shared his extreme disbelief. But they still took a moment to register what Georgia said. She didn't bother to move or even open her eyes, which made them feel a bit uncomfortable.

And when they failed to respond, she continued on from the same position. "Would you mind helping me up? I think I have icicles in my bloodstream."

Finally realizing that they left the poor girl lying in the snow, the three of them gently scrambled to lift her. As her rescuers sat her up, Miss Croft finally tightened up her face, using much more effort than normally required for a person to simply open their eyelids. "Thanks. If I could lift my arms I'd probably be giving you all hugs."

Always in need to be the hero, Travis positioned himself ready to lift the girl up. "You want us to carry you inside the truck?"

But she carefully waved away his offer before placing her hand against her tired face. "In a minute. Just let me remember how to be awake first."

The two men honored the girl's request. Nellie, however, was more interested in information, particularly about the dead body lying close by. "What happened? Did that thing chase you out here?"

"No. And if I could've run I don't think he would've been chasing me anywhere."

Curious by Georgia's comment, Nellie scrunched her brow before asking a follow-up. "What do you mean?"

"He was different than the ones people described on the phone. Different than my friend who attacked me. Crazy, sure, but not wild crazy. Slow and clunky. Sounded weird, too. Like he just didn't have the energy to be all psycho anymore."

The description made Nellie even more intrigued than before. She opened her mouth to ask another question, but before the words left her mouth, she was cut off by a loud, lengthy moan of agony and despair from deeper in the town. The long, monstrous wail rang out over Telluride's snowy rooftops. A strange noise that sounded like that of a twisted and deformed human voice.

Bill and those around him instantly turned to face the direction from which the freakish groan came from. And as the drawn out sound finally came to a stop, Georgia was the only one not surprised to hear it. "He sounded kinda like that."

***

Despite her current situation not being ideal, Beth felt lucky to be alive. She was neither dressed nor physically up for trekking through the deep snow that covered the streets. But anything was better than being left for dead.

She would've preferred to get somewhere safe or, at least, find a phone. Beth was curious as to how Peter was holding out, and she hadn't spoken to her boyfriend since the night before. Dr. Morris was adamant about fulfilling her journey to the pharmacy, though, and Beth felt a nagging obligation towards the woman. She didn't want to owe the doctor a debt. Beth made sure to have the upper hand in most relationships for this very reason. But she was grateful for what Dr. Morris did for her and wouldn't leave the woman's side until the favor was repaid.

In spite of the age gap between them, the two ladies made perfectly good small talk while venturing through the abandoned streets. Their conversation consisted of the usual topics. Where do you work? How long have you lived in Telly? Do you snowboard or ski? And when those talking points were exhausted, Beth moved on to a more pressing subject: the crisis at hand.

Anna had very little answers to her questions, though. The main one being where did all the crazy people go? The doctor had been cooped up inside her clinic for most of the attack. She hadn't even seen an infected person yet. Although she expected her clinic to be filled with them shortly. And that fear was the very reason that drove her to take this little expedition.

The two of them soon found the small pharmacy nestled neatly into a typical Telluride city block. The tight buildings gave the store that old Western charm, which the town was famous for. But both women, having lived here for some time, had gotten used to Telluride's nostalgic ambiance. They barely gave the pharmacy's snow-covered façade a second thought as they passed by it and opened the door.

What they found inside, though, was a different story entirely. As soon as the door creaked open both Beth and Anna's mouths dropped open in shock. The small, community pharmacy had been taken over by a large and diverse crowd of zombie-like guests. The strange people weren't violent, though. And none of them moved very fast. They just kind of lumbered about, moaning sporadically and roaming around the tight quarters in all different directions.

The two women standing at the doorway were more surprised than afraid and stood quietly for a solid minute while observing the weird scene before them. Neither one of them dared to move. Probably because the oblivious wanderers remained unaware (or uncaring) of their presence. But to Beth, the most bizarre part of all was the fresh blood covering the zombified people's faces. Every one of them seemed to be bleeding from every spot they could be bleeding from. Eyes. Ears. Nose. Their cheeks, chins, and mouths were completely drenched in crimson streaks that continued to drip to the floor.

For a second, Beth thought this might be the answer to the question pressing on her mind: what happened to the huge mob of people that attacked the town?

But there was a problem with her theory. One which Anna wanted to verbally confirm. "Are these the raging lunatics everyone's been talking about?"

In awe, Beth addressed her question while staring at the peculiar sight before her. "Maybe. But they're...different."

After continuing her observations for another second, Anna began digging into her pocket. "Well, one thing they definitely are is sick. So I'm not taking any chances."

Curious, Beth turned to the doctor and watched as she pulled out a surgical mask. "Do you have one for me?"

"Why? Are you planning on going in there, too?"

Anna then proceeded to put the mask on while Beth's face again grew long from shock. "You're going in there?!"

With the mask secured around her mouth, Dr. Morris carefully took a step forward into the pharmacy. "I came to get something, and I'm not leaving until I have it."

After her first step, Anna began tiptoeing around the sluggish zombies as they aimlessly moved about. Their slow movements made it easy for the brave (or stupid) woman to slip around and navigate through the tight crowd without touching anyone. Her deliberate and carefully placed steps took her all the way through the drug store aisles and to the pharmacy counter located at the back.

During the doctor's harrowing journey, Beth stood in the doorway, physically chewing the tips of her nails. Just watching her new companion fearlessly plunge into the crowd of hemorrhaging zombies filled her with enough anxiety to send her into a panic attic.

Beth wanted to take off. To just turn around and run away, never bothering to look back. She could find a nice hiding spot somewhere. Maybe even make it back to her boyfriend's house up in Mountain Village now that the gondola was on. His big mansion would be the perfect place to just wait for all this insanity to blow over.

Sticking with Anna was going to get her killed. This woman didn't know what she was doing. She hadn't seen what these things were really capable of. For all she knew every infected creature was just as harmless as the catatonic, moaning sleepwalkers they're dealing with now. How could she be a doctor? Only a mentally ill person would walk right in the middle of those things. She's crazy. But even knowing all that, Beth still couldn't abandon the person who saved her.

So she stood there anxiously waiting and watching as Dr. Morris searched through the pharmacy shelves in the back. It wasn't long before the doctor turned around and gave Beth a smiling wave, signaling that her mission was a success.

With a small plastic bag in hand, Anna hopped back over the counter and began retracing her steps. But Beth soon saw that Anna was moving much more quickly than she had on her first trip around. The excitement at having found what she was looking for made the doctor a little more confident in her steps. She took less time deciding where to place her feet and body as she moved about the bloody human carousel.

And as she drew within ten feet of Beth at the door, Dr. Morris placed her foot down on something that didn't feel quite like the floor.

Praying and hoping that she didn't step where she thought she did, Anna looked down to see that her boot was on top of a rather large, bloodstained sneaker.

The careless woman immediately cringed at the sight as a teeth-clattering shiver ran its way down her backside. She then slowly looked up, once again hoping that she wasn't going to see what she expected. But as the doctor's gaze came upright, she was met by a man's menacing, stone-like face covered in blood.

Anna didn't move, not so much because she was paralyzed by fear, but because she was wishing by some miracle the terrifying man would ignore that she had stepped on his foot. For a second it seemed like he would. The man's vacant, bloodshot eyes just blankly stared into Anna's, his gaze locked in a stranglehold around her face.

But just as she felt comfortable enough to lift her foot for another step, the man's jaw dropped open and unleashed a horrible, deafening moan louder than anything Beth had heard in her life. The sound almost seemed demonic in nature and rang out through the pharmacy door before echoing all across the valley. Beth and Anna both instinctively covered their ears but not without noticing that every other zombie in the building had now stopped their mindless walking and turned to face them.

The monstrous groan continued on much longer than any human voice should linger. And as soon as it was done, the rest of the crowd began closing in on Anna, reaching their arms out and grasping in her direction. Immediately recognizing the danger, the feisty doctor ducked her head and sprinted the remaining ten feet towards the door, barreling through a series of grabby hands and clunky bodies in her way.

Still holding onto the plastic bag, Anna joined Beth just outside the pharmacy, and the two began running back the way they came. With high knees, the women moved as fast as they could by placing their steps back in their pre-made footprints. It was an awkward yet effective way to traverse the deep snow.

At first, Beth and Anna continued running out of fear that the crowd from the pharmacy might be chasing after them. But as they pulled away from the block, a new threat forced them to keep up their pace. The doors to the buildings on either side of the street started opening one by one, unleashing wave after wave of the same blood-soaked zombies. As if the loud moan acted as a call to arms, crowds of the sluggish brutes emerged from the stores and poured out into the snowy streets.

Although they moved hastily, the bumbling fiends couldn't run. Their bodies just floundered around while moving forward in an uncoordinated speed-walk through the snow. They tripped and blundered about, even occasionally falling over one another.

Beth didn't consider any single one of them an immediate danger. Not like the ravenous mob that came barreling down the mountainside in the blizzard. But what they lacked in veracity, these new kind of monsters made up for in numbers.

Once they passed the spot where she was found, Beth quickly fell in line behind Anna. For several more blocks the two women refused to stop while the moaning creatures continued to close in on them, never bothering to pay any attention to the snow slowing them down. In typical zombie fashion, Beth's pursuers threw their arms around as they drew nearer, grasping at air with every close attempt.

It wasn't until the school came in sight that the two women finally departed from the town's streets and broke free from the rolling wave of deranged infected. But even though they started to pull away from the people chasing them, Beth locked onto Anna's back like a target as they continued on their path to the gymnasium's side door. The young girl began pushing through the small burn in her thighs for the last leg of their mad dash and then finally burst through the gym's entrance right behind Anna.

Out of breath and overheated, the two women fell back against the closing door just as a young male nurse approached them. "Anna! Where'd you go? You shouldn't be outside."

He then locked the door's handle above their heads as Dr. Morris addressed him with the surgical mask still covering her mouth. "It's OK. I got the meds. Start trying them out on the quarantined patients."

Anna held out the plastic bag still clutched in her hands, and the nurse accepted it with a confused look on his face before silently returning to the makeshift clinic. Dr. Morris watched him take several steps and then yelled out before the young man disappeared out of sight. "And double check the doors going outside!"

For a moment, the two women remained silent while staring out across the gymnasium. Neither said a word or bothered to look at one another. Despite their recent escape, they both felt content and relaxed.

The quiet remained for a solid minute before Beth eventually broke it without ever turning her head. "Tell me: you didn't think that mask was actually going to do anything, did you?"

Already having the answer ready, Anna still took a breath before deciding to respond. "Only for my bravery."

20

When the gondola car began its descent into town the sun was already on its way back behind the mountain range on the far side of the valley. It'd been a full minute since they relieved their cab of its unwelcome passenger, and unlike the ride up to the mid-mountain station, the group's nerves failed to fade away.

Peter, Chris, and Stephanie all sat at the edge of their seats, anxiously awaiting their arrival into town. After departing Mountain Village, they each felt composed and at least somewhat in control of the situation. Without any communication with the authorities in Telluride, their plan to head into town seemed logical, practical and the best option at the time.

But after their encounter with the strange horde of zombies infesting the mid-mountain station, the reality of the crisis started to sink in. They truly had no idea what they were up against. And if such a dangerous threat was hiding in such a small, inconvenient place, their imaginations ran wild as to what could be waiting for them in the town below.

The silent minute allowed their wandering minds to dwell on the grim truth of the situation until Chris became the first to vocalize what everyone was feeling. "I'm beginning to think this was a stupid idea."

Having been the one who thought of the plan (mainly out of desperation for his son), Peter felt it was his responsibility to respond. "Probably. But we need to assess the situation in town. With nobody answering their phone this was our only option."

Peter looked to Chris for a follow-up, but it was Steph who stated the obvious. "And if they're all dead?"

"Then we'll just hop back on the gondola."

Stephanie took the opportunity to stare at the Village Manager with an exaggerated girly smile before offering her response. "So we can venture into the zombie infested station again? Great."

Peter ignored the girl's sarcastic comment by turning his focus to the gondola's front facing window. In the few minutes since the second half of their ride began, the sun managed to creep downward a little below the Rocky Mountain ridgeline, showering the sky with the beginnings of a red sunset. There was still enough power behind the star's shine to light up the snow globe-like picture perfect view of Telluride only the gondola could provide. For Peter and Chris, both of whom had taken this ride more times than they could count, it was an odd display to see the town so engulfed in white.

But from their aerial view high off the mountainside, there was an odd addition that stood out from within the familiar sight. Between the buildings, they could see small specks littering the pristine sheets of white covering the unplowed streets. The two of them, along with Stephanie by their side, homed in on the numerous dots that moved back and forth until their approaching descent brought the figures into full view. Telluride's streets were littered with more of the walking bleeders the group had just narrowly escaped from. And one by one, the gondola's passengers dropped their jaws at the overwhelming realization that their short trip was for nothing.

By the time the cab pulled into the station, the transition from day to dusk was already in full swing. Situated more towards the base of the mountain than the town's streets, the gondola station and the surrounding area were free from the mindless, wandering murderers. So even with their spirits diminished, the group felt safe enough to exit the gondola car and enter the building. But there was little for them to do.

The discouraging sight of seeing the town so overrun by infected left the three survivors speechless. As if in a trance of disbelief, they all walked forward to the front of the station and looked out the window at the street before them.

Peter knew the isolated block they were seeing was just one corner of Telluride and not an accurate barometer for the entire town. Even from the gondola, he couldn't see every street corner. But he didn't know whether to be discouraged or comforted by that knowledge. There was always the chance, that for whatever reason, this area had the highest concentration of those things, and what he was witnessing was the whole extent of the infestation. Then again, there was also the chance that this scene was repeated on every street corner, and that the town was truly overrun.

As the gondola continued to run its course behind them, the group quietly watched for a short while longer. When the inevitable discussion began, Stephanie was once again the one to break the silence. "So, that's it? Game over?"

With his eyes still firmly locked ahead of him, Peter addressed the girl while shaking his head. "No. There might still be others out there trapped in their homes."

Chris turned to face him and struggled within himself to challenge Peter's optimism. "Maybe. But what would you have us do?"

Although it was tough to admit, Peter knew the ski patroller was right. He wanted to have a reasonable answer. Something that didn't reek of desperation and insanity. But the odds were stacked against him, and Peter could only remain silent as Chris drove his point home. "We came to see what the situation was like. And the situation is fucked. We should head back to the group we know is still alive and plan on how to get out of here."

Once again, the image of Ryan crazed and deranged slipped its way into Peter's mind. He knew coming into town was a long shot to saving his son. So long that he couldn't even see where he was aiming. But that didn't make his failure any easier to accept. He hoped that somewhere in this zombie infested town there was an answer that could save his son. And getting back on the gondola was as good as putting that twelve-year-old boy in his grave.

His companions could see Peter's logic and emotions wrestling one another in his mind. And with a face full of torment, he eventually turned to the girl standing next to him. "You agree with him?"

Almost as if she read his thoughts, Stephanie answered the question by addressing Peter's concern. "I don't have any family to worry about. So, yeah. I guess I do."

The group silently fell into an agreed acknowledgment. It was time to head back the way they came, regardless of what was waiting for them in the mid-mountain station.

The three of them lowered their heads in preparation to turn themselves around when the sound of a loud, revving engine caused them all to stop. One by one, they curiously turned back out the window to see the bumbling pack of zombies awkwardly cave in on itself in the middle of the street. The creatures in the center of the strange human funnel began clumsily running towards the back of the crowd as the engine noise grew louder.

Eventually, the wall of pushing zombies erupted when the front end of a massive truck plowed through them, entering the open space of snow in front of the station.

The group inside remained still and speechless as the truck came to a sliding stop in the snow. The four doors to the cab never opened, but a figure could be seen hopping out the bed of the truck and walking around to the front. "Hello? Is anybody here?"

As if the man's uniform didn't give him away, Peter immediately recognized the stranger as Marshal Travis Walker. He then made a move towards the door without saying a word to his companions, assuming they would simply follow him out.

Once outside, Peter waded through the snow on his way to the marshal, who squinted his eyes to get a better look at the man approaching him. "Peter, is that you?"

The Village Manager extended his arm for a greeting, which Travis readily accepted with a smile on his face. "It's good to see you, Marshal."

"We saw someone turned on the gondola and came to check it out. What are you doing here?"

"Nobody was answering their phones. I had to see how the town was doing."

Peter didn't phrase his comment as a question, but the marshal knew it had an answer. One which forced him to shamefully drop his head rather than discuss it. At that point, Stephanie and Chris joined them in front of the idling truck, and even though they hadn't been part of the conversation, Travis still addressed them alongside Peter. "There was nothing any of us could do. I just hope Mountain Village isn't as bad."

"It's quiet now but the courtyard was basically a massacre."

The marshal opened his mouth as if to continue the discussion, but a voice from the truck cut him off before he could speak. "This cute reunion is nice and all but our little game of zombie bowling kind of attracted some attention."

The four of them turned to the truck and found a man in a tarnished business suit leaning over the roof of the cab from the bed. The voice was new, but the man's face immediately struck Peter as a familiar sight. He scrunched his brow as if searching his mental database for a name to go along with it, and as the man went to speak again, the pieces clicked in Peter's mind.

He was looking at his Mountain Village neighbor: the infamous Scott Brooks. "So if you wouldn't mind getting in the fucking truck we would all greatly appreciate it."

The marshal let out an annoyed sigh, but quickly changed his reaction when he looked around the side of the truck to see a wave of bloody zombies pouring into the snow from the street. "Come on!"

Marshal Walker led the way around the truck and into the bed, where Mr. Brooks was accompanied by an older gentleman Peter didn't recognize. Once the four of them hopped in and slammed the tailgate, the old man slapped the side of the cab, signaling that it was time for them to be on their way. The loud rev of the engine was followed by a heavy clunk of shifting gears. The Ford truck then began spinning around in the snow, easily positioning itself to face the incoming flood of hobbling zombies head on.

After another rumble of a gearshift, the truck's tires rapidly sped around, searching for traction within the fluffy snow beneath them. It didn't take long for the rubber to catch, and the large pickup began clawing its way forward, barreling through the front of the galloping pack.

The first few people to connect with the truck's grill were immediately sucked underneath it. The vehicle bumped and shook as its large tires crushed those unfortunate enough to get caught in their wake, but the blood-soaked zombies' monotone moans never faltered for an instant.

Like a closing gate, those at the edges of the human wall collapsed all around the truck as it plowed on ahead. It wasn't long before the pickup moved deep enough into the never-ending mob that it became completely surrounded.

Although slow, the blundering buffoons swung their arms about trying to grab hold of the truck as it passed them by. Their bleeding bodies swayed back and forth, splashing sprays of blood against the windows.

The wave of zombies was building and growing more crowded as those around the truck pressed harder and harder to get to it. The vehicle moved just fast enough to keep it from being completely overwhelmed, though every once in a while a slow yet capable zombie managed to latch onto the side.

At first it was just one, which the marshal easily sent tumbling back to the ground with a swift kick to the head. But as more and more of the fiends began scaling the short walls of the truck, it became apparent to Peter that their moving fortress was far from impenetrable.

With six passengers in the bed, the cramped quarters made it all the more difficult to fight off the attack. Each one of them commanded a section of the pickup to defend from invaders, who were becoming more and more frequent. For the most part, they used their feet and fists to stop the agonizing faces of blood from climbing onto them, but the sound of sporadic gunfire would occasionally catch Peter by surprise. He turned back around to see the marshal and the old man standing in the middle of the bed intently aiming their side arms for more imminent threats.

Another contributing factor to the strange battle was that the truck struggled to keep up its speed. Every so often the engine would randomly rev as if the driver stepped on the gas but wouldn't go anywhere, their pace intermittently dropping against the push of the zombie horde.

Peter noticed it right away, as he assumed everyone in the truck did, but Scott Brooks was the only one to point it out to his fellow passengers in the bed. "I seem to remember us moving a lot faster on our drive down here."

As if he felt the need to defend both the truck and its driver, the old man was ready with a response. "We've added four more passengers since then."

From the opposite side of the truck as Peter, Chris chimed in while struggling with a persistent climber. "And we're going to add a lot more if we don't do something."

In regular hero fashion, Marshal Walker leaned on top of the young ski patroller and shot two bullets down into the zombie he was fighting. The creature promptly dropped off the side of the truck, and Travis stood valiantly over Chris and the others while trying to rally their spirits. "It's going to be all right. We're almost back at the Town Hall. Once there we can…" A raging savage suddenly leapt from one side of the bed to the other, cutting off the marshal's speech by tackling the man over the side of the truck.

Together, the bloodthirsty fiend and Marshal Walker tumbled down into the crowd, and the last sight Peter could see was a set of gnashing teeth drive their way into the marshal's face as the truck pulled away from him. "Travis!"

Peter hopelessly reached out for his friend. It was a weak attempt that he knew meant nothing. There was no saving someone from such an abrupt and violent end, but the old man held him back anyway while coughing under his breath.

The rest of the group remained stunned and speechless, except for Brooks, who coped with the loss by once again stating what was on everyone's mind. "I thought we were done with those crazy fucks?!?!"

Getting back to the matter at hand, Stephanie turned her attention to a crossing street, pointing out several rapid figures amidst the otherwise stumbling pack of moaners. "Apparently not."

The old man beside them followed the girl's finger and focused in on the moving objects, which soon became clear as the same rabid, deranged lunatics the resort was plagued by earlier in the day. "We've got incoming, Eleanor!"

Still in the middle of processing this new, startling information, the group's attention was suddenly snapped to the front of the truck by the loud smash of shattering glass. Peter leaned over the side of the truck to see the back end of a zombie sticking out of the passenger side window. A second later a gunshot rang out, and the zombie dropped out of the shattered window missing half its head.

The gruesome sight was just the latest added to an already long list of traumatizing events that had been thrust into Peter's life. In a matter of seconds he went from relative safety inside the gondola station to being completely surrounded on all sides by a gang of deformed, blood-drenched zombies.

He knew he needed to be strong. He needed to fight for his life and the lives of those around him. For the slim chance that his son could be saved. That his town could be saved. But after seeing Travis killed in an instant, after seeing a man (or thing) fall to the ground with half of its head torn off, Peter's mind made the decision to check out of its current location…if only for a moment.

That moment abruptly ended as the truck suddenly jerked towards the nearby sidewalk. The driver had yanked down hard on the wheel, sending the truck into a sharp turn towards the slim open space at the side of the street. As he tried to re-establish his bearings, Peter could sense the truck's brakes lock up and the tires begin their sliding halt through the snow.

Not a second after the truck came to a complete stop did the driver's door fling open and out stepped a mean, old woman holding a mini-hunting rifle in one hand. "Everybody out! Now!"

Her command was immediately followed by the other doors flying open and the passengers in the bed quickly hopping over the side. The woman moved through the snow around to the passenger side of the truck, where she helped another older gentlemen, injured with profuse amounts of blood pouring from his neck, out of the truck. Two other women came out of the backseat, but Peter was too caught up in their escape to get a good look at them.

"This way!" The rough, wheezing voice was that of the old man from the bed, who led the group off of the snowy street and towards a series of freestanding houses further up the block.

The free space around the truck wasn't free for long. The flowing wave of lumbering zombies flooded in that direction just as the few pale and bloodthirsty fiends broke free from the pack. They took off ahead of the others as the survivors made their way towards a small cabin isolated from the other houses.

The old man coughed horribly during the mad dash to the front door but still managed to be the first inside. He held it open as Peter and the others sprinted through. A few seconds later, the old woman, still clutching onto her rifle, made it with the injured man around her shoulder. Once inside, she moved to the back of the room and dropped him down to the floor. The old man at the door then slammed it shut just in time to lock out the lunatics approaching the front porch.

For a few more moments, the tension in the silent room lingered, just to make sure the crazed attackers didn't find some other way inside. And without the sound of a crash or any other type of forced entry, the whole group let out a unified sigh of relief, knowing that they were safe…at least for the moment.

Still at the front of the house, the old man leaned forward against the door as if to catch his breath along with the others but then spoke with an agitated grumble in his voice after a series of deep, hoarse coughs. "I shouldn't have let you drive, Eleanor. You didn't know what the fuck you were doing!"

He then turned around and began screaming in the faces of the shocked audience in the room. "And now it's your fault we're in this God damn…!"

A loud gunshot rang out from the back of the room and the top of the man's head suddenly exploded in an instant.

Although more intense and disgusted, the stunned expressions remained all around. Only now the onlookers shifted their dumbfounded stares to the back of the room, where the old woman was still aiming the mini-rifle to where her victim stood.

Nobody made a sound. Nobody made a move. They simply remained still, speechless and motionless, as the woman blankly lowered her rifle and took a slow, deep breath of reflection. "In over forty years of marriage, my husband never raised his voice to me. Not once. So whatever I just shot…wasn't him."

PART III
AVALANCHE

21

The air was strangely tense inside the barracks. Every one of the guardsmen felt it, but none had the courage to address the odd silence between them. As soldiers, they were certainly used to the extreme nerves and jitters that preceded an operation. The anticipation and impending excitement were nothing new. But something was different this time, and they all sensed it as they prepared for deployment.

Like most missions, the soldiers wouldn't know where they were going or any other details until they were called into the briefing room. But rumors and speculation were already slowly circulating around the room one quiet exchange of words at a time.

Something was happening in Telluride. And the massive blitzkrieg of a storm had nothing to do with it. Whatever little contact the men had with the outside world was driving both their imagination and fear of what was in store for them. Was it a riot? A plague? Some kind of hysteria fueled epidemic? Radio broadcasts and grainy (yet violent) cell phone videos had stopped coming out of the small ski resort. And the news reports (all of which the soldiers were only hearing about second hand) were scrambling to paint a picture of what was going on.

In the command center building adjacent to the barracks, the unit's three commanders were using the data available to them to do just that. There wasn't much in terms of intelligence. Besides several recorded phone calls from the mayor, the only evidence of the incident they had the media already made public.

The lingering storm patterns made any flyover of the mountainous terrain impossible. However, the air was clear enough over Telluride to allow satellites a clear shot of what became of the town. What the imagery showed, though, made the hardened military men curious, to say the least. The streets were barren, filled with a sleek sheet of untouched snow that extended over every rooftop in view. The blizzard ate up every building in the valley and spat it out with a pristine coating of snow. There was not a single body in sight, and the entire community had seemingly become a ghost town completely consumed by the storm.

The men didn't know what to make of it. Their superiors higher up on the military and political food chain weren't offering any guidance, either. One thing was clear, though: the governor wanted boots on the ground, and that made their decision simple enough.

But despite all the uncertainty and anxiety felt by the troops, the confidence in the command room was apparent to all who were in it. The only real obstacle was going to be getting through the unplowed road that normally brought cars to and from the isolated town. But the military surely had vehicles that were more than capable of making the trip.

Other than that, the commanders were hard pressed to imagine a scenario that could give them any trouble. After all, what problems could arise in a small town that was populated by hippies and the one percent? They would be armed with much more firepower than they would probably need and well equipped to handle any possible chemical or biological agent in the area.

Contrary to the publicity surrounding the mission, the commanders were expecting a relatively uneventful evening. So in a few short hours, with a planned ETA of just after midnight, their troops would enter the mountain town and bring order back to Telluride.

***

Stephanie still couldn't believe the old hag blew her husband's head off. What was even more shocking, though, was the manner in which she recruited help to move the body to the back of the house. The woman was cold and focused, but her determination felt familiar to Stephanie. It was a state of being that, in the past few hours, the teenage girl found herself experiencing for the first time.

She didn't know exactly the moment when her mind retreated into a hardened, callous shell. It could have been when her brother attacked her or when Chris drove his ski into her father's chest. Perhaps she fell into despair when they stumbled across the chairlift's wreckage. Or maybe even when she committed herself to dropping a crazed little boy with a single punch to the face. Most likely it was a combination of all those events that slowly chipped away at the soft girl she used to be at the surface. And looking back over the past twelve hours, Stephanie was surprised at how quickly she changed over the course of a single day.

Now she found herself in a strange house with six other people she didn't know when she woke up this morning. Upon arrival, the tension in the room was obvious. Their dramatic escape had rattled some nerves and put the survivors in an awkward position. But as the minutes ticked on, conversation began to percolate between them. At first, there were merely soft introductions. An exchange of names and a brief re-telling of stories while Chris used whatever was around the house to patch up the injured man's wound.

Then the more curious attendees started strolling over to the windows. Darkness had completely covered the town except for the small and quaint street lamps sporadically placed down the main streets. Within their faint light, silhouettes of the zombie crowd could be seen slowly roaming about without any cause or direction. It was hard to tell exactly through the blackness, but there seemed to be more of them than when the group first arrived. A lot more. So much so that the truck they drove in couldn't be seen, completely engulfed by the wandering horde.

As the scattered conversations picked up around the room, Stephanie noticed one set of voices starting to ring out above the rest. It was that of Peter and the old woman who killed her husband. She introduced herself earlier as Nellie Sheridan, and Steph recognized the name from a Telluride tourist guidebook.

But as the woman spoke, she didn't exactly come off as the fun-loving cowgirl her ad made her out to be. "All those years the council fought me and not once did you have my back. But I knew you personally placed restrictions on that mine. So don't tell me you didn't have an idea of what was going on."

Always the diplomat, Peter addressed her while doing his best to diffuse the tension. "You're desperate to place blame, Mrs. Sheridan. I get it. But nobody could've predicted this."

"Bullshit. I saw the men up there months ago in their white space suits. Nothing goes on in this valley without me knowing about it. And it certainly looked like you had something to hide."

Nellie's words froze the small chatter in the room as everyone turned to face her. They all had on the same curiously baffled expression, and the awkward silence persisted until Chris broke it by speaking directly to the village manager. "What's she talking about?"

Peter bashfully laughed off the insinuation. "It's not what you think."

But Chris pressed on. "Then start explaining."

Peter sighed and took a deep breath as he thought how best to tell the story. "A couple years ago we started thinking about expanding the ski resort's terrain towards the old mining settlement. The board of trustees finally started considering it, but first they sent an environmental team to survey the area. They found some…discrepancies with the soil. The team wanted to do additional testing but since the board already ruled against our proposal for expansion they didn't see the point."

The room collectively gasped, but Chris was again the one to vocalize his frustration. "Didn't see the point?! You're telling me this whole outbreak could've been prevented and…"

Peter put out his arms to defend himself from the verbal assault. "Whoa. Hold on a minute. It wasn't like they found some zombie virus in the dirt. There were abnormal minerals and bacteria. Nothing that could cause this."

After being emotionally exhausted from the day's events, Stephanie took the news with nothing more than a simple shrug of her shoulders. "Well, something did."

Knowing the sacrifices Peter had made for Telluride's sister community, Molly felt obligated to step in and defend him. "Leave the man alone. This isn't his fault."

However, Nellie was quick to scold her. "And I'm sure you have a better theory as to what caused this?"

"I do. The mine…it's cursed." Neither Nellie nor anyone else in the room knew how to respond. And Molly went on only after realizing they wanted her to explain. "I'm a history teacher so I know all about this region. Ute Native Americans used to make camp up and down the San Miguel River until Spanish explorers ran them out. But before they left, those Indians put a curse deep within the mountains to protect its riches. That's what happened to those miners. And it's happening to us now, too."

After another brief pause of bafflement, Scott threw his hands in the air as if the discussion was final. "There you go. Magic curses. Anybody else wanna add something?"

Georgia, from her position in the corner of the room, chimed in with a soft addition. "Don't forget about aliens."

The entire room, still processing Molly's theory, turned and gave the DJ a look of peculiar condemnation, which she readily accepted before continuing. "Some people believe that a mountain's 'back bowls' were formed by spaceships."

The silent stares persisted, and Georgia finally put her arms up to proclaim her innocent sanity. "Not that I'm one of them."

Nobody knew whether to discuss the current theories or come up with alternatives, so Chris broke the growing awkwardness with practicality. "Look, we can sit here all night debating why this is happening, but the cause is irrelevant. We need to figure out what we're going to do next."

Peter responded with a voice of calm composure. "Don't worry. The governor assured me the National Guard is on its way. He won't take my calls now, but all we have to do is hold out, find some more survivors, and help will be here before we know it."

But Nellie made it her duty to ground Mr. Hayden's optimism. "It's not that simple. We still don't know what we're dealing with or even how it spreads."

Uncomfortable with the seriousness of the conversation, Scott offered his two cents while giving himself a tour of the cabin. "Zombies one-oh-one: you get bit. You turn."

Remembering their injured comrade, Molly looked down at the old man sitting back against the far wall. "Hunter got bit."

He appeared to be in a daze, swaying back and forth as well as in and out of consciousness. Stephanie wanted to feel sorry for him, but she just couldn't muster the pity. "What should we do with him?"

Georgia, on the other hand, was a bit more concerned by Hunter's near zombie-like stupor. "Is he turning? He looks like he's turning."

Shaking his head, Chris eased the girl's worries. "No. That's just from the blood loss."

Even though she barely knew him, Molly still felt responsible to help the man she fought alongside. "Should we bring him with us?"

And on that note, Scott couldn't help throwing out a quip of his own. "I know little 'Miss Trigger-Happy' over there wouldn't mind putting him out of his misery."

Ignoring the joke, Nellie decided to answer it earnestly. "Not until he starts showing symptoms."

Through his wobbling haze, Hunter surprised the room by blurting out an opinion on his fate. "I'm fine on my own. Just let me be."

Everyone was a bit taken aback by the outburst, especially since he immediately went right back into his stupor. But after the old man's remarks settled in, Scott again had to put his own spin on it. "Yeah. That's what they all say…before they get a little brain hungry."

Pulling the conversation back to its practical nature, Stephanie offered further analysis on the subject. "But my brother wasn't bit. Neither was my father."

Peter lowered his head and solemnly added to her statement. "Or Ryan."

A short lull hit the discussion until Georgia made a reluctant admission. "I was."

The room collectively gasped, but Nellie was the only one brave enough to question the girl. "When?"

"I don't know. Couple hours ago."

"And how do you feel?"

"Cold. Tired. Hungry…but not crazy."

Chris then took that information and devised a theory. "So if being bit doesn't turn you, then what? It's airborne, and we're all just immune?"

But Molly was quick to amend his hypothesis. "Maybe it varies depending on the person. Some people turned right away. Others in a couple hours."

And with a grim interjection, Stephanie suddenly changed the tone of the dialogue. "But then we're not immune, are we? We're just taking longer than everyone else."

The tension in the room abruptly shifted as its occupants scanned one another with a sense of suspicion. The silence was brutal and had completely undone the minute trust they had built with one another.

At least until Nellie tore through the quiet with a distracting proclamation. "We need an avalanche to destroy the town."

An ecstatic jolt ran through the room, pulling everyone's gaze in Nellie's direction. They remained silent, wondering, maybe even hoping that the woman was joking. And they stayed that way until she elaborated. "There's no saving these people, and there's too many of them to fight. We have to end this here and now before it gets any worse. Destroying the town is the only way."

The room waited silently as its occupants slowly glanced around at each other to gauge their reactions. They remained speechless with blank expressions on all their faces until Scott Brooks was the first to break the quiet with a humored smile. "Well, this just got interesting."

Peter followed up Scott's remark by snapping in Nellie's direction. "Are you out of your fucking mind?"

With an almost cold chill to her voice, Nellie calmly retorted. "No. I'm not. In fact, I'm perfectly sane. But your friends and family, you know, the people outside trying to kill us, I'm pretty sure they are. And if we don't do something, we'll probably be joining them."

Adding a crack of her own, Georgia was fairly indifferent to the plan. "Well, it's an easy way to get out of my lease."

While Molly felt a nostalgic sadness. "I've lived here my entire adult life. Is this really our only option?"

The village manager, on the other hand, still fought the idea as best he could. "Only option? I can't believe it's even AN option."

The dissenting opinions started to squabble with the others and soon the discussion turned into a jumbled mess of voices. Stephanie stayed out of it, both literally and figuratively, from her position on the outskirts of the room. Through the heated debate though, she noticed Mr. Brooks had stopped his disinterested wandering and taken up shop at a similar position to hers on the other side of the room. He was listening intently to what everyone had to say and forming thoughts of his own. If Steph didn't know any better, she would've assumed those thoughts could further be labeled as plans.

But Scott caught sight of the girl staring at him and quickly turned in her direction, which she abruptly countered by loudly joining the hectic conversation. "She's right."

Stephanie's voice overpowered the others, and everyone stopped to allow the teenager to continue. "We don't know what this is or even how to fight it. I mean, just look what it did to a small town in a couple of hours. With tourists and locals! If the military comes here and fails…or worse, joins them…who knows what will happen."

The room once again fell flat, and Peter's passive objections had taken a more practical angle. "Is an avalanche even possible? I thought we have measures to prevent that."

With his extensive knowledge of the resort's operations, Chris was quick to answer. "We do, but the blizzard left a lot of loose snow on the mountain. Usually the skiers, CATs and patrolmen knock it down, but now it's just sitting on the trails ready to slide. A big enough explosion from inside Mountain Village will shake it all loose."

Peter persisted with his mild arguments. "Inside? You mean destroy Mountain Village? Just blow it all up. That's what you're proposing?"

Chris nodded his head in the affirmative. "There's explosives in the ski patrol office we could use."

And Nellie added to his inventory. "I brought some in the truck, too."

Trying to gather supporters, Peter pleaded to the others in the room. "So we're actually considering this? Demolishing our home?"

When no one joined in, Nellie offered the man a note of compassion. "It's not your home anymore. It's just a graveyard."

"But there might still be survivors hiding in their houses up there. And here in town, too. Are we just supposed to kill them all?"

Stephanie jumped in to add to the already developing plan. "What if we warn them somehow? Is there any way to get a message out?"

That idea sparked in Georgia a way for her to contribute. "We could try TORO. If anyone's alive, I bet they still have their radios on."

Feeling the pressure mounting against him, Peter continued his campaign against the plan. "I thought the radio went dead."

But Georgia optimistically squashed that objection. "It did, but I might be able to put something together. I probably won't be able to have any long range capabilities, but a weak signal might at least make it to the local receivers."

Not forgetting how all this came about, Nellie reminded them of the most important part. "Don't forget about the mine. We'll have to seal it off too, just in case."

As the logistical patroller, Chris started organizing their plans out loud. "So we're talking three teams. One for the radio station. One for the mine. And one up to the village."

Just as the scheme started to take shape, Peter suddenly began to lose his cool. "No. No. No! This is insane. Crazy! You're talking about annihilating this whole community. I can't let that happen."

Stephanie could sense each member of the group wanting to calm Peter down but ultimately hesitating to engage him. Even Nellie was reluctant to look the man in his eyes. But with nothing left to lose and a long way from home, the girl understood their situation better than most.

And that's why she confidently stepped forward to approach Peter with her head held high. "I know you're afraid."

"I'm not scared of those things."

Stephanie continued her forward march, eventually stopping right in front of Peter's feet. "Not of them. Of losing everything you've ever known. But it's already lost. All we can do now is make sure it doesn't happen to somebody else."

Peter lowered his eyes and took a deep breath, allowing a tumultuous wave of thoughts to calm down inside his head. Stephanie was ready to say more but chose to wait and let the gravity of reason return to the man before her.

Once it had, Peter opened his mouth to speak and out came a stronger, more decisive voice. "Our gas supplier keeps an underground reserve for emergencies in the basement of my office. It's piped underneath the buildings, and if you open all the valves an explosion there might take out the entire village square."

The group took his comment as a reluctant agreement, but Chris asked the obvious question just to make sure. "Does this mean you're in?"

"I've been lying to myself, hoping this place could be saved." Peter displayed a short, somber tone that quickly evaporated, replaced by the stern demands of a leader. "But nothing happens in that village until we're all ready. Agreed?"

A series of silent nods put everyone in acknowledgment, and although it wasn't ideal, the daring plan put the room's mood on a solid foundation. They had a goal and a course of action. All they had to do now was figure out who would be executing which part.

22

As she approached the gymnasium doors, Dr. Morris couldn't wipe the smile from her face. She'd done it. She'd really done it. She found a cure for the terror plaguing her town.

After she returned from her expedition to the pharmacy, the patients isolated in the classrooms began to turn one by one. Luckily, the nurses and volunteers were able to administer the medications before they became violent. Because it was a trial, every subject had to be given a different drug to try as many substances as possible. It was far from an ideal form of treatment. It was actually a desperate shot in the dark, but there was nothing left to lose. All Anna could do was cross her fingers and hope one of those unfortunate souls got better.

For well over an hour she randomly roamed the halls checking in on her patients one after the other. Some had yet to become ravenous and just continued to show standard flu like symptoms, which was a positive sign that there might be some way to slow down their transformation. It was hardly a solution. In fact, some of the patients degenerated from their insanity into a state of bloody sluggishness, similar to the zombies she encountered in the pharmacy.

Each failed patient further drowned Anna's hopes in a pot of inevitable doom. Her aspirations diminished with every classroom she visited. But she wouldn't stop checking on them. After all, she wrestled with herself for hours about possible courses of action and a shotgun drug trial approach was the only thing she could come up with. Now there was nothing left for her to do but pray for a miracle. And she found it in room 221B.

When the classroom came into view through the glass window on the door, Dr. Morris almost didn't believe what she was seeing. She'd been so accustomed to watching the sick and insane that it was strange to see a healthy, coherent man pacing at the front of the class. She blinked. Then blinked again. And when the man was still there the realization finally hit her: she had found a cure.

Upon seeing Anna outside the classroom, the man ran up to the door and tried to open it. The doorknob was locked, just as it'd been the first hundred times he tried it. But now that he saw someone the man assumed he would be let free. He banged on the glass, begging and pleading for her to let him out. However, Anna was still stuck in a state of disbelief from her discovery. After so much death and despair compounded into a single day, the doctor was almost shell-shocked by her success.

But even after regaining her senses, Anna never made a move to unlock the door. In fact, she didn't even register the man's desperate cries for help. There were still too many variables. What if it wasn't permanent? What if the change became intermittent? What if he was just faking it? (Could these things even fake?) There was still much more work to do. And for that reason, Anna ignored the man's yelling and instead focused on the piece of paper pinned to the door.

It had a brief description of the man's condition as well as the time and type of drug administered. It was some type of opiate compound Dr. Morris wasn't too familiar with. But that wasn't important. What mattered was that she had the information, and it was time to start spreading the news.

Like a gleeful madwoman, Anna tore through the empty halls back towards the gymnasium. And it was on that approach which she currently found herself, smiling from ear to ear with the knowledge that could save Telluride. In just a few short steps she would burst through the doors and begin planning on how best to deliver the cure to as many people as possible.

But upon stepping inside the temporary medical clinic she helped establish, Anna walked in on a scene of pure horror and chaos. Several of the patients had subtly turned into raging homicidal maniacs and were already well into the process of killing everyone in sight.

With most of the doors to the outside chained shut to prevent zombies from coming in, the frantic survivors were fearfully funneling towards the few exits available to them. In their path were ravenous madmen clawing and tearing their way from one unlucky bystander to the next. Their slaughter was random in its approach, and they spared no act of destruction as the fiends tossed and turned every cot and medical tray in their wake.

The once organized shelter had become a disaster itself. The sheer anarchy and terror of it all paralyzed Dr. Morris in her tracks. How could this be happening? She just gained the knowledge of their salvation only to have the hope of acting upon it ripped from her grasp.

But it wasn't too late. As long as she was alive she had the will to make a difference. That will was meaningless just a few minutes ago. She had no direction or way to change her fate. But now, with the information she had just learned, there was a chance to fight back. And she would be damned if she was just going to give up after coming so far.

With a newfound sense of urgency, Anna stormed over to the large medication cabinet turned over at the side of the gym. She climbed on top, swung open the doors, and began digging through the mess of vials for compounds matching the cure. Behind her she continued to hear the screams and cries of the innocent being murdered while running for their lives. But Dr. Morris had to drown the massacre out and focus on the task at hand. Her search was just too important to fail. She had to find something.

And she did! First there was one. Then Anna stumbled upon several more clustered together in the same spot of the cabinet. She wanted to continue searching but was suddenly startled by a hand on her shoulder. Anna turned around ready for an attack only to see Beth staring back at her.

The young woman obviously caught the doctor by surprise, but she also looked down with a shocked expression. "What are you doing? You need to get out of here."

Once Anna realized Beth was only concerned for their safety, the doctor went back to scrounging through the cabinets. "Just a second."

The baffled look upon Miss McCabe's face fell further into confusion. "Do you not see what's going on? People are dying."

"I know, and it's all pointless unless...aha!"

Dr. Morris cut off her own sentence by ripping out a small black case from deep within the cabinet. She then opened it up, revealing a series of small syringes before stuffing the vials she found inside.

Beth watched on as her worry morphed into curiosity. "What is that?"

The doctor finished loading the medicine, zipped the case closed, and looked up at the girl with a smile of pure satisfaction. "A cure."

Beth's lips slowly parted as her brain began processing Dr. Morris's revelation. The two women then remained in the same position while Anna allowed her time to absorb the information.

But the moment only lasted until Anna caught sight of a deranged man charging at them. "Look out!"

At the last second before impact, Dr. Morris tackled her former patient down and just out of the way of their would-be assailant's attack. The man's momentum took him flying into the cabinet at full speed, smashing the glass on the door and crumpling his body in on itself.

The loud noise of the crash echoed throughout the destroyed gymnasium, drawing the attention of the few other fiends finishing off their remaining victims. They all turned in the direction of the cabinet and slowly became less interested in the barely alive, bloody bodies around them.

Realizing what was about to happen, Beth and Anna both scrambled to their feet and took off in the direction of the gym's sole remaining exit. Without waiting for the chase to begin, the two women sprinted for the door while Dr. Morris clutched onto the small case like her life depended on it. With only a few steps remaining, they both heard the quick stomps behind them as the others began their pursuit. But by then it was too late. The running women slammed through the double doors without every turning around to see who was running after them.

Anna knew their immediate escape wouldn't be the end of the story. They still had to run. But that plan changed when her and Beth entered the mountain night only to be met by shrieks and cries of pain.

They both stopped just outside the door. They had to. Otherwise, the women would've run head first into an endless horde of zombies feasting upon the people that had escaped before them. The faint light flickering off the school barely illuminated the scene. It was hard to make out the faces of the deranged cannibals and their living meals through the darkness. Only bodies could be seen. But Anna recognized enough to know the situation wasn't in their favor.

In fact, their sudden emergence from the building got the attention of the infected in the crowd not preoccupied with food. Those zombies then turned and began making their way towards the two petrified women.

Upon first glance, Anna assumed the mob in front of her was the same one she narrowly escaped from when it was still daylight. But their body language, coupled with the moaning, which had now become an endless stream of monotone grunts, told her something was off. Any hop in their step (and there wasn't much to begin with) was replaced with a slow drone of a walk. Instead of a swift shuffle forward with a sense of urgency, the horde slumped along, moving one foot in front of the other without a single nimble bone in their bodies.

If it wasn't for the adrenaline pumping its way through her veins, Dr. Morris might've found their mobility amusing. But then she remembered the more immediate threat fast approaching them from behind.

She grabbed onto Beth's hand and together they ran along the side of the school, turning a corner around the building's edge. The two women then stopped and eagerly looked back to see what became of their pursuers.

The slow moving mob surely saw their meal's departure and began a sluggish shift in their direction. But no sooner had they fully turned themselves about than their more manic counterparts emerged through the double doors at full speed. Without missing a beat, the crazed savages locked onto the fading screams from the casualties in the crowd and barreled straight towards them. The whole throng slightly collapsed upon impact, tumbling over and disrupting their pursuit of the two women.

Grateful for the unlikely assist, Anna and Beth both shared a silent smile at their unusual luck. But the moment was brief. They had to keep moving and pressed on around to the other side of the school, where they began hopping through backyards in search of another shelter.

***

Since the other two plans couldn't get started until Georgia began hers, she and Molly were the first to leave. And for Scott, it wasn't a moment too soon. The punk girl's creepy purple hair was starting to freak him out.

As the local DJ, it was fairly obvious which task she was assigned to. And since Molly took a most personal interest in saving as many of her fellow townsfolk as possible, she readily volunteered to accompany Georgia on her mission.

Figuring out who would complete the other assignments was a bit more difficult. Given her personal history on the subject, everyone assumed Nellie would've jumped at the chance to close off the mine for good. But she declined, figuring setting the charges inside Mountain Village was the more important of the two explosions.

With that opening, the gears began to once again turn in the back of Brooks's mind. Ever since the crisis began, his plan to capitalize on the situation had to evolve along with the circumstances. First his plane failed to take off. Then his rescuers failed to escape when they had the chance. And now he was stuck in a cabin with people crazy enough to try and save the day.

But as if in some act of fate, he was presented with an opportunity to control the epidemic at its source. And he had to do his best to push down his rising excitement as he volunteered for the job old Mrs. Sheridan passed on.

At first, the group was a little skeptical of Scott's willingness to help. But this crowd was hardly the most difficult he'd ever had to sway in his favor. Talking was what the sharp businessman did best, and it wasn't long before everyone was convinced of his sincerity. Everyone except Peter.

On the flipside to Nellie, the group also assumed that Peter would be the one to join her in causing the avalanche. Seeing as how Mountain Village was his creation, they all thought he would want to be the one to destroy it. But to their surprise, he jumped at the chance to assist Scott in his effort to collapse the mine.

The only person who expected him to tag along was Scott himself. Although he never bothered to say hello, Scott knew he and Peter lived next door to one another. They were certainly aware of each other's existence, but neither one ever bothered to act upon it.

Now they were both forced into a situation where they had to confront their suspicions, which Scott could see were swirling around in Peter's mind as he volunteered to join him. Peter was mostly silent for the rest of the meeting, but Scott could tell from his leering eyes that his neighbor was wary of his intentions.

Once that was settled, Nellie's other partners fell into place. Only the girl and her ski patroller were left. It was obvious the two had formed some sort of bond in the few hours they'd known each other, and so they both would be joining Mrs. Sheridan on her way up to destroy the village.

Unfortunately, the last member of their group was in no shape to move. They briefly discussed putting Hunter out of his misery, but it was unanimous to just honor the man's wishes and let him be. Out of everyone, Chris took that decision particularly to heart. As a trained EMS professional, his job was to keep people alive no matter how close to death they were, but even he gave in to the group's grim consensus. After all, he knew better than anyone that without a proper doctor the odds of the old man surviving the night were practically nonexistent.

Once everyone finally accepted that sad reality, the two teams were ready to wait for the signal by the cabin's back door, away from the ever-growing crowd of zombies in front of the house. Before they did though, Peter secretly pulled the ski patroller to the side of the room. Scott was more than curious as to what his partner was scheming but couldn't get close enough to hear without drawing attention to himself.

Were they planning against him? How could they? Peter certainly knew he was up to something but didn't know enough to stop it. Besides, what could the young man possibly do from the other side of the valley?

Whatever it was they talked about didn't last more than a few exchanges. And both men soon returned to the back door ready to head outside. They still had to wait for the signal, but once outside they would be in a better position to move.

After receiving a quick nod from everyone behind her, Nellie pulled open the door only to be met by a rapidly approaching body on the porch. The quick event happened so fast that Nellie lifted her rifle up without ever having time to think. But she hesitated on pulling the trigger.

And lucky she did, for her hesitation was soon followed by a series of frightened pleas. "Don't shoot! Please, don't shoot!"

Scott purposely placed himself at the back of the group so that if they were bombarded by zombies he would have plenty of cannon fodder in front of him. But now he cursed himself for not being able to see who was at the door.

With the sudden burst of panic settling down, the group slowly piled outside onto the back porch. Scott was the last to leave and finally catch a glimpse of their new arrivals. The first was an older woman he didn't recognize who introduced herself as Dr. Anna Morris. The second was a younger blonde whose face was hidden behind Peter's chest as the two hugged each other.

At first glance, Scott swallowed deeply at the thought of who that might be. What other young woman would the village manager be excited for? His suspicions were then confirmed when the two released and Peter introduced her. "Everyone, this is Beth. She is...or was my assistant."

Beth gave a brief wave to the party but locked onto Scott's eyes for longer than anyone else. Besides a greeting, her stare and subtle smile had a whole nother meaning to it. But for now, Scott was just happy her message was silent. If he was to deal with Peter then she had to keep her mouth shut. The girl was smart, but he also knew how excited Beth could get when she was eager to please. Especially with emotions running high amidst a zombie Apocalypse.

Luckily, the crisis hadn't deterred Miss McCabe from playing the role he assigned her. How long she would be able to keep that up was another issue entirely. There was nothing Scott could do about it now, though, so he bit the bullet and prayed the girl could hold herself together long enough for him to succeed.

When the excitement of seeing new faces finally faded, Dr. Morris surveyed the ragtag group in front of her with a hint of disappointment. "This cabin was the only place with lights on. Are you all that's left of the town?"

Always figuring himself as the default leader, Peter answered the almost rhetorical question. "Well, we left a group of survivors up at the village. There might be others holed up in their homes, but that's probably the safest place for them right now."

Chris's guilty conscious then forced him to step up and include their fallen comrade. "We also left a man injured inside. He's lost a lot of blood, and I don't think he's gonna make it. He wanted to be left alone, though."

The doctor responded by turning to Beth and nodding her head. "I should give him the cure."

At the sound of those words, the entire group's face lit up at once. They remained speechlessly staring at the woman, hoping she would elaborate. But it took a moment for her to realize they were waiting for her to explain more. "We came from the temporary med clinic set up at the school. Before it was overrun, though, I did some drug trials. And one of them reversed the effects of the transformation."

Again, everyone was speechless. But Scott was the only one with a manipulative mind that allowed him to take notice of the case in the woman's hand. "Is that it there?"

Anna nodded. "I only have several doses, though. Not enough to cure everyone, but it's a common medication. If we can get a message to everyone, I'm sure we can stop this thing from spreading."

The situation was morphing quicker than Scott could adapt his plans. For now, though, his main concern was getting his hands on whatever was in that case.

He quickly thought of a reason to make her part with it but was surprised when Peter spoke up first, beating him to the punch. "Well, I can get the word out, but there's just too many infected to handle. As much as I hate to admit it, I've come to realize that a cure can't save Telluride. What it can do is keep this epidemic from leaving. First we need to contain it. That's where we were headed. It's a dangerous plan, though, and we can sure use all the help we can get."

His suggestion was subtle, but Peter's eyes, locked onto the case, made it clear what he wanted. Scott assumed the doctor would refuse. She obviously discovered this cure in the hopes of being Telluride's hero. But he was surprised to see her readily open the case with a smile. The doctor then proceeded to fill up two syringes from a vial and recap them before handing the needles over to the village manager.

Peter took one for himself and handed the other to Chris with a blinding stare. They each nodded in unison as if communicating some hidden message to one another. Once again, Scott was slightly concerned about this secret covenant the two had formed, but there was nothing he could do about it now. They had the syringes, and he would have to evolve his plan accordingly.

The bigger shocker was how silent Nellie had been to this news of a cure. She'd been the strongest advocate for destroying the mine, and Scott assumed that went hand in hand with utilizing a cure. But she failed to utter a word when the woman handed it over so easily.

In fact, she just as quickly dismissed the doctor when there was nothing left to say. "You should help the man inside."

Anna then nodded with a smile and took the remaining syringes inside the cabin as Chris yelled out to her. "Just keep a radio on and listen for the evacuation call."

As soon as the door shut behind her, Stephanie, who spent the entire conversation around the edge of the house, called out to everyone. "Guys, I think that's the signal."

Now with Beth added to the group, they all joined Stephanie at her position and could see the top of a large fire roaring in the distance. The tips of the flames reached up and over the rooftops between them, stretching high towards the full moon in the dark, star-filled sky. No one said a word, not even Scott, but they all knew that the fire signaled the beginning of Telluride's end.

23

Despite both being Telluride residents, the DJ and schoolteacher couldn't have been more different. And besides her job, that was one of the appeals that originally drew Georgia to the quaint mountain town. Even though it was small, Telluride managed to be populated by a wide range of people and families. Everything from old world cowboys to free-loving hippies.

Unfortunately, those differences didn't help the two women spark up any conversation between them. They just continued to sneak along through the town's side roads and dimly lit backyards, completely avoiding the overwhelming horde of zombies filling up the main streets.

Georgia wasn't much with a gun, so she held onto the handheld radio assigned to each team while Molly carried the weapon. Their first stop was a corner of the valley far away from the radio station where they were ultimately headed. But if the others were to have any chance of reaching their goals, Georgia and her partner had to take a short detour to conduct some arson.

The DJ was certainly feeling the nerves of excitement, but their journey was relatively calm and uneventful by design. The women went out of their way to ensure they avoided any unnecessary run-ins with a stray zombie lost from its pack.

But after about ten minutes of trudging through the snow, Molly decided the quiet was too much for her. "You don't really think aliens caused this, do you?"

It wasn't the question Georgia was expecting, but it interested her enough to pursue the conversation. "Do you really think it's an Indian curse?"

"Well, Native Americans did live in this valley."

A reflexive yet subtle smile appeared on Georgia's face. "And then cursed it?"

"I think whatever the reason all this is happening, knowing it won't make things any easier to accept."

The smile faded as Georgia nodded in strong, sober agreement. "Now that I can believe."

Georgia expected Molly to continue with a follow-up, but the schoolteacher remained silent as she led the way. Molly had an exact idea as to where they were going and stayed on a fixed route with unwavering determination. Georgia didn't know what direction they were headed but felt comfortable as long as they were out of danger.

In fact, she got so used to just following Molly's lead that it caught her by surprise when her guide suddenly stopped. Georgia looked up and found herself in a pretty unremarkable neighborhood of evenly spaced, cookie cutter houses. The street was an isolated corner of the valley. And as Georgia turned around, she noticed it was just outside the fringes of the zombie mass infesting the center of town. No matter how much Georgia focused, she could barely hear their moans.

Molly then drew the girl's attention as she continued on towards the house in front of them. "We're here."

Georgia turned back around but Molly was already halfway to the front door. Surprised, the young woman gave a quick jog to catch up to her older counterpart just inside the house. But when Georgia stopped, Molly kept moving deeper into the living room without missing a beat.

The place seemed tidy and organized like it was staged for sale. However, Georgia could sense a family's warm touch as her eyes darted around the room. "How do you know this place has what we need?"

Molly was too busy locked in her task to respond, but Georgia received an answer when her shifting gaze met a portrait of Molly smiling alongside her husband and kids. She stared at the photo, utterly mesmerized by how happy they all looked. That trance was soon broken, though, when the loud shattering of glass echoed throughout the house.

Georgia turned around to find Molly tossing liquor bottles randomly in every direction. The kitchen, dining, and bedrooms were already covered in broken bottles and the stench of alcohol. When she ran out, Molly returned to the living room's wet bar to restock. She then continued to further drench the room before retreating to the front door and stopping next to her young companion.

Georgia was fairly shocked by the emotionless display of savagery she had just witnessed. But for some reason, she was more frightened by the cold and deliberate manner in which Molly proceeded to remove a lighter from her pocket and stare at its flame.

A moment of quiet passed between them before Georgia finally asked the question that her conscience pressed on her mind. "Are you sure you want to do this?"

After a deep breath, Molly answered plainly without looking away from the flame. "Mrs. Sheridan was right. This isn't our home anymore."

She then tossed the lighter to the side and watched as it ignited a set of wet curtains dangling from the window. The fire quickly grew in just a few seconds, and the two women quickly exited the house without bothering to look back. They both could hear the roar of the flames expanding behind them, and judging by the limping army that was now inching its way in their direction, the blaze had already attracted the zombie horde's attention.

Of course, Georgia wasn't too certain as to how effective it would be, but she wasn't sticking around to find out. Both her and Molly took off towards the radio station on the other side of town, once again staying as far away from any unwanted encounters as possible.

***

Peter wasn't surprised that Beth decided to accompany them up to the mine. There were really only three options available to her; stay with Hunter, join the other team to Mountain Village or go with him and Scott. She wanted to help with the plan, and Chris's group already had three people. It just made sense that she would join the group of two. Besides, she was his secretary (or used to be at least). It figured that she would want to help him.

But that didn't stop the village manager from being frustrated by the situation. Not that Beth was a burden. He was more than confident that she could carry her own weight. Peter just wanted him and Scott Brooks to be alone. That way he could keep a better eye on the shady egomaniac without any distractions.

The man was obviously hiding something, and it bothered Peter that he hadn't yet figured out what that was. He didn't want to let on that he knew Brooks had an agenda, although the tension between them wasn't helping.

After Georgia and Molly's fire had grown up into the night's sky, the parade of dim-witted zombies lining the streets began gaping at the bright, blazing light in the distance. There wasn't much to see through the blackness, but under the moon's glow, the outline of the horde resembled a shadowy mass flowing together as one.

Chris and his team immediately took off through the adjacent backyard on their way towards the gondola. Peter's group, however, wasn't able to begin their assignment immediately. There were still too many of the moaning walkers surrounding the truck they needed to get up to the mine.

Instead, they continued to creep around the side of the house, hiding in the darkness while the slow moving crowd lumbered back and forth towards the fire like a mystified moth to a flame. It took longer than Peter expected, but eventually the crowd dispersed from around the truck in the direction of the burning house. He could feel Scott anxious to get going. With Peter in the front of the line, though, Mr. Brooks had to wait until their leader made the first move.

Even once the truck was completely free, the village manager still waited until the mob was at least a block away before darting out into the street in a dead sprint towards the vehicle. Beth and Scott kept up behind him, although the man they followed wasn't exactly sure where he was headed. He obviously knew where the truck was. Even with the town covered in darkness, it would've been hard to miss the only giant car shaped structure in the road. But the closer Peter got to the truck, the more it came into focus, and he could make out exactly where the driver's side door was located.

Even with the zombie swarm moving considerably slower than before, Peter still realized they were working on a tight window of time. He quickly opened the door and saw the keys exactly where Nellie said they would be: dangling from the ignition. A brief and subtle smile perked onto Peter's face. At least the plan was going well so far.

He reached forward, grabbed onto the door's inside handlebar and prepared to step up into the seat when a firm hand latched onto his shoulder. It was a man's grip, so there was only one option as to who it could've been. But even when the answer was so obvious, Peter still hoped, for whatever reason, that it wasn't Brooks.

This hope caused Peter to keep his head forward, refusing to look Scott in the eye. But that didn't keep Mr. Brooks from initiating a conversation. "What do you think you're doing?"

Peter finally turned to face the man keeping him from entering the truck. "What does it look like?"

Unexpectedly, Scott responded with an obnoxiously arrogant smile. "Didn't your parents ever tell you it's rude to answer a question with a question?"

"What the hell is your problem?"

"My problem is that you look like you're about to jump into the driver's seat of my truck."

Faced with a professional level of passive aggression, Peter felt his blood pressure rising. He knew he should've kept his anger down or at the very least hidden it. The situation, both with the zombies and his former neighbor, wouldn't benefit from him losing his temper.

But Peter just couldn't stop his frustration from showing. "You're seriously going to argue with me about this? Right now?"

"Hey, this truck was promised to me, and I'll be damned if I let some…"

Peter could see the needless argument starting to heat up, but to his surprise, Beth suddenly stepped up and cut off the brewing tension in its tracks. "Guys, come on. We're all going to the same place, right? What's the difference?"

Peter was glad Beth came to his aide. It was an unexpected surprise that bringing her along had the added benefit of diffusing standoffs like this in his favor. But when he turned to look at her, Peter noticed that Beth wasn't looking at Scott. She was looking at him, almost as if she was pleading for him to be the one to stand down.

He didn't know why Beth wouldn't take his side. He was her boss. It was her job to have his back. Maybe she didn't want to insult a stranger. Maybe she was compensating while trying not to play favorites. Whatever the reason, the situation wasn't really ideal for him to stay and analyze her decision.

In the background, Peter could see the zombie horde starting to lose interest in the giant fire that had nothing for them to kill. They were starting to become restless (at least as restless as a lethargic mob of zombies could be). And Scott Brooks knew it too. Peter could see it in his eyes.

The savvy man was playing a game of chicken, trying to assert his dominance in their relationship over something as trivial as driving a car. And judging by the cocky smile still lingering on his face, Peter knew Scott was willing to let their entire plan fall apart to accomplish it.

Realizing the importance of picking his battles, Peter released his hand from the side of the truck with an annoyed smirk. "Enjoy your ride."

He then casually walked around the hood to the passenger seat.

***

For anyone else the situation might've seemed awkward, but Nellie preferred being left out of her companions' conversation. Ever since they left her cabin, Chris and Stephanie had been chatting non-stop, exchanging impressions of the fellow survivors they just met. They never bothered to ask Mrs. Sheridan her opinion, and she never bothered to give it. All she cared about was making sure their voices weren't loud enough to attract any unwanted attention from the zombie horde on the street.

Sneaking through the backyards of adjacent houses, the group roughly backtracked parallel to the route they had taken in the truck. Nellie didn't think it was possible, but the streets they had driven through were even more packed with zombies than they had been only hours earlier.

She was able to catch glances of the moonlit crowd through breaks between the houses and saw that their movements were noticeably different than before. They walked slower, more rigid and awkward.

Even though their skin and faces were hidden in darkness, the zombies' body language alone was a far cry from the ferocious fiends who first appeared that morning. But given the change in their behavior after the storm disappeared, Nellie figured the creatures' evolution wasn't quite over yet.

Caught up in their conversation, Nellie's two comrades were too preoccupied to notice that their foe had once again transformed, and she wasn't about to tell them. The old rancher was content listening in to their chat as a cautious observer.

One might've called it gossip, but the information allowed her the chance to get a little insight into her allies' minds. If it were up to her, Nellie would've preferred to do this mission alone. But she knew she was going to need their help. The key was just making sure they provided the right amount of assistance without allowing them an opportunity to get in her way.

After a couple of blocks, Nellie began to notice the zombie procession was finally gaining ground in the direction of the house fire. The group transitioned their path over to the street, and Stephanie changed the topic to something Nellie found a bit more interesting. "Why did Peter pull you aside?"

The ski patroller responded with a comment that was more of a statement than a question. "Why do you think?"

"Ryan?"

Although monotone, Chris's answer held a slight hint of regret. "He asked me to put him out of his misery."

Stephanie took a deep breath of sad acceptance before asking a follow-up. "You think that's why he chose to blow up the mine instead? He wouldn't be able to kill his son?"

"Maybe. And in a way Mountain Village is like his child, too. He just doesn't have it in him to end them both."

"But once that doctor showed up with a cure you think he would've changed jobs."

Chris nodded in agreement before shifting the conversation's tone. "There's something else going on with him, though. I don't know why, but he didn't want to let that Brooks guy out of his sight."

He could've elaborated but chose not to. Probably because he sensed his fellow travel-mates knew exactly what he meant. She couldn't speak for Stephanie, but Nellie understood. You don't run a tourism business without learning to size people up on the fly. And something didn't sit right with Nellie about that Brooks character. From the moment they picked him up in that wreckage by the airport, she knew he was bad news. And now she had to rely on him to close up that mine for good.

She wasn't too concerned about it, though. Peter Hayden was with him, and despite their differences, Nellie knew she could count on him to get the job done. And hell, if they failed they failed. It was out of her control, which was why she left the more important task to herself.

A few more minutes passed before the gondola, still on and bringing cars up the mountain, came into view. Once it did, the teenage girl removed the handheld radio strapped to her belt and clicked it on. "We should tell the others we're about to get on board."

She then held down the receiver while talking into the speaker. "Hello? You guys there? It's Stephanie. We're about to jump on the gondola."

She continued walking alongside the others while waiting for a response. When one didn't come she tried again. "Hello? Did anybody get that?"

Slightly frustrated, the girl turned to Nellie, the one who supplied the devices from inside her cabin, looking for an explanation. "Do these things even work?"

Chris sighed, either from frustration or disappointment, before grabbing the radio from Stephanie and stuffing it in his jacket. "We should've checked them before we left."

Nellie was quick to reassure them, though. "The others probably still have theirs off. Don't worry. It's early. They'll turn them on when they get closer to their objectives."

She prepared herself to go into more depth if they probed further, but her simple excuse seemed to suffice…for now.

Quiet filled the air between them for the first time since their journey began. The faint light coming from inside the gondola station kept the group focused enough that they didn't need chatter to pass the time. Nellie used these last couple of steps to make sure her partners still had their side arms and the strap of her rifle was still firm around her shoulder. With their weapons confirmed, Nellie kept moving forward towards the station door.

It was only when she was about to cross the threshold inside that Chris stopped short, halting her movements as well. "Oh. I almost forgot."

Nellie turned to him perturbed that he waited until the last possible second to bring up something new. "Forgot what?"

"We ran into some trouble at the mid-mountain station on our way here."

The old rancher took the revelation in stride as she bluntly asked the next logical question. "What kind of trouble?

"The zombie kind."

Just moving her eyes, Nellie shifted her gaze over to the girl, whose grim expression confirmed the seriousness of the threat above them. Mrs. Sheridan then dropped her head down and sighed. It was a momentary show of frustration and discouragement that she quickly categorized as weakness.

So Nellie shot her head up with an eager smile instead. "Well, let's go say 'hello' then."

They all entered the station and hopped in the closest gondola car as it slowly completed its turn around the building. After gradually lurching towards the exit, the doors shut and the cab began to climb up the mountain, quietly approaching whatever horrors were waiting for its passengers at the mid-mountain station.

24

The pain was so great that Hunter could barely hear the voices outside the back door.

There'd been a lot of commotion in the cabin's main living room when the group first arrived, and he was coherent enough to understand most of it…during the beginning at least. They all muttered away about causes of the outbreak and various courses of action. His main concern, though, was not bleeding to death. That and turning into a zombie, of course.

Little by little he lost interest in the group's conversation until their words started blending together. Rather than fight the pain radiating from his neck, Hunter just rode it like a roller coaster, allowing the aches to flow through him and out the other side. This technique allowed his old body a chance to relax and not strain under the pressure. The downside to this was that the excruciating agony wreaked havoc on his senses. Unless he focused a great deal, Hunter couldn't really differentiate the shapes in front of his eyes. The same went for the rather intense discussion going on around him.

For a quick instant, he heard his name thrown out amidst the vocal noise, which briefly spiked his enthusiasm. Hunter didn't know exactly why his name was brought up but assumed it was because they were contemplating what to do with him. So without ever hearing a question or topic of discussion, the old man offered up an unsolicited response.

The folks around him quieted down a bit, enough for him to realize they acknowledged his remark, and then went on, once again, chatting amongst themselves. He might've never gone to college, but Hunter considered himself sharp enough to know that they'd already ruled him out of the fight. Nothing more than an old mountain dog limping along on the last leg of his life. Which he was actually fine with. After all, a grown man did just bite a huge chunk out of his neck.

Chris did a good job bandaging up the wound, but he could already feel the dressing completely soaked through. The ski patroller slowed down the bleeding a great deal. Didn't stop it, though. And now his patient began to sense the slow stream of blood trickle down his shoulder.

Focusing in on the injury had taken more effort than Hunter realized his attention span would allow. For an instant, his perception of time ran away from him. That's when he realized the room was empty and all of the distant voices were now emanating from the back door.

The group must have taken his proclamation quite literally and decided to leave him be. It was for the best. Hunter didn't know what the next ten minutes had in store for him. Hell, he didn't even know if he could last the next ten seconds. But at least he was alone.

The old, tired man closed his eyes, ready to drift off into either a temporary or eternal sleep. Either one would've been fine by him. But instead, his focus into nothingness was interrupted by creaky footsteps walking against the cabin's old wooden floor.

It was just one pair of shoes. Not a whole bunch that would've accompanied the entire group. Hunter's eyes remained closed (not that he had much confidence he could see if he opened them anyway), but the old man assumed one of his fellow survivors opted to stay behind and keep watch over him. He thought it might've been Molly. After all, besides him she was the only remaining member of the Marshal's ill-fated posse.

But that theory went out the window when a soft voice spoke into Hunter's ear. "It's going to be OK. I'm a doctor, and I'm here to help."

The voice wasn't strange. But it wasn't necessarily familiar either. Almost as if he had heard it at some point in time during his life. It could've been only once decades ago. And the curiosity still drove him to open his eyes.

A middle-aged woman had her head down in front of him and was toying with something in her hands. Hunter's eyes, the one part of his body that wasn't a struggle to move, followed her arms down to a spot where the woman prepared a syringe from a small vial. "It's a painkiller, so it'll make you feel better right away. The chances of you having an allergic reaction are slim."

The woman looked up, but Hunter's blurry vision could only make out the contours of what appeared to be a smile next to the needle she held by her face. "But don't worry. After this…"

She then moved in closer to Hunter's view and the distorted image slowly came into focus. "…you'll be cured."

It took a few seconds for her features to register, but as the woman moved the sharp tip closer to Hunter's arm, he immediately recognized her and desperately tried to squirm his deadened body away from her grasp. "Don't stick me with that, you crazy bitch!"

But the old man was too weak to fight. The syringe entered his arm and the medication's effects were instantaneous. His dulled senses drooped even further into a haze as the pain echoing through his body quickly faded. Another second or two passed by, and even the strong tormenting pulse from the gash in his neck was gone.

The drug swirled around Hunter's thoughts, and he could no longer remember why he protested it in the first place. He had some vague recollection that the woman who gave it to him shouldn't be trusted, but he couldn't remember a reason. Not that it mattered much anyway. He was still going to die. At least now he was going to die high out of his mind.

***

For the last couple hours, Austin sat both patiently and cautiously by his young fan's side. It became obvious when they set up shop in the village offices that he and the young boy's father were cut from different cloths. Austin had played many men of action in his movies but found the role much more difficult when it wasn't scripted for him ahead of time.

Peter Hayden, on the other hand, took charge like a natural born leader. Austin tried to keep up with him while they assembled their small caravan of survivors through the village, but the movie star struggled to match Peter's pace, determination, and fearlessness. Which wasn't all that surprising when he thought about it. The man did run the community's government, after all.

Austin wanted to help, though. He knew as well as anybody the responsibility that came with having a famous face. People were looking to him for guidance, if not some form of leadership. So he stepped up as the captain of the group when Peter made off for the gondola.

Not that he thought there was much to the job anyway. They had plenty of food and were fairly isolated up in the empty offices. All Austin had to do was keep the group calm until Peter got back. And if he never returned, which was always a possibility, then at least until the National Guard arrived, which Mr. Hayden assured was on its way.

At first, Austin was fine with his role. People tended to associate the actor with his characters rather than himself. And so they felt perfectly safe with a man they thought was more than capable of handling the situation.

But the reality was that the more time passed, the more Austin could feel himself growing anxious among the survivors. That was why he spent the majority of the afternoon at Ryan's side. Because a part of him still felt obligated to his fans. And even under the circumstances, with the boy never knowing who was next to him, the movie star sensed he was doing the right thing.

A part of him did feel ashamed for leaving the others, but he consciously rationalized to himself that the group was fine on their own. Things were quiet and help was on its way. What more could he do?

Ryan, on the other hand, needed to be looked after. The boy could wake up at any moment, and even with the chains restraining him to the wall, who knew what he would be like when he did. For the first hour or so, Austin assumed the kid would've shot up like the ravenous creature he was before he was knocked out. But he slowly began to notice a terrifying change in the unconscious boy's features.

It was around dusk when Austin first noticed Ryan's skin had somehow grown paler than it already was. It continued to do so until his face became abnormally veiny. Strange blotches soon rose to the surface under the boy's flesh, and it quickly became apparent to his caretaker that he was undergoing some type of transformation.

Still unsure about the child's condition, Austin tried to keep his distance. However, his curiosity was certainly getting the better of him. Inch by inch he crept closer, fascinated by the bizarre creature Ryan was becoming. Austin tried to stay on guard, to remember what kind of monster this boy had been. But hours of uneventful watching over an unconscious child had lulled the celebrity into a false sense of security.

He inched closer to his fan's seemingly peaceful face and noticed a small, dark pool in the corner of his orbits. Austin moved in even closer and could see a crimson tinge to the strange liquid. The substance continued to build until it flowed down his cheekbones, confirming Austin's suspicions that the boy was indeed bleeding from his eyes.

The movie star's face scrunched with a kind of perturbed disgust, but he remained intently intrigued by Ryan's physical changes. His continued observations then caught sight of a similar red streak flowing down the boy's neck. Tilting his head downward, Austin followed the trail to its source and discovered that the Hayden boy was also bleeding from his ear.

With his curiosity at its peak, Mr. Cage continued to stare deeply into the earlobe, trying to find the exact source of the bleed. And that's when Ryan's eyes shot open alongside a loud, monotone grunt of pain. The boy instantly leaned over in Austin's direction, but the action star was caught off guard, too close to evade the lumbering attack.

Ryan rolled right onto his surprised victim while carrying the same solitary moan the whole way. And in one fluid movement, sunk his teeth right into Austin's cheek. With the boy's mouth digging deep into his face, Austin unleashed a horrific scream of pain that echoed out of the office. Blood oozed from the wound and covered every surface in the vicinity until the actor finally tossed the small, lightweight child off of him.

Free from the attack, Austin took his time regaining his composure and standing to his feet. The whole event only lasted a few seconds, but in that short amount of time the entire area became drenched in blood. It wasn't an adrenaline-fueled incident, either. Austin's initial question of what Ryan would be like when he woke was answered by the sight of the slow, dumb-witted zombie in front of him. Contrary to what he was like before, the boy's current form was hardly a threat chained to a wall. But the damage had already been done.

Austin stood by the door, covered in blood and holding a hand up to the wound on his face. He waited there for a moment and watched as Ryan lumped around aimlessly, completely oblivious of the restraints holding him back. It was a pitiful sight and made Austin regret that he never had a chance to meet the boy before all this craziness.

At that moment, the door burst open and several of the other survivors rushed in to see what the commotion was about. Catching sight of Ryan and the blood was enough evidence for them to put the pieces together themselves. They then turned to Austin just as he removed his arm from his cheek and looked down at the contents of his hand. Lying on his palm was a large, bloody chunk of flesh the size of a golf ball.

Austin knew that wasn't a good sign. It probably meant that an equal sized piece was missing from his face. But he didn't realize just how bad it was until he looked up to see the horrified expressions of the survivors in front of him, a rather distant experience from the awes and smiles his movie star looks were used to.

25

Upon entering the TORO building, Molly Pullman was woefully unimpressed. She'd listen to the station all her life and often imagined what the inside of the recording booth looked like. The only experience she had with the technical aspect of broadcasting was what she'd seen in movies and on television. So Molly always pictured the DJ she was listening to inside some kind of fancy sound booth surrounded by recording equipment and microphones.

The reality was a lot less intriguing. TORO had a recording booth, sure, but it was far from comfortable. And the equipment was nothing special or impressive. In fact, putting a broadcast together seemed like a lot of hard (and boring) work. By the time Georgia showed her around, Ms. Pullman was convinced that somebody had to be crazy to want to be in this industry. Which actually made a lot of sense, since she thought the girl who brought her here wasn't quite right in the head to begin with.

Georgia was a sweet girl, though. Eccentric. But harmless in her own way. Her spirits were relatively up considering the amount of work the two women had ahead of them. Molly wasn't quite sure the status of the radio equipment when she signed on to this mission. And she was regretting not bringing it up beforehand or, at the very least, when they were on their way.

Besides the broken glass covering the entire sound booth, every piece of equipment was either flipped over or completely destroyed. Not to mention the console in the control room appeared like someone stomped on it. Whatever looked intact they simply prayed still worked. Everything that couldn't be salvaged but they had extras of was readily replaced. Headphones, microphones, cables, and wires were no big deal.

Molly didn't know what they were doing or where anything went. But Georgia's instructions were simple enough that she didn't necessarily need to know what was going on. And as long as no zombies were banging on the door, the schoolteacher was happy to help.

Although the carnage all around the station made her curious, Molly refrained from asking Georgia what caused it. That information wouldn't have helped them repair the destruction any faster. And besides, Molly had a feeling the story was too personal (not to mention traumatic) for Georgia to relive.

She realized this during the brief tour the DJ gave her of the facility. The two of them passed by an open door labeled "server room." Georgia neglected to show it any importance. When Molly peeked inside, though, she saw the bloody aftermath of a brutal battle. The most concerning part being the damage to what looked like very important (and expensive) equipment. But when Molly asked if they would need to fix anything inside, Georgia quickly passed by the room and dismissed the question by stating they could bypass the system. Of course, the simple schoolteacher had no clue if the girl was telling the truth or just avoiding a painful memory. She was just going to have to take Miss Croft's word for it.

Once the repairs were complete, Georgia took to a computer in the control room. She said she had to re-route the networks to get a workable signal. Molly had no idea what the experienced DJ was talking about. All she knew was that whatever Georgia was doing would take time. Time they didn't necessarily have.

So she stood armed and ready with both the pistol that had been so reliable for her since the crisis began and the radio Mrs. Sheridan gave her to inform the other groups of any complications. The building was still quiet, though, and there were no signs that the zombie mob they lured to her burning home had caught up with them. All Molly could do now was hope and pray that Georgia could finish her work before that happened.

***

Ever since she moved to the area, Beth had been meaning to take a summer tour up to Tomboy, the old mining settlement situated above Telluride. Unfortunately, her busy job seemed to always get in the way. An ironic coincidence considering that she would most likely be one of the last people to see it.

That was the bittersweet silver lining the young professional took from her current situation. Beth sat in the dead center of the massive pickup truck's backseat while it seamlessly climbed up the harrowing Tomboy Trail. The snow-covered road (if it could even be called that), was a thin patch of land carved out of the side of the valley that acted as a natural route up to the settlement's plateau.

Normally, tours were given in skinny jeeps that allowed customers to feel safe going up the mountain. But when two vehicles going in opposite directions passed each other by, which was bound to happen, the outside vehicle had just enough room to carefully hug the trail's edge without tumbling over. Needless to say, the truck Beth was in now easily took up the entire road.

Scott seemed to be handling it just fine, though, after setting the vehicle to its lowest gear, of course. Although the trail wasn't necessarily steep, the snow did pose more of a problem here than on the flat roads in town. But the Sheridans had the experience (and money) to outfit the vehicle with the top of the line snow tires it deserved.

What worried Beth more than the road, though, was the thick tension filling the inside of the cab. Her seat between the two men upfront also acted as a metaphorical position in their three-way relationship, one which her boss was still unaware of. And she would prefer it remained that way. Peter was a nice guy and all. Smart, too. That much was indisputable since she started working for him. But her loyalty always rested with Scott. And during this time of crisis, he would need her now more than ever. That reason and that reason alone was why she volunteered to tag along on this field trip.

But the strange feud that seemed to persist between her boss and boyfriend was going to be a problem. Beth didn't know how or why Peter was standoffish towards Scott. Especially since he was unaware that she'd been helping him. But the reason was irrelevant. This was a dangerous time and the last thing Beth needed was the two of them bickering with their lives on the line.

As the truck continued its steady climb, Beth tried to think of a topic to bring some form of positive communication to the group. But while her brain continued to churn, Scott beat her to the punch with his trademark sarcasm. "So what's the plan, fearless leader? Light the fuse and run like hell?"

Peter's attention remained focused out the window as he ignored the question, addressing his former assistant instead. "Beth, check under the seat and make sure the explosives are where Mrs. Sheridan said they were."

She ducked her head down and was immediately met by a thick, plastic container. "They're here."

Before she could look up, though, Scott had already turned the conversation in his favor. "Awesome. Maybe we can find one of those dynamite boxes and push the plunger down like Wile. E. Coyote."

Finally breaking his gaze out the window, Peter turned to the driver with a look halfway between agitation and disgust. "This really is a joke to you, isn't it?"

But Scott simply laughed off the tension. "Oh, don't be bitter just because you didn't get to drive the truck."

When he realized engaging the man was pointless, Peter exhaled a frustrated breath while turning his attention back out the windshield in front of him.

Beth could feel the tension rising through the silence and quickly began thinking of something, anything, that could get a dialogue going to preoccupy their minds. "You think we're going to run into any of those crazy people up there?"

Peter answered with eyes remaining fixated ahead. "Probably not."

Beth wasn't necessarily interested in the follow-up question that popped into her mind but asked it anyway. "Then why did we bring along that cure the lady found?"

Scott took it upon himself to respond. "The same reason we brought guns. It's better to have and not need than need and not have. Right, Peter?"

The question was aimed to antagonize Mr. Hayden more than anything else, and he again ignored it. But regardless of Scott's sarcasm, Peter didn't dispute his statement. Silence filled the cab once more, but the tension was vastly diminished because of the tone the conversation ended on. It was a small and somewhat obvious point they agreed on, yet that was all they needed to calm the air, even though their agreement wasn't said out loud.

On that note, Beth was happy to let the ride continue. And she then directed her attention out the window to see the same landscape Peter had been staring at. From the side of the trail, the view encompassed an angle of the valley that one didn't normally see. The moonlight did an alluring job illuminating the architecture of both Telluride and Mountain Village. Without anyone to turn on the lights, the communities looked far darker than usual. But the few street lamps scattered about gave the town an eerie beauty of ghostly desolation.

The picture reminded Beth that Telluride truly was a special place. One she admittedly had taken for granted in the time she'd lived there and felt saddened by the thought that it wouldn't be in existence for much longer.

***

The gondola ride up to the mid-mountain station was quite literally a calm before the storm. Stephanie, along with the cab's other two passengers, knew danger was waiting for them. What kind of danger was another issue entirely.

Was the mob that chased them out of the station still upstairs? Did the zombies still have the same overwhelming numbers or did some of them leave? Perhaps only a few stragglers remained, in which case the three survivors would have no problem overpowering them as the car passed through to the other side.

There was always the slim chance that all of them left. That the mindless fiends scattered across the mountainside looking for more ways to cause havoc. But Stephanie wouldn't even consider that as a possibility. Luck like that just hadn't been on her side.

As the gondola continued to climb its way upward, the group could see a wave of light pouring out from within the station above them. The closer they came, the brighter it glowed, until it lit up the mountainside like a flare in the darkness.

When the large structure finally came into full view, the group readied their weapons; Stephanie and Peter with their handguns and Nellie with her rifle. Not one of them said a word, but each understood the poor positioning they would have in a fight, cornered inside the tight space of the gondola cab. They silently prepared themselves anyway. After all, what choice did they have?

Eventually, the bright light fully illuminated the station's entrance as the gondola cab lifted over the ridge, bringing the building's large opening within view. The cab's passengers anxiously awaited a menacing threat, and their fears were confirmed when they spotted the entryway packed with a crowd of zombies.

But the horde huddled together there, moaning in unison like one loud concert of pain and torment, was unlike anything they were expecting. The maddened fiends that Stephanie and Chris encountered earlier had been replaced by the literal epitome of the living dead. Their faces, no longer pale and covered in blood, had grown dry, scaly and cracked like that of a freshly decomposed corpse. The zombies had stopped hastily lumbering their deadened bodies around and were now just walking around in circles at an agonizingly slow pace, almost as if every step they took required every ounce of energy they could muster.

Their sudden change in appearance, even more drastic than the previous one, took the group by surprise. Stephanie wanted to say something. To converse with the others about the meaning behind the monsters' evolution. But there wasn't a single moment for any of them to discuss it.

Right after seeing the creatures for the first time, the gondola cab rode up into the station, plowing straight into the densely packed mob of roaming zombies.

Upon impact, the first series of undead were either dragged under the cab or knocked aside into the surrounding fodder. The next wave, however, had nowhere to go other than to be pinned by those behind them, pressing their crusty faces up against the gondola's glass. The zombies had previously left a path for the gondola cars to pass by. But the entire hellish crowd collapsed in on itself when they found out there were people inside the newest one to arrive. The cab continued to move forward fully into the station and was quickly enveloped by a massive swarm closing in around it.

With ample supply of the grotesque faces before her, Stephanie was finally able to get a good look at how truly hideous these unfortunate souls had become. Their grey, worn skin had degraded into a dry canvas of brittle flesh, crumbling off their bodies from even the softest contact against the cab. Deep pocks and sores littered every inch of their faces, and nothing could be seen inside their sockets except the blank, glossy clouds that had become their eyes.

It was hard for Stephanie to see through and above the tightly packed crowd that encompassed them, but from what she could tell, the floor was completely covered wall to wall with fiends. Their first escape must've drawn everyone from the building's multiple levels to the gondola floor. A process that probably continued long after the survivors had left. There were a couple hundred of them at least, all moaning incessantly like a flock of injured animals. Far too many for the speechless passengers inside the gondola to count.

And it was at that moment the cab's doors slowly began to open.

None of the zombies pressing on that side of the cab rushed inside it. At least, not like they did before. Without the wall holding them up, the walking corpses in the front toppled forward from those pushing behind them.

Stephanie leaned back in her seat and began kicking any object that crossed the threshold into the cab. Some of the dry, brittle body parts exploded in a puff of ash from the impact of her boot. Others she could only push back outside to get lost among the next wave that persisted to claw and climb their way inside.

Backed up against the wall of the cab, Chris and Nellie aimed their weapons and took carefully placed shots at the attackers that Stephanie missed. For the most part, their combined efforts were able to keep up with the moaning crowd that incessantly forced its way forward. But as the gondola continued to move slowly through the station, so did the endless wave of zombies that never ceased its attempts to get inside. The whole mass of walking dead acted like a glacier, slowly creeping in the same direction as an unstoppable force, never stalling or breaking for an instant.

For a solid minute, the battle raged on with the three survivors holding back the assault from inside their tight quarters. Then, at about halfway through the station, Nellie's rifle clicked empty. At first, she reached inside her coat for additional ammo, but when the zombie wall at the door started to press forward, she realized reloading wasn't an option. Frantic to take back the ground she had lost, Nellie turned her weapon around and began banging the butt of the rifle against any gnashing head that poked through the doorway.

The group showed an awkward display of teamwork to keep the zombies at bay, but it seemed to work. Although arms would occasionally grasp at air inside the cab, not a single zombie had succeeded to gain full entry. Their slow and deliberate movements allowed the survivors time to pace themselves in a well-timed system of defense. After all, there was no sense rushing the fight. The gondola was more than halfway through the station and would continue to slowly move towards the exit. Eventually, the group would be free, all they had to do was hold out for a few more minutes.

That plan changed, however, when a loud crunch of the gondola track above their heads rang out over the moaning of the crowd and was immediately followed by the cab coming to a jerky halt.

The sudden stop took all three passengers by surprise, but none of them had the luxury to look up at what caused it. Nellie gritted her teeth as she twisted the rifle around like a staff to keep the top portion of the door blocked. This allowed her to look back at Chris with a silent expression that demanded he explain what just happened.

He opened his mouth to answer but was also unexpectedly met with an empty click from his gun. The patroller then proceeded to sit back and repeatedly kick at the door alongside Stephanie while answering Nellie's concern. "The added resistance must've triggered a failsafe."

Still pushing back against the onslaught, Nellie wasted no time with a follow-up. "How do we get it back on?"

"A red button in the control booth behind us."

Upon hearing those words, Stephanie stopped kicking and quickly swung her feet down into a sprinter's position. "I'm going."

Although Chris wanted to stop kicking and talk to the girl, he had to speak while continuing to fight off the limbs reaching through the doorway. "But you won't have time to make it back."

"I don't plan on it."

"What?"

Nellie quickly interrupted the brewing conversation to cut it off before it began. "If she's going to go she has to go now."

Stephanie squatted, ready to propel herself forward, but kept her gaze in Chris's direction. He paused his defenses to look at her for the briefest moment. And in that short second, she could tell how badly he wanted to discuss options with her. To formulate some sort of plan to save her.

There just wasn't enough time, though. All they had was a single instant to make a decision. So with a quick nod of his head, Chris told Stephanie all he was able to.

And the girl responded by shooting herself out into the zombie wall that barricaded the doorway.

Although her frame was small, Steph's quick blast caught the crowd off guard. The zombies' frail bodies tumbled over like bowling pins, and gave the girl just enough free space to pivot in the direction of the control booth.

In a dead sprint, Stephanie darted straight into the horde in front of her, fearlessly meeting them head on. At first, the mob gave way like it did when she exited the gondola. But there were too many to power through.

Eventually, Stephanie's sprint got caught up in the zombie wall, slowing to nothing more than a single person working their way through a crowd of people. Only these people weren't just in the way. The zombies' grabbing hands and ravenous teeth pulled and snapped at the girl from every direction. Spikes of pain attacked her skin, each one trying to drag her down to the floor. More scratches and bites littered her bleeding body with every passing second, but that didn't stop her from pressing forward.

In a combination of agility and power, Stephanie muscled her way through the moving sea of ghouls and freaks, never looking anywhere other than the booth in front of her. She swam her arms forward, using every ounce of her weight as leverage against the force pushing back against her. And despite the agony surging up and down her core, the determined girl chose to bite down hard into her lower lip rather than add her screams to the noise already coursing through the room.

With her body burning and covered in blood, Stephanie finally broke out into the free space of the control booth. Once inside, she stumbled forward onto the control panel and practically dropped right on top of the blinking red button marked as her target. Almost immediately, a bell rang out through the station followed by a series of loud clicks and shifting gears as the gondola once again began moving.

From her fatigued position against the control panel, Stephanie looked up to see that there weren't nearly as many zombies surrounding the cab as when she left it. In her dramatic charge through the station, the girl managed to attract the attention of almost every hungry fiend on the floor. Her partners now had practically a clear shot out of the station and, in a few moments, would be on their descent down into Mountain Village.

It was a strange and awkward feeling of success for Stephanie. Mainly because she had never before in her life been so determined to accomplish a single goal. Over the course of one day, her life, not only physically, but mentally and emotionally, had been turned upside down and inside out. Truths had become falsehoods. And fears that she never knew she had become real. But with her family gone and nothing left to lose, she'd given herself to a cause. It didn't matter if that cause was right. What mattered was that she believed in it and, for the first time since she could remember, felt pride in that fact.

It was a new emotion that caused Stephanie to smile for this bittersweet ending. A smile that remained even as the zombies dragged her to the floor and began devouring her body.

26

Anna awoke to the faint sound of grumbling from across the room. It barely stood out amongst the soft, continuous moaning that persisted outside the cabin. But she'd gotten so used to the zombies' death cry that it practically lulled her to sleep while waiting for the man in front of her to be cured.

She didn't know how long it'd been since she injected him (or how long she'd been asleep for that matter), but the quick rest gave Anna the jump-start she needed to see her patient's treatment to its end.

He passed out immediately after receiving the cure, which was to be expected. The compound was originally used as a sedative, after all. But a short time later the man started developing a fever, breaking out into a deep, cold sweat across his forehead.

At first, Anna feared that he was allergic to the medicine. Then she recalled that she hadn't observed how the cure worked on the test subject back at the school. Maybe the fever was a normal part of the process as it burned the sickness out of the body.

Whatever the case may have been, Dr. Morris knew her patient wasn't regaining consciousness anytime soon. She took a seat across the room, planning only to rest her eyes. But the tired woman fell asleep instead, and only recently woke up to the odd noise bubbling from the man's mouth.

He was starting to come to, and Anna cautiously approached him while listening intently to his muffled words. His eyes were still closed, so Dr. Morris just assumed he was dreaming. But the activity was a good sign that the cure was staving off whatever was in his system, at least for the time being.

She continued to move closer and stopped once she realized he was merely speaking the pointless gibberish old men occasionally ramble off in their sleep. Unsatisfied by his drivel, Anna was about ready to stand when she realized she wasn't quite looking at the same person as before.

The man's aged, wrinkly face had grown even rougher than it was earlier. His once sunburned, mountain skin became pale enough to make out a spider web of veins across his still sweaty cheeks and forehead. But most troubling of all was that despite appearing unconscious, his chest continued to rise and drop rapidly as if the man was panting from an all-out sprint.

Already crouching closely to examine his face, Anna curiously lifted her patient's hand to take a pulse. She found the arm to be dead weight, completely devoid of life as the man slept despite his rapidly pounding chest. Dr. Morris placed her fingers against his wrist and immediately felt a pulse jumping out at her.

She then looked over to the watch on her other arm but felt silly when it wasn't there. She must've forgotten to put it on before leaving her house for work.

This scattered brain revelation was followed by the man suddenly springing to life and latching his mouth firmly onto Anna's other arm still placed against his neck.

Although she couldn't see them, the doctor could feel sharp teeth sinking deep into her flesh. Once secured, the man's jaw took its time digging towards the bone while a continuous stream of blood oozed past his lips.

The pain was enormous, but Anna didn't scream. The utter and complete surprise of the moment robbed the air right out of her lungs, preventing the doctor from uttering a sound. Instead, all Anna could do was stare in disbelief as the man chomped down harder and harder into her limb.

Eventually, the chunk of meat in his mouth satisfied the man enough for him to pull back and rip out a large section of his victim's arm. Blood poured from the gaping hole as Anna stumbled back in a near paralyzing state of shock. She continued to stare at the wound, and through the torn and shredded pieces of flesh, Anna could sporadically see straight through to the white of her bone.

Movement from the rejuvenated man then began to catch the doctor's attention. She shifted her gaze over to him and was speechless at the frenzied look glaring from his eyes. The man stood calmly and carefully in direct contrast with the expression of bloodthirsty rage on his face. The blood still smothering his mouth bubbled as the man hissed down at Anna like an animal sizing up its prey.

But even though a compounding terror shook her entire body, Anna still didn't scream. In fact, fear never even entered her thoughts. All she could wonder was what went wrong to create the monster that stood before her. Why wasn't he cured? It should've worked. No. More than that. It was supposed to work. It had to. It was their last chance. Their only hope of salvation. And she was going to be the hero that rescued Telluride from the horror that tore it apart.

But not anymore. Her dreams of being the savior were over. And that was the only thing she could think about as the man lunged for her face.

***

When she first volunteered herself for this mission, Georgia didn't know how difficult it would be to get a workable signal through the building's tower. That didn't mean her decision to go was wrong. The others were most likely going to destroy the town one way or another, and TORO was their best bet to inform as many people as they could of the impending disaster. As the only station employee currently in the valley, getting it up and running fell solely on her shoulders. Unfortunately, it wasn't proving to be as easy as she hoped.

The control room where she now worked was still in disarray and the window separating it from the broadcast booth was still smashed to pieces from when Malcolm crashed through it. The repair of the station's equipment went smoothly enough, though. But now that they were finished, there was nothing for Molly to do but wait as Georgia tried to get the system up and running.

Through the small window on the door, Georgia could see the schoolteacher getting restless, pacing out in the quiet hallway. Molly wasn't an idiot, either. Although this wasn't her expertise, she knew it shouldn't have taken this long. And the faster Georgia watched her walk back and forth, the more nervous she became that she wouldn't be able to finish the job.

The DJ forced her gaze back to the screen, but her eyes struggled to focus on the work. The nerves churning inside Georgia's stomach were starting to get to her. And for the first time since she sat in front of the computer, the tired girl realized there was a strong possibility that she wouldn't be able to get the job done, which in turn made it harder to concentrate.

The affair turned into a perpetuating cycle of frustration and self-doubt. A downward spiral that she only snapped out of when the sound of the door swinging open grabbed her attention.

Molly entered the room along with an aura of anxious energy. "Making progress?"

Georgia continued to stare at the screen, though, trying her best to refrain from making any eye contact. "I think so."

Her partner wasn't thrilled with the answer. "You think?"

"I'm a DJ. Not an engineer."

Molly gave the girl an unnerving stare. It was a look that made Georgia feel both guilty and ashamed. Not because she wasn't able to get the system working but because she was too much of a coward to do it the right way. All they had to do was rewire the network and rework the mainframe to bypass the damaged equipment in the server room.

But that required her to deal with Malcolm's corpse and blood spread out over the floor. She'd been avoiding even looking into the room (much less confronting the memory of being in it), since they entered the building. Mainly because Georgia didn't think she had to. There were other ways to get a signal up the tower, and Georgia assured herself she had the ability to get it done. But now she realized her confidence was nothing more than a weak justification for her fear.

Despite her hardened shell, the frightened girl just didn't want to face what she'd done. And now she had to accept that her denial had possibly put hundreds of lives in danger.

The guilt weighing her down must've showed on her face because Molly could tell something was wrong. But before the schoolteacher had a chance to bring it up, a loud bang grabbed both of the women's attention.

Georgia felt her heart, already aching from the emotional plight tearing her apart, drop further into her stomach. She froze in her chair as Molly quickly went into the hallway through the still open door.

From her seat, Georgia could see Molly staring down the hall, and the expression of confused terror that took over her face spoke volumes about what was in front of her. A steady stream of moans echoing their way through the building was growing louder by the second, and Georgia could only imagine how many mindless zombies it took to create such a deafening noise.

But despite her obvious fear, Molly wasn't panicking. In fact, she wasn't moving at all. She just stood there in complete awe of whatever threat was coming towards her.

Which for Georgia was an unseen horror that piqued her curiosity. "What is it?"

Molly answered the question while squinting her eyes to make sure what she was seeing was real. "They're here. And they're...different."

"Different how?"

Finally filled with urgency, Molly darted inside the room and quickly slammed the door behind her. "Just keep working."

Georgia dove back into the screen, frantic to pick up where she left off. But as she typed away, her mind continually failed to focus on the mission. "Why didn't you shoot them?"

Molly pressed her back against the door while trying her best to see down the hall through the door's small window. "I'd run out of bullets...fast."

The picture of a zombie filled hallway kept creeping into Georgia's thoughts, distracting her from the task at hand. She couldn't think. She couldn't focus. And no matter how hard she tried to block it out, the feeling of impending doom began to overwhelm every aspect of Georgia's being.

The stoic expression of solidarity chiseled into Molly's face, said that she'd already accepted her fate. But the hard truth that she wasn't going to make it out of the building alive hit Georgia like a brick wall, especially when she just barely escaped it with her life only hours earlier.

In the back of her mind, she always knew that this was a possibility. That she agreed to a suicide mission for a selfless, noble cause. But there's a difference between believing you're ready for death and actually embracing it when the end is staring you in the face.

And that's when a series of grey, dried up faces appeared all bunched together in the door's window. Their harrowing moans paralyzed Georgia with an incalculable fear as she tried to wrap her muddled mind around what she was seeing. Are these the same zombies? What happened to them? Are they even still considered alive?

The horrific ghouls began banging on the door, demanding to be let in as Molly firmly pressed her back against it. "Georgia. Georgia! Focus! You need to finish."

Her words snapped the DJ back to reality and filled her with a new sense of determination. Frantic to finish what she started, Georgia's fingers danced around the keyboard. One after the other, she tried every avenue available to her, hoping a signal would stick in the system. But something was preventing her. Nothing seemed to hold. She tried harder and harder, pressing the program to its limits until it eventually gave out and locked her out of the network.

The red error message that flashed across the screen was the final nail in the coffin of Georgia's dreams for success, and her eyes slowly looked to the floor in a stupor of disbelief.

From her position against the door, Molly watched Georgia intently and questioned the girl with a tone of optimistic hope. "Did you do it?"

But instead of answering, the DJ lifted her gaze in a speechless trance. Molly continued to press on, though, looking for a definitive reply. "Georgia, did you fix the signal?!"

She took a moment to think of the best way to communicate her failure, but Georgia could only muster enough will to slowly shake her head with a blank stare.

Surprisingly, Molly took the grim news with nothing more than an accepting sigh. She then wasted no time dealing with the situation the best way she knew how. "Get on the radio and tell the others."

Scanning the computer desk, Georgia caught sight of the handheld radio and scrambled to lift it up to her mouth. "Hello? Hello, come in! This is Georgia. We couldn't get the radio working and we're being overrun."

She paused and anxiously waited for a response that never came. "Can anybody hear me? Come in!"

A mixture of despair and confusion manifested in her voice as Georgia tried one last, desperate plea. "Hello?"

When no one answered, she finally looked up at Molly with an expression of hopelessness. "It's not working."

Her words immediately coincided with the door in the broadcast booth bursting open. Through the broken glass in front of them, the two women watched as a flood of walking corpses sluggishly dragged into the room. They were moving so slowly it was almost strange to consider them a threat. But their agonizing moans and deathly stares told Georgia all she needed to know.

One after another, they poured into the room, and Molly raised her weapon ready to shoot. She didn't, though. Instead, she waited, biding her time as her targets inched closer with every passing second. Then, when there was no chance of missing, Molly calmly and carefully squeezed the trigger, making sure each bullet hit its mark right between the eyes.

The gun was loud and shocked Georgia back into the corner of the room. She wanted to fight but didn't know how. There were so many of them, and they just kept coming.

Molly continued to pace herself, dropping each zombie with a single shot. The bodies quickly began to pile up on top of each other. But that didn't stop the droning fiends from climbing over their fallen brethren on their way through the broken glass and into the control room.

With each new casualty, Molly allowed the next one to draw closer. Before long, the endless wave of zombies was right in front of her face but would only come barely within reach before dropping to the floor. The schoolteacher never considered herself a killer but, at that moment, appeared to be in some sort of murderous zone. Molly hit her mark with every shot and felt confident enough to take every last one of them down.

And that's when she pulled the trigger expecting to hear a bang but was met with only the sound of a solitary click. Molly's brief realization that she failed to keep track of her ammo was short lived. The zombies she had confidently let in so close were already on top of her. So much so that the click of her empty gun was immediately followed by her scream as they sunk their hungry mouths onto her body.

Without pause or delay, the next wave of zombies turned their attention towards Georgia, still backed into the corner. Even with the horde moving at a snail's pace, she only had a few moments before they reached her.

The facts told her there was no other outcome. There were at least a dozen of them between her and the exit with more continuing to enter the room. She didn't have a gun, not that it made much of a difference for Molly. And the radio didn't work, so nobody was coming to her rescue.

But even given all that, Georgia still found it hard to accept her fate and felt the urge to fight. She frantically kicked in front of her, pushing and smacking the soles of her feet at every zombie that came close. Her futile struggle only lasted a few pointless seconds, though, as her desperate pants of panic soon became screams of horror when the mob became too many to stop.

27

After Stephanie's sacrifice, the rest of the gondola ride down to Mountain Village was silent. Nellie knew there was plenty to talk about. They should've been formulating a plan and developing some sort of strategy for dealing with whatever pandemonium they might encounter. But the old woman could also feel the loss weighing heavy on her partner's heart and knew he needed the time to grieve.

She just hoped his moment of silence didn't last long. In just a few minutes, the gondola would enter Mountain Village station, and Chris would have to be focused for them to complete their mission.

Personally, Mrs. Sheridan didn't feel the need to give the girl's death any more than a passing thought. And to be fair, Chris never looked to the woman for sympathy anyway. How could he when he saw her blow her own husband's head off without even batting an eye.

As soon as the outbreak began, Nellie knew that a battlefield line was drawn between the infected and the survivors alongside her. She wouldn't go so far as to call them soldiers, but death was a known hazard to all involved. Besides, in Nellie's mind, everyone in this valley was already dead.

To her joy (and somewhat surprise), Chris sat up in his seat ready for action as they pulled into the station. Nellie nodded her head approvingly and was taken aback even further when the ski patroller darted out of the cab as the doors opened.

It seemed that Stephanie's death had filled young Mr. Chambers with a revitalized sense of conviction. He was determined to make sure the girl did not sacrifice herself in vain. And luckily for Nellie, she was all too willing to use that drive to her advantage.

She followed him into the station and the unlikely duo stopped just in front of the exit to gain a sense of their surroundings. What they found under the bright lights of the heated walkway was a similar scene to the one they had left in the streets of Telluride. Every inch of Mountain Village courtyard was packed with a moving mass of the same walking corpses they encountered up at the mid-mountain station. Chris assured her that the place was empty earlier this afternoon, but like in town, the infected must've been hiding until the time when they would emerge into the darkness as the decomposed creatures they'd become.

From his position, Chris intently scoured the crowd. But his attention was mainly focused on a building closer to them and on the outskirts of the village square. "There's too many to get to Peter's office from here. But the basement he was talking about runs through the village. If we can get to the ski patrol building where the explosives are located, we can just head downstairs and take the tunnels across."

After hearing the plan, Nellie carefully observed the zombie stragglers between them and the building, who roamed around aimlessly, free from the much larger, denser pack in the center of the village. "We'll still have to go through a fair amount of those things."

"You got a better idea?"

Nellie was almost insulted by the question. She was merely stating a fact, not complaining. So she simply responded to the patroller's comment by lifting her rifle and leaving the station.

She never bothered to look back to see if Chris followed her out, but Nellie wasted no time taking aim at the nearest zombie. Calmly and carefully moving ahead, Nellie squeezed the trigger while looking down her rifle's sight. The bullet found its mark, but it also rang out a deafening gunshot across the village square. The loud bang overcame the chaotic symphony of moans bellowed by the zombie orchestra, grabbing their attention in the process.

The giant mass in the village courtyard began swaying back and forth as their slow move towards the gondola began. At which point it became a race against time for Nellie to reach her destination before being engulfed by the crowd approaching her.

Without running, she quickly scuttled forward, selectively picking off the zombies in her way, each one with nothing more than a single bullet between the eyes. Nellie was careful not to get distracted by taking out too many. She didn't want to waste time focusing on those that weren't an immediate threat.

But the fringes of the zombie horde started trickling into her path on the heated walkway. Nellie was quickly finding that her time between shots was growing shorter and shorter, and she was still a good hundred feet away from her destination.

The seasoned shooter didn't panic, though. Or even look away from her task when another gunshot fired that didn't come from her rifle. Nellie kept her concentrating eyes ahead and could sense Chris move up alongside her. Together they alternated shots at the zombie wave that was on the verge of overtaking them. To keep the fiends away, they began rapidly squeezing their triggers for the last few steps until finally barging through the glass front door of the ski patrol offices.

Chris quickly locked the door behind them before leading Nellie deeper into the building. But it only took a matter of seconds before the massive crowd busted through the glass door and windows, storming the lobby like a slow, unstoppable juggernaut. Neither of the survivors looked back, though, as Chris led Nellie down a stairwell, unconcerned about the danger behind them.

The couple then approached a steel cage positioned in the corner of the immaculately clean boiler room-like basement. With the zombie moans echoing out from the lobby, Chris casually entered a combination into a padlock on the chain door. Once unlocked, he and Nellie both entered the cage and stopped to survey the well-kept, organized shelves of equipment before them.

With labels meticulously categorizing every piece of hardware, Nellie's eyes scanned each shelf to figure out exactly what they needed. Her gaze immediately passed by a series of rifles, mortars and other kinds of launchers, what most would consider a safe and distant delivery system for avalanche control. For their purposes, though, Nellie was more interested in the bombs themselves, along with the other explosive devices found on the top tier of the shelf.

At her side, Nellie could sense Chris preparing to point the equipment out to her. But Nellie didn't wait for his instructions. She already took it upon herself to grab a duffle bag from the floor and began piling in everything she needed. Picking and choosing from the stockpile, Nellie found a good assortment of charges and fuses for a controlled demolition.

Once the duffle bag was full, Nellie threw the strap over her shoulder and turned back around to face the patroller. "Now where?"

"This way."

Nellie followed Chris out of the cage, but they both soon stopped when a series of loud crashes from the stairwell overtook the continuous moaning that had become their natural ambience. The noise drew their attention as several of the weak, flimsy bodies came tumbling into the basement in the form of a zombie avalanche.

After slamming into the floor at the base of the steps, the living corpses just laid on the ground motionless. And despite the danger of having the creatures right in front of them, Nellie and Chris just stood there, curiously watching to see what they might do. And after a brief moment of suspense, the zombies started moaning again as they awkwardly began the slow process of rising to their feet.

Again, Nellie and Chris didn't feel the urge to flee. Even as another series of bangs brought a second group of zombies down into the basement.

The danger, although apparent, wasn't immediate. But there was something chilling about the scene before them that made Nellie uncomfortable. The sight of stumbling zombies endlessly pursuing them without thought, logic or reason was a discouraging image. No matter where they went. No matter how far they ran. These creatures would always be following behind them.

It didn't fill her with fear, though. Just made Nellie feel all the more justified in her actions.

When the first set of invaders finally got to their feet (and a third began their rough trip down the steps), Nellie and Chris resumed their quest to a tunnel entrance on the other side of the basement.

They weren't necessarily running, neither felt the need to rush, but the couple jogged with a mild sense of urgency. Although still a way from catching up, the zombies were surely on their way. And whatever distance the survivors could put between them and their pursuers would certainly alleviate a great deal of stress, which was always a good idea when setting a series of live explosives in a high-pressure situation.

In line with Mountain Village's recent construction, the tunnel was fairly modern and updated as far as underground passageways went. Besides four well-formed concrete walls, a series of pipes traversed the length of the tunnel, veering off and elbowing in different directions at various intersections. Nellie had no idea where they were going, but Chris kept on a steady path dead ahead and looked perfectly confident in the route he was taking.

By the time the group entered another basement, much larger yet similar to the one they just left, the moaning that followed them down the tunnel had faded.

But Nellie grew a little concerned when she looked to Chris for further direction and saw that he was just as lost as she was. "I assume we're under the right building. So then, what're we looking for?"

"I'm not sure. Hopefully, we'll know it when we see it."

Nellie took it upon herself to start following the pipes above their heads in search of the gas reserve. Chris then followed her lead, and it wasn't long before they both met in a separate room housing a large tank completely outfitted with an assortment of valves and gauges. Nellie felt completely dwarfed by its size and was a bit intimidated by the number of pipes, both large and small, that fed into the top of it.

After a few seconds of standing in awe as well, Chris broke the silence between them. "You have any idea how to work this thing?"

But instead of answering right away, Nellie took her time by examining every inch of the tank. Little by little, she began breaking down the whole contraption into its most basic components. The equipment, capable of accommodating the whole village, was certainly more massive than the facilities she'd been used to working with. But isolated out, the tank's parts were nothing she hadn't seen in the past while helping her father and brothers maintain their properties around town. It was a fairly simple system, just on a much grander scale.

Once she became familiar enough to recognize what she had to do, a sly smile broke out on Nellie's face as she finally answered his question. "I think I do."

She handed Chris the duffle bag before approaching the tank. Then, after a final, quick scan of the system, Nellie began turning knobs, valves and levers in an orchestrated combo.

Chris initially took a step back as the pipes began to grumble with the gauges coming to life, but Nellie quickly pulled his attention back to her as she reached a hand out to him. "Start handing me the charges."

Although still unsure of the situation, Chris opened up the duffel bag and started handing her the devices inside. One by one, Nellie placed the explosives around the room in no particular design. She wasn't quite sure what set up would be the most effective. But then again, the old rancher figured if she had to worry about creating an optimal explosion in a room filled with bombs then something was dearly wrong.

When everything was finally set, Nellie turned back to Chris but found that the patroller was gone. All that remained was the limp duffel back resting on the ground where he had stood.

Nellie wasn't too concerned that he took off. She didn't really have a need for him now, anyway. But her instincts told her that he didn't leave empty handed. It was a fear that she confirmed when Nellie looked inside the empty duffel bag and saw that the last piece of crucial equipment was missing. Chris had taken the detonator.

***

As a ski patroller, Chris developed a knack for figuring out when people weren't telling him the whole truth. EMS, in particular, was known for catching people in vulnerable situations, but being on the mountain added a whole nother level to a patient's humility. It didn't matter if they were a snowboarding bum or a skiing executive, a person would say anything to keep their pride intact.

Which was why there was something about Nellie that concerned Chris. From what he could tell, the woman's pride was infallible. It would have to take a lot to unnerve anybody who would shoot their spouse in front of a room filled with strangers. Yet Chris couldn't shake the feeling that she was hiding something. Or at least, not being completely upfront with him. And if it had nothing to do with her pride, then Chris was a bit nervous as to what she had up her sleeve.

But then again, he wasn't completely honest with her either, which was the main reason he never pressed the issue with the old woman. Ever since they left the cabin, Peter had given Chris his own agenda. And not a subtle one at that. Chris was pretty sure Nellie was at least aware that he had an ulterior motive. After all, Stephanie pretty much gave it away on their walk to the gondola.

So as he quickly climbed the stairwell up to Peter's office, Chris had little remorse about running off with the detonator in hand. Before blowing up the village, he had to make sure the other survivors were ready to get going. He just hoped they were all still safe and sound where he had left them.

Unfortunately, that prayer was immediately shattered upon entering the building's top floor hallway.

Blood and body parts were sprawled out from wall to wall, covering almost every inch of surface in sight. The supplies, food and clothing, were all over the floor, probably tossed around during the panic. Chris had encountered this scene before and was easily able to deduce what transpired, but he tried his best to stop himself from recreating the horror in his mind. It was the pure definition of carnage, and as Chris carefully walked through the massacre, he noticed one distinct face was missing among the brutalized men, women and children: Austin Cage.

The movie star was nowhere in sight, and if by some off chance he wasn't the one responsible, he could've been anywhere by now. The crazed attackers the infected became in the first stage of their transformation weren't exactly known for sticking around.

It was a shame that Chris found no one alive, but strangely enough, the person he came to see wouldn't exactly be classified as a survivor. After tiptoeing through the grotesque bloodbath, Chris turned into Peter's office and caught sight of young Ryan still chained to the wall. The boy was eerily standing with his head down and slowly looked up when he felt another presence in the room.

Chris patiently waited by the doorway and wasn't surprised to see that Ryan stood in a daze with his face dripping a copious amount of blood. He had already entered the second stage of the infection. Chris only hoped that the cure would still be effective in someone so far gone.

With the detonator still in his other hand, Chris reached into his jacket and carefully removed the full syringe Peter had handed to him. The cautious patroller then briefly thought about how best to approach the situation. It seemed as though Ryan was relatively docile. The boy stood in place while continuously taking the same long, raspy breaths. His body subtly swayed back and forth while his eyes rolled around in their sockets, refusing to take notice of anything surrounding him.

Without any other option presenting itself, Chris finally decided to just go right in and stick the boy square in the neck. But first the patroller widened his stance before flicking the syringe's cap off with his thumb and cautiously sliding his feet forward one at a time. As he slowly moved towards him, Chris kept his eyes straight on Ryan and nothing else.

He knew there was little chance that the boy was coherent enough to talk to, but that didn't stop him from trying. "Ryan, I know you're in there somewhere. And I'm not done fighting for you. I made Sarah and your father a promise. I'm going to get you out of here, OK? Just hold on and I'll…"

His words were cut off by a loud bang as the left side of Ryan's unsuspecting face exploded off the rest of his head. Blood and brain matter shot out all over the window behind him, and the body appeared to hover in place for a moment longer before dropping to the floor.

With his jaw open in a complete state of shock, Chris quickly turned around to see Nellie still aiming her rifle in the doorway. "What did you just do?!

The old woman casually lowered her rifle and answered the rhetorical question as simply as she could. "Killed a zombie. What did it look like?"

Still holding the detonator firmly in one hand, Chris raised the syringe clutched in the other. "I was going to cure him."

Nellie shook her head as she again responded with a dry tone. "That's not a cure."

"Of course, it is. Dr. Morris said that…"

"Anna Morris is not a doctor. She's a drug addict."

The peculiar statement forced Chris's face to scrunch as he paused for a moment to process the confusing information. "What?"

"She was a hippie teenager that came here in the sixties, dropped acid, and never left. It seems Mr. Hayden would've known that if he stepped off his pedestal in the mountains every once in a while."

Chris's eyes sank to the floor as a large weight fell from his shoulders into the pit of his stomach. He could feel his insides begin to churn. And his whole being tied into knots while his mind was pulled in a million directions.

He then approached the office window to look out over the infested village square as he spoke, not so much to Nellie but more to himself. "All those people. We have to save them."

Although still keeping a fair distance between them, Nellie approached the large window as well, but looked through it with a small chuckle of pity. "What's there to save? Just look at them, Christopher. Little by little their bodies and minds have been slowly fading away.

They're dying. There's no cure for that."

The truth had already smacked him in the face, but the dense reality of the situation was still working its way through Chris's mind. The force of it all was so thick it caused him to bury himself into his forearm as he fell against the glass. "I knew all the doctors on the mountain, too. I should've known she was lying."

"You wanted to believe in hope. There's nothing wrong with that."

Chris's thoughts immediately brought him images of Sarah. But not of her laughing or smiling. All Chris could see was her beaten body lying in a pool of her own blood. And then a wave of guilt forced his eyes to move from the window over to Ryan's mutilated corpse on the floor. "How could you do it then? Just kill someone you loved so much without a second thought."

"Because hope can only get you so far."

Realizing he'd come to the end of the road, Chris looked at the syringe one last time before letting it slide out of his hand. He watched it fall all the way to the floor before reaching into his jacket and pulling out the hand radio. He clicked the receiver and opened his mouth to speak but caught Nellie plainly staring at him with an odd expression. Her face was flat and dull of emotion. That's when a series of puzzle pieces began to click in Chris's mind.

Slowly taking his hand away from his mouth, the patroller gave the radio one last look before turning his attention back to Nellie. "It doesn't work, does it?"

With the same blank expression remaining on her face, Nellie simply shook her head in a slow yet deliberate manner. Chris then deduced the rest of her plans as a follow up to his original question. "We're not warning anybody. You're just going to blow the village right here and now."

Although he couldn't have known her intentions for sure, Chris's words were in the form of a statement, not a question.

But rather than confirm his suspicions, Nellie went right into explaining her actions. "Sooner or later, we're all going to change into those monsters. No one's immune to this thing. And if we don't stop it here while it's contained in this valley…" Nellie paused to take a deep sigh and then finished her sentence. "…it won't be stopped at all."

With the sting of betrayal already getting to him, Chris squeezed hard on the detonator's handle yet kept his finger off the trigger. "What makes you think I'm going to let you do this?"

Nellie remained strong, though, and stayed perfectly relaxed in her position. Chris half expected the woman to lift her rifle but was taken by surprise when she spoke straight into his eyes with a motherly tone instead. "Because I can see it in your face. The pain. The loss. I'd recognize it anywhere. The despair that fuels us when hope runs out."

Chris wanted to be angry. He wanted to fight back. But Nellie's words fit into his heart like a key, opening up a sea of emotional agony that'd been building since the day began. It was a connection that caused him to release the tense grip of anger around his body, allowing his shoulders to physically relax as he fell back onto his heels.

Nellie saw the patroller finally lower his guard and moved in close by placing a compassionate hand on his shoulder. "It's easy to regret the choices we've failed to make. To accept the guilt of letting down those we love. But that doesn't make us weak. It makes us understand that sometimes the hard choices are the right ones…"

With her hand still on his shoulder, Nellie held out her other one, asking for him to make his final decision, "…even when others refuse to see it."

He didn't find absolution in her speech, but deep down, Chris knew this story never had a happy ending. He always pictured that his life would eventually work itself out. Regardless of how much he avoided the issue, he knew, just knew, that he and Sarah were destined to spend their lives together.

But that didn't matter now. All that mattered was the truth. And Nellie Sheridan saw it better than most.

Chris lifted the detonator and looked at it one last time before placing it firmly into the old woman's open hand. "You could've just shot me and taken it."

Without any pause or hesitation, Nellie's finger released the safety from the device. "That was my backup plan."

And she squeezed the trigger.

28

It sure was a good night for the Apocalypse. Or at least, Scott Brooks thought so.

Despite the raging storm that started off the day, the evening air was calm, clear, and still. Even though the Tomboy settlement was only a few hundred feet more above sea level, Scott noticed the stars shone brighter up here than down in the valley. It also might've had something to do with the fact that the majority of residents were out roaming the streets as zombies and weren't home to turn on their lights. Mountain Village, especially, glimmered as a faint light of its former self with only its streetlamps illuminating the mountainside.

From a cliff overlooking the canyon, Scott stood alone and felt oddly content with the quiet. The scenic view was tranquil, serene, peaceful even. Which was strange given the violence the community had seen. The incessant moaning from the infected roaming the streets gradually faded as the truck made its way up the trail to the point where it couldn't be heard at all. The only thing that remained was an eerie silence, the calm before an explosive storm that would bury everything Scott saw before him in a pile of snow and ruined civilization. Everything except the settlement's original nineteenth century style wooden buildings behind him, which hadn't been touched since the last mining crew vanished during their shift over a century ago.

Another minute passed before Scott could hear the soft crunch of footsteps approaching behind him. It seemed as if it was just one set of feet, but Scott didn't care enough to turn around. He was going to be annoyed regardless of who it was, so he continued to absorb the natural bliss in front of him for as long as he could.

The footsteps slowly grew louder until they were finally interrupted by Beth's annoyingly chirpy voice. "The fuses are all set, but Peter went to explore the mine. Can't imagine why, though. That's the last place I would want to be."

Scott, once again, didn't bother to turn around, or even respond much at all. He just continued to stare out over the moonlit valley, even as Beth wrapped her arms around his neck and lovingly pressed her face against his back. "And now we're finally alone."

If Beth had been on the other side of him, she would've seen Scott's clearly agitated face. His mouth curled up on the edge of becoming a sneer and stayed there until Beth pushed herself off him with sudden excitement. "Oh, I wanted to tell you! He approved the budget request."

Scott's face morphed from annoyance to confusion. He turned around to face her with a raised eyebrow and quietly waited until she elaborated further. "I didn't try to convince him. Just said exactly what Peter wanted to hear and he decided on his own."

Finally breaking his silence, Scott spoke with an irritated tone. "What are you talking about?"

"The poor people building. He's making the one you wanted him to. I did it just like you said."

With all that had happened over the course of the day, it took a moment for Scott to remember the assignment he'd given her. But when it finally came back to him, Scott was so surprised that he couldn't help but laugh with a smile at the girl's almost unbelievable idiocy. "Really? You're bringing that up now?"

Beth immediately realized she was being mocked, and her cheerful demeanor quickly shifted to a mixture of confusion and betrayal. "You're not happy?"

With agitation still bubbling under the surface, Scott threw his arms in the air as his anger fueled a sarcastic cackle. "The entire town turned into a bunch of homicidal maniacs! You think I care about a stupid, fucking building?!"

Beth could obviously see how the conversation was turning and looked away as she took to the defensive. "You don't need to yell."

Continuing his sarcasm, Scott spun around while bellowing his voice out over the valley. "Why not? Because there's so many people around to hear us?"

"Peter might."

In one swoop, Scott's arrogant self became coldly serious as he held out his hand towards Beth. "Not for long. Give me the detonator."

But she just shook her head with a face verging on the cusp of fear. "I don't have it. He took it in with him."

Scott lifted his extended hand into a shrug as he rolled his eyes in exaggerated disappointment. "Oh, wonderful. Another fantastic way you've pulled through for me."

Beth's fear then faded, though, as she squinted her eyes to carefully examine the face in front of her. "Scott, baby, you don't look so well."

But her concern was instantly overwhelmed by Scott's escalating ferocity. He began to encircle her, like a predator stalking its prey. And she feebly retreated into herself with each repeated verbal assault more intense than the last. "How do I look then, huh? Like someone who's just been chased around by murderous lunatics? Or maybe a victim of a plane crash, hmm? Perhaps a guy just frustrated because he's been dealing with fucking morons. ALL. DAY. LONG!"

He then stopped in front of Beth for a final insult just as her eyes began to swell with tears. "And you think I would be used to that last one by now. Considering that I have you in my life."

Beth tightened her face to prevent herself from overtly weeping, but she couldn't stop the tears from streaming down her cheeks. She then lowered her head to shamefully hide her cries.

Sensing her modesty as an opening for another attack, Scott gently placed his hands on Beth's shoulders and spoke with a sarcastically caring voice to further berate her. "Awww. Did I hurt your feelings, Beth? Well, what did you think was going to happen? That we would get married and live in a mansion on the California coast? I'm sorry, but you're a tool, sweetie. A means to get a job done. A job that's pointless now. And you know what happens to a useless tool, right?"

Beth looked up and her puffy eyes shone with a glimmer of beaten innocence. It was obvious that she hoped and prayed, even still, that Scott was playing some kind of joke. That his cruel words were nothing more than his way of lashing out. A desperate man taking his frustration out on the one closest to him.

But if that were true, Scott wouldn't have been disgusted by her hopeless feelings. He would've felt sorry for the misguided, love-struck girl before him. Or at the very least, pity the fact that she fell for such a cold, impassionate man.

Instead, he only saved her the horror of hearing an answer to his rhetorical question by spinning around and tossing her off the side of the cliff.

***

Peter saw nothing of any particular interest inside the mine. Not that he was planning to find anything but figured he might as well have a look anyway. People had most certainly been in there as recently as the day before, which was as likely a culprit for the outbreak as anything (meaning he still hadn't a clue as to what caused it). But even though the mine was sealed off for tourists, state officials and other workers had been in there before. If it was truly the source for whatever was causing this epidemic, then why now?

The question gently buzzed around Peter's mind like an annoying gnat. But in the end, the why didn't matter. All that mattered was that if there was even a chance this mine was to blame for the destruction of his home, then it had to be destroyed.

Neither he nor Beth had set explosives before but arming the charges was fairly simple. Also, it didn't hurt that he and his former assistant had already formed a working relationship. She was someone whom he trusted enough to literally place his life in her hands. Unlike their third companion.

Not for a second did Peter think he was going to allow Scott Brooks to place dangerous charges in his vicinity. He still didn't know what the weasel was up to, but Peter was content to simply let Brooks hang around the abandoned settlement until the plan was in place. That was the only reason he still carried the detonator in his hand. Not that he thought the man would do anything as malicious as blow the mine up with him still inside. But Peter would be damned if he was going to let an egomaniac control the situation.

Eventually, Peter realized his meandering around the darkened tunnels was a waste of time and decided to backtrack to the mine's entrance. With the detonator in one hand, he used the flashlight in his other to guide a way through the rugged, cave-like walls. Soon the mine's dirt floor showed glimpses of snow that had blown in from outside. The trail of white started to build up until Peter was distracted by a speck of moonlight growing in the distance. As he moved towards it, the speck gradually opened up to become the mine's entrance.

But as he came closer, Peter also started to hear the faint echo of a yell rushing at him. Although Peter still couldn't make out the words, the booming voice grew louder with every step. The concerned village manager picked up his pace just as he entered a flood of moonlight peering into the mine. It was a trail of celestial glow that carried Peter outside just in time to see Scott spin around and toss Beth off the side of the settlement plateau.

The unbelievable sight was accompanied by a scream of terror as Beth plummeted down the mountainside, and it wasn't until the girl's shrieking voice faded away that Peter was able to yell out to her murderer. "What did you just do?!"

Refusing to move right away, Scott stood firm with his back to Peter as he answered succinctly. "Took care of a problem."

The cold, callous remark hit Peter like a truck. His mind went blank, completely unable to respond. But the brief silence was shattered when Scott turned around while removing the handgun from his jacket. "And I'm about to take care of another one."

Still standing in the mine's entrance, Peter's shock prevented him from even registering the gun pointed straight at him. Instead, he mumbled out a set of words to no one in particular, still struggling to accept that his assistant had just been murdered right in front of him. "You...you killed her."

With the gun held out casually in his hand, Scott began to slowly walk forward through the snow. "She was a good lay and all but super high maintenance. Then again, you would know that, wouldn't you?"

Although he had the detonator and flashlight in either hand, Peter's attention kept reminding him of the handgun in his own jacket pocket. It was an inconspicuous tendency that Scott easily picked up on as he reached out and carefully took the weapon out himself. "Hold on there, Petey. Don't want you hurting yourself now, do we?"

Scott flicked his wrist, tossing the gun deep into the abandoned settlement. And Peter simply watched helplessly as he held his own occupied hands off to the side. "Why are you doing this?"

Actually amazed by the question, Scott tilted his head to look at Peter with a surprised smile. "You really have to ask? We're standing before one of the greatest discoveries in the history of mankind. Do you have any idea how much something like this is worth? Billions. And you just want to blow it up?"

Peter was just as shocked by Scott's answer. But instead of surprise, Mr. Hayden had to refrain from showing his disgust. "Money? That's what this is about?"

"Of course! This thing is literally a gold mine! Well, not literally. But you know what I mean."

Peter was utterly appalled by the man's uncompromising greed. He knew Scott Brooks was a shady character, at best. But never had he imagined such an immoral snake of a human being living next door to him. There was no way someone could be so recklessly stupid.

And that's when Peter noticed Scott wasn't looking like his normal self. "You're sick."

Brooks laughed off the assertion as a meaningless insult. "Why? Because I make the most of what's in front of me? That's what I do. I see an opportunity and take it. Anywhere and from anyone."

But he didn't realize Peter's statement was a literal observation on his physical appearance. "No. You're actually sick, Your face is pale. Your eyes are bloodshot. You're turning into one of them."

The smile on Scott's face slowly faded when the grave truth made its way into his mind. "You don't know what you're talking about."

"My own son attacked me. I think I do."

Scott shook his head in disbelief as a sudden despair began to take over. "No. No. No! This can't be happening. I...I can't be one of those things."

A part of Peter actually felt good about his rival's doomed fate, but he wasn't able to show it. Instead, all he could muster was a cheap taunt. "I guess even assholes aren't immune."

Ignoring the insult, Scott's hand shook as he pushed the gun further into Peter's face. "Give me the cure."

Watching the barrel wave around in front of his eyes, Peter quickly deduced the situation wasn't working in his favor. It was bad enough when Scott just wanted to kill him as a normal person, but now the regular lunatic was going to become a bloodthirsty one. He could give him the cure, but then he would still be left alone with a murderer. Either way, Peter had to do something.

And then he realized that he had yet to see a zombie use a gun. At some point, Scott would have to ditch it during the heat of his transformation. That would be the moment for Peter to strike.

If he were to survive, he had to throw his attacker off guard. Agitate him so that he would get lost between the man he is and the monster he would become.

And right now, that meant frustrating the shit out of him by playing dumb. "What cure?"

"The one from the doctor. It's in one of your pockets."

Peter stupidly tried to grab the syringe while still holding the flashlight and detonator. "But my hands are full."

"Then drop something."

"Like what? The detonator? But then the mine could blow."

The beads of sweat building on Scott's furrowed forehead started popping as they dripped down his tightened, angry face. "Just shut up and do it!"

"I thought you didn't want to blow it up, though?"

Scott let out a frustrated puff of air and bared his teeth before screaming out in a fit of rage. "Give it to me now!"

In one sudden, wrathful moment, Brooks threw his arms back to dive forward at Peter, tossing the gun behind him in the process. Scott's attack caught Peter by surprise as he tackled into him, bringing both men down to the ground. Although the snow certainly cushioned the fall, Peter still hit the ground with enough unexpected force to cause the detonator to fly out of his hand.

Now on top of his foe, Scott frantically searched through the pockets of Peter's jacket. His face had been taken over by a desperate ferocity, but the man still clung to the last bits of his sanity as he continued his search for the cure. "Where is it? Where is it?!"

Still recovering from the blow, Peter grunted off the last remnants of pain in his back just in time to see Scott find the syringe tucked deep into his breast pocket. In one fluid motion, Brooks used the last of his conscious thoughts to flick off the safety cap and jab the needle straight into the top of his neck.

The sight was a little unnerving for Peter to watch, but he understood that in Scott's desperation, it was the most convenient patch of skin available to him. Whether or not the substance would work, though, was another issue entirely. Did he inject it in the right location? Or the more pressing question: did he use it in time?

For a moment, Scott's breathing slowed down as he looked up with an easy sense of calm. Peter couldn't see Brooks's face, but the man's body relaxed back, the stress and tension shedding off his shoulders. He continued to stare up, though, refusing to look down at the victim he continued to pin into the snow. And for his part, Peter was reluctant to grab his attacker's attention, afraid at what kind of monster, human or otherwise, he would be talking to.

The village manager just cautiously waited for what seemed like an eternity before finally calling out in a soft, gentle voice. "Scott...?"

Brooks didn't respond, though. He just remained still in the same calm position, either ignoring or not hearing his name. Peter waited for another moment before trying again.

But when he opened his mouth to speak, Scott unleashed a sudden animalistic roar as his arms shot down towards his target's throat. Reacting on pure instinct, Peter pushed the flashlight up with both hands against Scott's chest to keep the savage attack at arm's length.

Peter wanted to stop for a moment and think about what to do. About how to handle the situation. But he wasn't able. All he could do was stay strong as Scott continued to press down on top of him, gnashing his teeth and swiping his hands like deadly claws in front of his prey's face.

Adrenaline poured through Peter's veins, forcing his body into action. He pulled his legs up to his chest, quickly sliding his knees under the assault before thrusting his feet in a hard push against Scott's body.

The bloodthirsty fiend fell backwards, but no sooner did he hit the snow had the crazy creature already sprung up ready to attack again. Sensing another onslaught, Peter quickly rolled to his feet just in time to see Scott charging at him full speed. With the flashlight still in hand, Peter took a fighting stance and readied himself.

Then, at the last possible second, Peter stepped to the side and swung his flashlight around, connecting it to the side of the maniac's head. Scott's momentum took him flying past Peter and into the mine, but his flailing arms still managed to scratch at Peter's face as it just barely dodged out of the way. The attack spun Peter around, knocking him to his knees, where he then looked down to see droplets of blood falling into the snow. A slow wave of pain rushed through his face, and he dropped the flashlight to run his hand across the freshly torn skin on his cheek.

Inside the mine, Scott stumbled over from the blow to his head. But it only took a moment for him to recover by letting out a ravenous roar that echoed out of the mine. He rolled back over and began clawing his way to his feet in another dead charge ahead.

The beast-like shrill brought Peter back to the battle, and he peeked over his shoulder into the mine to see Brooks clamoring towards him like a crazed animal. Another spike of adrenaline flooded his limbs as Peter scrambled, too, climbing through the snow on his hands and knees.

He could feel Scott on his trail, the maddened predator ready to pounce on him at any second. And in a last desperate lunge, Peter reached out for the detonator lying peacefully in the snow. He snuck his hand under the device and without a second thought pressed down on the trigger.

At first, he heard a series of loud booms as the charges popped behind him. Peter then spun around on his back to see Scott's ferocious face diving head first at him just as the blast dropped a large boulder on top of his flying body. The explosion continued to shake the mountainside, bringing down more rocks and rubble to clog up the mine's entrance. But once the dust all cleared, Peter could still see Scott's hand protruding out from the middle of the debris.

A sudden panic caused him to drop the detonator and scramble over to the gun next to him that Scott had tossed into the snow. Once he picked it up, Peter pointed it with both hands at the collapsed cave entrance and fearfully zoomed in on the lifeless hand lying still amidst the rock. He then waited in that position for a solid minute before finally breathing easy while dropping his hands into his lap.

The sigh of relief was accompanied by Peter slowly standing and walking over to the settlement's edge. On his way, he stopped by the empty case of explosives and other supplies he and Beth removed from the truck. Peter then pulled out the group's handheld radio from within the pile and brought it, along with the gun still glued to his hand, over to the cliff.

Although it didn't exactly go as smoothly as he hoped, Peter's part of the plan was complete. With that in mind, he felt content enough to allow his exhausted body the luxury of dropping down into the snow. He could feel the blood from the wound on his face still trickling down his chin, but was just too tired to do anything about it. For now, all he wanted to do was check in and make sure the others were all right.

Looking out over the valley, Peter brought the radio to his face and spoke as if he was talking directly to the town and village below. "This is Peter. The mine's been sealed. How's everyone else coming along?"

Peter took the radio away from his face and waited for a response. When one didn't come after several seconds, he tried again. "Did anybody get that? I said the mine is sealed."

Again, no voice responded to his call, and Peter's desperate words started to show a sign of hopeless dread. "Hello? Please…somebody say something."

The radio's continued silence filled the village manager with anxious worry. Why weren't they answering? What could it mean? He could feel his breath starting to get worked up as a number of many frightful scenarios rushed through his head.

But then Peter realized that the day's events had trained him to fear for the worst. He could've not been able to reach the other groups for any number of reasons. His radio could've been broken. Their radios could've been broken. Their radios could've been off. Or maybe the others were just too busy to answer. They were in the middle of preventing the zombie Apocalypse, after all.

After confronting his own fabricated anxiety, Peter breathed another sigh to calm his nerves and relax his mind. Everything was probably fine. And Chris was surely on his way to give Ryan the cure, if he hadn't already. Just because it didn't work on Scott, didn't mean it wouldn't for Ryan. There could've been a hundred medical reasons why it couldn't save the devious man. But it would for his son. It had to. After today, the Haydens deserved a happy ending. And in just a few short hours the town would be evacuated, the zombies would be destroyed, and he and Ryan would be united once again.

Peter's thought was a reassuring one that filled him with a calm, overdue happiness. It was then immediately followed by a gigantic explosion that ripped through the center of Mountain Village.

The loud boom shook the whole valley as a large ball of fire erupted on the mountainside. A chain reaction of flames tore its way around the village square, destroying everything in its path. And it wasn't long before the entire community lifted from its firm home and began tumbling towards the valley floor.

Up above it, Peter could easily spot every ski trail release a torrential wave of snow and debris that only added to the already enormous tidal wave rushing down the mountain. A deathly glow of moonlight shone upon the white cascade, and it appeared in slow motion as it came barreling into the town below. The first crest of snow hit the base of the resort hard and began flooding its way outward as it covered everything in its path. About half-way through the streets, it almost appeared as if the deluge was actually slowing down. But the final barrage of snow bringing up the rear pushed the landslide forward until all of Telluride was lost in its wake.

The whole flood only lasted a few seconds, and by the time it settled throughout the canyon there was not a trace of the town buried beneath it. All that remained was a heavy plume of fluffy powder that floated up throughout the valley. The white cloud continued to climb, even reaching as high as the Tomboy settlement, where Peter still sat speechless on the cliff edge after watching the entire wintery destruction.

His mind immediately turned into a blank sheet of total despair and disbelief, unable to form a single comprehensive thought. He had trouble processing the sight in front of him. In just a few short moments, he went from finally feeling a ray of hope to watching everything he'd built over the course of his adult life crumble into nothingness. It was a scene of total physical and emotional devastation, and one which Peter could only respond to with the release of a single, involuntary whimper.

That was it. The end. Blowing the village was the final part of the plan, and now that it was done there was nothing left. For a brief moment, Peter contemplated how it could've happened so soon. But as with the outbreak, the why didn't matter. All that mattered was that no one could've escaped that. There wasn't enough time. Not in Mountain Village or Telluride below. And certainly not for Ryan.

Peter's son was dead. There was no denying it now. Sure, he was probably gone hours earlier. But Peter had clung to the hope that there was some sliver of a chance that Ryan could be saved. Not anymore.

So what was left? Peter searched through the depths of his shattered mind looking for salvation. Something, anything that could lift him up from the tumultuous pit of depression he was falling into. But the only release the distraught man could grasp was the cold metal of the pistol still clutched in his hand.

Peter lifted the gun to examine it, barely even contemplating the grave finality of his decision. He saw no other way out, and as the last human being left alive in the valley, he frankly didn't care. Without another second to delay, Peter brought the gun's barrel up to the side of his head while looking out over the vast desolation of the snowy ruins before him. But such destruction was not the last thing he wanted to see. So he closed his eyes and pictured the smiling faces of his wife and child one last time before smiling himself and squeezing the trigger.

EPILOGUE

During the initial hours of the epidemic, it didn't take long for Georgia's broadcast to generate the largest internet audience in TORO's history.

While she was on the air, Miss Croft was the only real source of news coming out of the canyon. All attempts from national network stations to get in contact with someone from Telluride failed miserably. The anchors futilely pleaded for anyone inside experiencing the horror to call them, but the people inside the town weren't even watching the news. They were too busy trying to survive. Besides unconfirmed cell phone videos, the only guests the producers could get on the air were people who recollected second-hand accounts of the chaos. A family member or friend who received a short, desperate phone call during their loved one's final moments.

Likewise, no outside callers were getting through to Georgia's show either. Sure, people tried. But the lines were being dominated by local traffic, which the DJ felt a responsibility to answer. Maybe if she had an assistant, Georgia could've managed the outside calls better and gotten a reporter on the air. But Malcolm was the only one around to help, and her boss was busy dealing with...other issues. Besides, Georgia's top priority in the moment was chronicling the horrifying tales of those around her. Sickening stories that went out over the internet for the whole world to hear.

Men and women around the country huddled over in office cubicles to hear the faint volume of their computer screens turned down to just above a whisper. Across the Atlantic, European commuters on their way back from work turned on their radios to the breaking news terrorizing a small town in the Colorado Rockies. And in Asia, families came home hoping to have dinner only to hear about gruesome accounts of murder and mayhem.

The planet was shocked, fearful, and surprisingly intrigued by the terror in Telluride. It was a disaster without a cause. A tragedy without explanation. And no matter who you were or where you were listening from, there was only one thing you wanted: more.

Especially after Georgia's broadcast suddenly went dark.

Why did the radio go silent? Was she attacked? Or did she run away? Perhaps she was never in danger to begin with. Maybe this was all some sick, elaborate hoax. A marketing stunt for an upcoming movie.

Then why were other news station around the globe reporting it as true? Surely no one would ever let a cruel joke get so far. Especially not the governor, who would only give a vague comment through his press secretary that he was, "handling the matter cautiously."

Private humanitarian expeditions out to the valley were already being planned, but they were still at least a day away from getting through the aftermath of the storm. It seemed as if for the time being all anybody could do was speculate as to the how or why any of this was happening.

One thing was for sure, though: the longer Georgia was off the air, the more people tuned in hoping she would come back on. As the day progressed, word spread through news or gossip about the havoc being raged in a small mountain town. Speculation and mystery fueled a media firestorm of blogs and conspiracy websites until it drove anyone with an interest to sign in.

One by one, potential listeners logged on hoping to hear the young DJ's spunky voice return. But it never did. And ultimately, it was their very drive and thirst for more information that kept her off the air. Unbeknownst to Georgia, it was that very swarm of internet traffic which jammed the station's already fragile systems, preventing her from broadcasting the call to evacuate. Maybe, just maybe, if the damaged servers were still intact she might've gotten a signal out. But her warning wasn't meant to be.

And so the millions upon millions of concerned, eager, frightened, and (unfortunately), excited listeners would never get to hear the fate of the small mountain town and the zombies who destroyed it. Including the caravan of soldiers and guardsmen already on their way to the ruined civilization formerly known as Telluride, Colorado.

CHECK OUT OTHER GREAT ZOMBIE NOVELS

Z BURBIA
by Jake Bible

Whispering Pines is a classic, quiet, private American subdivision on the edge of Asheville, NC, set in the pristine Blue Ridge Mountains. Which is good since the zombie apocalypse has come to Western North Carolina and really put suburban living to the test!

Surrounded by a sea of the undead, the residents of Whispering Pines have adapted their bucolic life of block parties to scavenging parties, common area groundskeeping to immediate area warfare, neighborhood beautification to neighborhood fortification.

But, even in the best of times, suburban living has its ups and downs what with nosy neighbors, a strict Home Owners' Association, and a property management company that believes the words "strict interpretation" are holy words when applied to the HOA covenants. Now with the zombie apocalypse upon them even those innocuous, daily irritations quickly become dramatic struggles for personal identity, family security, and straight up survival.

ZOMBIE RULES
by David Achord

Zach Gunderson's life sucked and then the zombie apocalypse began.

Rick, an aging Vietnam veteran, alcoholic, and prepper, convinces Zach that the apocalypse is on the horizon. The two of them take refuge at a remote farm. As the zombie plague rages, they face a terrifying fight for survival.

They soon learn however that the walking dead are not the only monsters.

CHECK OUT OTHER GREAT ZOMBIE NOVELS

RUN
by Rich Restucci

The dead have risen, and they are hungry.

Slow and plodding, they are Legion. The undead hunt the living. Stop and they will catch you. Hide and they will find you. If you have a heartbeat you do the only thing you can: You run.

Survivors escape to an island stronghold: A cop and his daughter, a computer nerd, a garbage man with a piece of rebar, and an escapee from a mental hospital with a life-saving secret. After reaching Alcatraz, the ever expanding group of survivors realize that the infected are not the only threat.

Caught between the viciousness of the undead, and the heartlessness of the living, what choice is there? Run.

THE DEAD WALK THE EARTH
by Luke Duffy

As the flames of war threaten to engulf the globe, a new threat emerges.

A 'deadly flu', the like of which no one has ever seen or imagined, relentlessly spreads, gripping the world by the throat and slowly squeezing the life from humanity.

Eight soldiers, accustomed to operating below the radar, carrying out the dirty work of a modern democracy, become trapped within the carnage of a new and terrifying world.

Deniable and completely expendable. That is how their government considers them, and as the dead begin to walk, Stan and his men must fight to survive.

CHECK OUT OTHER GREAT ZOMBIE NOVELS

900 MILES
by S. Johnathan Davis

John is a killer, but that wasn't his day job before the Apocalypse.

In a harrowing 900 mile race against time to get to his wife just as the dead begin to rise, John, a business man trapped in New York, soon learns that the zombies are the least of his worries, as he sees first-hand the horror of what man is capable of with no rules, no consequences and death at every turn.

Teaming up with an ex-army pilot named Kyle, they escape New York only to stumble across a man who says that he has the key to a rumored underground stronghold called Avalon..... Will they find safety? Will they make it to Johns wife before it's too late?

Get ready to follow John and Kyle in this fast paced thriller that mixes zombie horror with gladiator style arena action!

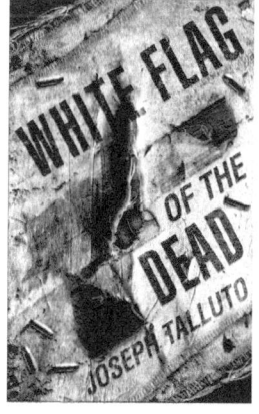

WHITE FLAG OF THE DEAD
by Joseph Talluto

Millions died when the Enillo Virus swept the earth. Millions more were lost when the victims of the plague refused to stay dead, instead rising to slaughter and feed on those left alive. For survivors like John Talon and his son Jake, they are faced with a choice: Do they submit to the dead, raising the white flag of surrender? Or do they find the will to fight, to try and hang on to the last shreds or humanity?